THE WEB
SHE WEAVES

THE WEB SHE WEAVES

An Anthology of Mystery and
Suspense Stories by Women

Edited by
MARCIA MULLER & BILL PRONZINI

AVENEL BOOKS
New York

Grateful acknowledgement is extended to the following for permission to reprint:

"Postiche," by Mignon Eberhart. Copyright © 1935 by The Butterick Company; copyright renewed © 1962 by Mignon G. Eberhart. Reprinted by permission of Brandt & Brandt Literary Agents, Inc.

"Suspicion," by Dorothy L. Sayers. From *In the Teeth of the Evidence*. Copyright © 1940 by Dorothy L. Sayers. Reprinted by permission of A. Watkins, Inc.

"Harlequin's Lane," by Agatha Christie. Copyright © 1930 by Dodd, Mead and Company; renewed © 1957 by Agatha Christie Mallowan. Reprinted by permission of Harold Ober Associates, Inc.

"His Heart Could Break," by Craig Rice. Copyright © 1943 by The American Mercury, Inc. Reprinted by permission of Scott Meredith Literary Agency, Inc., 845 Third Avenue, New York, N.Y. 10022, agents for the estate of Craig Rice.

"Chinoiserie," by Helen McCloy. Copyright © 1946 by Helen McCloy; renewed © 1977 by Helen McCloy. Reprinted by permission of the author.

"Good-bye, Miss Lizzie Borden," by Lillian de la Torre. Copyright © 1947 by Lillian de la Torre; renewed © 1974 by Lillian de la Torre McCue. Reprinted by permission of Harold Ober Associates, Inc.

"McGowney's Miracle," by Margaret Millar. Copyright © 1954 by Hearst International, Inc.; renewed © 1982 by Margaret Millar. Reprinted by permission of Harold Ober Associates, Inc.

"St. Patrick's Day in the Morning," by Charlotte Armstrong. Copyright © 1959 by Davis Publications, Inc. First published in *Ellery Queen's Mystery Magazine*. Reprinted by permission of Brandt & Brandt Literary Agents, Inc.

"The Possibility of Evil," by Shirley Jackson. Copyright © 1965 by Stanley Edgar Hyman. First published in *The Saturday Evening Post*. Reprinted by permission of Brandt & Brandt Literary Agents, Inc.

"The Snail-Watcher," by Patricia Highsmith. Copyright © 1964 by Patricia Highsmith. First published in *Gamma Magazine*. Reprinted by permission of the author and her agent, Diogenes Verlag AG, Zurich, Switzerland.

"The Locked Room," by Celia Fremlin. Copyright © 1968 by Celia Fremlin. First published in *Ellery Queen's Mystery Magazine* as "From the Locked Room Upstairs." Reprinted by permission of the author.

"The Fall of a Coin," by Ruth Rendell. Copyright © 1975 by Ruth Rendell. First published in *Ellery Queen's Mystery Magazine*. Reprinted by permission of the author and Georges Borchardt, Inc.

"Double Jeopardy," by Susan Dunlap. Copyright © 1978 by Susan Dunlap. First published in *Ellery Queen's Mystery Magazine* as "Death Threat." Reprinted by permission of the author.

"My Neighbor, Ay," by Joyce Harrington. Copyright © 1974 by Joyce Harrington. First published in *Ellery Queen's Mystery Magazine*. Reprinted by permission of the author.

"Norman and the Killer," by Joyce Carol Oates. Copyright © 1965, 1966 by Joyce Carol Oates. Reprinted by permission of the author.

"Cattails," by Marcia Muller. Copyright © 1983 by Marcia Muller. An original story published by permission of the author.

"Great-Aunt Allie's Flypapers," by P. D. James. Copyright © 1978 by Faber and Faber, Ltd. First published in *Verdict of 13*. Reprinted by permission of the author and her agents, International Creative Management, Inc.

This 1988 edition is published by Avenel Books, distributed by Crown Publishers, Inc., 225 Park Avenue South, New York, New York 10003, by arrangement with William Morrow & Co., Inc.

Manufactured in the United of America

Library of Congress Cataloging-in-Publication Data
The Web she weaves: an anthology of mystery and suspense stories by women/edited by Marcia Muller & Bill Pronzini.
  1. Detective and mystery stories. American—Women authors.
2. Detective and mystery stories. English—Women authors.
I. Muller, Marcia. II. Pronzini, Bill.
PS648.D4W4 1988
813'.0872'089287—dc19   87-35136
                                                CIP

ISBN 0-517-66208-6
h g f e d c b a

CONTENTS

INTRODUCTION

With the exception of such legendary figures as Agatha Christie and Dorothy L. Sayers, mystery and suspense fiction is thought by the general readership to be largely the domain of men. In truth, however, it is difficult to find any supportable basis for the idea of the male writer as owner and sole shaper of the genre.

Witness the following evidence to the contrary:

As early as 1867—twenty years prior to the appearance of the first Sherlock Holmes story—Seely Regester (the pseudonym of Mrs. Metta Victoria Fuller Victor, 1831–1886) published the first American detective novel authored by a woman, *The Dead Letter.* Although tedious and full of such trappings as illegitimacy, robbery, clairvoyance, strange suitors, and a final assembly in the parlor, Miss Regester's novel paved the way for more competent efforts on both sides of the Atlantic.

In 1878, American writer Anna Katharine Green's (1846–1935) *The Leavenworth Case* became an overnight success. Miss Green also gave us the first spinster sleuth, Amelia Butterworth, who began her unabashed snooping in *The Affair Next Door* (1897) and continued it in *Lost Man's Lane* (1898). Younger but equally nosy was Miss Green's Violet Strange, who appeared in *The Golden Slipper* (1915) and who was assisted by—the Watson of all Watsons—a bloodhound.

Another early female detective, Loveday Brooke, was the creation of Catherine Louisa Pirkis. In addition to *The Experiences of Loveday Brooke,* a collection of seven stories published in 1894, Mrs. Pirkis wrote thirteen other thrillers, many of them featuring amateur female sleuths.

In England, Lillie Thomas Meade (1854–1914), in collaboration with the pseudonymous Dr. Clifford Halifax, produced a series of medical mysteries about a country doctor for *The Strand* in 1894. For the same magazine four years later, the versatile Miss Meade then created, in collaboration with Robert Eustace, one of the first female master criminals, Madame Koluchy, who sent a gang of Italian thugs out to do her dirty work for her. Another of Miss Meade's heroines, Madame Sara of *The Sorceress of the Strand* (1903), took matters into her own hands to become one of our most prolific of fictional female murderers.

The Hungarian-born Baroness Emmuska Orczy contributed one of the first and most important armchair detectives, The Old Man in the Corner, in 1901 ("the corner" being a booth in a London tearoom from which the old man seldom ventures). Another of her heroes, the eccentric Scarlet Pimpernel, outfoxed nearly everyone during the French Revolution; and Lady Molly Robertson-Kirk joined the ranks of professionals at Scotland Yard in 1910 as she sought to overturn her husband's murder conviction.

An important contribution in the area of psychological suspense came in 1913, with the publication of Marie Belloc Lowndes's *The Lodger.* Many of Mrs. Lowndes's works are based on historical events, but in this one, which explores the Jack the Ripper murders, the outward happenings are not nearly so important as the tensions of the relationships between the characters involved. This, too, was an important innovation in the field.

Back in America, Mary Roberts Rinehart was busy establishing what has come to be called the "Had I But Known" school of suspense writing. Replete with fluttery and sometimes foolish heroines, Mrs. Rinehart's novels and stories contain numerous confrontations with the dark forces of evil, during which the lady would be heard to murmur, "Had I but known then what I know now . . ." The author, a nurse herself, also gave us Miss Pinkerton, an early nurse-detective.

Carolyn Wells (1869–1942) began one of the longest-running detective series when she introduced private investigator Fleming Stone in *The Clue* (1909). Stone went on to solve a previously unprecedented total of sixty-one cases over the ensuing four decades. Miss Wells was more accomplished as a teacher than as a writer, however; her major offering to the genre is *The Technique of the Mystery Story* (1913), in which she sets forth rules for writing which are as valid today as they were then.

During the "Golden Age" of crime fiction (the period 1925 to 1940), women writers flourished. The most famous of these, of course, is Agatha Christie. Recipient of the first Mystery Writers of America Grand Master Award in 1954, Mrs. Christie gave us sixty-eight novels over her long career, beginning with *The Mysterious Affair at Styles* in 1920, as well as such celebrated sleuths as Hercule Poirot, Miss Jane Marple, Parker Pyne, the mysterious Harley Quin, and the husband-and-wife team of Tommy and Tuppence. Her play, *The Mousetrap,* which opened in 1952 and has yet to close, is the longest-running production on the British stage.

Other acclaimed and still popular British mystery novelists who began writing during the Golden Age include Dorothy L. Sayers, the creator of the aristocratic Lord Peter Wimsey and his "right-hand woman," Miss Climpson, who star in such novels as *Unnatural Death* and *Strong Poison,* and such short story collections as *Lord Peter Views the Body;* New Zealander Ngaio Marsh, who brought us the sophisticated Roderick Alleyn in *A Man Lay Dead* in 1934; Daphne du Maurier, who was and still is a Gothic novelist with an unparalleled hand at atmospheric suspense, as seen in *Rebecca* (1938); Margery Allingham, who wrote both fast-moving, action-packed adventure stories and novels of deep psychological characterization; and Scotswoman Josephine Tey (Elizabeth Mackintosh), who gave us Miss Pym, an amateur sleuth in an academic setting, and the elegant Alan Grant of Scotland Yard, hero of the classic *The Daughter of Time*.

On this side of the Atlantic, Golden Age authors were fewer, but their contributions are equally significant. Two of the most notable are Mignon G. Eberhart, whose career began with the publication of *The Patient in Room 18* in 1929, progressed through sixty additional novels of quality, and reached its high point in 1970 when she was presented with MWA's Grand Master Award; and Helen McCloy, the creator of the first psychiatrist detective, Dr. Basil Willing, who made his first bow in *Dance of Death* (1938).

During World War II and in the years following, many other women established themselves as important mystery writers. The works of Canadian Margaret Millar, whose first novel, *The Invisible Worm,* appeared in 1942, have been widely acclaimed for their sensitive, psychologically oriented suspense and sharp character development. Charlotte Armstrong's novels and short stories *(The Unsuspected, A Dram of Poison)* often explore the theme of peril to the very young and the very old with considerable deftness. The prolific Craig Rice, in such novels as *The Sunday Pigeon Murders* (1942) and *Home Sweet Homicide* (1944), gave us a kind of wacky humor that at that time was rare in the genre.

A number of Dorothy B. Hughes's excellent novels *(Ride the Pink Horse, The Candy Kid)* offered vivid portraits of Mexico and her native Southwest during the postwar years, and she is an award-winning reviewer in the field as well, having received the 1950 Edgar for her critical acumen. Dorothy Salisbury Davis demonstrated her keen insight and sympathy for the underdog in such novels as *A Gentle Murderer* (1951). Lillian de la Torre, a true-crime expert and aficionado of the theater, created the award-winning series of historical detective stories in which Dr. Samuel Johnson appears as sleuth. American expatriate Patricia Highsmith began writing such chilling and memorable psychological suspense novels as *Strangers on a Train*. And Helen MacInnes proved a woman *could* write first-rate spy novels by publishing more than fifteen, including *The Double Image* and *The Snare of the Hunter*.

Perhaps the best known of the present-day "women of mystery" is P. D. James, whose Chief Superintendent Adam Dalgliesh and private eye Cordelia Gray have delighted millions. Also notable among modern practitioners are Ruth Rendell, with her excellent police procedurals featuring Chief Inspector Wexford of Scotland Yard, as well as with such straight suspense novels as *Master of the Moor* (1982); the prolific Elizabeth Linington, who writes series under her own name (Sergeant Ivor Maddox) and the pseudonyms of Dell Shannon (police detective Luis Mendoza) and Lesley Egan (Jesse Falkenstein and Vic Varallo); the collaborative team of Mary J. Latis and Martha Hennissart, who, under their pen names of Emma Lathen and R. B. Dominic, have been hailed as mistresses of witty and charming detective stories; Maj Söwall, the Swedish poet who co-authored, with her late husband, Per Wahlöö, a fine series of police procedurals set in Stockholm *(The Laughing Policeman, The Terrorists);* and Carolyn Weston, also a writer of procedurals, whose novels such as *Poor, Poor Ophelia* (1972) became the basis for the TV series *The Streets of San Francisco*.

In keeping with the expansion of occupational opportunity for women, other contemporary authors have begun placing their heroines in jobs they would not have held ten years ago. Lillian O'Donnell's Norah Mulcahaney *(The Phone Calls, Don't Wear Your Wedding Ring)* detects for New York's finest, often taking on cases of special interest to women. Equally effective as a public crimefighter is Dorothy Uhnak's Christie Opara *(The Bait, The Ledger);* a former policewoman herself, Uhnak has also written a number of other novels, such as *Law and Order,* which draw on her police experience. Sue Grafton and Marcia Muller have created believable female private investigators, with their own unique personalities, that are anything but distaff imitations of Sam Spade and Philip Marlowe.

And finally, contributions to the genre have not been limited to those authors we generally think of as mystery writers. Louisa May Alcott, for example, put aside her genteel tales for young people long enough to produce several stories in the Gothic-suspense mode. Edith Wharton used her fine sense of characterization to build both psychological and supernatural suspense. Katherine Mansfield, Dorothy Parker, Edna St. Vincent Millay, Willa Cather, and Fannie Hurst, among others, dabbled in matters criminous with great success. One of the best known of modern literary writers, Joyce Carol Oates, has often worked in the mystery-Gothic mode, notably in her National Book Award-winning novel *Them* (1969); much of her fiction, in fact, contains marked suspense elements.

The volume of evidence presented above, it seems to us, makes the case for women as primary forces in the shaping of the mystery genre a conclusive one. If further evidence is needed, we offer the stories in the pages that follow. They span close to one hundred years of mystery and suspense writing, and exhibit a wide variety of subject matter, style, and approach. We're quite sure you'll find them every bit as entertaining and expert as any produced by their male counterparts during that same time frame.

The defense rests.

—MARCIA MULLER and BILL PRONZINI
San Francisco, California

THE WEB
SHE WEAVES

THE LODGER

Marie Belloc Lowndes

Marie Belloc Lowndes (1868–1947) was born into a distinguished family, whose members included literary figures, barristers, and scientists. She claimed to have written every day of her life from the age of sixteen, and her finely crafted novels, plays, and short stories are evidence of the continual rewriting and polishing that her perfectionist nature demanded. Mrs. Belloc Lowndes is primarily known for her crime and suspense novels, which rely heavily on character development and the relationships between men and women. "The Lodger," which the author later expanded into a novel of the same title, is a tale of psychological suspense based on the Jack the Ripper murders. The story has so fascinated filmmakers that four versions have been produced, beginning with Alfred Hitchcock's 1926 adaptation.

"**T**here he is at last, and I'm glad of it, Ellen. 'Tain't a night you would wish a dog to be out in."

Mr. Bunting's voice was full of unmistakable relief. He was close to the fire, sitting back in a deep leather armchair —a clean-shaven, dapper man, still in outward appearance what he had been so long, and now no longer was—a self-respecting butler.

"You needn't feel so nervous about him; Mr. Sleuth can look out for himself, all right." Mrs. Bunting spoke in a dry, rather tart tone. She was less emotional, better balanced, than was her husband. On her the marks of past servitude were less apparent, but they were there all the same—especially in her neat black stuff dress and scrupulously clean, plain collar and cuffs. Mrs. Bunting, as a single woman, had been for long years what is known as a useful maid.

"I can't think why he wants to go out in such weather. He did it in last week's fog, too," Bunting went on complainingly.

"Well, it's none of your business—now, is it?"

"No; that's true enough. Still, 'twould be a very bad thing for us if anything happened to him. This lodger's the first bit of luck we've had for a very long time."

Mrs. Bunting made no answer to this remark. It was too obviously true to be worth answering. Also she was listening —following in imagination her lodger's quick, singularly quiet—"stealthy," she called it to herself—progress through the dark, fog-filled hall and up the staircase.

"It isn't safe for decent folk to be out in such weather —not unless they have something to do that won't wait till tomorrow." Bunting had at last turned round. He was now looking straight into his wife's narrow, colorless face; he was an obstinate man, and liked to prove himself right. "I read you out the accidents in *Lloyd's* yesterday—shocking, they

18

were, and all brought about by the fog! And then, that 'orrid monster at his work again—"

"Monster?" repeated Mrs. Bunting absently. She was trying to hear the lodger's footsteps overhead; but her husband went on as if there had been no interruption:

"It wouldn't be very pleasant to run up against such a party as that in the fog, eh?"

"What stuff you do talk!" she said sharply; and then she got up suddenly. Her husband's remark had disturbed her. She hated to think of such things as the terrible series of murders that were just then horrifying and exciting the nether world of London. Though she enjoyed pathos and sentiment—Mrs. Bunting would listen with mild amusement to the details of a breach-of-promise action—she shrank from stories of either immorality or physical violence.

Mrs. Bunting got up from the straight-backed chair on which she had been sitting. It would soon be time for supper.

She moved about the sitting room, flecking off an imperceptible touch of dust here, straightening a piece of furniture there.

Bunting looked around once or twice. He would have liked to ask Ellen to leave off fidgeting, but he was mild and fond of peace, so he refrained. However, she soon gave over what irritated him of her own accord.

But even then Mrs. Bunting did not at once go down to the cold kitchen, where everything was in readiness for her simple cooking. Instead, she opened the door leading into the bedroom behind, and there, closing the door quietly, stepped back into the darkness and stood motionless, listening.

At first she heard nothing, but gradually there came the sound of someone moving about in the room just overhead; try as she might, however, it was impossible for her to guess what her lodger was doing. At last she heard him open the door leading out on the landing. That meant that he would spend the rest of the evening in the rather cheerless room above the drawing-room floor—oddly enough, he liked sitting there best, though the only warmth obtainable was from a gas stove fed by a shilling-in-the-slot arrangement.

It was indeed true that Mr. Sleuth had brought the Buntings luck, for at the time he had taken their rooms it had been touch and go with them.

After having each separately led the sheltered, impersonal, and, above all, the financially easy existence that is the compensation life offers to those men and women who deliberately take upon themselves the yoke of domestic service, these two, butler and useful maid, had suddenly, in middle age, determined to join their fortunes and savings.

Bunting was a widower; he had one pretty daughter, a girl of seventeen, who now lived, as had been the case ever since the death of her mother, with a prosperous aunt. His second wife had been reared in the Foundling Hospital, but she had gradually worked her way up into the higher ranks of the servant class and as useful maid she had saved quite a tidy sum of money.

Unluckily, misfortune had dogged Mr. and Mrs. Bunting from the very first. The seaside place where they had begun by taking a lodging house became the scene of an epidemic. Then had followed a business experiment which had proved disastrous. But before going back into service, either together or separately, they had made up their minds to make one last effort, and, with the little money that remained to them, they had taken over the lease of a small house in the Marylebone Road.

Bunting, whose appearance was very good, had retained a connection with old employers and their friends, so he occasionally got a good job as waiter. During this last month his jobs had perceptibly increased in number and in profit; Mrs. Bunting was not superstitious, but it seemed that in this matter, as in everything else, Mr. Sleuth, their new lodger, had brought them luck.

As she stood there, still listening intently in the darkness of the bedroom, she told herself, not for the first time, what

Mr. Sleuth's departure would mean to her and Bunting. It would almost certainly mean ruin.

Luckily, the lodger seemed entirely pleased both with the rooms and with his landlady. There was really no reason why he should ever leave such nice lodgings. Mrs. Bunting shook off her vague sense of apprehension and unease. She turned round, took a step forward, and, feeling for the handle of the door giving into the passage, she opened it, and went down with light, firm steps into the kitchen.

She lit the gas and put a frying pan on the stove, and then once more her mind reverted, as if in spite of herself, to her lodger, and there came back to Mrs. Bunting, very vividly, the memory of all that had happened the day Mr. Sleuth had taken her rooms.

The date of this excellent lodger's coming had been the twenty-ninth of December, and the time late afternoon. She and Bunting had been sitting, gloomily enough, over their small banked-up fire. They had dined in the middle of the day—he on a couple of sausages, she on a little cold ham. They were utterly out of heart, each trying to pluck up courage to tell the other that it was no use trying anymore. The two had also had a little tiff on that dreary afternoon. A newspaper seller had come yelling down the Marylebone Road, shouting out, "'Orrible murder in Whitechapel!" and just because Bunting had an old uncle living in the East End he had gone and bought a paper, and at a time, too, when every penny, nay, every halfpenny, had its full value! Mrs. Bunting remembered the circumstances because that murder in Whitechapel had been the first of these terrible crimes—there had been four since—which she would never allow Bunting to discuss in her presence, and yet which had of late begun to interest curiously, uncomfortably, even her refined mind.

But, to return to the lodger. It was then, on that dreary afternoon, that suddenly there had come to the front door a tremulous, uncertain double knock.

Bunting ought to have got up, but he had gone on reading the paper and so Mrs. Bunting, with the woman's greater courage, had gone out into the passage, turned up the gas, and opened the door to see who it could be. She remembered, as if it were yesterday instead of nigh on a month ago, Mr. Sleuth's peculiar appearance. Tall, dark, lanky, an old-fashioned top hat concealing his high bald forehead, he had stood there, an odd figure of a man, blinking at her.

"I believe—is it not a fact that you let lodgings?" he had asked in a hesitating, whistling voice, a voice that she had known in a moment to be that of an educated man—of a gentleman. As he had stepped into the hall, she had noticed that in his right hand he held a narrow bag—a quite new bag of strong brown leather.

Everything had been settled in less than a quarter of an hour. Mr. Sleuth had at once "taken" to the drawing-room floor, and then, as Mrs. Bunting eagerly lit the gas in the front room above, he had looked around him and said, rubbing his hands with a nervous movement, "Capital—capital! This is just what I've been looking for!"

The sink had specially pleased him—the sink and the gas stove. "This is quite first-rate!" he had exclaimed, "for I make all sorts of experiments. I am, you must understand, Mrs.—er—Bunting, a man of science." Then he had sat down—suddenly. "I'm very tired," he had said in a low tone, "very tired indeed! I have been walking about all day."

From the very first the lodger's manner had been odd, sometimes distant and abrupt, and then, for no reason at all that she could see, confidential and plaintively confiding. But Mrs. Bunting was aware that eccentricity has always been a perquisite, as it were the special luxury, of the well born and well educated. Scholars and such-like are never quite like other people.

And then, this particular gentleman had proved himself so eminently satisfactory as to the one thing that really matters to those who let lodgings. "My name is Sleuth," he said, "S-l-e-u-t-h. Think of a hound, Mrs. Bunting, and you'll never forget my name. I could give you references," he had

added, giving her, as she now remembered, a funny sidewise look, "but I prefer to dispense with them. How much
did you say? Twenty-three shillings a week, with attend-
ance? Yes, that will suit me perfectly; and I'll begin by paying my first month's rent in advance. Now, four times
twenty-three shillings is"—he looked at Mrs. Bunting, and
for the first time he smiled, a queer, wry smile—"ninety-two
shillings."

He had taken a handful of sovereigns out of his pocket
and put them down on the table. "Look here," he had said,
"there's five pounds; and you can keep the change, for I shall
want you to do a little shopping for me tomorrow."

After he had been in the house about an hour, the bell
had rung, and the new lodger had asked Mrs. Bunting if she
could oblige him with the loan of a Bible. She brought up to
him her best Bible, the one that had been given to her as a
wedding present by a lady with whose mother she had lived
for several years. This Bible and one other book, of which
the odd name was Cruden's Concordance, formed Mr.
Sleuth's only reading: he spent hours each day poring over
the Old Testament and over the volume which Mrs. Bunting
had at last decided to be a queer kind of index to the Book.

However, to return to the lodger's first arrival. He had
had no luggage with him, barring the small brown bag, but
very soon parcels had begun to arrive addressed to Mr.
Sleuth, and it was then that Mrs. Bunting first became curious. These parcels were full of clothes; but it was quite clear
to the landlady's feminine eye that none of these clothes had
been made for Mr. Sleuth. They were, in fact, secondhand
clothes, bought at good secondhand places, each marked,
when marked at all, with a different name. And the really
extraordinary thing was that occasionally a complete suit
disappeared—became, as it were, obliterated from the
lodger's wardrobe.

As for the bag he had brought with him, Mrs. Bunting
had never caught sight of it again. And this also was certainly
very strange.

Mrs. Bunting thought a great deal about that bag. She often wondered what had been in it; not a nightshirt and comb and brush, as she had at first supposed, for Mr. Sleuth had asked her to go out and buy him a brush and comb and toothbrush the morning after his arrival. That fact was specially impressed on her memory, for at the little shop, a barber's, where she had purchased the brush and comb, the foreigner who had served her had insisted on telling her some of the horrible details of the murder that had taken place the day before in Whitechapel, and it had upset her very much.

As to where the bag was now, it was probably locked up in the lower part of a chiffonnier in the front sitting room. Mr. Sleuth evidently always carried the key of the little cupboard on his person, for Mrs. Bunting, though she looked well for it, had never been able to find it.

And yet, never was there a more confiding or trusting gentleman. The first four days that he had been with them he had allowed his money—the considerable sum of one hundred and eighty-four pounds in gold—to lie about wrapped up in pieces of paper on his dressing table. This was a very foolish, indeed a wrong thing to do, as she had allowed herself respectfully to point out to him; but as only answer he had laughed, a loud, discordant shout of laughter.

Mr. Sleuth had many other odd ways; but Mrs. Bunting, a true woman in spite of her prim manner and love of order, had an infinite patience with masculine vagaries.

On the first morning of Mr. Sleuth's stay in the Buntings' house, while Mrs. Bunting was out buying things for him, the new lodger had turned most of the pictures and photographs hanging in his sitting room with their faces to the wall! But this queer action on Mr. Sleuth's part had not surprised Mrs. Bunting as much as it might have done; it recalled an incident of her long-past youth—something that had happened a matter of twenty years ago, at a time when Mrs. Bunting, then the still youthful Ellen Cottrell, had been maid to an old lady. The old lady had a favorite nephew, a bright, jolly young gentleman who had been learning to paint animals in Paris; and it was he who had had the impudence, early one summer morning, to turn to the wall six beautiful engravings of paintings done by the famous Mr. Landseer! The old lady thought the world of those pictures, but her nephew, as only excuse for the extraordinary thing he had done, had observed that "they put his eye out."

Mr. Sleuth's excuse had been much the same; for, when Mrs. Bunting had come into his sitting room and found all her pictures, or at any rate all those of her pictures that happened to be portraits of ladies, with their faces to the wall, he had offered as only explanation, "Those women's eyes follow me about."

Mrs. Bunting had gradually become aware that Mr. Sleuth had a fear and dislike of women. When she was "doing" the staircase and landing, she often heard him reading bits of the Bible aloud to himself, and in the majority of instances the texts he chose contained uncomplimentary reference to her own sex. Only today she had stopped and listened while he uttered threateningly the awful words, "A strange woman is a narrow pit. She also lieth in wait as for a prey, and increaseth the transgressors among men." There had been a pause, and then had come, in a high singsong, "Her house is the way to hell, going down to the chambers of death." It had made Mrs. Bunting feel quite queer.

The lodger's daily habits were also peculiar. He stayed in bed all the morning, and sometimes part of the afternoon, and he never went out before the streetlamps were alight. Then, there was his dislike of an open fire; he generally sat in the top front room, and while there he always used the large gas stove, not only for his experiments, which he carried on at night, but also in the daytime, for warmth.

But there! Where was the use of worrying about the lodger's funny ways? Of course, Mr. Sleuth was eccentric; if he hadn't been "just a leetle 'touched' upstairs"—as Bunting had once described it—he wouldn't be their lodger now; he would be living in a quite different sort of way with some of his relations, or with a friend of his own class.

Mrs. Bunting, while these thoughts galloped disconnectedly through her brain, went on with her cooking, doing everything with a certain delicate and cleanly precision.

While in the middle of making the toast on which was to be poured some melted cheese, she suddenly heard a noise, or rather a series of noises. Shuffling, hesitating steps were creaking down the house above. She looked up and listened. Surely Mr. Sleuth was not going out again into the cold, foggy night? But no; for the sounds did not continue down the passage leading to the front door.

The heavy steps were coming slowly down the kitchen stairs. Nearer and nearer came the thudding sounds, and Mrs. Bunting's heart began to beat as if in response. She put out the gas stove, unheedful of the fact that the cheese would stiffen and spoil in the cold air; and then she turned and faced the door. There was a fumbling at the handle, and a moment later the door opened and revealed, as she had known it would, her lodger.

Mr. Sleuth was clad in a plaid dressing gown, and in his hand was a candle. When he saw the lit-up kitchen, and the woman standing in it, he looked inexplicably taken aback, almost aghast.

"Yes, sir? What can I do for you, sir? I hope you didn't ring, sir?" Mrs. Bunting did not come forward to meet her lodger; instead, she held her ground in front of the stove. Mr. Sleuth had no business to come down like this into her kitchen.

"No, I—I didn't ring," he stammered; "I didn't know you were down here, Mrs. Bunting. Please excuse my costume. The truth is, my gas stove has gone wrong, or, rather, that shilling-in-the-slot arrangement has done so. I came down to see if *you* had a gas stove. I am going to ask leave to use it tonight for an experiment I want to make."

Mrs. Bunting felt troubled—oddly, unnaturally troubled. Why couldn't the lodger's experiment wait till tomorrow? "Oh, certainly, sir; but you will find it very cold down here." She looked round her dubiously.

"It seems most pleasantly warm," he observed, "warm and cozy after my cold room upstairs."

"Won't you let me make you a fire?" Mrs. Bunting's housewifely instincts were roused. "Do let me make you a fire in your bedroom, sir; I'm sure you ought to have one there these cold nights."

"By no means—I mean, I would prefer not. I do not like an open fire, Mrs. Bunting." He frowned, and still stood, a strange-looking figure, just inside the kitchen door.

"Do you want to use this stove now, sir? Is there anything I can do to help you?"

"No, not now—thank you all the same, Mrs. Bunting. I shall come down later, altogether later—probably after you and your husband have gone to bed. But I should be much obliged if you would see that the gas people come tomorrow and put my stove in order."

"Perhaps Bunting could put it right for you, sir. I'll ask him to go up."

"No, no—I don't want anything of that sort done tonight. Besides, he couldn't put it right. The cause of the trouble is quite simple. The machine is choked up with shillings: a foolish plan, so I have always felt it to be."

Mr. Sleuth spoke very pettishly, with far more heat than he was wont to speak; but Mrs. Bunting sympathized with him. She had always suspected those slot-machines to be as dishonest as if they were human. It was dreadful, the way they swallowed up the shillings!

As if he were divining her thoughts, Mr. Sleuth, walking forward, stared up at the kitchen slot-machine. "Is it nearly full?" he asked abruptly. "I expect my experiment will take some time, Mrs. Bunting."

"Oh, no, sir; there's plenty of room for shillings there still. We don't use our stove as much as you do yours, sir. I'm never in the kitchen a minute longer than I can help this cold weather."

And then, with him preceding her, Mrs. Bunting and her lodger made a slow progress to the ground floor. There Mr. Sleuth courteously bade his landlady good night, and proceeded upstairs to his own apartments.

Mrs. Bunting again went down into her kitchen, again she lit the stove, and again she cooked the toasted cheese. But she felt unnerved, afraid of she knew not what. The place seemed to her alive with alien presences, and once she caught herself listening, which was absurd, for of course she could not hope to hear what her lodger was doing two, if not three, flights upstairs. She had never been able to discover what Mr. Sleuth's experiments really were; all she knew was that they required a very high degree of heat.

The Buntings went to bed early that night. But Mrs. Bunting intended to stay awake. She wanted to know at what hour of the night her lodger would come down into the kitchen, and, above all, she was anxious as to how long he would stay there. But she had had a long day, and presently she fell asleep.

The church clock hard by struck two in the morning, and suddenly Mrs. Bunting awoke. She felt sharply annoyed with herself. How could she have dropped off like that? Mr. Sleuth must have been down and up again hours ago.

Then, gradually, she became aware of a faint acrid odor; elusive, almost intangible, it yet seemed to encompass her and the snoring man by her side almost as a vapor might have done.

Mrs. Bunting sat up in bed and sniffed; and then, in spite of the cold, she quietly crept out of the nice, warm bed-clothes and crawled along to the bottom of the bed. There Mr. Sleuth's landlady did a very curious thing; she leaned over the brass rail and put her face close to the hinge of the door. Yes, it was from there that this strange, horrible odor was coming; the smell must be very strong in the passage. Mrs. Bunting thought she knew now what became of those suits of clothes of Mr. Sleuth's that disappeared.

As she crept back, shivering, under the bedclothes, she

longed to give her sleeping husband a good shake, and in fancy she heard herself saying: "Bunting, get up! There is something strange going on downstairs that we ought to know about."

But Mr. Sleuth's landlady, as she lay by her husband's side, listening with painful intentness, knew very well that she would do nothing of the sort. The lodger had a right to destroy his clothes by burning if the fancy took him. What if he did make a certain amount of mess, a certain amount of smell, in her nice kitchen? Was he not—was he not such a good lodger! If they did anything to upset him, where could they ever hope to get another like him?

Three o'clock struck before Mrs. Bunting heard slow, heavy steps creaking up her kitchen stairs. But Mr. Sleuth did not go straight up to his own quarters, as she expected him to do. Instead, he went to the front door, and, opening it, put it on the chain. At the end of ten minutes or so he closed the front door, and by that time Mrs. Bunting had divined why the lodger had behaved in this strange fashion —it must have been to get the strong acrid smell of burning wool out of the passage. But Mrs. Bunting felt as if she herself would never get rid of the horrible odor. She felt herself to be all smell.

At last the unhappy woman fell into a deep, troubled sleep; and then she dreamed a most terrible and unnatural dream; hoarse voices seemed to be shouting in her ear, " 'Orrible murder off the Edgeware Road!" Then three words, indistinctly uttered, followed by "—at his work again! Awful details!"

Even in her dream Mrs. Bunting felt angered and impatient; she knew so well why she was being disturbed by this horrid nightmare. It was because of Bunting—Bunting, who insisted on talking to her of those frightful murders, in which only morbid, vulgar-minded people took any interest. Why, even now, in her dream, she could hear her husband speaking to her about it.

"Ellen"—so she heard Bunting say in her ear—"Ellen,

my dear, I am just going to get up to get a paper. It's after seven o'clock."

Mrs. Bunting sat up in bed. The shouting, nay, worse, the sound of tramping, hurrying feet smote on her ears. It had been no nightmare, then, but something infinitely worse—reality. Why couldn't Bunting have lain quietly in bed awhile longer, and let his poor wife go on dreaming? The most awful dream would have been easier to bear than this awakening.

She heard her husband go to the front door, and, as he bought the paper, exchange a few excited words with the newspaper boy. Then he came back and began silently moving about the room.

"Well!" she cried. "Why don't you tell me about it?"

"I thought you'd rather not hear."

"Of course I like to know what happens close to our own front door!" she snapped out.

And then he read out a piece of the newspaper—only a few lines, after all—telling in brief, unemotional language that the body of a woman, apparently done to death in a peculiarly atrocious fashion some hours before, had been found in a passage leading to a disused warehouse off the Marylebone Road.

"It serves that sort of hussy right!" was Mrs. Bunting's only comment.

When Mrs. Bunting went down into the kitchen, everything there looked just as she had left it, and there was no trace of the acrid smell she had expected to find there. Instead, the cavernous whitewashed room was full of fog, and she noticed that, though the shutters were bolted and barred as she had left them, the windows behind them had been widely opened to the air. She, of course, had left them shut.

She stooped and flung open the oven door of her gas-stove. Yes, it was as she had expected; a fierce heat had been generated there since she had last used the oven, and a mass of black, gluey soot had fallen through to the stone floor below.

Mrs. Bunting took the ham and eggs that she had bought the previous day for her own and Bunting's breakfast, and broiled them over the gas ring in their sitting room. Her husband watched her in surprised silence. She had never done such a thing before.

"I couldn't stay down there," she said, "it was so cold and foggy. I thought I'd make breakfast up here, just for today."

"Yes," he said kindly; "that's quite right, Ellen. I think you've done quite right, my dear."

But, when it came to the point, his wife could not eat any of the nice breakfast she had got ready; she only had another cup of tea.

"Are you ill?" Bunting asked solicitously.

"No," she said shortly; "of course I'm not ill. Don't be silly! The thought of that horrible thing happening so close by has upset me. Just hark to them, now!"

Through their closed windows penetrated the sound of scurrying feet and loud, ribald laughter. A crowd, nay, a mob, hastened to and from the scene of the murder.

Mrs. Bunting made her husband lock the front gate. "I don't want any of those ghouls in here!" she exclaimed angrily. And then, "What a lot of idle people there must be in the world," she said.

The coming and going went on all day. Mrs. Bunting stayed indoors; Bunting went out. After all, the ex-butler was human—it was natural that he should feel thrilled and excited. All their neighbors were the same. His wife wasn't reasonable about such things. She quarreled with him when he didn't tell her anything, and yet he was sure she would have been angry with him if he had said very much about it.

The lodger's bell rang about two o'clock, and Mrs. Bunting prepared the simple luncheon that was also his breakfast. As she rested the tray a minute on the drawing-room floor landing, she heard Mr. Sleuth's high, quavering voice reading aloud the words:

"She saith to him, Stolen waters are sweet, and bread

eaten in secret is pleasant. But he knoweth not that the dead are there; and that her guests are in the depths of hell."

The landlady turned the handle of the door and walked in with the tray. Mr. Sleuth was sitting close by the window, and Mrs. Bunting's Bible lay open before him. As she came in he hastily closed the Bible and looked down at the crowd walking along the Marylebone Road.

"There seem a great many people out today," he observed, without looking round.

"Yes, sir, there do." Mrs. Bunting said nothing more, and offered no other explanation; and the lodger, as he at last turned to his landlady, smiled pleasantly. He had acquired a great liking and respect for this well-behaved, taciturn woman; she was the first person for whom he had felt any such feeling for many years past.

He took a half sovereign out of his waistcoat pocket; Mrs. Bunting noticed that it was not the same waistcoat Mr. Sleuth had been wearing the day before. "Will you please accept this half sovereign for the use of your kitchen last night?" he said. "I made as little mess as I could, but I was carrying on a rather elaborate experiment."

She held out her hand, hesitated, and then took the coin.

As she walked down the stairs, the winter sun, a yellow ball hanging in the smoky sky, glinted in on Mrs. Bunting, and lent bloodred gleams, or so it seemed to her, to the piece of gold she was holding in her hand.

It was a very cold night—so cold, so windy, so snow-laden the atmosphere, that everyone who could do so stayed indoors. Bunting, however, was on his way home from what had proved a very pleasant job; he had been acting as waiter at a young lady's birthday party, and a remarkable piece of luck had come his way. The young lady had come into a fortune that day, and she had had the gracious, the surprising thought of presenting each of the hired waiters with a sovereign.

This birthday treat had put him in mind of another

birthday. His daughter Daisy would be eighteen the following Saturday. Why shouldn't he send her a postal order for half a sovereign, so that she might come up and spend her birthday in London?

Having Daisy for three or four days would cheer up Ellen. Mr. Bunting, slackening his footsteps, began to think with puzzled concern of how queer his wife had seemed lately. She had become so nervous, so "jumpy," that he didn't know what to make of her sometimes. She had never been a really good-tempered woman—your capable, self-respecting woman seldom is—but she had never been like what she was now. Of late she sometimes got quite hysterical; he had let fall a sharp word to her the other day, and she had sat down on a chair, thrown her black apron over her face, and burst out sobbing violently.

During the last ten days Ellen had taken to talking in her sleep. "No, no, no!" she had cried out, only the night before. "It isn't true! I won't have it said! It's a lie!" And there had been a wail of horrible fear and revolt in her unusually quiet, mincing voice. Yes, it would certainly be a good thing for her to have Daisy's company for a bit. Whew! It *was* cold; and Bunting had stupidly forgotten his gloves. He put his hands in his pockets to keep them warm.

Suddenly he became aware that Mr. Sleuth, the lodger who seemed to have "turned their luck," as it were, was walking along on the opposite side of the solitary street.

Mr. Sleuth's tall, thin figure was rather bowed, his head bent toward the ground. His right arm was thrust into his long Inverness cape; the other occasionally sawed the air, doubtless in order to help him keep warm. He was walking rather quickly. It was clear that he had not yet become aware of the proximity of his landlord.

Bunting felt pleased to see his lodger; it increased his feeling of general satisfaction. Strange, was it not, that that odd, peculiar-looking figure should have made all the difference to his (Bunting's) and Mrs. Bunting's happiness and comfort in life?

Naturally, Bunting saw far less of the lodger than did Mrs. Bunting. Their gentleman had made it very clear that he did not like either the husband or wife to come up to his rooms without being definitely asked to do so, and Bunting had been up there only once since Mr. Sleuth's arrival five weeks before. This seemed to be a good opportunity for a little genial conversation.

Bunting, still an active man for his years, crossed the road, and, stepping briskly forward, tried to overtake Mr. Sleuth; but the more he hurried, the more the other hastened, and that without even turning to see whose steps he heard echoing behind him on the now freezing pavement.

Mr. Sleuth's own footsteps were quite inaudible—an odd circumstance, when you came to think of it, as Bunting did think of it later, lying awake by Ellen's side in the pitch-darkness. What it meant was, of course, that the lodger had rubber soles on his shoes.

The two men, the pursued and the pursuer, at last turned into the Marylebone Road. They were now within a hundred yards of home; and so, plucking up courage, Bunting called out, his voice echoing freshly on the still air:

"Mr. Sleuth, sir! Mr. Sleuth!"

The lodger stopped and turned round. He had been walking so quickly, and he was in so poor a physical condition, that the sweat was pouring down his face.

"Ah! So it's you, Mr. Bunting? I heard footsteps behind me, and I hurried on. I wish I'd known that it was only you; there are so many queer characters about at night in London."

"Not on a night like this, sir. Only honest folk who have business out of doors would be out such a night as this. It *is* cold, sir!" And then into Bunting's slow and honest mind there suddenly crept the query as to what Mr. Sleuth's own business out could be on this cold, bitter night.

"Cold?" the lodger repeated. "I can't say that I find it cold, Mr. Bunting. When the snow falls the air always becomes milder."

"Yes, sir; but tonight there's such a sharp east wind. Why, it freezes the very marrow in one's bones!"

Bunting noticed that Mr. Sleuth kept his distance in a rather strange way: he walked at the edge of the pavement, leaving the rest of it, on the wall side, to his landlord.

"I lost my way," he said abruptly. "I've been over Primrose Hill to see a friend of mine, and then, coming back, I lost my way."

Bunting could well believe that, for when he had first noticed Mr. Sleuth he was coming from the east, and not, as he should have done if walking home from Primrose Hill, from the north.

They had now reached the little gate that gave onto the shabby, paved court in front of the house. Mr. Sleuth was walking up the flagged path, when, with a "By your leave, sir," the ex-butler, stepping aside, slipped in front of his lodger, in order to open the front door for him.

As he passed by Mr. Sleuth, the back of Bunting's bare left hand brushed lightly against the long Inverness cape the other man was wearing, and, to his surprise, the stretch of cloth against which his hand lay for a moment was not only damp, damp from the flakes of snow that had settled upon it, but wet—wet and gluey. Bunting thrust his left hand into his pocket; it was with the other that he placed the key in the lock of the door.

The two men passed into the hall together. The house seemed blackly dark in comparison with the lighted-up road outside; and then, quite suddenly, there came over Bunting a feeling of mortal terror, an instinctive knowledge that some terrible and immediate danger was near him. A voice —the voice of his first wife, the long-dead girl to whom his mind so seldom reverted nowadays—uttered in his ear the words, "Take care!"

"I'm afraid, Mr. Bunting, that you must have felt something dirty, foul, on my coat? It's too long a story to tell you now, but I brushed up against a dead animal—a dead rabbit lying across a bench on Primrose Hill."

Mr. Sleuth spoke in a very quiet voice, almost in a whisper.

"No, sir; no, I didn't notice nothing. I scarcely touched you, sir." It seemed as if a power outside himself compelled Bunting to utter these lying words. "And now, sir, I'll be saying good night to you," he added.

He waited until the lodger had gone upstairs, and then he turned into his own sitting room. There he sat down, for he felt very queer. He did not draw his left hand out of his pocket till he heard the other man moving about in the room above. Then he lit the gas and held up his left hand; he put it close to his face. It was flecked, streaked with blood.

He took off his boots, and then, very quietly, he went into the room where his wife lay asleep. Stealthily he walked across to the toilet table, and dipped his hand into the water jug.

The next morning Mr. Sleuth's landlord awoke with a start; he felt curiously heavy about the limbs and tired about the eyes.

Drawing his watch from under his pillow, he saw that it was nearly nine o'clock. He and Ellen had overslept. Without waking her, he got out of bed and pulled up the blind. It was snowing heavily, and, as is the way when it snows, even in London, it was strangely, curiously still.

After he had dressed he went out into the passage. A newspaper and a letter were lying on the mat. Fancy having slept through the postman's knock! He picked them both up and went into the sitting room; then he carefully shut the door behind him, and, tossing the letter aside, spread the newspaper wide open on the table and bent over it.

As Bunting at last looked up and straightened himself, a look of inexpressible relief shone upon his stolid face. The item of news he had felt certain would be there, printed in big type on the middle sheet, was not there.

He folded the paper and laid it on a chair, and then eagerly took up his letter.

Dear Father [it ran]: I hope this finds you as well as it leaves me. Mrs. Puddle's youngest child has got scarlet fever, and aunt thinks I had better come away at once, just to stay with you for a few days. Please tell Ellen I won't give her no trouble.

Your loving daughter,
Daisy

Bunting felt amazingly lighthearted; and, as he walked into the next room, he smiled broadly.

"Ellen," he cried out, "here's news! Daisy's coming today. There's scarlet fever in their house, and Martha thinks she had better come away for a few days. She'll be here for her birthday!"

Mrs. Bunting listened in silence; she did not even open her eyes. "I can't have the girl here just now," she said shortly; "I've got just as much as I can manage to do."

But Bunting felt pugnacious, and so cheerful as to be almost light-headed. Deep down in his heart he looked back to last night with a feeling of shame and self-rebuke. Whatever had made such horrible thoughts and suspicions come into his head?

"Of course Daisy will come here," he said shortly. "If it comes to that, she'll be able to help you with the work, and she'll brisk us both up a bit."

Rather to his surprise, Mrs. Bunting said nothing in answer to this, and he changed the subject abruptly. "The lodger and me came in together last night," he observed. "He's certainly a funny kind of gentleman. It wasn't the sort of night one would choose to go for a walk over Primrose Hill, and yet that was what he had been doing—so he said."

It stopped snowing about ten o'clock, and the morning wore itself away.

Just as twelve was striking, a four-wheeler drew up to the gate. It was Daisy—pink-cheeked, excited, laughing-eyed Daisy, a sight to gladden any father's heart. "Aunt said I was to have a cab if the weather was bad," she said.

There was a bit of a wrangle over the fare. King's Cross, as all the world knows, is nothing like two miles from the Marylebone Road, but the man clamored for one-and-six-pence, and hinted darkly that he had done the young lady a favor in bringing her at all.

While he and Bunting were having words, Daisy, leaving them to it, walked up the path to the door where her stepmother was awaiting her.

Suddenly there fell loud shouts on the still air. They sounded strangely eerie, breaking sharply across the muffled, snowy air.

"What's that?" said Bunting, with a look of startled fear. "Why, whatever's that?"

The cabman lowered his voice: "Them are crying out that 'orrible affair at King's Cross. He's done for two of 'em this time! That's what I meant when I said I might have got a better fare; I wouldn't say anything before Missy there, but folk 'ave been coming from all over London—like a fire; plenty of toffs, too. But there—there's nothing to see now!"

"What! Another woman murdered last night?" Bunting felt and looked convulsed with horror.

The cabman stared at him, surprised. "Two of 'em, I tell yer—within a few yards of one another. He 'ave got a nerve—"

"Have they caught him?" asked Bunting perfunctorily.

"Lord, no! They'll never catch 'im! It must 'ave happened hours and hours ago—they was both stone-cold. One each end of an archway. That's why they didn't see 'em before."

The hoarse cries were coming nearer and nearer—two news vendors trying to outshout each other.

"'Orrible discovery near King's Cross!" they yelled exultantly. And as Bunting, with his daughter's bag in his hand, hurried up the path and passed through his front door, the words pursued him like a dreadful threat.

Angrily he shut out the hoarse, insistent cries. No, he had no wish to buy a paper. That kind of crime wasn't fit reading for a young girl, such a girl as was his Daisy, brought up as carefully as if she had been a young lady by her strict Methody aunt.

As he stood in his little hall, trying to feel "all right" again, he could hear Daisy's voice—high, voluble, excited— giving her stepmother a long account of the scarlet-fever case to which she owed her presence in London. But, as Bunting pushed open the door of the sitting room, there came a note of sharp alarm in his daughter's voice, and he heard her say: "Why, Ellen! Whatever is the matter? You do look bad!" and his wife's muffled answer: "Open the window —do."

Rushing across the room, Bunting pushed up the sash. The newspaper sellers were now just outside the house. "Horrible discovery near King's Cross—a clue to the murderer!" they yelled. And then, helplessly, Mrs. Bunting began to laugh. She laughed and laughed and laughed, rocking herself to and fro as if in an ecstasy of mirth.

"Why, father, whatever's the matter with her?" Daisy looked quite scared.

"She's in 'sterics—that's what it is," he said shortly. "I'll just get the water jug. Wait a minute."

Bunting felt very put out, and yet glad, too, for this queer seizure of Ellen's almost made him forget the sick terror with which he had been possessed a moment before. That he and his wife should be obsessed by the same fear, the same terror, never crossed his simple, slow-working mind.

The lodger's bell rang. That, or the threat of the water jug, had a magical effect on Mrs. Bunting. She rose to her feet, still trembling, but composed.

As Mrs. Bunting went upstairs she felt her legs trembling under her, and put out a shaking hand to clutch at the banister for support. She waited a few minutes on the landing, and then knocked at the door of her lodger's parlor.

But Mr. Sleuth's voice answered her from the bedroom. "I'm not well," he called out querulously; "I think I caught a chill going out to see a friend last night. I'd be obliged if you'll bring me up a cup of tea and put it outside my door, Mrs. Bunting."

"Very well, sir."

Mrs. Bunting went downstairs and made her lodger a cup of tea over the gas ring, Bunting watching her the while in heavy silence.

During their midday dinner the husband and wife had a little discussion as to where Daisy should sleep. It had already been settled that a bed should be made up for her in the sitting room, but Bunting saw reason to change this plan. As the two women were clearing away the dishes, he looked up and said shortly: "I think 'twould be better if Daisy were to sleep with you, Ellen, and I were to sleep in the sitting room."

Ellen acquiesced quietly.

Daisy was a good-natured girl; she liked London, and wanted to make herself useful to her stepmother. "I'll wash up; don't you bother to come downstairs," she said.

Bunting began to walk up and down the room. His wife gave him a furtive glance; she wondered what he was thinking about.

"Didn't you get a paper?" she said at last.

"There's the paper," he said crossly, "the paper we always do take in, the *Telegraph.*" His look challenged her to a further question.

"I thought they was shouting something in the street— I mean just before I was took bad."

But he made no answer; instead, he went to the top of the staircase and called out sharply: "Daisy! Daisy, child, are you there?"

"Yes, father," she answered from below.

"Better come upstairs out of that cold kitchen."

He came back into the sitting room again.

"Ellen, is the lodger in? I haven't heard him moving

about. I don't want Daisy to be mixed up with him."

"Mr. Sleuth is not well today," his wife answered; "he is remaining in bed a bit. Daisy needn't have anything to do with him. She'll have her work cut out looking after things down here. That's where I want her to help me."

"Agreed," he said.

When it grew dark, Bunting went out and bought an evening paper. He read it out of doors in the biting cold, standing beneath a streetlamp. He wanted to see what was the clue to the murderer.

The clue proved to be a very slender one—merely the imprint in the snowy slush of a half-worn rubber sole; and it was, of course, by no means certain that the sole belonged to the boot or shoe of the murderer of the two doomed women who had met so swift and awful a death in the arch near King's Cross station. The paper's special investigator pointed out that there were thousands of such soles being worn in London. Bunting found comfort in that obvious fact. He felt grateful to the special investigator for having stated it so clearly.

As he approached his house, he heard curious sounds coming from the inner side of the low wall that shut off the courtyard from the pavement. Under ordinary circumstances Bunting would have gone at once to drive whoever was there out into the roadway. Now he stayed outside, sick with suspense and anxiety. Was it possible that their place was being watched—already?

But it was only Mr. Sleuth. To Bunting's astonishment, the lodger suddenly stepped forward from behind the wall onto the flagged path. He was carrying a brown-paper parcel, and, as he walked along, the new boots he was wearing creaked and the tap-tap of wooden heels rang out on the stones.

Bunting, still hidden outside the gate, suddenly understood what his lodger had been doing the other side of the wall. Mr. Sleuth had been out to buy himself a pair of boots, and had gone inside the gate to put them on, placing his old footgear in the paper in which the new boots had been wrapped.

Bunting waited until Mr. Sleuth had let himself into the house; then he also walked up the flagged pathway, and put his latchkey in the door.

In the next three days each of Bunting's waking hours held its meed of aching fear and suspense. From his point of view, almost any alternative would be preferable to that which to most people would have seemed the only one open to him. He told himself that it would be ruin for him and for his Ellen to be mixed up publicly in such a terrible affair. It would track them to their dying day.

Bunting was also always debating within himself as to whether he should tell Ellen of his frightful suspicion. He could not believe that what had become so plain to himself could long be concealed from all the world, and yet he did not credit his wife with the same intelligence. He did not even notice that, although she waited on Mr. Sleuth as assiduously as ever, Mrs. Bunting never mentioned the lodger.

Mr. Sleuth, meanwhile, kept upstairs; he had given up going out altogether. He still felt, so he assured his landlady, far from well.

Daisy was another complication, the more so that the girl, whom her father longed to send away and whom he would hardly let out of his sight, showed herself inconveniently inquisitive concerning the lodger.

"Whatever does he do with himself all day?" she asked her stepmother.

"Well, just now he's reading the Bible," Mrs. Bunting had answered, very shortly and dryly.

"Well, I never! That's a funny thing for a gentleman to do!" Such had been Daisy's pert remark, and her stepmother had snubbed her well for it.

Daisy's eighteenth birthday dawned uneventfully. Her father gave her what he had always promised she should have on her eighteenth birthday—a watch. It was a pretty little silver watch, which Bunting had bought secondhand on the last day he had been happy; it seemed a long time ago now.

Mrs. Bunting thought a silver watch a very extravagant present, but she had always had the good sense not to interfere between her husband and his child. Besides, her mind was now full of other things. She was beginning to fear that Bunting suspected something, and she was filled with watchful anxiety and unease. What if he were to do anything silly—mix them up with the police, for instance? It certainly would be ruination to them both. But there—one never knew, with men! Her husband, however, kept his own counsel absolutely.

Daisy's birthday was on Saturday. In the middle of the morning Ellen and Daisy went down into the kitchen. Bunting didn't like the feeling that there was only one flight of stairs between Mr. Sleuth and himself, so he quietly slipped out of the house and went to buy himself an ounce of tobacco.

In the last four days Bunting had avoided his usual haunts. But today the unfortunate man had a curious longing for human companionship—companionship, that is, other than that of Ellen and Daisy. This feeling led him into a small, populous thoroughfare hard by the Edgeware Road. There were more people there than usual, for the housewives of the neighborhood were doing their marketing for Sunday.

Bunting passed the time of day with the tobacconist, and the two fell into desultory talk. To the ex-butler's surprise, the man said nothing at all to him on the subject of which all the neighborhood must still be talking.

And then, quite suddenly, while still standing by the counter, and before he had paid for the packet of tobacco he held in his hand, Bunting, through the open door, saw, with horrified surprise, that his wife was standing outside a greengrocer's shop just opposite. Muttering a word of apology, he rushed out of the shop and across the road.

"Ellen!" he gasped hoarsely. "You've never gone and left my little girl alone in the house?"

Mrs. Bunting's face went chalky white. "I thought you were indoors," she said. "You *were* indoors. Whatever made you come out for, without first making sure I was there?"

Bunting made no answer; but, as they stared at each other in exasperated silence, *each knew that the other knew.*

They turned and scurried down the street.

"Don't run," he said suddenly; "we shall get there just as quickly if we walk fast. People are noticing you, Ellen. Don't run."

He spoke breathlessly, but it was breathlessness induced by fear and excitement, not by the quick pace at which they were walking.

At last they reached their own gate. Bunting pushed past in front of his wife. After all, Daisy was his child—Ellen couldn't know how he was feeling. He made the path almost in one leap, and fumbled for a moment with his latchkey. The door opened.

"Daisy!" he called out in a wailing voice. "Daisy, my dear, where are you?"

"Here I am, father; what is it?"

"She's all right!" Bunting turned his gray face to his wife. "She's all right, Ellen!" Then he waited a moment, leaning against the wall of the passage. "It did give me a turn," he said; and then, warningly, "Don't frighten the girl, Ellen."

Daisy was standing before the fire in the sitting room, admiring herself in the glass. "Oh, father," she said, without turning round, "I've seen the lodger! He's quite a nice gentleman—though, to be sure, he does look a cure! He came down to ask Ellen for something, and we had quite a nice little chat. I told him it was my birthday, and he asked me to go to Madame Tussaud's with him this afternoon." She laughed a little self-consciously. "Of course I could see he was 'centric, and then at first he spoke so funnily. 'And who be you?' he says, threatening-like. And I says to him, 'I'm Mr. Bunting's daughter, sir.' 'Then you're a very fortunate girl'—that's what he said, Ellen—'to 'ave such a nice stepmother as you've got. That's why,' he says, 'you look such a good, innocent girl.' And then he quoted a bit of the prayer book at me. 'Keep innocency,' he says, wagging his head at me. Lor'! It made me feel as if I was with aunt again."

"I won't have you going out with the lodger—that's flat." He was wiping his forehead with one hand, while with the other he mechanically squeezed the little packet of tobacco, for which, as he now remembered, he had forgotten to pay.

Daisy pouted. "Oh, father, I think you might let me have a treat on my birthday! I told him Saturday wasn't a very good day—at least, so I'd heard—for Madame Tussaud's. Then he said we could go early, while the fine folk are still having their dinners. He wants you to come, too." She turned to her stepmother, then giggled happily. "The lodger has a wonderful fancy for you, Ellen; if I was father, I'd feel quite jealous!"

Her last words were cut across by a loud knock on the door. Bunting and his wife looked at each other apprehensively.

Both felt a curious thrill of relief when they saw that it was only Mr. Sleuth—Mr. Sleuth dressed to go out: the tall hat he had worn when he first came to them was in his hand, and he was wearing a heavy overcoat.

"I saw you had come in"—he addressed Mrs. Bunting in his high, whistling, hesitating voice—"and so I've come down to ask if you and Miss Bunting will come to Madame Tussaud's now. I have never seen these famous waxworks, though I've heard of the place all my life."

As Bunting forced himself to look fixedly at his lodger, a sudden doubt, bringing with it a sense of immeasurable relief, came to him. Surely it was inconceivable that this gentle, mild-mannered gentleman could be the monster of cruelty and cunning that Bunting had but a moment ago believed him to be!

"You're very kind, sir, I'm sure." He tried to catch his wife's eye, but Mrs. Bunting was looking away, staring into vacancy. She still, of course, wore the bonnet and cloak in which she had just been out to do her marketing. Daisy was already putting on her hat and coat.

Madame Tussaud's had hitherto held pleasant memories for Mrs. Bunting. In the days when she and Bunting were courting they often spent part of their "afternoon out" there. The butler had an acquaintance, a man named Hopkins, who was one of the waxworks' staff, and this man had sometimes given him passes for "self and lady." But this was the first time Mrs. Bunting had been inside the place since she had come to live almost next door, as it were, to the big building.

The ill-sorted trio walked up the great staircase and into the first gallery; and there Mr. Sleuth suddenly stopped short. The presence of those curious, still figures, suggesting death in life, seemed to surprise and affright him.

Daisy took quick advantage of the lodger's hesitation and unease.

"Oh, Ellen," she cried, "do let us begin by going into the Chamber of Horrors! I've never been in there. Aunt made father promise he wouldn't take me, the only time I've ever been here. But now that I'm eighteen I can do just as I like; besides, aunt will never know!"

Mr. Sleuth looked down at her.

"Yes," he said, "let us go into the Chamber of Horrors; that's a good idea, Miss Bunting."

They turned into the great room in which the Napoleonic relics are kept, and which leads into the curious, vault-like chamber where waxen effigies of dead criminals stand grouped in wooden docks. Mrs. Bunting was at once disturbed and relieved to see her husband's old acquaintance, Mr. Hopkins, in charge of the turnstile admitting the public to the Chamber of Horrors.

"Well, you *are* a stranger," the man observed genially. "I do believe this is the very first time I've seen you in here, Mrs. Bunting, since you married!"

"Yes," she said; "that is so. And this is my husband's daughter, Daisy; I expect you've heard of her, Mr. Hopkins. And this"—she hesitated a moment—"is our lodger, Mr. Sleuth."

But Mr. Sleuth frowned and shuffled away. Daisy, leaving her stepmother's side, joined him.

Mrs. Bunting put down three sixpences.

"Wait a minute," said Hopkins; "you can't go into the Chamber of Horrors just yet. But you won't have to wait more than four or five minutes, Mrs. Bunting. It's this way, you see; our boss is in there, showing a party round." He lowered his voice. "It's Sir John Burney—I suppose you know who Sir John Burney is?"

"No," she answered indifferently; "I don't know that I ever heard of him." She felt slightly—oh, very slightly— uneasy about Daisy. She would like her stepdaughter to keep well within sight and sound. Mr. Sleuth was taking the girl to the other end of the room.

"Well, I hope you never *will* know him—not in any personal sense, Mrs. Bunting." The man chuckled. "He's the Head Commissioner of Police—that's what Sir John Burney is. One of the gentlemen he's showing round our place is the Paris Prefect of Police, whose job is on all fours, so to speak, with Sir John's. The Frenchy has brought his daughter with him, and there are several other ladies. Ladies always like 'orrors, Mrs. Bunting; that's our experience here. 'Oh, take me to the Chamber of 'Orrors!'—that's what they say the minute they gets into the building."

A group of people, all talking and laughing together, were advancing from within toward the turnstile.

Mrs. Bunting stared at them nervously. She wondered which of them was the gentleman with whom Mr. Hopkins had hoped she would never be brought into personal contact. She quickly picked him out. He was a tall, powerful, nice-looking gentleman with a commanding manner. Just now he was smiling down into the face of a young lady. "Monsieur Barberoux is quite right," he was saying; "the English law is too kind to the criminal, especially to the murderer. If we conducted our trials in the French fashion, the place we have just left would be very much fuller than it is today! A man of whose guilt we are absolutely assured is oftener than not acquitted, and then the public taunt us with 'another undiscovered crime'!"

"D'you mean, Sir John, that murderers sometimes escape scot-free? Take the man who has been committing all those awful murders this last month. Of course, I don't know much about it, for father won't let me read about it, but I can't help being interested!" Her girlish voice rang out, and Mrs. Bunting heard every word distinctly.

The party gathered round, listening eagerly to hear what the Head Commissioner would say next.

"Yes." He spoke very deliberately. "I think we may say —now, don't give me away to a newspaper fellow, Miss Rose —that we do know perfectly well who the murderer in question is—"

Several of those standing nearby uttered expressions of surprise and incredulity.

"Then why don't you catch him?" cried the girl indignantly.

"I didn't say we know *where* he is; I only said we know *who* he is; or, rather, perhaps I ought to say that we have a very strong suspicion of his identity."

Sir John's French colleague looked up quickly. "The Hamburg and Liverpool man?" he said interrogatively.

The other nodded. "Yes; I suppose you've had the case turned up?"

Then, speaking very quickly, as if he wished to dismiss the subject from his own mind and from that of his auditors, he went on:

"Two murders of the kind were committed eight years ago—one in Hamburg, the other just afterward in

Liverpool, and there were certain peculiarities connected with the crimes which made it clear they were committed by the same hand. The perpetrator was caught, fortunately for us red-handed, just as he was leaving the house of his victim, for in Liverpool the murder was committed in a house. I myself saw the unhappy man—I say unhappy, for there is no doubt at all that he was mad"—he hesitated, and added in a lower tone—"suffering from an acute form of religious mania. I myself saw him, at some length. But now comes the really interesting point. Just a month ago this criminal lunatic, as we must regard him, made his escape from the asylum where he was confined. He arranged the whole thing with extraordinary cunning and intelligence, and we should probably have caught him long ago were it not that he managed, when on his way out of the place, to annex a considerable sum of money in gold with which the wages of the staff were about to be paid."

The Frenchman again spoke. "Why have you not circulated a description?" he asked.

"We did that at once"—Sir John Burney smiled a little grimly—"but only among our own people. We dare not circulate the man's description among the general public. You see, we may be mistaken, after all."

"That is not very probable!" The Frenchman smiled a satirical little smile.

A moment later the party were walking in Indian file through the turnstile, Sir John Burney leading the way.

Mrs. Bunting looked straight before her. Even had she wished to do so, she had neither time nor power to warn her lodger of his danger.

Daisy and her companion were now coming down the room, bearing straight for the Head Commissioner of Police. In another moment Mr. Sleuth and Sir John Burney would be face to face.

Suddenly Mr. Sleuth swerved to one side. A terrible change came over his pale, narrow face; it became discomposed, livid with rage and terror.

But, to Mrs. Bunting's relief—yes, to her inexpressible relief—Sir John Burney and his friends swept on. They passed by Mr. Sleuth unconcernedly, unaware, or so it seemed to her, that there was anyone else in the room but themselves.

"Hurry up, Mrs. Bunting," said the turnstile keeper; "you and your friends will have the place all to yourselves." From an official he had become a man, and it was the man in Mr. Hopkins that gallantly addressed pretty Daisy Bunting. "It seems strange that a young lady like you should want to go in and see all those 'orrible frights," he said jestingly.

"Mrs. Bunting, may I trouble you to come over here for a moment?" The words were hissed rather than spoken by Mr. Sleuth's lips.

His landlady took a doubtful step forward.

"A last word with you, Mrs. Bunting." The lodger's face was still distorted with fear and passion. "Do you think to escape the consequences of your hideous treachery? I trusted you, Mrs. Bunting, and you betrayed me! But I am protected by a higher power, for I still have work to do. Your end will be bitter as wormwood and sharp as a two-edged sword. Your feet shall go down to death, and your steps take hold on hell." Even while Mr. Sleuth was uttering these strange, dreadful words, he was looking around, his eyes glancing this way and that, seeking a way of escape.

At last his eyes became fixed on a small placard placed about a curtain. "Emergency Exit" was written there. Leaving his landlady's side, he walked over to the turnstile. He fumbled in his pocket for a moment, and then touched the man on the arm. "I feel ill," he said, speaking very rapidly; "very ill indeed! It's the atmosphere of this place. I want you to let me out by the quickest way. It would be a pity for me to faint here—especially with ladies about." His left hand shot out and placed what he had been fumbling for in his pocket on the other's bare palm. "I see there's an emergency exit over there. Would it be possible for me to get out that way?"

"Well, yes, sir; I think so." The man hesitated; he felt a slight, a very slight, feeling of misgiving. He looked at Daisy, flushed and smiling, happy and unconcerned, and then at Mrs. Bunting. She was very pale; but surely her lodger's sudden seizure was enough to make her feel worried. Hopkins felt the half sovereign pleasantly tickling his palm. The Prefect of Police had given him only half a crown—mean, shabby foreigner!

"Yes, I can let you out that way," he said at last, "and perhaps when you're standing out in the air on the iron balcony you'll feel better. But then, you know, sir, you'll have to come round to the front if you want to come in again, for those emergency doors only open outward."

"Yes, yes," said Mr. Sleuth hurriedly; "I quite understand! If I feel better I'll come in by the front way, and pay another shilling—that's only fair."

"You needn't do that if you'll just explain what happened here."

The man went and pulled the curtain aside, and put his shoulder against the door. It burst open, and the light for a moment blinded Mr. Sleuth. He passed his hand over his eyes.

"Thank you," he said; "thank you. I shall get all right here."

Five days later Bunting identified the body of a man found drowned in the Regent's Canal as that of his late lodger; and, the morning following, a gardener working in the Regent's Park found a newspaper in which were wrapped, together with a half-worn pair of rubber-soled shoes, two surgical knives. This fact was not chronicled in any newspaper; but a very pretty and picturesque paragraph went the round of the press, about the same time, concerning a small box filled with sovereigns which had been forwarded anonymously to the Governor of the Foundling Hospital.

Mr. and Mrs. Bunting are now in the service of an old lady, by whom they are feared as well as respected, and whom they make very comfortable.

THE DUCHESS AT PRAYER

Edith Wharton

Born into a socially prominent New York family, Edith Wharton (1862–1937) overcame a troubled childhood and a disastrous early marriage to become one of America's foremost novelists. Her work, as evidenced by such classics as Ethan Frome, *is noted for its depth of characterization and sympathy for human suffering. In "The Duchess at Prayer" we are caught up in the hopelessness of three persons—a husband, his wife, and her lover—bound by the conventions and prohibitions of their times. Although the story is narrated as past history, two hundred years after the events, its ending is no less horrifying than if it had happened yesterday.*

Have you ever questioned the long shuttered front of an old Italian house, that motionless mask, smooth, mute, equivocal as the face of a priest behind which buzz the secrets of the confessional? Other houses declare the activities they shelter; they are the clear expressive cuticle of a life flowing close to the surface; but the old palace in its narrow street, the villa on its cypress-hooded hill, are as impenetrable as death. The tall windows are like blind eyes, the great door is a shut mouth. Inside there may be sunshine, the scent of myrtles, and a pulse of life through all the arteries of the huge frame; or a mortal solitude, where bats lodge in the disjointed stones and the keys rust in unused doors. . . .

II

From the loggia, with its vanishing frescoes, I looked down an avenue barred by a ladder of cypress-shadows to the ducal escutcheon and mutilated vases of the gate. Flat noon lay on the gardens, on fountains, porticoes and grottoes. Below the terrace, where a chrome-colored lichen had sheeted the balustrade as with fine *laminæ* of gold, vineyards stooped to the rich valley clasped in hills. The lower slopes were strewn with white villages like stars spangling a summer dusk; and beyond these, fold on fold of blue mountain, clear as gauze against the sky. The August air was lifeless, but it seemed light and vivifying after the atmosphere of the shrouded rooms through which I had been led. Their chill was on me and I hugged the sunshine.

"The Duchess's apartments are beyond," said the old man.

He was the oldest man I had ever seen; so sucked back into the past that he seemed more like a memory than a living being. The one trait linking him with the actual was the fixity with which his small saurian eye held the pocket that, as I entered, had yielded a lira to the gatekeeper's child. He went on, without removing his eye:

"For two hundred years nothing has been changed in the apartments of the Duchess."

"And no one lives here now?"

"No one, sir. The Duke goes to Como for the summer season."

I had moved to the other end of the loggia. Below me, through hanging groves, white roofs and domes flashed like a smile.

"And that's Vicenza?"

"Proprio!" The old man extended fingers as lean as the hands fading from the walls behind us. "You see the palace roof over there, just to the left of the Basilica? The one with the row of statues like birds taking flight? That's the Duke's town palace, built by Palladio."

"And does the Duke come there?"

"Never. In winter he goes to Rome."

"And the palace and the villa are always closed?"

"As you see—always."

"How long has this been?"

"Since I can remember."

I looked into his eyes: they were like tarnished metal mirrors reflecting nothing. "That must be a long time," I said involuntarily.

"A long time," he assented.

I looked down on the gardens. An opulence of dahlias overran the box-borders, between cypresses that cut the sunshine like basalt shafts. Bees hung above the lavender; lizards sunned themselves on the benches and slipped through the cracks of the dry basins. Everywhere were vanishing traces of that fantastic horticulture of which our dull age has lost the art. Down the alleys maimed statues stretched their arms like rows of whining beggars; faun-eared terms grinned in the thickets, and above the laurustinus walls rose the mock ruin of a temple, falling into real ruin in the bright disintegrating air. The glare was blinding.

"Let us go in," I said.

The old man pushed open a heavy door, behind which the cold lurked like a knife.

"The Duchess's apartments," he said.

Overhead and around us the same evanescent frescoes, under foot the same scagliola volutes, unrolled themselves interminably. Ebony cabinets, with inlay of precious marbles in cunning perspective, alternated down the room with the tarnished efflorescence of gilt consoles supporting Chinese monsters; and from the chimney panel a gentleman in the Spanish habit haughtily ignored us.

"Duke Ercole II," the old man explained, "by the Genoese Priest."

It was a narrow-browed face, sallow as a wax effigy, high-nosed and cautious-lidded, as though modeled by priestly hands; the lips weak and vain rather than cruel; a quibbling mouth that would have snapped at verbal errors like a lizard catching flies, but had never learned the shape of a round yes or no. One of the Duke's hands rested on the head of a dwarf, a simian creature with pearl earrings and fantastic dress; the other turned the pages of a folio propped on a skull.

"Beyond is the Duchess's bedroom," the old man reminded me.

Here the shutters admitted but two narrow shafts of light, gold bars deepening the subaqueous gloom. On a dais the bedstead, grim, nuptial, official, lifted its baldachin; a yellow Christ agonized between the curtains, and across the room a lady smiled at us from the chimney breast.

The old man unbarred a shutter and the light touched her face. Such a face it was, with a flicker of laughter over it like the wind on a June meadow, and a singular tender pliancy of mien, as though one of Tiepolo's lenient goddesses had been busked into the stiff sheath of a seventeenth-century dress!

"No one has slept here," said the old man, "since the Duchess Violante."

"And she was—?"

"The lady there—first Duchess of Duke Ercole II."

He drew a key from his pocket and unlocked a door at the farther end of the room. "The chapel," he said. "This is the Duchess's balcony." As I turned to follow him the Duchess tossed me a sidelong smile.

I stepped into a grated tribune above a chapel festooned with stucco. Pictures of bituminous saints mouldered between the pilasters; the artificial roses in the altar vases were gray with dust and age, and under the cobwebby rosettes of the vaulting a bird's nest clung. Before the altar stood a row of tattered armchairs, and I drew back at sight of a figure kneeling near them.

"The Duchess," the old man whispered. "By the Cavaliere Bernini."

It was the image of a woman in furred robes and spreading fraise, her hand lifted, her face addressed to the tabernacle. There was a strangeness in the sight of that immovable presence locked in prayer before an abandoned shrine. Her face was hidden, and I wondered whether it were grief or gratitude that raised her hands and drew her eyes to the altar, where no living prayer joined her marble invocation. I followed my guide down the tribune steps, impatient to see what mystic version of such terrestrial graces the ingenious artist had found—the Cavaliere was master of such arts. The Duchess's attitude was one of transport, as though heavenly airs fluttered her laces and the lovelocks escaping from her coif. I saw how admirably the sculptor had caught the poise of her head, the tender slope of the shoulder; then I crossed over and looked into her face—it was a frozen horror. Never have hate, revolt and agony so possessed a human countenance. . . .

The old man crossed himself and shuffled his feet on the marble.

"The Duchess Violante," he repeated.

"The same as in the picture?"

"Eh—the same."

"But the face—what does it mean?"

He shrugged his shoulders and turned deaf eyes on me. Then he shot a glance round the sepulchral place, clutched my sleeve and said, close to my ear: "It was not always so."

"What was not?"

"The face—so terrible."

"The Duchess's face?"

"The statue's. It changed after—"

"After?"

"It was put here."

"The statue's face *changed*—?"

He mistook my bewilderment for incredulity and his confidential finger dropped from my sleeve. "Eh, that's the story. I tell what I've heard. What do I know?" He resumed his senile shuffle across the marble. "This is a bad place to stay in—no one comes here. It's too cold. But the gentleman said, *I must see everything!*"

I let the lire sound. "So I must—and hear everything. This story, now—from whom did you have it?"

His hand stole back. "One that saw it, by God!"

"That saw it?"

"My grandmother, then. I'm a very old man."

"Your grandmother? Your grandmother was—?"

"The Duchess's serving girl, with respect to you."

"Your grandmother? Two hundred years ago?"

"Is it too long ago? That's as God pleases. I am a very old man and she was a very old woman when I was born. When she died she was as black as a miraculous Virgin and her breath whistled like the wind in a keyhole. She told me the story when I was a little boy. She told it to me out there in the garden, on a bench by the fishpond, one summer night of the year she died. It must be true, for I can show you the very bench we sat on. . . ."

III

Noon lay heavier on the gardens; not our live humming warmth but the stale exhalation of dead summers. The very statues seemed to drowse like watchers by a deathbed. Lizards shot out of the cracked soil like flames and the bench in the laurustinus niche was strewn with the blue varnished bodies of dead flies. Before us lay the fishpond, a yellow marble slab above rotting secrets. The villa looked across it, composed as a dead face, with the cypresses flanking it for candles. . . .

IV

"Impossible, you say, that my mother's mother should have been the Duchess's maid? What do I know? It is so long since anything has happened here that the old things seem nearer, perhaps, than to those who live in cities. . . . But how else did she know about the statue then? Answer me that, sir! That she saw with her eyes, I can swear to, and never smiled again, so she told me, till they put her first child in her arms . . . for she was taken to wife by the steward's son, Antonio, the same who had carried the letters. . . . But where am I? Ah, well . . . she was a mere slip, you understand, my grandmother, when the Duchess died, a niece of the upper maid, Nencia, and suffered about the Duchess because of her pranks and the funny songs she knew. It's possible, you think, she may have heard from others what she afterward fancied she had seen herself? How that is, it's not for an unlettered man to say; though indeed I myself seem to have seen many of the things she told me. This is a strange place. No one comes here, nothing changes, and the old memories stand up as distinct as the statues in the garden. . . .

"It began the summer after they came back from the Brenta. Duke Ercole had married the lady from Venice, you must know; it was a gay city, then, I'm told, with laughter

and music on the water, and the days slipped by like boats
running with the tide. Well, to humor her he took her back
the first autumn to the Brenta. Her father, it appears, had
a grand palace there, with such gardens, bowling alleys,
grottoes and casinos as never were; gondolas bobbing at the
water gates, a stable full of gilt coaches, a theater full of
players, and kitchens and offices full of cooks and lackeys to
serve up chocolate all day long to the fine ladies in masks and
furbelows, with their pet dogs and their blackamoors and
their *abates.* Eh! I know it all as if I'd been there, for Nencia,
you see, my grandmother's aunt, traveled with the Duchess,
and came back with her eyes round as platters, and not a
word to say for the rest of the year to any of the lads who'd
courted her here in Vicenza.

"What happened there I don't know—my grandmother
could never get at the rights of it, for Nencia was mute as
a fish where her lady was concerned—but when they came
back to Vicenza the Duke ordered the villa set in order; and
in the spring he brought the Duchess here and left her. She
looked happy enough, my grandmother said, and seemed no
object for pity. Perhaps, after all, it was better than being
shut up in Vicenza, in the tall painted rooms where priests
came and went as softly as cats prowling for birds, and the
Duke was forever closeted in his library, talking with
learned men. The Duke was a scholar; you noticed he was
painted with a book? Well, those that can read 'em make out
that they're full of wonderful things; as a man that's been to
a fair across the mountains will always tell his people at
home it was beyond anything *they'll* ever see. As for the
Duchess, she was all for music, playacting and young company. The Duke was a silent man, stepping quietly, with his
eyes down, as though he'd just come from confession; when
the Duchess's lapdog yapped at his heels he danced like a
man in a swarm of hornets; when the Duchess laughed he
winced as if you'd drawn a diamond across a windowpane.
And the Duchess was always laughing.

"When she first came to the villa she was very busy

laying out the gardens, designing grottoes, planting groves and planning all manner of agreeable surprises in the way of water jets that drenched you unexpectedly, and hermits in caves, and wild men that jumped at you out of thickets. She had a very pretty taste in such matters, but after a while she tired of it, and there being no one for her to talk to but her maids and the chaplain—a clumsy man deep in his books —why, she would have strolling players out from Vicenza, mountebanks and fortune-tellers from the marketplace, traveling doctors and astrologers, and all manner of trained animals. Still it could be seen that the poor lady pined for company, and her waiting women, who loved her, were glad when the Cavaliere Ascanio, the Duke's cousin, came to live at the vineyard across the valley—you see the pinkish house over there in the mulberries, with a red roof and a pigeon-cote?

"The Cavaliere Ascanio was a cadet of one of the great Venetian houses, *pezzi grossi* of the Golden Book. He had been meant for the Church, I believe, but what! he set fighting above praying and cast in his lot with the captain of the Duke of Mantua's *bravi*, himself a Venetian of good standing, but a little at odds with the law. Well, the next I know, the Cavaliere was in Venice again, perhaps not in good odor on account of his connection with the gentleman I speak of. Some say he tried to carry off a nun from the convent of Santa Croce; how that may be I can't say, but my grandmother declared he had enemies there, and the end of it was that on some pretext or other the Ten banished him to Vicenza. There, of course, the Duke, being his kinsman, had to show him a civil face; and that was how he first came to the villa.

"He was a fine young man, beautiful as a Saint Sebastian, a rare musician, who sang his own songs to the lute in a way that used to make my grandmother's heart melt and run through her body like mulled wine. He had a good word for everybody, too, and was always dressed in the French fashion, and smelt as sweet as a bean field; and every soul about the place welcomed the sight of him.

"Well, the Duchess, it seemed, welcomed it too; youth will have youth, and laughter turns to laughter; and the two matched each other like the candlesticks on an altar. The Duchess—you've seen her portrait—but to hear my grandmother, sir, it no more approached her than a weed comes up to a rose. The Cavaliere, indeed, as became a poet, paragoned her in his song to all the pagan goddesses of antiquity; and doubtless these were finer to look at than mere women; but so, it seemed, was she; for, to believe my grandmother, she made other women look no more than the big French fashion doll that used to be shown on Ascension days in the Piazza. She was one, at any rate, that needed no outlandish finery to beautify her; whatever dress she wore became her as feathers fit the bird; and her hair didn't get its color by bleaching on the housetop. It glittered of itself like the threads in an Easter chasuble, and her skin was whiter than fine wheaten bread and her mouth as sweet as a ripe fig. . . .

"Well, sir, you could no more keep them apart than the bees and the lavender. They were always together, singing, bowling, playing cup and ball, walking in the gardens, visiting the aviaries and petting her grace's trick dogs and monkeys. The Duchess was as gay as a foal, always playing pranks and laughing, tricking out her animals like comedians, disguising herself as a peasant or a nun (you should have seen her one day pass herself off to the chaplain as a mendicant sister), or teaching the lads and girls of the vineyards to dance and sing madrigals together. The Cavaliere had a singular ingenuity in planning such entertainments and the days were hardly long enough for their diversions. But toward the end of the summer the Duchess fell quiet and would hear only sad music, and the two sat much together in the gazebo at the end of the garden. It was there the Duke found them one day when he drove out from Vicenza in his gilt coach. He came but once or twice a year to the villa, and it was, as my grandmother said, just a part of her poor lady's ill luck to be wearing that day the Venetian habit, which uncovered the shoulders in a way the Duke always scowled at, and her curls loose and powdered with gold. Well, the three drank chocolate in the gazebo, and what happened no one knew, except that the Duke, on taking leave, gave his cousin a seat in his carriage; but the Cavaliere never returned.

"Winter approaching, and the poor lady thus finding herself once more alone, it was surmised among her women that she must fall into a deeper depression of spirits. But far from this being the case, she displayed such cheerfulness and equanimity of humor that my grandmother, for one, was half vexed with her for giving no more thought to the poor young man who, all this time, was eating his heart out in the house across the valley. It is true she quitted her gold-laced gowns and wore a veil over her head; but Nencia would have it she looked the lovelier for the change and so gave the Duke greater displeasure. Certain it is that the Duke drove out oftener to the villa, and though he found his lady always engaged in some innocent pursuit, such as embroidery or music, or playing games with her young women, yet he always went away with a sour look and a whispered word to the chaplain. Now as to the chaplain, my grandmother owned there had been a time when her grace had not handled him overwisely. For, according to Nencia, it seems that his reverence, who seldom approached the Duchess, being buried in his library like a mouse in a cheese —well, one day he made bold to appeal to her for a sum of money, a large sum, Nencia said, to buy certain tall books, a chest full of them, that a foreign pedlar had brought him; whereupon the Duchess, who could never abide a book, breaks out at him with a laugh and a flash of her old spirit —'Holy Mother of God, must I have more books about me? I was nearly smothered with them in the first year of my marriage'; and the chaplain turning red at the affront, she added: 'You may buy them and welcome, my good chaplain, if you can find the money; but as for me, I am yet seeking a way to pay for my turquoise necklace, and the statue of Daphne at the end of the bowling green, and the Indian parrot that my black boy brought me last Michaelmas from the Bohemians—so you see I've no money to waste on trifles'; and as he backs out awkwardly she tosses at him over her shoulder: 'You should pray to Saint Blandina to open the Duke's pocket!' to which he returned, very quietly, 'Your excellency's suggestion is an admirable one, and I have already entreated that blessed martyr to open the Duke's understanding.'

"Thereat, Nencia said (who was standing by), the Duchess flushed wonderfully red and waved him out of the room; and then 'Quick!' she cried to my grandmother (who was too glad to run on such errands), 'Call me Antonio, the gardener's boy, to the box-garden; I've a word to say to him about the new clove carnations. . . .'

"Now I may not have told you, sir, that in the crypt under the chapel there has stood, for more generations than a man can count, a stone coffin containing a thighbone of the blessed Saint Blandina of Lyons, a relic offered, I've been told, by some great Duke of France to one of our own dukes when they fought the Turk together, and the object, ever since, of particular veneration in this illustrious family. Now, since the Duchess had been left to herself, it was observed she affected a fervent devotion to this relic, praying often in the chapel and even causing the stone slab that covered the entrance to the crypt to be replaced by a wooden one, that she might at will descend and kneel by the coffin. This was matter of edification to all the household and should have been peculiarly pleasing to the chaplain; but, with respect to you, he was the kind of man who brings a sour mouth to the eating of the sweetest apple.

"However that may be, the Duchess, when she dismissed him, was seen running to the garden, where she talked earnestly with the boy Antonio about the new clove carnations; and the rest of the day she sat indoors and played sweetly on the virginal. Now Nencia always had it in mind that her grace had made a mistake in refusing that request of the chaplain's; but she said nothing, for to talk reason to the Duchess was of no more use than praying for rain in a drought.

"Winter came early that year, there was snow on the hills by All Souls, the wind stripped the gardens, and the lemon-trees were nipped in the lemon-house. The Duchess kept her room in this black season, sitting over the fire, embroidering, reading books of devotion (which was a thing she had never done) and praying frequently in the chapel. As for the chaplain, it was a place he never set foot in but to say mass in the morning, with the Duchess overhead in the tribune, and the servants aching with rheumatism on the marble floor. The chaplain himself hated the cold, and galloped through the mass like a man with witches after him. The rest of the day he spent in his library, over a brazier, with his eternal books. . . .

"You'll wonder, sir, if I'm ever to get to the gist of the story; and I've gone slowly, I own, for fear of what's coming. Well, the winter was long and hard. When it fell cold the Duke ceased to come out from Vicenza, and not a soul had the Duchess to speak to but her maidservants and the gardeners about the place. Yet it was wonderful, my grandmother said, how she kept her brave colors and her spirits; only it was remarked that she prayed longer in the chapel, where a brazier was kept burning for her all day. When the young are denied their natural pleasures they turn often enough to religion; and it was a mercy, as my grandmother said, that she, who had scarce a live sinner to speak to, should take such comfort in a dead saint.

"My grandmother seldom saw her that winter, for though she showed a brave front to all she kept more and more to herself, choosing to have only Nencia about her and dismissing even her when she went to pray. For her devotion had that mark of true piety, that she wished it not to be observed; so that Nencia had strict orders, on the chaplain's approach, to warn her mistress if she happened to be in prayer.

"Well, the winter passed, and spring was well forward,

when my grandmother one evening had a bad fright. That it was her own fault I won't deny, for she'd been down the lime-walk with Antonio when her aunt fancied her to be stitching in her chamber; and seeing a sudden light in Nencia's window, she took fright lest her disobedience be found out, and ran up quickly through the laurel grove to the house. Her way lay by the chapel, and as she crept past it, meaning to slip in through the scullery, and groping her way, for the dark had fallen and the moon was scarce up, she heard a crash close behind her, as though someone had dropped from a window of the chapel. The young fool's heart turned over, but she looked round as she ran, and there, sure enough, was a man scuttling across the terrace; and as he doubled the corner of the house my grandmother swore she caught the whisk of the chaplain's skirts. Now that was a strange thing, certainly; for why should the chaplain be getting out of the chapel window when he might have passed through the door? For you may have noticed, sir, there's a door leads from the chapel into the saloon on the ground floor, the only other way out being through the Duchess's tribune.

"Well, my grandmother turned the matter over, and next time she met Antonio in the lime-walk (which, by reason of her fright, was not for some days) she laid before him what had happened; but to her surprise he only laughed and said, 'You little simpleton, he wasn't getting out of the window, he was trying to look in'; and not another word could she get from him.

"So the season moved on to Easter, and news came the Duke had gone to Rome for that holy festivity. His comings and goings made no change at the villa, and yet there was no one there but felt easier to think his yellow face was on the far side of the Apennines, unless perhaps it was the chaplain.

"Well, it was one day in May that the Duchess, who had walked long with Nencia on the terrace, rejoicing at the sweetness of the prospect and the pleasant scent of the gillyflowers in the stone vases, the Duchess toward midday withdrew to her rooms, giving orders that her dinner should be served in her bedchamber. My grandmother helped to carry in the dishes, and observed, she said, the singular beauty of the Duchess, who in honor of the fine weather had put on a gown of shot silver and hung her bare shoulders with pearls, so that she looked fit to dance at court with an emperor. She had ordered, too, a rare repast for a lady that heeded so little what she ate—jellies, game pasties, fruits in syrup, spiced cakes and a flagon of Greek wine; and she nodded and clapped her hands as the women set it before her, saying again and again, 'I shall eat well to-day.'

"But presently another mood seized her; she turned from the table, called for her rosary, and said to Nencia: 'The fine weather has made me neglect my devotions. I must say a litany before I dine.'

"She ordered the women out and barred the door, as her custom was; and Nencia and my grandmother went downstairs to work in the linen room.

"Now the linen room gives on the courtyard, and suddenly my grandmother saw a strange sight approaching. First up the avenue came the Duke's carriage (whom all thought to be in Rome), and after it, drawn by a long string of mules and oxen, a cart carrying what looked like a kneeling figure wrapped in death clothes. The strangeness of it struck the girl dumb and the Duke's coach was at the door before she had the wit to cry out that it was coming. Nencia, when she saw it, went white and ran out of the room. My grandmother followed, scared by her face, and the two fled along the corridor to the chapel. On the way they met the chaplain, deep in a book, who asked in surprise where they were running, and when they said, to announce the Duke's arrival, he fell into such astonishment and asked them so many questions and uttered such ohs and ahs, that by the time he left them by, the Duke was at their heels. Nencia reached the chapel door first and cried out that the Duke was coming; and before she had a reply he was at her side, with the chaplain following.

"A moment later the door opened and there stood the Duchess. She held her rosary in one hand and had drawn a scarf over her shoulders; but they shone through it like the moon in a mist, and her countenance sparkled with beauty.

"The Duke took her hand with a bow. 'Madam,' he said, 'I could have had no greater happiness than thus to surprise you at your devotions.'

"'My own happiness,' she replied, 'would have been greater had your excellency prolonged it by giving me notice of your arrival.'

"'Had you expected me, Madam,' said he, 'your appearance could scarcely have been more fitted to the occasion. Few ladies of your youth and beauty array themselves to venerate a saint as they would to welcome a lover.'

"'Sir,' she answered, 'having never enjoyed the latter opportunity, I am constrained to make the most of the former.—What's that?' she cried, falling back, and the rosary dropped from her hand.

"There was a loud noise at the other end of the saloon, as of a heavy object being dragged down the passage; and presently a dozen men were seen haling across the threshold the shrouded thing from the oxcart. The Duke waved his hand toward it. 'That,' said he, 'Madam, is a tribute to your extraordinary piety. I have heard with peculiar satisfaction of your devotion to the blessed relics in this chapel, and to commemorate a zeal which neither the rigors of winter nor the sultriness of summer could abate I have ordered a sculptured image of you, marvelously executed by the Cavaliere Bernini, to be placed before the altar over the entrance to the crypt.'

"The Duchess, who had grown pale, nevertheless smiled playfully at this. 'As to commemorating my piety,' she said, 'I recognize there one of your excellency's pleasantries—'

"'A pleasantry?' the Duke interrupted; and he made a sign to the men, who had now reached the threshold of the chapel. In an instant the wrappings fell from the figure, and there knelt the Duchess to the life. A cry of wonder rose from all, but the Duchess herself stood whiter than the marble.

" 'You will see,' says the Duke, 'this is no pleasantry, but a triumph of the incomparable Bernini's chisel. The likeness was done from your miniature portrait by the divine Elisabetta Sirani, which I sent to the master some six months ago, with what results all must admire.'

" 'Six months!' cried the Duchess, and seemed about to fall; but his excellency caught her by the hand.

" 'Nothing,' he said, 'could better please me than the excessive emotion you display, for true piety is ever modest, and your thanks could not take a form that better became you. And now,' says he to the men, 'let the image be put in place.'

"By this, life seemed to have returned to the Duchess, and she answered him with a deep reverence. 'That I should be overcome by so unexpected a grace, your excellency admits to be natural; but what honors you accord it is my privilege to accept, and I entreat only that in mercy to my modesty the image be placed in the remotest part of the chapel.'

"At that the Duke darkened. 'What! You would have this masterpiece of a renowned chisel, which, I disguise not, cost me the price of a good vineyard in gold pieces, you would have it thrust out of sight like the work of a village stonecutter?'

" 'It is my semblance, not the sculptor's work, I desire to conceal.'

" 'If you are fit for my house, Madam, you are fit for God's, and entitled to the place of honor in both. Bring the statue forward, you dawdlers!' he called out to the men.

"The Duchess fell back submissively. 'You are right, sir, as always; but I would at least have the image stand on the left of the altar, that, looking up, it may behold your excellency's seat in the tribune.'

" 'A pretty thought, Madam, for which I thank you; but

I design before long to put my companion image on the other side of the altar; and the wife's place, as you know, is at her husband's right hand.'

" 'True, my lord—but, again, if my poor presentment is to have the unmerited honor of kneeling beside yours, why not place both before the altar, where it is our habit to pray in life?'

" 'And where, Madam, should we kneel if they took our places? Besides,' says the Duke, still speaking very blandly, 'I have a more particular purpose in placing your image over the entrance to the crypt; for not only would I thereby mark your special devotion to the blessed saint who rests there, but, by sealing up the opening in the pavement, would assure the perpetual preservation of that holy martyr's bones, which hitherto have been too thoughtlessly exposed to sacrilegious attempts.'

" 'What attempts, my lord?' cries the Duchess. 'No one enters this chapel without my leave.'

" 'So I have understood, and can well believe from what I have learned of your piety; yet at night a malefactor might break in through a window, Madam, and your excellency not know it.'

" 'I'm a light sleeper,' said the Duchess.

"The Duke looked at her gravely. 'Indeed?' said he. 'A bad sign at your age. I must see that you are provided with a sleeping draught.'

"The Duchess's eyes filled. 'You would deprive me, then, of the consolation of visiting those venerable relics?'

" 'I would have you keep eternal guard over them, knowing no one to whose care they may more fittingly be entrusted.'

"By this the image was brought close to the wooden slab that covered the entrance to the crypt, when the Duchess, springing forward, placed herself in the way.

" 'Sir, let the statue be put in place tomorrow, and suffer me, tonight, to say a last prayer beside those holy bones.'

"The Duke stepped instantly to her side. 'Well thought, Madam; I will go down with you now, and we will pray together.'

" 'Sir, your long absences have, alas! given me the habit of solitary devotion, and I confess that any presence is distracting.'

" 'Madam, I accept your rebuke. Hitherto, it is true, the duties of my station have constrained me to long absences; but henceforward I remain with you while you live. Shall we go down into the crypt together?'

" 'No; for I fear for your excellency's ague. The air there is excessively damp.'

" 'The more reason you should no longer be exposed to it; and to prevent the intemperance of your zeal I will at once make the place inaccessible.'

"The Duchess at this fell on her knees on the slab, weeping excessively and lifting her hands to heaven.

" 'Oh,' she cried, 'you are cruel, sir, to deprive me of access to the sacred relics that have enabled me to support with resignation the solitude to which your excellency's duties have condemned me; and if prayer and meditation give me any authority to pronounce on such matters, suffer me to warn you, sir, that I fear the blessed Saint Blandina will punish us for thus abandoning her venerable remains!'

"The Duke at this seemed to pause, for he was a pious man, and my grandmother thought she saw him exchange a glance with the chaplain, who, stepping timidly forward, with his eyes on the ground, said, 'There is indeed much wisdom in her excellency's words, but I would suggest, sir, that her pious wish might be met, and the saint more conspicuously honored, by transferring the relics from the crypt to a place beneath the altar.'

" 'True!' cried the Duke, 'and it shall be done at once.'

"But thereat the Duchess rose to her feet with a terrible look.

" 'No,' she cried, 'by the body of God! For it shall not be said that, after your excellency has chosen to deny every request I addressed to him, I owe his consent to the solicitation of another!'

"The chaplain turned red and the Duke yellow, and for a moment neither spoke.

"Then the Duke said, 'Here are words enough, Madam. Do you wish the relics brought up from the crypt?'

" 'I wish nothing that I owe to another's intervention!'

" 'Put the image in place then,' says the Duke furiously, and handed her grace to a chair.

"She sat there, my grandmother said, straight as an arrow, her hands locked, her head high, her eyes on the Duke, while the statue was dragged to its place; then she stood up and turned away. As she passed by Nencia, 'Call me Antonio,' she whispered; but before the words were out of her mouth the Duke stepped between them.

" 'Madam,' says he, all smiles now, 'I have traveled straight from Rome to bring you the sooner this proof of my esteem. I lay last night at Monselice and I have been on the road since daybreak. Will you not invite me to supper?'

" 'Surely, my lord,' said the Duchess. 'It shall be laid in the dining parlor within the hour.'

" 'Why not in your chamber and at once, Madam? Since I believe it is your custom to sup there.'

" 'In my chamber?' says the Duchess, in disorder.

" 'Have you anything against it?' he asked.

" 'Assuredly not, sir, if you will give me time to prepare myself.'

" 'I will wait in your cabinet,' said the Duke.

"At that, said my grandmother, the Duchess gave one look, as the souls in hell may have looked when the gates closed on our Lord; then she called Nencia and passed to her chamber.

"What happened there my grandmother could never learn, but that the Duchess, in great haste, dressed herself with extraordinary splendor, powdering her hair with gold, painting her face and bosom, and covering herself with jewels till she shone like our Lady of Loreto; and hardly were these preparations complete when the Duke entered from the cabinet, followed by the servants carrying supper. Thereupon the Duchess dismissed Nencia, and what follows my grandmother learned from a pantry lad who brought up the dishes and waited in the cabinet; for only the Duke's body servant entered the bedchamber.

"Well, according to this boy, sir, who was looking and listening with his whole body, as it were, because he had never before been suffered so near the Duchess, it appears that the noble couple sat down in great good humor, the Duchess playfully reproving her husband for his long absence, while the Duke swore that to look so beautiful was the best way of punishing him. In this tone the talk continued, with such gay sallies on the part of the Duchess, such tender advances on the Duke's, that the lad declared they were for all the world like a pair of lovers courting on a summer's night in the vineyard; and so it went till the servant brought in the mulled wine.

" 'Ah,' the Duke was saying at that moment, 'this agreeable evening repays me for the many dull ones I have spent away from you; nor do I remember to have enjoyed such laughter since the afternoon last year when we drank chocolate in the gazebo with my cousin Ascanio. And that reminds me,' he said, 'is my cousin in good health?'

" 'I have no reports of it,' says the Duchess. 'But your excellency should taste these figs stewed in malmsey—'

" 'I am in the mood to taste whatever you offer,' said he; and as she helped him to the figs he added, 'If my enjoyment were not complete as it is, I could almost wish my cousin Ascanio were with us. The fellow is rare good company at supper. What do you say, Madam? I hear he's still in the country; shall we send for him to join us?'

" 'Ah,' said the Duchess, with a sigh and a languishing look, 'I see your excellency wearies of me already.'

" 'I, Madam? Ascanio is a capital good fellow, but to my mind his chief merit at this moment is his absence. It inclines me so tenderly to him that, by God, I could empty a glass to his good health.'

"With that the Duke caught up his goblet and signed to the servant to fill the Duchess's.

" 'Here's to the cousin,' he cried, standing, 'who has the good taste to stay away when he's not wanted. I drink to his very long life—and you, Madam?'

"At this the Duchess, who had sat staring at him with a changed face, rose also and lifted her glass to her lips.

" 'And I to his happy death,' says she in a wild voice; and as she spoke the empty goblet dropped from her hand and she fell face down on the floor.

"The Duke shouted to her women that she had swooned, and they came and lifted her to the bed. . . . She suffered horribly all night, Nencia said, twisting herself like a heretic at the stake, but without a word escaping her. The Duke watched by her, and toward daylight sent for the chaplain; but by this she was unconscious and, her teeth being locked, our Lord's body could not be passed through them.

"The Duke announced to his relations that his lady had died after partaking too freely of spiced wine and an omelet of carp's roe, at a supper she had prepared in honor of his return; and the next year he brought home a new Duchess, who gave him a son and five daughters. . . ."

V

The sky had turned to a steel gray, against which the villa stood out sallow and inscrutable. A wind strayed through the gardens, loosening here and there a yellow leaf from the sycamores; and the hills across the valley were purple as thunderclouds.

"And the statue—?" I asked.

"Ah, the statue. Well, sir, this is what my grandmother

told me, here on this very bench where we're sitting. The poor child, who worshiped the Duchess as a girl of her years will worship a beautiful kind mistress, spent a night of horror, you may fancy, shut out from her lady's room, hearing the cries that came from it, and seeing, as she crouched in her corner, the women rush to and fro with wild looks, the Duke's lean face in the door, and the chaplain skulking in the antechamber with his eyes on his breviary. No one minded her that night or the next morning; and toward dusk, when it became known the Duchess was no more, the poor girl felt the pious wish to say a prayer for her dead mistress. She crept to the chapel and stole in unobserved. The place was empty and dim, but as she advanced she heard a low moaning, and coming in front of the statue she saw that its face, the day before so sweet and smiling, had the look on it that you know—and the moaning seemed to come from its lips. My grandmother turned cold, but something, she said afterward, kept her from calling or shrieking out, and she turned and ran from the place. In the passage she fell in a swoon; and when she came to her senses, in her own chamber, she heard that the Duke had locked the chapel door and forbidden any to set foot there. . . . The place was never opened again till the Duke died, some ten years later; and then it was that the other servants, going in with the new heir, saw for the first time the horror that my grandmother had kept in her bosom. . . ."

"And the crypt?" I asked. "Has it never been opened?"

"Heaven forbid, sir!" cried the old man, crossing himself. "Was it not the Duchess's express wish that the relics should not be disturbed?"

THE MAN IN THE INVERNESS CAPE

Baroness Orczy

Hungarian-English Baroness Emmuska Orczy (1865–1947) spoke no English until the age of fifteen, but her somewhat late mastery of the language did not prevent her from successfully depicting the nuances of British society, as shown in her excellent novels and short stories. Her colorful and eccentric characters—The Old Man in the Corner, the Scarlet Pimpernel, and Lady Molly Robertson-Kirk— accurately reflect the England the baroness came to know and love. In "The Man in the Inverness Cape," Lady Molly —head of the "female department of Scotland Yard," who in a later exploit clears her own husband of murder—investigates a particularly baffling disappearance.

Well, you know, some say she is the daughter of a duke, others that she was born in the gutter, and that the handle has been soldered onto her name in order to give her style and influence.

I could say a lot, of course, but "my lips are sealed," as the poets say. All through her successful career at the Yard she honoured me with her friendship and confidence, but when she took me in partnership, as it were, she made me promise that I would never breathe a word of her private life, and this I swore on my Bible oath—"wish I may die," and all the rest of it.

Yes, we always called her "my lady," from the moment that she was put at the head of our section; and the chief called her "Lady Molly" in our presence. We of the Female Department are dreadfully snubbed by the men, though don't tell me that women have not ten times as much intuition as the blundering and sterner sex; my firm belief is that we shouldn't have half so many undetected crimes if some of the so-called mysteries were put to the test of feminine investigation.

Many people say—people, too, mind you, who read their daily paper regularly—that it is quite impossible for anyone to "disappear" within the confines of the British Isles. At the same time these wise people invariably admit one great exception to their otherwise unimpeachable theory, and that is the case of Mr. Leonard Marvell, who, as you know, walked out one afternoon from the Scotia Hotel in Cromwell Road and has never been seen or heard of since.

Information had originally been given to the police by Mr. Marvell's sister Olive, a Scotchwoman of the usually accepted type: tall, bony, with sandy-coloured hair, and a somewhat melancholy expression in her blue-grey eyes.

Her brother, she said, had gone out on a rather foggy afternoon. I think it was the third of February, just about a year ago. His intention had been to go and consult a solicitor in the City—whose address had been given him recently by a friend—about some private business of his own.

Mr. Marvell had told his sister that he would get a train at South Kensington Station to Moorgate Street, and walk thence to Finsbury Square. She was to expect him home by dinnertime.

As he was, however, very irregular in his habits, being fond of spending his evenings at restaurants and music-halls, the sister did not feel the least anxious when he did not return home at the appointed time. She had her dinner in the *table d'hôte* room, and went to bed soon after ten.

She and her brother occupied two bedrooms and a sitting-room on the second floor of the little private hotel. Miss Marvell, moreover, had a maid always with her, as she was somewhat of an invalid. This girl, Rosie Campbell, a nice-looking Scotch lassie, slept on the top floor.

It was only on the following morning, when Mr. Leonard did not put in an appearance at breakfast, that Miss Marvell began to feel anxious. According to her own account, she sent Rosie in to see if anything was the matter, and the girl, wide-eyed and not a little frightened, came back with the news that Mr. Marvell was not in his room, and that his bed had not been slept in that night.

With characteristic Scottish reserve, Miss Olive said nothing about the matter at the time to anyone, nor did she give information to the police until two days later, when she herself had exhausted every means in her power to discover her brother's whereabouts.

She had seen the lawyer to whose office Leonard Marvell had intended going that afternoon, but Mr. Statham, the solicitor in question, had seen nothing of the missing man.

With great adroitness Rosie, the maid, had made inquiries at South Kensington and Moorgate Street stations. At the former, the booking-clerk, who knew Mr. Marvell by

sight, distinctly remembered selling him a first-class ticket
to one of the City stations in the early part of the afternoon;
but at Moorgate Street, which is a very busy station, no one
recollected seeing a tall, red-haired Scotchman in an Inverness cape—such was the description given of the missing
man. By that time the fog had become very thick in the City;
traffic was disorganized, and everyone felt fussy, ill-tem-
pered, and self-centred.

These, in substance, were the details which Miss Marvell gave to the police on the subject of her brother's strange
disappearance.

At first she did not appear very anxious; she seemed to
have great faith in Mr. Marvell's power to look after himself;
moreover, she declared positively that her brother had neither valuables nor money about his person when he went
out that afternoon.

But as day succeeded day and no trace of the missing
man had yet been found, matters became more serious, and
the search instituted by our fellows at the Yard waxed more
keen.

A description of Mr. Leonard Marvell was published in
the leading London and provincial dailies. Unfortunately,
there was no good photograph of him extant, and descriptions are apt to prove vague.

Very little was known about the man beyond his disappearance, which had rendered him famous. He and his sister
had arrived at the Scotia Hotel about a month previously,
and subsequently they were joined by the maid, Campbell.

Scotch people are far too reserved ever to speak of
themselves or their affairs to strangers. Brother and sister
spoke very little to anyone at the hotel. They had their meals
in their sitting-room, waited on by the maid, who messed
with the staff. But, in face of the present terrible calamity,
Miss Marvell's frigidity relaxed before the police inspector,
to whom she gave what information she could about her
brother.

"He was like a son to me," she explained with scarcely

restrained tears, "for we lost our parents early in life, and as we were left very, very badly off, our relations took but little notice of us. My brother was years younger than I am—and though he was a little wild and fond of pleasure, he was as good as gold to me, and has supported us both for years by journalistic work. We came to London from Glasgow about a month ago, because Leonard got a very good appointment on the staff of the *Daily Post*."

All this, of course, was soon proved to be true; and although, on minute inquiries being instituted in Glasgow, but little seemed to be known about Mr. Leonard Marvell in that city, there seemed no doubt that he had done some reporting for the *Courier,* and that latterly, in response to an advertisement, he had applied for and obtained regular employment on the *Daily Post.*

The latter enterprising halfpenny journal, with characteristic magnanimity, made an offer of £50 reward to any of its subscribers who gave information which would lead to the discovery of the whereabouts of Mr. Leonard Marvell.

But time went by, and that £50 remained unclaimed.

Lady Molly had not seemed as interested as she usually was in cases of this sort. With strange flippancy—wholly unlike herself—she remarked that one Scotch journalist more or less in London did not vastly matter.

I was much amused, therefore, one morning about three weeks after the mysterious disappearance of Mr. Leonard Marvell, when Jane, our little parlourmaid, brought in a card accompanied by a letter.

The card bore the name MISS OLIVE MARVELL. The letter was the usual formula from the chief, asking Lady Molly to have a talk with the lady in question, and to come and see him on the subject after the interview.

With a smothered yawn my dear lady told Jane to show in Miss Marvell.

"There are two of them, my lady," said Jane, as she prepared to obey.

"Two what?" asked Lady Molly with a laugh.

"Two ladies, I mean," explained Jane.

"Well! Show them both into the drawing-room," said Lady Molly, impatiently.

Then, as Jane went off on this errand, a very funny thing happened; funny, because during the entire course of my intimate association with my dear lady, I had never known her act with such marked indifference in the face of an obviously interesting case. She turned to me and said:

"Mary, you had better see these two women, whoever they may be; I feel that they would bore me to distraction. Take note of what they say, and let me know. Now, don't argue," she added with a laugh, which peremptorily put a stop to my rising protest, "but go and interview Miss Marvell and Co."

Needless to say, I promptly did as I was told, and the next few seconds saw me installed in our little drawing-room, saying polite preliminaries to the two ladies who sat opposite to me.

I had no need to ask which of them was Miss Marvell. Tall, ill-dressed in deep black, with a heavy crape veil over her face, and black-cotton gloves, she looked the uncompromising Scotchwoman to the life. In strange contrast to her depressing appearance, there sat beside her an overdressed, much behatted, peroxided young woman, who bore the stamp of the theatrical profession all over her pretty, painted face.

Miss Marvell, I was glad to note, was not long in plunging into the subject which had brought her here.

"I saw a gentleman at Scotland Yard," she explained, after a short preamble, "because Miss—er—Lulu Fay came to me at the hotel this very morning with a story which, in my opinion, should have been told to the police directly my brother's disappearance became known, and not three weeks later."

The emphasis which she laid on the last few words, and the stern look with which she regarded the golden-haired young woman beside her, showed the disapproval with which the rigid Scotchwoman viewed any connection which her brother might have had with the lady, whose very name seemed unpleasant to her lips.

Miss—er—Lulu Fay blushed even through her rouge, and turned a pair of large, liquid eyes imploringly upon me.

"I—I didn't know. I was frightened," she stammered.

"There's no occasion to be frightened now," retorted Miss Marvell, "and the sooner you try and be truthful about the whole matter, the better it will be for all of us."

And the stern woman's lips closed with a snap, as she deliberately turned her back on Miss Fay and began turning over the leaves of a magazine which happened to be on a table close to her hand.

I muttered a few words of encouragement, for the little actress looked ready to cry. I spoke as kindly as I could, telling her that if indeed she could throw some light on Mr. Marvell's present whereabouts it was her duty to be quite frank on the subject.

She "hem"-ed and "ha"-ed for a while, and her simpering ways were just beginning to tell on my nerves, when she suddenly started talking very fast.

"I am principal boy at the Grand," she explained with great volubility, "and I knew Mr. Leonard Marvell well—in fact—er—he paid me a good deal of attention and—"

"Yes—and—" I queried, for the girl was obviously nervous.

There was a pause. Miss Fay began to cry.

"And it seems that my brother took this young—er—lady to supper on the night of February 3rd, after which no one has ever seen or heard of him again," here interposed Miss Marvell, quietly.

"Is that so?" I asked.

Lulu Fay nodded, whilst heavy tears fell upon her clasped hands.

"But why did you not tell this to the police three weeks ago?" I ejaculated, with all the sternness at my command.

"I—I was frightened," she stammered.

"Frightened? Of what?"

"I am engaged to Lord Mountnewte and—"

"And you did not wish him to know that you were accepting the attentions of Mr. Leonard Marvell—was that it? Well," I added, with involuntary impatience, "what happened after you had supper with Mr. Marvell?"

"Oh! I hope—I hope that nothing happened," she said through more tears. "We had supper at the Trocadero, and he saw me into my brougham. Suddenly, just as I was driving away, I saw Lord Mountnewte standing quite close to us in the crowd."

"Did the two men know one another?" I asked.

"No," replied Miss Fay. "At least, I didn't think so, but when I looked back through the window of my carriage I saw them standing on the curb talking to each other for a moment, and then walk off together towards Piccadilly Circus. That is the last I have seen of either of them," continued the little actress with a fresh flood of tears. "Lord Mountnewte hasn't spoken to me since, and Mr. Marvell has disappeared with my money and my diamonds."

"Your money and your diamonds?" I gasped in amazement.

"Yes; he told me he was a jeweller, and that my diamonds wanted resetting. He took them with him that evening, for he said that London jewellers were clumsy thieves, and that he would love to do the work for me himself. I also gave him two hundred pounds which he said he would want for buying the gold and platinum required for the settings. And now he has disappeared—and my diamonds—and my money! Oh! I have been very—very foolish—and—"

Her voice broke down completely. Of course, one often hears of the idiocy of girls giving money and jewels unquestioningly to clever adventurers who know how to trade upon their inordinate vanity. There was, therefore, nothing very out of the way in the story just told me by Miss—er— Lulu Fay, until the moment when Miss Marvell's quiet voice, with its marked Scotch burr, broke in upon the short silence which had followed the actress's narrative.

"As I explained to the chief detective inspector at Scotland Yard," she said calmly, "the story which this young—er—lady tells is only partly true. She may have had supper with Mr. Leonard Marvell on the night of February 3rd, and he may have paid her certain attentions; but he never deceived her by telling her that he was a jeweller, nor did he obtain possession of her diamonds and her money through false statements. My brother was the soul of honour and loyalty. If, for some reason which Miss—er—Lulu Fay chooses to keep secret, he had her jewels and money in his possession on the fatal February 3rd, then I think his disappearance is accounted for. He has been robbed and perhaps murdered."

Like a true Scotchwoman she did not give way to tears, but even her harsh voice trembled slightly when she thus bore witness to her brother's honesty, and expressed the fears which assailed her as to his fate.

Imagine my plight! I could ill forgive my dear lady for leaving me in this unpleasant position—a sort of peacemaker between two women who evidently hated one another, and each of whom was trying her best to give the other "the lie direct."

I ventured to ring for our faithful Jane and to send her with an imploring message to Lady Molly, begging her to come and disentangle the threads of this muddled skein with her clever fingers; but Jane returned with a curt note from my dear lady, telling me not to worry about such a silly case, and to bow the two women out of the flat as soon as possible and then come for a nice walk.

I wore my official manner as well as I could, trying not to betray the 'prentice hand. Of course, the interview lasted a great deal longer, and there was considerably more talk than I can tell you of in a brief narrative. But the gist of it all was just as I have said. Miss Lulu Fay stuck to every point of the story which she had originally told Miss Marvell. It was the latter uncompromising lady who had immediately marched the younger woman off to Scotland Yard in order that she might repeat her tale to the police. I did not wonder that the chief promptly referred them both to Lady Molly.

Anyway, I made excellent shorthand notes of the conflicting stories which I heard; and I finally saw, with real relief, the two women walk out of our little front door.

Our fellows at the Yard were abnormally active. It seemed, on the face of it, impossible that a man, healthy, vigorous, and admittedly sober, should vanish in London between Piccadilly Circus and Cromwell Road without leaving the slightest trace of himself or of the valuables said to have been in his possession.

Of course, Lord Mountnewte was closely questioned. He was a young Guardsman of the usual pattern, and, after a great deal of vapid talk which irritated Detective Inspector Saunders not a little, he made the following statement:

"I certainly am acquainted with Miss Lulu Fay. On the night in question I was standing outside the Troc, when I saw this young lady at her own carriage window talking to a tall man in an Inverness cape. She had, earlier in the day, refused my invitation to supper, saying that she was not feeling very well, and would go home directly after the theatre; therefore I felt, naturally, a little vexed. I was just about to hail a taxi, meaning to go on to the club, when, to my intense astonishment, the man in the Inverness cape came up to me and asked me if I could tell him the best way to get back to Cromwell Road."

"And what did you do?" asked Saunders.

"I walked a few steps with him and put him on his way," replied Lord Mountnewte, blandly.

In Saunders's own expressive words, he thought that story "fishy." He could not imagine the arm of coincidence being quite so long as to cause these two men—who presumably were both in love with the same girl, and who had just met at a moment when one of them was obviously suffering pangs of jealousy—to hold merely a topographical conversation with one another. But it was equally difficult to suppose that the eldest son and heir of the Marquis of Loam should murder a successful rival and then rob him in the streets of London.

Moreover, here came the eternal and unanswerable questions: If Lord Mountnewte had murdered Leonard Marvell, where and how had he done it, and what had he done with the body?

I daresay you are wondering by this time why I have said nothing about the maid, Rosie Campbell.

Well, plenty of very clever people (I mean those who write letters to the papers and give suggestions to every official department in the kingdom) thought that the police ought to keep a very strict eye upon that pretty Scotch lassie. For she was very pretty, and had quaint, demure ways which rendered her singularly attractive, in spite of the fact that, for most masculine tastes, she would have been considered too tall. Of course, Saunders and Danvers kept an eye on her—you may be sure of that—and got a good deal of information about her from the people at the hotel. Most of it, unfortunately, was irrelevant to the case. She was maid-attendant to Miss Marvell, who was feeble in health, and who went out but little. Rosie waited on her master and mistress upstairs, carrying their meals to their private room, and doing their bedrooms. The rest of the day she was fairly free, and was quite sociable downstairs with the hotel staff.

With regard to her movements and actions on that memorable 3rd of February, Saunders—though he worked very hard—could glean but little useful information. You see, in a hotel of that kind, with an average of thirty to forty guests at one time, it is extremely difficult to state positively what any one person did or did not do on that particular day.

Most people at the Scotia remembered that Miss Marvell dined in the *table d'hôte* room on that 3rd of February; this she did about once a fortnight, when her maid had an evening "out."

The hotel staff also recollected fairly distinctly that Miss Rosie Campbell was not in the steward's room at supper-time that evening, but no one could remember definitely when she came in.

One of the chambermaids who occupied the bedroom adjoining hers said that she heard her moving about soon after midnight; the hall porter declared that he saw her come in just before half-past twelve when he closed the doors for the night.

But one of the ground-floor valets said that, on the morning of the 4th, he saw Miss Marvell's maid, in hat and coat, slip into the house and upstairs, very quickly and quietly, soon after the front doors were opened, namely, about 7:00 A.M.

Here, of course, was a direct contradiction between the chambermaid and hall porter on the one side, and the valet on the other, whilst Miss Marvell said that Campbell came into her room and made her some tea long before seven o'clock every morning, including that of the 4th.

I assure you our fellows at the Yard were ready to tear their hair out by the roots, from sheer aggravation at this maze of contradictions which met them at every turn.

The whole thing seemed so simple. There was nothing "to it" as it were, and but very little real suggestion of foul play, and yet Mr. Leonard Marvell had disappeared, and no trace of him could be found.

Everyone now talked freely of murder. London is a big town, and this would not have been the first instance of a stranger—for Mr. Leonard Marvell was practically a stranger in London—being enticed to a lonely part of the city on a foggy night, and there done away with and robbed, and the body hidden in an out-of-the-way cellar, where it might not be discovered for months to come.

But the newspaper-reading public is notably fickle, and Mr. Leonard Marvell was soon forgotten by everyone save the chief and the batch of our fellows who had charge of the case.

Thus I heard through Danvers one day that Rosie Campbell had left Miss Marvell's employ, and was living in rooms in Findlater Terrace, near Walham Green.

I was alone in our Maida Vale flat at the time, my dear lady having gone to spend the week-end with the Dowager Lady Loam, who was an old friend of hers; nor, when she returned, did she seem any more interested in Rosie Campbell's movements than she had been hitherto.

Yet another month went by, and I for one had absolutely ceased to think of the man in the Inverness cape, who had so mysteriously and so completely vanished in the very midst of busy London, when, one morning early in January, Lady Molly made her appearance in my room, looking more like the landlady of a disreputable gambling-house than anything else I could imagine.

"What in the world—" I began.

"Yes! I think I look the part," she replied, surveying with obvious complacency the extraordinary figure which confronted her in the glass.

My dear lady had on a purple-cloth coat and skirt of a peculiarly vivid hue, and of a singular cut, which made her matchless figure look like a sack of potatoes. Her soft-brown hair was quite hidden beneath a "transformation," of that yellow-reddish tint only to be met with in very cheap dyes.

As for her hat—I won't attempt to describe it. It towered above and around her face, which was plentifully covered with brick-red and with that kind of powder which causes the cheeks to look a deep mauve.

My dear lady looked, indeed, a perfect picture of appalling vulgarity.

"Where are you going in this elegant attire?" I asked in amazement.

"I have taken rooms in Findlater Terrace," she replied lightly. "I feel that the air of Walham Green will do us both good. Our amiable, if somewhat slatternly, landlady expects us in time for luncheon. You will have to keep rigidly in the background, Mary, all the while we are there. I said that I was bringing an invalid niece with me, and, as a preliminary, you may as well tie two or three thick veils over your face. I think I may safely promise that you won't be dull."

And we certainly were not dull during our brief stay at 34, Findlater Terrace, Walham Green. Fully equipped, and arrayed in our extraordinary garments, we duly arrived there, in a rickety four-wheeler, on the top of which were perched two seedy-looking boxes.

The landlady was a toothless old creature, who apparently thought washing a quite unnecessary proceeding. In this she was evidently at one with every one of her neighbours. Findlater Terrace looked unspeakably squalid; groups of dirty children congregated in the gutters and gave forth discordant shrieks as our cab drove up.

Through my thick veils I thought that, some distance down the road, I spied a horsy-looking man in ill-fitting riding-breeches and gaiters, who vaguely reminded me of Danvers.

Within half an hour of our installation, and whilst we were eating a tough steak over a doubtful tablecloth, my dear lady told me that she had been waiting a full month, until rooms in this particular house happened to be vacant. Fortunately the population in Findlater Terrace is always a shifting one, and Lady Molly had kept a sharp eye on No. 34, where, on the floor above, lived Miss Rosie Campbell. Directly the last set of lodgers walked out of the ground-floor rooms, we were ready to walk in.

My dear lady's manners and customs, whilst living at the above aristocratic address, were fully in keeping with her appearance. The shrill, rasping voice which she assumed echoed from attic to cellar.

One day I heard her giving vague hints to the landlady that her husband, Mr. Marcus Stone, had had a little trouble with the police about a small hotel which he had kept somewhere near Fitzroy Square, and where "young gentlemen used to come and play cards of a night." The landlady was also made to understand that the worthy Mr. Stone was now living temporarily at His Majesty's expense, whilst Mrs. Stone had to live a somewhat secluded life, away from her fashionable friends.

The misfortunes of the pseudo Mrs. Stone in no way marred the amiability of Mrs. Tredwen, our landlady. The inhabitants of Findlater Terrace care very little about the antecedents of their lodgers, so long as they pay their week's rent in advance, and settle their "extras" without much murmur.

This Lady Molly did, with a generosity characteristic of an ex-lady of means. She never grumbled at the quantity of jam and marmalade which we were supposed to have consumed every week, and which anon reached titanic proportions. She tolerated Mrs. Tredwen's cat, tipped Ermyntrude —the tousled lodging-house slavey—lavishly, and lent the upstairs lodger her spirit-lamp and curling-tongs when Miss Rosie Campbell's got out of order.

A certain degree of intimacy followed the loan of those curling-tongs. Miss Campbell, reserved and demure, greatly sympathized with the lady who was not on the best of terms with the police. I kept steadily in the background. The two ladies did not visit each other's rooms, but they held long and confidential conversations on the landings, and I gathered, presently, that the pseudo Mrs. Stone had succeeded in persuading Rosie Campbell that, if the police were watching No. 34, Findlater Terrace at all, it was undoubtedly on account of the unfortunate Mr. Stone's faithful wife.

I found it a little difficult to fathom Lady Molly's intentions. We had been in the house over three weeks, and nothing whatever had happened. Once I ventured on a discreet query as to whether we were to expect the sudden re-appearance of Mr. Leonard Marvell.

"For if that's what it's about," I argued, "then surely the men from the Yard could have kept the house in view, without all this inconvenience and masquerading on our part."

But to this tirade my dear lady vouchsafed no reply.

She and her newly acquired friend were, about this time, deeply interested in the case known as the "West End Shop Robberies," which no doubt you recollect, since they occurred such a very little while ago. Ladies who were shopping in the large drapers' emporiums during the crowded and busy sale time lost reticules, purses, and valuable parcels without any trace of the clever thief being found.

The drapers, during sale time, invariably employ detectives in plain clothes to look after their goods, but in this case it was the customers who were robbed, and the detectives, attentive to every attempt at "shop-lifting," had had no eyes for the more subtle thief.

I had already noticed Miss Rosie Campbell's keen look of excitement whenever the pseudo Mrs. Stone discussed these cases with her. I was not a bit surprised, therefore, when, one afternoon at about tea-time, my dear lady came home from her habitual walk, and, at the top of her shrill voice, called out to me from the hall:

"Mary! Mary! They've got the man of the shop robberies. He's given the silly police the slip this time, but they know who he is now, and I suppose they'll get him presently. 'Tisn't anybody I know," she added, with that harsh, common laugh which she had adopted for her part.

I had come out of the room in response to her call, and was standing just outside our own sitting-room door. Mrs. Tredwen, too, bedraggled and unkempt, as usual, had sneaked up the area steps, closely followed by Ermyntrude.

But on the half-landing just above us the trembling figure of Rosie Campbell, with scared white face and dilated eyes, looked on the verge of a sudden fall.

Still talking shrilly and volubly, Lady Molly ran up to her, but Campbell met her halfway, and the pseudo Mrs. Stone, taking vigorous hold of her wrist, dragged her into our own sitting-room.

"Pull yourself together, now," she said with rough kindness. "That owl Tredwen is listening, and you needn't let her know too much. Shut the door, Mary. Lor' bless you, m'dear,

I've gone through worse scares than these. There! You just lie down on this sofa a bit. My niece'll make you a cup o' tea; and I'll go and get an evening paper, and see what's going on. I suppose you are very interested in the shop-robbery man, or you wouldn't have took on so."

Without waiting for Campbell's contradiction to this statement, Lady Molly flounced out of the house.

Miss Campbell hardly spoke during the next ten minutes that she and I were left alone together. She lay on the sofa with eyes wide-open, staring up at the ceiling, evidently still in a great state of fear.

I had just got tea ready when Lady Molly came back. She had an evening paper in her hand, but threw this down on the table directly she came in.

"I could only get an early edition," she said breathlessly, "and the silly thing hasn't got anything in it about the matter."

She drew near to the sofa, and, subduing the shrillness of her voice, she whispered rapidly, bending down towards Campbell:

"There's a man hanging about at the corner down there. No, no; it's not the police," she added quickly, in response to the girl's sudden start of alarm. "Trust me, my dear, for knowing a 'tec when I see one! Why, I'd smell one half a mile off. No; my opinion is that it's your man, my dear, and that he's in a devil of a hole."

"Oh! He oughtn't to come here," ejaculated Campbell in great alarm. "He'll get me into trouble and do himself no good. He's been a fool!" she added, with a fierceness wholly unlike her usual demure placidity, "getting himself caught like that. Now I suppose we shall have to hook it—if there's time."

"Can I do anything to help you?" asked the pseudo Mrs. Stone. "You know I've been through all this myself, when they was after Mr. Stone. Or perhaps Mary could do something."

"Well, yes," said the girl, after a slight pause, during

which she seemed to be gathering her wits together. "I'll write a note, and you shall take it, if you will, to a friend of mine—a lady who lives in the Cromwell Road. But if you still see a man lurking about at the corner of the street, then, just as you pass him, say the word 'Campbell,' and if he replies 'Rosie,' then give *him* the note. Will you do that?"

"Of course I will, my dear. Just you leave it all to me."

And the pseudo Mrs. Stone brought ink and paper and placed them on the table. Rosie Campbell wrote a brief note, and then fastened it down with a bit of sealing-wax before she handed it over to Lady Molly. The note was addressed to Miss Marvell, Scotia Hotel, Cromwell Road.

"You understand?" she said eagerly. "Don't give the note to the man unless he says 'Rosie' in reply to the word 'Campbell.' "

"All right—all right!" said Lady Molly, slipping the note into her reticule. "And you go up to your room, Miss Campbell; it's no good giving that old fool Tredwen too much to gossip about."

Rosie Campbell went upstairs, and presently my dear lady and I were walking rapidly down the badly lighted street.

"Where is the man?" I whispered eagerly as soon as we were out of earshot of No. 34.

"There is no man," replied Lady Molly, quickly.

"But the West End shop thief?" I asked.

"He hasn't been caught yet, and won't be either, for he is far too clever a scoundrel to fall into an ordinary trap."

She did not give me time to ask further questions, for presently, when we had reached Reporton Square, my dear lady handed me the note written by Campbell, and said:

"Go straight on to the Scotia Hotel, and ask for Miss Marvell; send up the note to her, but don't let her see you, as she knows you by sight. I must see the chief first, and will be with you as soon as possible. Having delivered the note, you must hang about outside as long as you can. Use your wits; she must not leave the hotel before I see her."

There was no hansom to be got in this elegant quarter of the town, so, having parted from my dear lady, I made for the nearest Underground station, and took a train for South Kensington.

Thus it was nearly seven o'clock before I reached the Scotia. In answer to my inquiries for Miss Marvell, I was told that she was ill in bed and could see no one. I replied that I had only brought a note for her, and would wait for a reply.

Acting on my dear lady's instructions, I was as slow in my movements as ever I could be, and was some time in finding the note and handing it to a waiter, who then took it upstairs.

Presently he returned with the message: "Miss Marvell says there is no answer."

Whereupon I asked for pen and paper at the office, and wrote the following brief note on my own responsibility, using my wits as my dear lady had bidden me to do.

Please, madam, I wrote, *will you send just a line to Miss Rosie Campbell? She seems very upset and frightened at some news she has had.*

Once more the waiter ran upstairs, and returned with a sealed envelope, which I slipped into my reticule.

Time was slipping by very slowly. I did not know how long I should have to wait about outside in the cold, when, to my horror, I heard a hard voice, with a marked Scotch accent, saying:

"I am going out, waiter, and shan't be back to dinner. Tell them to lay a little cold supper upstairs in my room."

The next moment Miss Marvell, with coat, hat, and veil, was descending the stairs.

My plight was awkward. I certainly did not think it safe to present myself before the lady; she would undoubtedly recollect my face. Yet I had orders to detain her until the appearance of Lady Molly.

Miss Marvell seemed in no hurry. She was putting on her gloves as she came downstairs. In the hall she gave a few more instructions to the porter, whilst I, in a dark corner in the background, was vaguely planning an assault or an alarm of fire.

Suddenly, at the hotel entrance, where the porter was obsequiously holding open the door for Miss Marvell to pass through, I saw the latter's figure stiffen; she took one step back as if involuntarily, then, equally quickly, attempted to dart across the threshold, on which a group—composed of my dear lady, of Saunders, and of two or three people scarcely distinguishable in the gloom beyond—had suddenly made its appearance.

Miss Marvell was forced to retreat into the hall; already I had heard Saunders's hurriedly whispered words:

"Try and not make a fuss in this place, now. Everything can go off quietly, you know."

Danvers and Cotton, whom I knew well, were already standing one each side of Miss Marvell, whilst suddenly amongst this group I recognized Fanny, the wife of Danvers, who is one of our female searchers at the Yard.

"Shall we go up to your own room?" suggested Saunders.

"I think that is quite unnecessary," interposed Lady Molly. "I feel convinced that *Mr.* Leonard Marvell will yield to the inevitable quietly, and follow you without giving any trouble."

Marvell, however, did make a bold dash for liberty. As Lady Molly had said previously, he was far too clever to allow himself to be captured easily. But my dear lady had been cleverer. As she told me subsequently, she had from the first suspected that the trio who lodged at the Scotia Hotel were really only a duo—namely, Leonard Marvell and his wife, Rosie Campbell. The latter impersonated a maid most of the time; but among these two clever people the three characters were interchangeable. *Of course, there was no Miss Marvell at all!* Leonard was alternately dressed up as man or woman, according to the requirements of his villainies.

"As soon as I heard that Miss Marvell was very tall and

bony," said Lady Molly, "I thought that there might be a possibility of her being merely a man in disguise. Then there was the extraordinarily suggestive fact—but little dwelt on by either the police or public—that no one seems ever to have seen brother and sister together, nor was the entire trio ever seen at one and the same time.

"On that 3rd of February Leonard Marvell went out. No doubt he changed his attire in a lady's waiting-room at one of the railway stations; subsequently he came home, now dressed as Miss Marvell, and had dinner in the *table d'hôte* room so as to set up a fairly plausible alibi. But ultimately it was his wife, Rosie Campbell, who stayed indoors that night, whilst he, Leonard Marvell, when going out after dinner, impersonated the maid until he was clear of the hotel; then he reassumed his male clothes once more, no doubt in the deserted waiting-room of some railway station, and met Miss Lulu Fay at supper, subsequently returning to the hotel in the guise of the maid.

"You see the game of criss-cross, don't you? This interchanging of characters was bound to baffle everyone. Many clever scoundrels have assumed disguises, sometimes impersonating members of the opposite sex, but never before have I known *two people play the part of three!* Thus, endless contradictions followed as to the hour when Campbell the maid went out and when she came in, for at one time it was she herself who was seen by the valet, and at another it was Leonard Marvell dressed in her clothes."

He was also clever enough to accost Lord Mountnewte in the open street, thus bringing further complications into this strange case.

After the successful robbery of Miss Fay's diamonds, Leonard Marvell and his wife parted for a while. They were waiting for an opportunity to get across the Channel and there turn their booty into solid cash. Whilst Mrs. Marvell, alias Rosie Campbell, led a retired life in Findlater Terrace, Leonard kept his hand in with West End shop robberies.

Then Lady Molly entered the lists. As usual, her scheme

was bold and daring; she trusted her own intuition and acted accordingly.

When she brought home the false news that the author of the shop robberies had been spotted by the police, Rosie Campbell's obvious terror confirmed her suspicions. The note written by the latter to the so-called Miss Marvell, though it contained nothing in any way incriminating, was the crowning certitude that my dear lady was right, as usual, in all her surmises.

And now Mr. Leonard Marvell will be living for two years at the taxpayers' expense; he has "disappeared" temporarily from the public eye.

THE WOMAN
IN THE STORE

Katherine Mansfield

Born in New Zealand in 1888, Katherine Mansfield (whose real name was Kathleen Beauchamp Murry) was one of the outstanding short-story writers of the early years of this century. Several collections of stories were published during her short life and posthumously, among them In a German Pension (1911), Bliss (1920), and The Little Girl *(1924). "The Woman at the Store" is an excellent example of her talent—a stark and realistic portrait of a* crime passionel, *and of the New Zealand outback of seventy-five years ago; it is also notable for its surprising sexual theme and content. Mansfield, who also wrote poetry and a published journal, died of tuberculosis in 1923, at the age of thirty-five.*

All that day the heat was terrible. The wind blew close to the ground; it rooted among the tussock grass, slithered along the road, so that the white pumice dust swirled in our faces, settled and sifted over us and was like a dry-skin itching for growth on our bodies. The horses stumbled along, coughing and chuffing. The pack horse was sick—with a big, open sore rubbed under the belly. Now and again she stopped short, threw back her head, looked at us as though she were going to cry, and whinnied. Hundreds of larks shrilled; the sky was slate colour, and the sound of the larks reminded me of slate pencils scraping over its surface. There was nothing to be seen but wave after wave of tussock grass, patched with purple orchids and manuka bushes covered with thick spider webs.

Jo rode ahead. He wore a blue galatea shirt, corduroy trousers and riding boots. A white handkerchief, spotted with red—it looked as though his nose had been bleeding on it—was knotted round his throat. Wisps of white hair straggled from under his wideawake—his moustache and eyebrows were called white—he slouched in the saddle, grunting. Not once that day had he sung:

> *"I don't care, for don't you see,*
> *My wife's mother was in front of me!"*

It was the first day we had been without it for a month, and now there seemed something uncanny in his silence. Jim rode beside me, white as a clown; his black eyes glittered, and he kept shooting out his tongue and moistening his lips. He was dressed in a Jaeger vest, and a pair of blue duck trousers, fastened round the waist with a plaited leather belt. We had hardly spoken since dawn. At noon we had lunched off fly biscuits and apricots by the side of a swampy creek.

"My stomach feels like the crop of a hen," said Jo. "Now then, Jim, you're the bright boy of the party—where's this 'ere store you kep' on talking about? 'Oh, yes,' you says, 'I know a fine store, with a paddock for the horses and a creek runnin' through, owned by a friend of mine who'll give yer a bottle of whisky before 'e shakes hands with yer.' I'd like ter see that place—merely as a matter of curiosity—not that I'd ever doubt yer word—as yer know very well—but . . ."

Jim laughed. "Don't forget there's a woman too, Jo, with blue eyes and yellow hair, who'll promise you something else before she shakes hands with you. Put that in your pipe and smoke it."

"The heat's making you balmy," said Jo. But he dug his knees into the horse. We shambled on. I half fell asleep, and had a sort of uneasy dream that the horses were not moving forward at all—then that I was on a rocking-horse, and my old mother was scolding me for raising such a fearful dust from the drawing-room carpet. "You've entirely worn off the pattern of the carpet," I heard her saying, and she gave the reins a tug. I snivelled and woke to find Jim leaning over me, maliciously smiling.

"That was a case of all but," said he. "I just caught you. What's up? Been bye-bye?"

"No!" I raised my head. "Thank the Lord we're arriving somewhere."

We were on the brow of the hill, and below us there was a whare roofed with corrugated iron. It stood in a garden, rather far back from the road—a big paddock opposite, and a creek and a clump of young willow trees. A thin line of blue smoke stood up straight from the chimney of the whare; and as I looked a woman came out, followed by a child and a sheep-dog—the woman carrying what appeared to me a black stick. She made gestures at us. The horses put on a final spurt, Jo took off his wideawake, shouted, threw out his chest, and began singing, "I don't care, for don't you see . . ." The sun pushed through the pale clouds and shed a vivid light over the scene. It gleamed on the woman's yellow hair, over her flapping pinafore and the rifle she was carrying. The child hid behind her, and the yellow dog, a mangy beast, scuttled back into the whare, his tail between his legs. We drew rein and dismounted.

"Hallo," screamed the woman. "I thought you was three 'awks. My kid comes runnin' in ter me. 'Mumma,' says she, 'there's three brown things comin' over the 'ill,' says she. An' I comes out smart, I can tell yer. 'They'll be 'awks,' I says to her. Oh, the 'awks about 'ere yer wouldn't believe."

The "kid" gave us the benefit of one eye from behind the woman's pinafore—then retired again.

"Where's your old man?" asked Jim.

The woman blinked rapidly, screwing up her face.

"Away shearin'. Bin away a month. I suppose yer not goin' to stop, are yer? There's a storm comin' up."

"You bet we are," said Jo. "So you're on your lonely, missus?"

She stood, pleating the frills of her pinafore, and glancing from one to the other of us, like a hungry bird. I smiled at the thought of how Jim had pulled Jo's leg about her. Certainly her eyes were blue, and what hair she had was yellow, but ugly. She was a figure of fun. Looking at her, you felt there was nothing but sticks and wires under that pinafore—her front teeth were knocked out, she had red pulpy hands, and she wore on her feet a pair of dirty bluchers.

"I'll go and turn out the horses," said Jim. "Got any embrocation? Poi's rubbed herself to hell!"

" 'Arf a mo!" The woman stood silent a moment, her nostrils expanding as she breathed. Then she shouted violently. "I'd rather you didn't stop. . . . You *can't*, and there's the end of it. I don't let out that paddock anymore. You'll have to go on; I ain't got nothing!"

"Well, I'm blest!" said Jo, heavily. He pulled me aside. "Gone a bit off 'er dot," he whispered. "Too much alone, *you know*," very significantly. "Turn the sympathetic tap on 'er, she'll come round all right."

But there was no need—she had come round by herself.

"Stop if yer like!" she muttered, shrugging her shoulders. To me—"I'll give yer the embrocation if yer come along."

"Right-o, I'll take it down to them." We walked together up the garden path. It was planted on both sides with cabbages. They smelled like stale dish-water. Of flowers there were double poppies and sweet-williams. One little patch was divided off by pawa shells—presumably it belonged to the child—for she ran from her mother and began to grub in it with a broken clothes-peg. The yellow dog lay across the doorstep, biting fleas; the woman kicked him away.

"Gar-r, get away, you beast . . . the place ain't tidy. I 'aven't 'ad time ter fix things to-day—been ironing. Come right in."

It was a large room, the walls plastered with old pages of English periodicals. Queen Victoria's Jubilee appeared to be the most recent number. A table with an ironing-board and wash-tub on it, some wooden forms, a black horsehair sofa, and some broken cane chairs pushed against the walls. The mantelpiece above the stove was draped in pink paper, further ornamented with dried grasses and ferns and a coloured print of Richard Seddon. There were four doors—one, judging from the smell, let into the "Store," one onto the "back yard," through a third I saw the bedroom. Flies buzzed in circles round the ceiling, and treacle papers and bundles of dried clover were pinned to the window curtains.

I was alone in the room; she had gone into the store for the embrocation. I heard her stamping about and muttering to herself: "I got some, now where did I put that bottle? . . . It's behind the pickles . . . no, it ain't." I cleared a place on the table and sat there, swinging my legs. Down in the paddock I could hear Jo singing and the sound of hammer strokes as Jim drove in the tent-pegs. It was sunset. There is no twilight in our New Zealand days, but a curious half-hour when everything appears grotesque—it frightens—as though the savage spirit of the country walked abroad and sneered at what it saw. Sitting alone in the hideous room I grew afraid. The woman next door was a long time finding that stuff. What was she doing in there? Once I thought I heard her bang her hands down on the counter, and once she half moaned, turning it into a cough and clearing her throat. I wanted to shout "Buck up!" but I kept silent.

"Good Lord, what a life!" I thought. "Imagine being here day in, day out, with that rat of a child and a mangy dog. Imagine bothering about ironing. *Mad*, of course she's mad! Wonder how long she's been here—wonder if I could get her to talk."

At that moment she poked her head round the door.

"Wot was it yer wanted?" she asked.

"Embrocation."

"Oh, I forgot. I got it, it was in front of the pickle jars." She handed me the bottle.

"My, you do look tired, you do! Shall I knock yer up a few scones for supper? There's some tongue in the store, too, and I'll cook yer a cabbage if you fancy it."

"Right-o." I smiled at her. "Come down to the paddock and bring the kid for tea."

She shook her head, pursing up her mouth.

"Oh no. I don't fancy it. I'll send the kid down with the things and a billy of milk. Shall I knock up a few extry scones to take with yer ter-morrow?"

"Thanks."

She came and stood by the door.

"How old is the kid?"

"Six—come next Christmas. I 'ad a bit of trouble with 'er one way an' another. I 'adn't any milk till a month after she was born and she sickened like a cow."

"She's not like you—takes after her father?" Just as the woman had shouted her refusal at us before, she shouted at me then.

"No, she don't! She's the dead spit of me. Any fool could see that. Come on in now, Else, you stop messing in the dirt."

I met Jo climbing over the paddock fence.

"What's the old bitch got in the store?" he asked.

"Don't know—didn't look."

"Well, of all the fools. Jim's slanging you. What have you been doing all the time?"

"She couldn't find this stuff. Oh, my shakes, you are smart!"

Jo had washed, combed his wet hair in a line across his forehead, and buttoned a coat over his shirt. He grinned.

Jim snatched the embrocation from me. I went to the end of the paddock where the willows grew and bathed in the creek. The water was clear and soft as oil. Along the edges held by the grass and rushes, white foam tumbled and bubbled. I lay in the water and looked up at the trees that were still a moment, then quivered lightly, and again were still. The air smelt of rain. I forgot about the woman and the kid until I came back to the tent. Jim lay by the fire, watching the billy boil.

I asked where Jo was, and if the kid had brought our supper.

"Pooh," said Jim, rolling over and looking up at the sky. "Didn't you see how Jo had been titivating? He said to me before he went up to the whare, 'Dang it! she'll look better by night light—at any rate, my buck, she's female flesh!'"

"You had Jo about her looks—you had me, too."

"No—look here. I can't make it out. It's four years since I came past this way, and I stopped here two days. The husband was a pal of mine once, down the West Coast —a fine, big chap, with a voice on him like a trombone. She'd been barmaid down the Coast—as pretty as a wax doll. The coach used to come this way then once a fortnight, that was before they opened the railway up Napier way, and she had no end of a time! Told me once in a confidential moment that she knew one hundred and twenty-five different ways of kissing!"

"Oh, go on, Jim! She isn't the same woman!"

"Course she is. . . . I can't make it out. What I think is the old man's cleared out and left her: that's all my eye about shearing. Sweet life! The only people who come through now are Maoris and sundowners!"

Through the dark we saw the gleam of the kid's pinafore. She trailed over to us with a basket in her hand, the milk billy in the other. I unpacked the basket, the child standing by.

"Come over here," said Jim, snapping his fingers at her.

She went; the lamp from inside of the tent cast a bright light over her. A mean, undersized brat, with whitish hair, and weak eyes. She stood, legs wide apart and her stomach protruding.

"What do you do all day?" asked Jim.

She scraped out one ear with her little finger, looked at the result and said, "Draw."

"Huh! What do you draw? Leave your ears alone!"

"Pictures."

"What on?"

"Bits of butter paper an' a pencil of my Mumma's."

"Boh! What a lot of words at one time!" Jim rolled his eyes at her. "Baa-lambs and moo-cows?"

"No, everything. I'll draw all of you when you're gone, and your horses and the tent, and that one"—she pointed to me—"with no clothes on in the creek. I looked at her where she couldn't see me from."

"Thanks very much. How ripping of you," said Jim. "Where's Dad?"

The kid pouted. "I won't tell you because I don't like yer face!" She started operations on the other ear.

"Here," I said. "Take the basket, get along home and tell the other man supper's ready."

"I don't want to."

"I'll give you a box on the ear if you don't," said Jim, savagely.

"Hie! I'll tell Mumma. I'll tell Mumma." The kid fled.

We ate until we were full, and had arrived at the smoke

stage before Jo came back, very flushed and jaunty, a whisky bottle in his hand.

" 'Ave a drink—you two!" he shouted, carrying off matters with a high hand. " 'Ere, shove along the cups."

"One hundred and twenty-five different ways," I murmured to Jim.

"What's that? Oh! stow it!" said Jo. "Why 'ave you always got your knife into me? You gas like a kid at a Sunday School beano. She wants us to go up there to-night, and have a comfortable chat. I"—he waved his hand airily—"I got 'er round."

"Trust you for that," laughed Jim. "But did she tell you where the old man's got to?"

Jo looked up. "Shearing! You 'eard 'er, you fool!"

The woman had fixed up the room, even to a light bouquet of sweet-williams on the table. She and I sat one side of the table, Jo and Jim the other. An oil-lamp was set between us, the whisky bottle and glasses, and a jug of water. The kid knelt against one of the forms, drawing on butter paper. I wondered, grimly, if she was attempting the creek episode. But Jo had been right about night time. The woman's hair was tumbled—two red spots burned in her cheeks—her eyes shone—and we knew that they were kissing feet under the table. She had changed the blue pinafore for a white calico dressing-jacket and a black skirt—the kid was decorated to the extent of a blue sateen hair ribbon. In the stifling room, with the flies buzzing against the ceiling and dropping onto the table, we got slowly drunk.

"Now listen to me," shouted the woman, banging her fist on the table. "It's six years since I was married, and four miscarriages. I says to 'im, I says, what do you think I'm doin' up 'ere? If you was back at the coast, I'd 'ave you lynched for child murder. Over and over I tells 'im—you've broken my spirit and spoiled my looks, and wot for—that's wot I'm driving at." She clutched her head with her hands and stared round at us. Speaking rapidly, "Oh, some days—an'

months of them—I 'ear them two words knockin' inside me
all the time—'Wot for!' but sometimes I'll be cooking the
spuds an' I lifts the lid off to give 'em a prong and I 'ears,
quite sudden again, 'Wot for!' Oh! I don't mean only the
spuds and the kid—I mean—I mean," she hiccoughed—
"you know what I mean, Mr. Jo."

"I know," said Jo, scratching his head.

"Trouble with me is," she leaned across the table, "he
left me too much alone. When the coach stopped coming,
sometimes he'd go away days, sometimes he'd go away
weeks, and leave me ter look after the store. Back 'e'd
come—pleased as Punch. 'Oh, 'allo,' 'e'd say. ' 'Ow are you
gettin' on? Come and give us a kiss.' Sometimes I'd turn a
bit nasty, and then 'e'd go off again, and if I took it all
right, 'e'd wait till 'e could twist me round 'is finger, then
'e'd say, 'Well, so long, I'm off,' and do you think I could
keep 'im?—not me!"

"Mumma," bleated the kid, "I made a picture of them
on the 'ill, an' you an' me, an' the dog down below."

"Shut your mouth!" said the woman.

A vivid flash of lightning played over the room—we
heard the mutter of thunder.

"Good thing that's broke loose," said Jo. "I've 'ad it in
me 'ead for three days."

"Where's your old man now?" asked Jim, slowly.

The woman blubbered and dropped her head onto the
table. "Jim, 'e's gone shearin' and left me alone again," she
wailed.

" 'Ere, look out for the glasses," said Jo. "Cheer-o, 'ave
another drop. No good cryin' over spilt 'usbands! You Jim,
you blasted cuckoo!"

"Mr. Jo," said the woman, drying her eyes on her jacket
frill, "you're a gent, an' if I was a secret woman, I'd place any
confidence in your 'ands. I don't mind if I do 'ave a glass on
that."

Every moment the lightning grew more vivid and the
thunder sounded nearer. Jim and I were silent—the kid

never moved from her bench. She poked her tongue out and blew on her paper as she drew.

"It's the loneliness," said the woman, addressing Jo—he made sheep's eyes at her—"and bein' shut up 'ere like a broody 'en." He reached his hand across the table and held hers, and though the position looked most uncomfortable when they wanted to pass the water and whisky, their hands stuck together as though glued. I pushed back my chair and went over to the kid, who immediately sat flat down on her artistic achievements and made a face at me.

"You're not to look," said she.

"Oh, come on, don't be nasty!" Jim came over to us, and we were just drunk enough to wheedle the kid into showing us. And those drawings of hers were extraordinary and repulsively vulgar. The creations of a lunatic with a lunatic's cleverness. There was no doubt about it, the kid's mind was diseased. While she showed them to us, she worked herself up into a mad excitement, laughing and trembling, and shooting out her arms.

"Mumma," she yelled. "Now I'm going to draw them what you told me I never was to—now I am."

The woman rushed from the table and beat the child's head with the flat of her hand.

"I'll smack you with yer clothes turned up if yer dare say that again," she bawled.

Jo was too drunk to notice, but Jim caught her by the arm. The kid did not utter a cry. She drifted over to the window and began picking flies from the treacle paper.

We returned to the table—Jim and I sitting one side, the woman and Jo, touching shoulders, the other. We listened to the thunder, saying stupidly, "That was a near one," "There it goes again," and Jo, at a heavy hit, "Now we're off," "Steady on the brake," until rain began to fall, sharp as cannon-shot on the iron roof.

"You'd better doss here for the night," said the woman.

"That's right," assented Jo, evidently in the know about this move.

"Bring up yer things from the tent. You two can doss in the store along with the kid—she's used to sleep in there and won't mind you."

"Oh Mumma, I never did," interrupted the kid.

"Shut yer lies! An' Mr. Jo can 'ave this room."

It sounded a ridiculous arrangement, but it was useless to attempt to cross them, they were too far gone. While the woman sketched the plan of action, Jo sat, abnormally solemn and red, his eyes bulging, and pulling at his moustache.

"Give us a lantern," said Jim, "I'll go down to the paddock." We two went together. Rain whipped in our faces, the land was light as though a bush fire was raging. We behaved like two children let loose in the thick of an adventure, laughed and shouted to each other, and came back to the whare to find the kid already bedded in the counter of the store. The woman brought us a lamp. Jo took his bundle from Jim, the door was shut.

"Good-night all," shouted Jo.

Jim and I sat on two sacks of potatoes. For the life of us we could not stop laughing. Strings of onions and half-hams dangled from the ceiling—wherever we looked there were advertisements for "Camp Coffee" and tinned meats. We pointed at them, tried to read them aloud—overcome with laughter and hiccoughs. The kid in the counter stared at us. She threw off her blanket and scrambled to the floor, where she stood in her grey flannel night-gown, rubbing one leg against the other. We paid no attention to her.

"Wot are you laughing at?" she said, uneasily.

"You!" shouted Jim. "The red tribe of you, my child."

She flew into a rage and beat herself with her hands. "I won't be laughed at, you curs—you." He swooped down upon the child and swung her onto the counter.

"Go to sleep, Miss Smarty—or make a drawing—here's a pencil—you can use Mumma's account book."

Through the rain we heard Jo creak over the boarding of the next room—the sound of a door being opened—then shut to.

"It's the loneliness," whispered Jim.

"One hundred and twenty-five different ways—alas! my poor brother!"

The kid tore out a page and flung it at me.

"There you are," she said. "Now I done it ter spite Mumma for shutting me up 'ere with you two. I done the one she told me I never ought to. I done the one she told me she'd shoot me if I did. Don't care! Don't care!"

The kid had drawn the picture of the woman shooting at a man with a rook rifle and then digging a hole to bury him in.

She jumped off the counter and squirmed about on the floor biting her nails.

Jim and I sat till dawn with the drawing beside us. The rain ceased, the little kid fell asleep, breathing loudly. We got up, stole out of the whare, down into the paddock. White clouds floated over a pink sky—a chill wind blew; the air smelled of wet grass. Just as we swung into the saddle Jo came out of the whare—he motioned to us to ride on.

"I'll pick you up later," he shouted.

A bend in the road, and the whole place disappeared.

MURDER IN THE FISHING CAT

Edna St. Vincent Millay

Edna St. Vincent Millay (1892–1950) holds the unusual distinction of being a poet beloved by both the common people and the intelligentsia. The quality of her poetry is evidenced by the fact she was awarded the Pulitzer Prize in 1923. In addition, she was a dramatist, writing three plays in verse and the libretto for an opera. She ventured into the shadowy world of crime fiction only once, with "The Murder in the Fishing Cat," and her poet's touch shows in her descriptions of the minute details of the protagonist's life as he moves toward his highly symbolic murder.

Nobody came anymore to the *Restaurant du Chat qui Pêche.* It was difficult to say just why.

The popularity of a restaurant does not depend on the excellence of its cuisine or the cobwebs on the bottles in its cellar. And you might have in the window ten glass tanks instead of one in which moved obscurely shadowy eels and shrimps, yet you could be no surer of success. Jean-Pierre knew this, and he did not reproach himself for his failure. It is something that may happen to the best of us.

For fourteen years he had served as good *lapin sauté* as was to be found in Paris; and if the *petits pois* were rather big and hard, and the Vouvray rather like thin cider, and you got no more than a teaspoonful of sugar with your strawberries, well, what could you expect for seven francs, all told? Not the world, surely. As for the rest, where else might you, while sitting comfortably at your table under a red-and-white awning, choose your eel, and see it captured for you deftly in a napkin, and borne off, writhing muscularly, to the kitchen, to be delivered to you five minutes later on a platter, fried? That was more than you could do at Ciro's.

It might be, of course, because Margot had scolded him much too audibly. But where was the man among his clients whose wife had not at some time or other addressed him as *saligaud,* or *espèce de soupe au lait?* Let him stand forth.

And, anyway, she had gone now. After fourteen years at his side, stamping the butter, whacking the long loaves of bread, sitting down with a sigh to a bowl of onion soup after nine o'clock, she had gone. She had run off with a taxi driver who had red mustaches that curled naturally. And the place was very still.

Jean-Pierre stood in the doorway with a damp cloth in his hand, and watched the people go by. They all went by. Once he had been sure that all were coming in, but now he

114

knew better. They were going to the *Rendezvous des Co-chers et Camionneurs,* next door.

"*J'ai pas la veine,*" said Jean-Pierre. He stepped out upon the pavement and busily passed the damp cloth over a table which was not yet dry.

A man and a girl went by. Two men went by. A woman went past, selling papers: "*L'Intran'! L'Intran-sigeant! La Liberté—troisième édition! L'Intran'! L'In-transigeant!*" Two young men went by; one was wearing a smock, the other had a painted picture under his arm. A man and a girl went past with their arms about each other. The man was saying, "*Si, si, c'est vrai.*" A very little girl came along, carrying a basket of small fringe-pet-aled pinks and fading roses. She had a serious face. She held out the flowers earnestly to a woman, with a coat over her arm, pushing a baby carriage; to an old man reading a newspaper as he walked; to two young women, dressed precisely alike, who were hurrying somewhere, chattering.

A priest went by, taking long steps, his black gown flap-ping about his large shoes, his stiff, shallow hat on the back of his head. He was trying to catch a bus. He began to run. The little girl watched him go by, seriously. Still watching him, she held out her flowers to a soldier in a uniform of horizon-blue. Then she went to the restaurant next door and moved among the tables.

"*Sentez, madame,*" she said without emotion, and im-passively thrust a bunch of pinks under the nose of a young woman, with a very red mouth, whose fork dangled lan-guidly from her hand as she conversed with the man across from her.

"*Merci, merci,*" said the woman, and motioned her away without looking at her.

An American boy was dining alone, reading from a yel-low book. He looked up from his book, and followed the little girl with his eyes as she moved about the terrace. As she approached him he spoke to her.

"C'est combien, ça, ma petite?" he asked.

She came up to him, and pressed her small stomach against the table.

"Dix sous," she answered lispingly, staring at his forehead.

He put an arm about her while he selected a nosegay from the basket, stood it up in his empty wineglass, and poured Vichy for it. Then he gave her a franc and told her to keep the change.

She stared at him, and went off up the street, holding out her basket to the passersby.

Jean-Pierre came to himself with a start: the proprietor of a flourishing café does not stand all the afternoon gaping at the goings-on in the café next door. No wonder people did not come to the *Restaurant du Chat:* it had an absent-minded *patron.* He hurriedly passed the damp cloth over two of the iron-legged tables, plucked a brown leaf from the laurel which hedged the terrace from the pavement proper, and went back into the restaurant.

"Ça va, Philippe?" he questioned jovially of the large eel which was now the sole occupant of the tank.

Not for the life of him could Jean-Pierre have told you why he had addressed the eel as Philippe; but having done so, he was glad. For from the moment he had given the creature a name, it possessed an identity, it was a person, something he could talk to.

He went to the kitchen, and returned with a morsel of lobster from a salad of the night before and tossed it into the pool.

Two men and two women, finding the *Rendezvous des Cochers* crowded, turned in at the *Restaurant du Chat qui Pêche* and seated themselves.

They heard Jean-Pierre singing:

> *"Oh, madame, voilà du bon fromage!*
> *Oh, madame, voilà du bon fromage!*
> *Voilà du bon fromage au lait!"*

One of the men rapped on the table with his stick. Jean-Pierre stopped short in his song, caught up the *carte du jour,* smoothed down his black beard, and hurried out.

"Very good, the rabbit," he suggested. And, "What will you have, sirs, in the way of wine?"

For half a year there had been only three of them to do the work—he, his wife, and Maurice, the waiter. Maurice had come to them when he was sixteen; but very soon he was nineteen, and the War Department, which knows about everything, had found out about that also, and had taken him away to put him into the army.

Then for two months there had been only two of them, but it was quite enough. Now Margot was gone, and he was alone. But business was worse and worse; and very rarely was he hurried with all the cooking and the serving and the cleaning up.

Jean-Pierre had made few friends in Paris in these fourteen years. He had dealt pleasantly with his clients, his neighbors, and the tradespeople with whom he had to do; but he had been content with his wife. She was a pretty woman from the frontier of Spain and more Spanish than French. He had met her for the first time right over there, in the Luxembourg Gardens. He could almost see from his doorway the very tree under which she had been sitting. She was wearing a hat of pink straw sloping down over her forehead, with many little roses piled high under the back of it; and she was very small about the waist. She was embroidering something white.

Several times he passed the chair in which she was sitting, and every time she looked up, and then looked down again. When she arose to go, he fell into step beside her.

"Mademoiselle, may I accompany you?" he asked.

"No, please," she answered hurriedly, without looking at him, and quickened her step.

He kept pace with her, however, and bent over her and spoke again more softly.

"It is wrong for one so beautiful to be so cruel."

"*Veux-tu me laisser!*" she scolded, tossing her head, and hastened out of sight.

But the next afternoon she was there again.

"You remember my wife, Philippe?" said Jean-Pierre. "Margot of the naughty eyes and the pretty ankles?"

Philippe said nothing.

"You do, all the same," Jean-Pierre averred. "She used to stir the water to make you mad." After a moment he said again, "Philippe, you remember Margot, don't you?"

Philippe said nothing.

"Well, anyhow," said Jean-Pierre, "she's gone."

For three months now Philippe had been alone in the tank. Nobody ate eels anymore. The few customers that came ordered rabbit, mutton, or beefsteak and potatoes. It would be foolish to have more eels sent in from the basin in the country. Jean-Pierre had explained that he would need for a time no more eels or shrimps, that he was making some changes.

Every morning when the proprietor of the *Chat qui Pêche* came down to open the door and put the tables and chairs out upon the pavement, Philippe lay sluggishly on the green bottom of his tank, the sunshine bringing out colors on his back that one had not known were there.

It was an oblong glass tank with brass edges. Fresh water came up through a little spout in the middle of it, and the stale water was sucked away through a pipe in one corner, which was covered with a bubble-shaped piece of netting. Looking into the tank one day, Jean-Pierre wondered why the netting was shaped like that; then he reflected that if the wire had been flat over the mouth of the pipe, it would have been clogged always with bits of dirt and food, which would float up to settle on it. He felt very proud when he had come to this conclusion.

Philippe had been at one time gray-green in color, and thin and very active. Now he was green-black, with a valance standing up along his spine of transparent purple, and with two little pale-green fins behind his head. He was big now, but as lithe as ever.

Jean-Pierre had heard queer tales about eels; he did not know how much truth there was in them. He had heard that their mothers came ashore to give birth to them; that they were born, like little animals, not laid, like eggs. And when they were small they were called "elvers." And he had been told that after they were born, their mothers left them, and went away. And in a little while the elvers started out for themselves in search of pools to live in. And if it so happened that the pools nearby had dried up with the heat, they went farther. And it was said that they have gone as far as twenty miles, across the land, in search of water, thousands of them, an army of little eels. And no human eye had witnessed their sinuous migration. Only from time to time there was found a dead elver in the grass, and people knew the eels had passed that way.

"Dis-moi un peu, Philippe," said Jean-Pierre. "You are a droll one, aren't you?"

The days went by, and nothing happened in them. Every day a few people came to eat there. Once there had been ten at a time, and Jean-Pierre had said to himself that if this kept on, he would have to get a waiter. But it did not keep on.

Every day he missed his wife more keenly. One day he went across the *rue de Médicis* into the Luxembourg Gardens, and walked up and down past the place where he had first seen her. A young woman was sitting under the tree, embroidering, but she was not Margot. She had two children with her, two little girls, dressed just alike, in very short dresses made all of pale-blue silk ruffles. They were chasing one another up and down the walk and calling in shrill voices. One of them lost her hair ribbon, a pale-blue silk bow, and ran sidewise up to her mother, holding in one hand the ribbon and lifting with the other a lock of straight blond hair at the top of her head; but all the time calling to her sister, and pawing the earth with brown, impatient legs.

Jean-Pierre wished very much that his only child, his and Margot's, had not died of diphtheria. She would have been much prettier than either of these little girls; she had looked like her mother. And she would be a companion for him now. If she were here this afternoon, he would take her to the *Jardin des Plantes* and show her all the different-colored birds. And after that they would go to the *Café des Deux Magots* and sit outside, and he would have a half-blond beer, and she would have a grenadine. And he would buy her one of those small white-and-brown rabbits made all of real fur that hop when you press a bulb, such as old men are always peddling along the pavement from trays suspended in front of their stomachs by a cord about their necks.

The days went by and went by. May passed, and June passed. One day there came a postcard from Maurice, a picture bearing the title, *Panorama de Metz*. On it was written carefully in pencil, *Bon souvenir d'un nouveau poilu aviateur*. Jean-Pierre was very excited about the postcard. Four times that day he drew it from his pocket and read it aloud, then turned it over and read with happiness his own name on the front of it. Late in the afternoon it occurred to him with pleasure that he had not yet read it to Philippe, and he hastened to do so. But from his wife there had come no word.

It seemed to Jean-Pierre that he would give everything he had in the world if he might once again hear Margot wail from the terrace, *"Un-e sou-u-u-u-u-pe!"* And, oh, to be called once more a dirty camel, a robber, or a species of dog!

He went to the tank and leaned over the quivering water.

"You are my wife, Philippe. You know?" said Jean-Pierre. "You are a *salope!*"

Having delivered himself of which genial insult, he felt happier, and stood for some moments in his doorway with his arms folded, looking boldly out upon the world.

* * *

"*Ça va, mon vieux?*" he accosted the eel one morning, and stirred the top of the water with a lobster claw. But Philippe scarcely moved. Jean-Pierre reached down with the lobster claw and tickled his back. The flat tail flapped slightly, but that was all. Jean-Pierre straightened up and pulled at his beard in astonishment. Then he leaned far over, so that his head made a shadow in which the eel was clearly visible, and shouted down to him:

"Philippe, Philippe, my friend, you are not sick, are you?"

He waited eagerly, but there was no responsive motion. The eel lay still.

"Oh, my God!" cried the *patron* of the *Chat qui Pêche*, and clutched his hair in his hands. Then for the first time he noticed that the surface of the water was unusually quiet. No fresh water bubbled up from the tap in the middle.

"Oh, my God!" cried Jean-Pierre again, and rushed to the kitchen.

There was nothing there with which to clean a clogged waterpipe. Everything that was long enough was much too thick. One tine of a fork would go in, but was probably not long enough. Nevertheless, he would try.

He ran back to the window and prodded the tube with a tine of the fork. Then he straightened up and waited, breathless. The water did not come. He rushed again to the kitchen, and scratched about among the cooking utensils. Was there no piece of wire anywhere in the world? A pipe cleaner! That was it! He searched feverishly through all his pockets, but he knew all the time that he had none. It occurred to him that if Margot were there, she would have a hairpin, which could be straightened out, and he cursed her savagely that she had gone.

Suddenly his eye fell on the broom, which was standing in a corner. He went over to it and tore forth a handful of splints, with which he rushed back to the tank.

"Wait, wait, Philippe!" he called as he approached.

"Don't die! Wait just a very little minute!" And he thrust a splint down into the tube. It broke, and he had difficulty in extracting it. Sweat came out on his forehead. He put two splints together, and inserted them with care.

"Don't die! don't die!" he moaned, but softly, lest the splints should break.

Suddenly, incredibly, the water came, and dust and particles of food began to travel slowly toward the outlet. Jean-Pierre thrust his hands in up to the wrists, and shooed the stale water down the tank.

The next morning Philippe was quite himself again. Fearfully, Jean-Pierre crept into the room and approached the window.

"Comment ça va ce matin?" he questioned in a timid voice, and put a finger into the pool.

The eel aroused, and wriggled sullenly to the other end of the glass.

Jean-Pierre giggled sharply with delight, and all that morning he went about with a grin on his face, singing, *"Madame, voilà du bon fromage!"*

Jean-Pierre hated the room in which he slept. It seemed to have become, since Margot left, every day dirtier and more untidy. For one thing, of course, he never made the bed. When he crawled into it at night it was just as he had crawled out of it in the morning. The thin blanket dragged always to the floor on one side, the counterpane on the other. The sheets grew grayer and grayer, and the bolster flatter. And he seemed always to have fallen asleep on the button side of the square pillow.

Infrequently he drew off the soiled sheets and put on clean ones. But at such times he became more than usually unhappy; he missed Margot more. She had been used to exclaim always over the fresh bed that it smelled sweet, and to pass her hand with pleasure over the smooth old linen. Often she would say with pride: "I tell you frankly, my little cabbage, in many of the big hotels today, rich hotels, full of

Americans, they make up the beds with cotton. I don't see how the clients sleep. I could not."

Every morning on awaking, Jean-Pierre groaned once and turned heavily. Then he rubbed the back of his wrist across his eyes, and stared out at the daylight. He saw on the shelf above the narrow fireplace a pale photograph of himself and his brother when they were children. They were seated in an imitation rowboat. Into his hand had been thrust an imitation oar, which it supported without interest; from the hand of his brother dangled listlessly a handsome string of imitation fish.

He saw also the swathed and ghostly bulk of what he knew to be a clock—a clock so elegant and fine, so ornamented with whorls of shiny brass, that his wife had kept it lovingly wrapped in a towel. To be sure, the face of the clock could not be seen; but what will you? One cannot have everything. Between the clock and the photograph was a marvelous object—a large melon growing serenely in a small-necked bottle. A great trick, that. But Jean-Pierre was very tired of the melon.

He was tired of everything in the room, everything in his life, but particularly of the things on the mantelpiece. And most of all was he tired of the candlestick that stood between the clock and the wreath of wax gardenias—a candlestick which had never known a candle, a flat lily pad with a green frog squatting on it. Jean-Pierre did not know that it was a green frog squatting on a lily pad. It had been there so long that when he looked at it he no longer saw it. It was only one of the things on the mantelpiece.

One morning, however, as he awoke and groaned and turned and looked out with dull eyes on still another yesterday, it so happened that he stared for some moments at the candlestick. And presently he said, *"Tiens! tiens!"* and laid his forefinger alongside his nose.

That morning he dressed hurriedly, with a little smile going and coming at his lips. And when he was dressed he thrust the candlestick into his pocket and ran downstairs.

"Bonjour, Philippe!" he called as he entered the restaurant. "Regard, species of wild man, I bring you a little friend!"

Happily, and with excessive care, he installed the green frog at the bottom of the tank. The eel moved away from it in beautiful curves.

"There is somebody for you to talk to, Philippe," said Jean-Pierre, "as you are for me."

He went to the door and opened it. The morning air came freshly in from the trees and fountains of the Luxembourg.

The days went by and went by, and nothing happened in them. One afternoon Jean-Pierre stood for a long time outside the window of a shop which had the sign up, *Fleurs Naturelles.* It was unfortunate for Margot, he told you frankly, that she had left him, because otherwise on this day she would be receiving a bouquet of flowers, *pois de senteur,* purple, pink, and mauve, and big white *pivoines.* It was the anniversary of their wedding. There were water lilies in the window, too.

Suddenly Jean-Pierre burst into the flower shop with the face of a boy in love, and after much shrugging and gesticulation and interchange of commonplace insults, he parted from the shopkeeper, and went home to Philippe, bearing a long-stemmed lily.

At twenty minutes to one of an afternoon a week later a man might have been seen to walk along the *quai* of the Seine to the *Place St. Michel,* and then up the *Boulevard St. Michel* to the *rue de Médicis.* On the corner of the *rue de Médicis* he hesitated and looked both ways. Just then a very little girl came up the *boulevard* and held out to him a basket of pinks and roses. He shook his head.

It happened that for that moment these two were the only people on that corner. The little girl stood for a moment beside him, hesitating, looking both ways. Then she tucked her basket under her arm and started up the *rue de*

Médicis. And because she had turned that way, the man turned that way, too, letting her decision take the place of his own.

He walked slowly, glancing as he passed at the many people taking their luncheon under the awnings in front of the cafés. He was looking for a place to eat, and it happened that he wished to be alone.

Before the *Restaurant du Chat qui Pêche* there were six oblong, iron-legged tables, on each of which stood a warted blue-glass vase containing a sprig of faded sweet william and the wilted stamens of a rose from which the petals had dropped. The place was deserted. There was no sign of life anywhere about, saving only that in one of the windows there was a glass tank filled with slightly quivering water, on the surface of which floated a lily, and on the bottom of which, beside an artificial bright-green frog, dozed a large and sluggish eel.

The man seated himself at one of the tables and tapped upon the table with the vase. There was no response. He tapped again.

"*Voilà!*" called Jean-Pierre from the back of the restaurant, and came eagerly out, holding in his hand the *carte du jour.*

"The rabbit is very good," he suggested, "also the gigot. And what will you have, sir, in the way of wine?"

"White wine," said the man, "a half-bottle. A salad of tomatoes, an onion soup, and an *anguille.*"

"*Oui, monsieur,*" said Jean-Pierre. "And after the *andouilles,* what?" *Andouilles* are a kind of sausage.

"Not *andouilles,*" replied the man, with some impatience, "*anguille.*"

"*Oui, monsieur,*" said Jean-Pierre, trembling. He passed his damp cloth over the table and went back into the restaurant. He sat down upon a chair, and his head dropped to one side, his eyes bulging. "*O-o, là là!*" said Jean-Pierre.

Several moments passed. The man on the terrace outside rapped sharply on the table.

"Voilà!" called Jean-Pierre, leaping to his feet. Hurriedly he gathered up a folded napkin, a thick white plate, a knife, fork, and spoon, two round bits of bread, and an unlabeled bottle of white wine. With these he issued forth.

When the table was fairly set, he curved one hand behind his ear and leaned down to listen.

"Will *monsieur* kindly repeat his order?" he requested in a half-whisper.

The gentleman did so, with annoyance, glanced up into the face bending over him, frowned, and reached for the wine.

Jean-Pierre went away and returned with the tomato salad. It was very pretty. There were green bits of chopped onion scattered over it. Presently he brought the onion soup. This was not very good. It was composed chiefly of soaked bits of bread, and it was not hot, but with grated cheese it could be made to do.

When the soup was finished, Jean-Pierre appeared again and cleared away the dishes.

"And for the rest, sir," said he, fixing the eyes of his client with his own, which glittered meaningly, "it will be necessary to wait a few moments, you understand."

"Yes, yes," said the man, and shrugged. He wished vaguely he had gone elsewhere for his food.

"Because he is living," Jean-Pierre pursued in a clear voice of unaccountable pride, "and it will be necessary first to kill him. See, he lives!" And pulling the man by the sleeve, he pointed with his thumb to the brass-bound tank in the window.

The man glanced askance at the window, and twitched his sleeve free.

"Encore une demi-bouteille de vin blanc," he replied.

Jean-Pierre stood for a moment looking down into the water. The eel was stretched along the bottom of the tank, dozing in the sunshine. Once he idly flipped his thick tail, then lay still again. His dark back shone with a somber iridescence.

"*Philippe,*" whispered Jean-Pierre, thrusting his face close to the surface of the pool—"*Philippe, mon petit, adieu!*"

At this, tears rushed from his eyes, and his neck and chest tried horridly to sob, working out and in like the shoulders of a cat that is sick.

"O Holy Virgin!" he moaned, and wound the clean white napkin firmly about his hand.

The eel came writhing out into the air. It was muscular and strong. It struck backward with its heavy body. It wound itself about Jean-Pierre's wrist. It was difficult to hold. It was difficult to shift from one hand to the other while one rushed to the kitchen.

Jean-Pierre held the eel to the table and reached for the knife. The knife was gone. Sweat rolled from his forehead, down his cheeks, and into his beard.

He ran wildly from one end of the kitchen to the other, the eel all the time plunging and twisting in his hand. He could not think what it was he was looking for.

The broom! But, no, it was not that. At length he saw the handle of the knife, Margot's knife, with which she used to kill the bread. It was peering at him from under a clutter of red and white onion skins. It had been watching him all this time.

He walked slowly past it, then turned sharply, and snatched it with his hand. He held Philippe firmly down upon the table, turned away his face, and struck with closed eyes. When he looked again, the knife was wedged in the table; Philippe had not been touched. He eased the knife free; the eel struck it with his lashing tail, and it fell to the floor. He stooped to pick it up; the eel reared in his grasp and smote him across the face.

"Ah-h-h!" cried Jean-Pierre, "you would, would you!" Smarting and furious from the blow, he clutched the knife and rose.

"You would, would you!" he said again, between his teeth. His throat thickened. Flames danced before his eyes. *"Eh bien, on verra!* Name of a name! We shall see, my little pigeon!" The flames roared and crackled. His eyes smarted, and his lungs were full of smoke. His heart swelled, burst, and the stored resentment and pain of his long isolation raced through his body, poisoning his blood.

"Take *that* for your lying face!" he cried. "Spaniard! Take *that* for your ankles! *That* for your red mustaches! Take *that*! Take *that*!"

Kneeling on the floor, he beat in the head of Philippe with the handle of the knife.

All the time that the stranger was eating, Jean-Pierre watched him slyly from the door. Twice a small giggle arose to his lips, but he caught at his beard and pulled it down. He was happy for the first time in many months. He had killed the taxi driver with the red mustaches, he had fried him in six pieces that leaped, and the stranger was eating him.

When the stranger had gone, Jean-Pierre gathered up the dishes and bore them to the kitchen, chuckling as he did so. He saw the head of the eel in the corner whither he had kicked it, and he spat upon it. But when he came back for the wine bottles and the salt and pepper and vinegar and oil, his eyes fell on the tank in the window, with its bright-green frog and its floating lily and its quiet emptiness. Then he remembered that it was Margot that he had killed.

He put his hand to his throat and stared. Margot! Now, how had that happened? He was sure that he had never intended to kill Margot. What a terrible mistake! But, no, it was not true that he had killed Margot. It was an ugly and tiresome dream. There was sun on the trees in the Gardens of the Luxembourg. Was not that proof enough that Margot was not dead, if one had needed proof?

Still, come to think of it, it was a long time since she had been about the house. It was fully a year, if you pressed the point, since he had heard her voice. There was something very dead about her, come to think of it.

But certainly he had killed Margot! How silly of him! He remembered the circumstances now perfectly. They had been out together in a rowboat on a river whose banks were brass. In Margot's hand was an oar, in his a handsome string of fish. At one end of the river was a dam covered by a dome of netted wire. At the other end water bubbled up continuously from a hidden spring.

He looked at Margot. As he looked, the oar slipped softly from her hand into the water; on the other side of the boat the string of fish slipped softly from his hand into the water. Then he noted with disquiet that the water in the river was steadily receding. He looked at the banks; they were like high walls of brass. He looked at them again; they were like tall cliffs of brass. He looked at the river; it was as shallow as a plate of soup.

It occurred to him that if he wanted to drown Margot, he would best be quick about it, as soon there would be no water in which to drown her. "But I do not wish to drown Margot!" he protested. But the man kept rapping on the table with a sprig of sweet william. And even as he said it, he stepped from the boat, seized her by the waist with both hands, and plunged her beneath the surface.

Her lithe body doubled powerfully in his grasp. He was astonished at the litheness of her body. Her feet, in elegant shoes of patent leather with six straps, appeared above the water, the ankles crossed. The top of her head was not even wet. Yet, for all that, the life came out of her. It rose to the surface in a great colored bubble, and floated off into the sunshine.

Jean-Pierre gazed across at the Luxembourg. A child in a white dress passed through a gate into the garden, holding in its hand by a string a blue balloon. Jean-Pierre smiled, and watched the balloon float off.

Over there, under a tree whose blossoms of white and

mauve wire drifted like lilies on the air, wearing a white dress and a pink hat with roses piled beneath the brim, forever and ever sat Margot. Over her head, tethered to her wrist by its string, floated forever and ever the blue balloon.

She was very near to him. It was a matter of a moment only to go across to her and lift the hat and say, *"Mademoiselle,* may I accompany you?"

Save that between them, flowing level with its brassy banks past the curb before his door, forever and ever ran the sunny river, full of rolling motor buses and rocking red taxicabs, too broad, too broad to swim. People went paddling past the window, this way and that way. A priest sailed by in a flapping gown, square boats upon his feet. A little girl went drifting by in a basket; her eyes were closed; her hands were full of brown carnations. Two gendarmes passed, their short capes winging in thick folds.

At the sight of the gendarmes Jean-Pierre started violently and stepped back from the window. There was something he must be about, and that without more delay, but he could not think what it was. Memories of Margot flew at his mind with sharp beaks. He waved his arms about his head to scare them off. There was something he must be about, and that at once.

Something touched him lightly on the shoulder. He uttered an indrawn scream, and swung on his heel. It was only the wall. He had backed into the wall. Yet even as he said to himself, "It is only the wall," and wiped his sleeve across his forehead, he saw them beside him, the two gendarmes, one on the left of him and one on the right. The one on the right of him said to the other:

"This is he, the man who drowned his wife in a plate of soup."

But the other answered: "Not at all. He beat in her head with a knife. Do you not see the onion skins?"

Then for the first time Jean-Pierre saw that both had red mustaches, and he knew that he was lost.

"Come, my man," they said, and stepped back, and he was left standing alone.

Suddenly that part of the floor on which he was standing slipped backward like a jerked rug under his feet, and he was thrown forward on his face. There came a rush of cold wind on the nape of his neck.

"No, you don't!" he shrieked, and, rolling over violently, leaped into the kitchen and bolted the door.

He knelt behind the door, and addressed them craftily through the keyhole.

"Messieurs," he said, "upstairs in my chamber is a melon as big as my head, in a bottle with a neck the size of a pipestem. It is the marvel of all Paris. I will give ten thousand francs to the man who can divine me how it came there."

Then he put his ear to the hole and listened, with difficulty restraining himself from chuckling aloud.

In a moment he heard their feet upon the stairs.

He counted the stairs with them as they ascended, nodding his head at each. When he knew that they were at the top, he slipped quietly forth, and bolted the stairway door.

His head was very clear; it was as light as a balloon on his shoulders. He knew precisely what he must do. He must bury the body, remove all traces of his guilt, and get away. And he must lose no time. He took his hat and coat from the peg where they were hanging, and placed them in readiness over a chair by the street door. Then he went softly and swiftly into the kitchen.

He gathered up from the table six sections of a broken backbone, a large knife, and an unwashed platter; from the stove a greasy frying pan; and from the floor a crushed and bloodstained head. These objects he wrapped in a newspaper, laid upon a chair, and then covered with a cloth.

Hark! Was that a step in the room above? No.

Hastily, he washed the table, scrubbing feverishly until the last stain was removed, scrubbed a wide stain from the floor, and set the kitchen in order.

Hark! Was that a step on the stair? No.

He lifted the newspaper parcel from the chair and bore it, shielded from sight by his apron, into the small backyard behind the restaurant, a yard bare save for a tree of empty bottles, some flowerpots full of dry earth and withered stalks, and a rusted birdcage with crushed and dented wires.

There he laid his burden down, and after an hour of terror and sweating toil buried it in a hole much bigger than was required.

The afternoon advanced, and evening came. A light flashed on in the *Rendezvous des Cochers et Camionneurs;* farther up the street another light. The street was ablaze. Gay people walked up and down, sat at tables eating, talked eagerly together.

In the *Restaurant du Chat qui Pêche* the dusk thickened into dark, the darkness into blackness, and no lights came on. The door was wide open. The night wind came in through the door, and moved about the empty rooms.

At midnight a gendarme, seeing that the door was open and the restaurant in darkness, approached, rapped sharply on the open door, and called. There was no answer.

He closed the door, and went on.

THE LIPSTICK

Mary Roberts Rinehart

Mary Roberts Rinehart (1876–1958) has been called the "Queen of the Gothic Romance" and the inventor (not entirely to her credit) of the "Had I But Known" school of mystery writing—a reputation based on such novels as The Circular Staircase *(1908),* The Man in Lower Ten *(1909), and* The Case of Jennie Brice *(1913). But Mrs. Rinehart was also a prolific writer of adventure novels, plays (notably, with Avery Hopwood,* The Bat*), humorous sketches, autobiographical works, and short stories. The best of her fiction —"The Lipstick" is certainly in this category—supports the contention of eminent critic Howard Haycraft that she was the "dean of crime writing by and for women" in the United States during the first half of this century.*

I walked home after the coroner's inquest. Mother had gone on in the car, looking rather sick, as indeed she had done ever since Elinor's death. Not that she had particularly cared for Elinor. She has a pattern of life which divides people into conformers and nonconformers. The conformers pay their bills the first of the month, go to church—the Episcopal, of course—never by any chance get into anything but the society columns of the newspapers, and regard marriage as the *sine qua non* of every female over twenty.

My cousin Elinor Hammond had openly flouted all this. She had gone gaily through life, as if she wakened each morning wondering what would be the most fun that day, stretching her long lovely body between her silk sheets—how mother resented those sheets!—and calling to poor tired old Fred in his dressing room.

"Let's have some people in for cocktails, Fred."

"Anything you say, darling."

It was always like that. Anything Elinor said was all right with Fred. He worshiped her. As I walked home that day I was remembering his face at the inquest. He had looked dazed.

"You know of no reason why your—why Mrs. Hammond should take her own life?"

"None whatever."

"There was nothing in her state of health to have caused her anxiety?"

"Nothing. She had always seemed to be in perfect health."

"She was consulting Doctor Barclay."

"She was tired. She was doing too much," he said unhappily.

Yet there it was. Elinor had either fallen or jumped from that tenth-floor window of Doctor Barclay's waiting

134

room, and the coroner plainly believed she had jumped. The doctor had not seen her at all that day. Only the nurse.

"There was no one else in the reception room," she testified. "The doctor was busy with a patient. Mrs. Hammond sat down by the window and took off her hat. Then she lit a cigarette and picked up a magazine. After that I went back to my office to copy some records. I didn't see her again until—"

She was a pretty little thing. She looked pale.

"Tell us what happened next," said the coroner gently.

"I heard the other patient leave about five minutes later. She went out from the consulting room. There's a door there into the hall. We have that arrangement, so—well, so that patients don't meet. When he buzzed for the next case, I went in to get Mrs. Hammond. She wasn't there. I saw her hat, but her bag was gone. I thought she had gone to the lavatory. Then—" She stopped and gulped. "Then I heard people shouting in the street and I looked out the window."

The coroner gave her a little time. She got out a handkerchief and dabbed at her eyes.

"What would you say was her mental condition that morning, Miss Comings? Was she depressed?"

"I thought she seemed very cheerful," she said.

"The window was open beside her?"

"Yes. I couldn't believe it until I—"

He excused her then. She was openly crying by that time, and it was clear that she had told all she knew.

When Doctor Barclay was called—he had come in late —I was surprised. I had expected an elderly man, but he was only in the late thirties and quite good-looking. Knowing Elinor, I wondered. She had had a passion for handsome men, except for Fred, who had no looks whatever. Beside me I heard mother give a ladylike snort.

"So that's it!" she said. "She had as much need for a psychiatrist as I need a third leg."

But the doctor added little to what we already knew. He had not seen Elinor at all that morning. When he rang the buzzer and nobody came he had gone forward to the reception room. Miss Comings was leaning out the window. All at once she began to scream. Fortunately a Mrs. Thompson arrived at that time and took charge of her. He had gone down to the street, but the ambulance had already arrived.

He was frank enough up to that time. Queried about the reason for Elinor's consulting him, he tightened, however.

"I have many patients like Mrs. Hammond," he said. "Women who live on their nerves. Mrs. Hammond had been doing that for years."

"That is all? She mentioned no particular trouble?"

He smiled faintly.

"We all have troubles," he said. "Some we imagine, some we magnify, some are real. But I would say that Mrs. Hammond was an unusually normal person. I had recommended that she go away for a rest. I believe she meant to do so."

His voice was clipped and professional. If Elinor had been attracted to him it had been apparently a one-sided affair. Fred, however, was watching him intently.

"You did not gather that she contemplated suicide?"

"No. Not at any time."

That is all they got out of him. He evaded them on anything Elinor had imagined, or magnified. In fact he did as fine a piece of dodging as I have ever seen. His relations with his patients, he said, were particularly confidential. If he knew anything of value he would tell it, but he did not.

Mother nudged me as he finished.

"Probably in love with her," she said. "He's had a shock. That's certain."

He sat down near us, and I watched him. I saw him reach for a cigarette, then abandon the idea, and I saw him more or less come to attention when the next witness was called. It was the Mrs. Thompson who had looked after the nurse, and she was a strangely incongruous figure in that group of Elinor's family and friends. She was a large moth-

erly-looking woman, perspiring freely and fanning herself
with a small folding fan.

She stated at once that she was not a patient.

"I clean his apartment for him once a week," she said.
"He has a Jap, but he's no cleaner. That day I needed a little
money in advance, so I went to see him."

She had not entered the office at once. She had looked
in and seen Elinor, so she had waited in the hall, where there
was a breeze. She had seen the last patient, a woman, leave
by the consulting room door and go down in the elevator.
A minute or so later she heard the nurse scream.

"She was leaning out the window yelling her head off,"
she said. "Then the doctor ran in and we got her on a couch.
She said somebody had fallen out, but she didn't say who it
was."

Asked how long she had been in the hall, she thought
about a quarter of an hour. She was certain no other patient
had entered during that time. She would have seen them if
they had.

"You are certain of that?"

"Well, I was waiting my chance to see the doctor. I was
watching pretty close. And I was never more than a few feet
from the door."

"You found something belonging to Mrs. Hammond,
didn't you? In the office?"

"Yes, sir. I found her bag."

The bag, it seemed, had been behind the radiator in
front of the window.

"I thought myself it was a queer place for it, if she was
going to—do what she did." And she added naïvely, "I gave
it to the police when they came."

So that was that. Elinor, having put her hat on the table,
had dropped her bag behind the radiator before she
jumped. Somehow it didn't make sense to me, and later on,
of course, it made no sense at all.

The verdict was of suicide while of unsound mind. The
window had been examined, but there was the radiator in

front of it, and the general opinion seemed to be that a fall would have to be ruled out. Nobody of course mentioned murder. In the face of Mrs. Thompson's testimony it looked impossible. Fred listened to the verdict with blank eyes. His sister Margaret, sitting beside him and dressed in heavy mourning, picked up her bag and rose. And Doctor Barclay stared straight ahead of him as though he did not hear it. Then he got up and went out, and while I put mother in the car I saw him driving away, still with that queer fixed look on his face.

I was in a fine state of fury as I walked home. I had always liked Elinor, even when, as mother rather inelegantly said, she had snatched Fred from under my nose. As a matter of cold fact, Fred Hammond never saw me after he first met her. He had worshiped her from the start, and his white, stunned face at the inquest only added to the mystery.

The fools, I thought. As though Elinor would ever have jumped out that window. Even if she was in trouble she would never have done it that way. There were so many less horrible ways. Sleeping tablets, or Fred's automatic, or even her smart new car and carbon-monoxide gas. But I refused to believe that she had done it at all. She had never cared what people thought. I remembered almost the last time I had seen her. Somebody had given a suppressed-desire party, and Elinor had gone with a huge red letter "A" on the front of her white satin dress.

Mother nearly had a fit when she saw it.

"I trust, Elinor," she said, "that your scarlet letter does not mean what it appears to mean."

Elinor had laughed.

"What do you think, Aunt Emma?" she said. "Would you swear that never in your life—"

"That will do, Elinor," mother said. "Only I am glad my dear sister is not alive, to see you."

She had been very gay that night, and she had enjoyed the little run-in with mother. Perhaps that was one of the reasons I had liked her. She could cope with mother. She could, of course. She wasn't an only daughter, living at home and on an allowance which was threatened every now and then. And she had brought laughter and gaiety into my own small world. Even her flirtations—and she was too lovely not to have plenty of them—had been lighthearted affairs, although mother had never believed it.

She was having tea when I got home. She sat stiffly behind the tea tray and inspected me.

"I can't see why you worry about all this, Louise. You look dreadful," she said. "What's done is done. After all, she led Fred a miserable life."

"She made him happy, and now she's dead," I said shortly. "Also I don't believe she threw herself out that window."

"Then she fell."

"I don't believe that either," I said shortly.

"Nonsense! What do you believe?"

But I had had enough. I left her there and went upstairs to my room. It wasn't necessary for mother to tell me that I looked like something any decent dog would have buried. I could see that for myself. I sat down at my toilet table and rubbed some cream into my face, but my mind was running in circles. Somebody had killed Elinor and had gotten away with it. Yet who could have hated her enough for that? A jealous wife? It was possible. She had a way of taking a woman's husband and playing around with him until she tired of him. But she had not been doing that lately. She had been, for her, rather quiet.

Plenty of people of course had not liked her. She had a way of riding roughshod over them, ignoring their most sensitive feelings or laughing at them. She never snubbed anyone. She said what she had to say, and sometimes it wasn't pleasant. Even to Fred. But he had never resented it. He was like that.

I could see the Hammond place from my window, and the thought of Fred sitting there alone was more than I

could bear. Not that I had ever been in love with him, in
spite of mother's hopes. I dressed and went down to dinner, but I was still out of favor. I couldn't eat, either. Luckily it was mother's bridge night, and after she and her
three cronies were settled at the table I managed to slip
out through the kitchen. Annie, the cook, was making
sandwiches and cutting cake.

"It beats all, the way those old ladies can eat," she said
resignedly.

I told her if I was asked for to say I had gone to bed, and
went out. Fred's house was only two blocks away, set in its
own grounds like ours, and as I entered the driveway I saw
a man standing there, looking at it. I must have surprised
him, for he turned suddenly and looked at me. It was Doctor
Barclay.

He didn't recognize me, however. I suppose he had not
even seen me at the inquest. He touched his hat and went
out to the street, and a moment later I heard his car start off.
But if he had been in the house Fred did not mention it. I
rang and he himself opened the door. He seemed relieved
when he saw me.

"I thought you were the damned police again," he said.
"Come in. I've sent the servants to bed. They're all pretty
well shot."

We went into the library. It looked as if it hadn't been
dusted for a month. Elinor's house had always looked that
way, full of people and cigarette smoke and used highball
glasses. But at least it had looked alive. Now—well, now it
didn't. So it was a surprise to see her bag lying on the table.
Fred saw me looking at it.

"Police returned it today," he said. "Want a drink?"

"I'll have some White Rock. May I look inside it, Fred?"

"Go to it," he said dully. "There's nothing there that
doesn't belong. No note, if that's what you mean."

I opened the bag. It was crammed as usual: compact,
rouge, coin purse, a zipper compartment with some bills in
it, a small memorandum book, a handkerchief smeared with

lipstick, a tiny perfume vial, and some samples of dress material with a card pinned to them, "Match slippers to these." Fred was watching me over his glass, his eyes red and sunken.

"I told you. Nothing."

I searched the bag again, but I could not find the one thing which should have been there. I closed the bag and put it back on the table. But he wasn't paying any attention to me anyhow. He was staring at a photograph of Elinor in a silver frame, on the desk.

"All this police stuff," he said. "Why can't they just let her rest? She's asleep now, and she never got enough sleep. She was beautiful, wasn't she, Lou?"

"She was indeed," I said honestly.

"People said things. Margaret thought she was foolish and extravagant." He glanced at the desk in the corner, piled high with what looked like unopened bills. "Maybe she was, but what the hell did I care?"

He seemed to expect some comment, watching me out of haggard eyes. So I said:

"You didn't have to buy her, Fred. You had her. She was devoted to you."

He gave me a faint smile, like a frightened small boy who has been reassured.

"She was, you know, Lou," he said. "I wasn't only her husband. I was her father too. She told me everything. Why she had to go to that damned doctor—"

"Didn't you know she was going, Fred?"

"Not until I found a bill from him," he said grimly. "I told her I could prescribe a rest for her, instead of her sitting for hours with that young puppy. But she only laughed."

He talked on, as if he was glad of an audience. He had made her happy. She went her own way sometimes, but she always came back to him. He considered the coroner's verdict an outrage. "She fell. She was always reckless about heights." And he had made no plans, except that Margaret was coming to stay until he closed the place. And as if the mere mention of her had summoned her, at that minute Margaret walked in.

I had never liked Margaret Hammond. She was a tall angular woman, older than Fred, and she merely nodded to me.

"I decided to come tonight," she said. "I don't like your being alone. And tomorrow I want to inventory the house. I'd like to have father's portrait, Fred."

He winced at that. There had been a long quarrel about old Joe Hammond's portrait ever since Fred's marriage. Not that Elinor had cared about it, but because Margaret had always wanted it she had held onto it. I looked at Margaret. Perhaps she was the nearest to a real enemy Elinor had ever had. She had hated the marriage, had resented Elinor's easygoing extravagant life. Even now she could not help looking at the desk, piled high with bills.

"I'd better straighten that for you," she said. "We'll have to find out how you stand."

"I know how I stand."

He got up and they confronted each other, Fred with his back to the desk, as if even then he was protecting Elinor from Margaret's prying eyes.

She shrugged and let it go. Yet as I left the house I was fairly confident she would spend the night at that desk. Fred asleep, the exhausted sleep of fatigue and escape, and Margaret creeping down to the desk, perhaps finding that bill of Doctor Barclay's and showing it to him in the morning.

"So that's how she put in her time! And you pay for it!"

It was warm that night. I walked slowly home, hoping the bridge game was not over. But it seemed my night for unexpected encounters, for I had gone nearly half the way when I realized I was being followed. That is, someone was walking softly behind me. I felt the hair rising on my scalp as I stopped and turned. But it was only a girl. When I stopped she stopped too. Then she came on, and spoke my name.

"You're Miss Baring, aren't you?"

"Yes. You scared me half to death."

"I'm sorry. I saw you coming out of the inquest today, and a reporter told me your name. You've been to the Hammonds', haven't you?"

"Yes. What about it?"

She seemed uncertain. She stood still, fiddling with her handbag. She was quite young, and definitely uneasy.

"Were you a friend of Mrs. Hammond's?" she inquired.

"She was my cousin. Why?"

She seemed to make a decision, although she took her time to do it. She opened her bag, got out a cigarette and lit it before she answered.

"Because I think she was pushed out that window," she said defiantly. "I'm in an office across the street, and I was looking out. I didn't know who she was, of course."

"Do you mean that you saw it happen?" I said incredulously.

"No. But I saw her at the window, just before it happened, and she was using a lipstick. When I looked out again she was—she was on the pavement." She shivered, and threw away the cigarette. "I don't think a woman would use a lipstick just before she was going to do a thing like that, do you?"

"No," I said. "How long was it between that and when you saw her, down below?"

"Hardly a minute."

"You're sure it was Mrs. Hammond?"

"Yes. She had on a green dress, and I had noticed her hair. She didn't have a hat on. I—well, I went back tonight to see if the lipstick was somewhere on the pavement. I couldn't find it. The street was crowded. Anyhow someone may have picked it up. It's three days ago. But I'm pretty sure she still had it when she fell."

That was what I had not told Fred, that Elinor's gold lipstick was missing from her bag.

I looked at my watch. It was only eleven o'clock, and mother was good for another hour.

"We might go and look again," I said. "Do you mind?"

She didn't mind. She was a quiet-spoken girl, certain that Elinor had not killed herself. But she didn't want her name used. In fact, she would not tell me her name.

"Just call me Smith," she said. "I don't want any part of this. I've got a job to hold."

I never saw her again, and unless she reads this she will probably never know that she took the first step that solved the case. Because I found the lipstick that night. It was in the gutter, and a dozen cars must have run over it. It was crushed flat, but after I had wiped the mud off, Elinor's monogram was perfectly readable.

Miss Smith saw it and gasped.

"So I was right," she said.

The next minute she had hailed a bus and got on it, and as I say, I have never seen her since.

I slept badly that night. I heard the party below breaking up and the cars driving away. When mother came upstairs she opened my door, but I had turned off the light and closed my eyes, which was the only escape I knew of. I knew then that I had a murder to consider, and it seemed unimportant whether she had won two dollars or lost it that evening. But I got up after she had settled down for the night, and hid that battered lipstick in the lining of my hatbox.

It was late when I got to Doctor Barclay's office the next morning. The reception-room door was unlocked and I walked in. The room was empty, so I went to the window and looked down. I tried to think that I was going to jump, and whether I would use a lipstick or not if I were. It only made me dizzy and weak in the knees, however, and when the nurse came in I felt like holding onto her.

If she recognized me she gave no sign of it.

"I don't think you have an appointment, have you?" she inquired.

"No. I'm sorry. Should I?"

She looked as though I had committed *lèse-majesté*, no

less; and when I gave my name she seemed even more suspicious. She agreed, however, to tell Doctor Barclay I was there, and after a short wait she took me back to the consulting room.

The doctor got up when he saw me, and I merely put Elinor's lipstick on the desk in front of him and sat down.

"I don't think I understand," he said, staring at it.

"Mrs. Hammond was at the window in your reception room, using that lipstick, only a minute before she fell."

"I see." He looked at it again. "I suppose you mean it fell with her."

"I mean that she never killed herself, doctor. Do you think a woman would rouge her mouth just before she meant to do—what we're supposed to think she did?"

He smiled wryly.

"My dear girl," he said, "if you saw as much of human nature as I do that wouldn't surprise you."

"So Elinor Hammond jumped out your window with a lipstick in her hand, and you watch the Hammond house last night and then make a bolt for it when I appear. If that makes sense—"

It shocked him. He hadn't recognized me before. He leaned back in his chair and looked at me as if he was seeing me for the first time.

"I see," he said. "So it was you in the driveway."

"It was indeed."

He seemed to come to a decision then. He leaned forward in his chair.

"I suppose I'd better tell you, and trust you to keep it to yourself. I hadn't liked the way Mr. Hammond looked at the inquest. That sort of thing is my business. I was afraid he might—well, put a bullet through his head."

"You couldn't stop it, standing in the driveway," I said skeptically.

He laughed a little at that. It made him look less professional, more like a human being. Then he sobered.

"I see," he said. "Well, Miss Baring, whatever happened

to Mrs. Hammond, I assure you I didn't do it. As for being outside the house, I've told you the truth. I was wondering how to get in when you came. His sister had called me up. She was worried."

"I wouldn't rely too much on what Margaret Hammond says. She hated Elinor like poison."

I got up on that and retrieved the lipstick. He got up too, and surveyed me unsmilingly.

"You're a very young and attractive woman, Miss Baring. Why don't you let this drop? After all you can't bring her back. You know that."

"I know she never killed herself," I said stubbornly, and went out.

I was less surprised than I might have been to find Margaret in the reception room when I reached it. She was standing close to the open window from which Elinor had fallen, and for one awful minute I thought she was going to jump herself.

"Margaret!" I said sharply.

She jerked and turned. She never used makeup, and her face was a dead white. But I was surprised to find her looking absolutely terrified when she saw me. She pulled herself together, however.

"Oh, it's you, Louise," she said. "You frightened me." She sat down abruptly and wiped her face with her handkerchief. "She must have slipped, Lou. It would be easy. Try it yourself."

But I shook my head. I had no intention of leaning out that window. Not with Margaret behind me. She said she had come to pay Fred's bill for Elinor, and I let it go at that. Nevertheless, there was something queer about her that day, and I felt shivery as I went down in the elevator. Women at her time of life sometimes go off-balance to the point of insanity.

I had some trouble in starting my car, which is how I happened to see her when she came out of the building. And then she did something that made me stop and watch her.

There was no question about it. She was looking over the pavement and in the gutter. So she knew Elinor's lipstick had fallen with her. Either that or she had missed it out of the bag.

She didn't see me. She hailed a taxi and got into it, her tall figure in its deep mourning conspicuous in that summer crowd of thin light dresses. To this day I don't know why I followed her, except that she was the only suspect I had. Not that I really believed then that she had killed Elinor. All I knew was that someone had done it.

I did follow her, however. The taxi went on and on. I began to feel rather silly as it passed through the business section and into the residential part of town. Here the traffic was lighter and I had to fall back. But on a thinly settled street the taxi stopped and Margaret got out. She did not see me or my car. She was looking at a frame house, set back from the street, and with a narrow porch in front of it, and as I watched her she climbed the steps and rang the bell.

She was there, inside the house, for almost an hour. I began to feel more idiotic than ever. There were so many possible reasons for her being there, reasons which had nothing to do with Elinor. But when she finally came out I sat up in amazement.

The woman seeing her off on the porch was the Mrs. Thompson of the inquest.

I stooped to fix my shoe as the taxi passed me, but I don't believe Margaret even saw the car. Nor did Mrs. Thompson. She didn't go into the house at once. Instead she sat down on the porch and fanned herself with her apron, and she was still there when I went up the steps.

She looked surprised rather than apprehensive. I don't suppose she had seen me at the inquest. She didn't move.

"I hope you're not selling anything," she said, not unpleasantly. "If you are you needn't waste your time."

It was impossible to connect her with crime. Any crime. By the time a woman has reached fifty what she is is written indelibly on her. Not only on her face. On her hands, on the clothes she wears and the way she wears them. She was the sort who got up in the morning and cooked breakfast for a large family. Probably did her own washing, too. Her knuckles were large and the skin on them red, as if they were too much in hot water. But her eyes were shrewd as she surveyed me.

"I'm not selling anything," I said. "May I sit down and talk to you?"

"What about?" She was suspicious now. "I've got lunch to get. The children will be coming home from school."

She got up, and I saw I would have to be quick.

"It's about a murder," I said shortly. "There's such a thing as being accessory after the fact, and I think you know something you didn't tell at the Hammond inquest."

Her florid color faded somewhat.

"It wasn't a murder," she said. "The verdict—"

"I know all about that. Nevertheless, I think it was a murder. What was Mrs. Hammond's sister-in-law doing here if it wasn't?"

She looked startled, but she recovered quickly.

"I never saw her before," she said. "She came to thank me for my testimony. Because it showed the poor thing did it herself."

"And to pay you for it, I suppose?"

She flushed angrily.

"Nobody paid me anything," she said. "And now I think you'd better go. If you think anybody can bribe me to lie you're wrong. That's all."

She went in and slammed the door, and I drove back to town, puzzled over the whole business. Was she telling the truth? Or had there been something she had not told at the inquest? Certainly I believed that the doctor had known more than he had told. But why conceal anything? I began to feel as though there was a sort of conspiracy around me, and it was rather frightening.

I was late for lunch that day, and mother was indignant.

"I can't imagine why, with nothing to do, you are always late for meals," she said.

"I've had plenty to do, mother," I told her. "I've been working on Elinor's murder."

She gave a small ladylike squeal.

"Murder?" she said. "Of course she wasn't murdered. Who would do such a thing?"

"Well, Margaret for one. She always loathed her."

"Women in Margaret's position in life do not commit crimes," she said pontifically. "Really I don't know what has happened to you, Louise. The idea of suspecting your friends—"

"She is no friend of mine. And Elinor was."

"So you'll stir up all sorts of scandal. Murder indeed! I warn you, Louise, if you keep on with this idiotic idea you will find yourself spread all over the newspapers. And I shall definitely stop your allowance."

With this dire threat she departed, and I spent the afternoon wondering what Doctor Barclay and the Thompson woman either knew or suspected, and in getting a shampoo and wave at Elinor's hairdresser's.

The girls there were more than willing to talk about her, and the one who set my hair told me something I hadn't known.

"Here I was, waiting for her," she said. "And she was always so prompt. Of course she never came, and—"

"You mean you expected her here, the day it happened?"

"That's right," she agreed. "She had an appointment for four o'clock. When I got the paper on my way home I simply couldn't believe it. She'd always been so gay. Of course the last few weeks she hadn't been quite the same, but naturally I never dreamed—"

"How long since you noticed a change in her?" I asked.

"Well, let me see. About Easter, I think. I remember I liked a new hat she had, and she gave it to me then and there! Walked out in her bare head. I ran after her with it, but she wouldn't take it back. She said a funny thing, now I think of it. She said sometimes new hats were dangerous!"

I may have looked better when I left the shop, but what I call my mind was doing pinwheels. Why were new hats dangerous? And why had Elinor changed since Easter?

Fred had dinner with us that evening. At least he sat at the table and pushed his food around with a fork. Margaret hadn't come. He said she was in bed with a headache, and he spent most of the time talking about Elinor.

It was ghastly, of course. Even mother looked unhappy. "I wish you'd eat something, Fred," she said. "Try to forget the whole thing. It doesn't do any good to go over and over it. You made her very happy. Always remember that."

Sometime during the meal I asked him if anything had happened to upset Elinor in the spring. He stared at me.

"In the spring? When?"

"About Easter," I said. "I thought she'd been different after that. As if she wasn't well, or something."

"Easter?" he said. "I don't remember anything, Lou. Except that she started going to that damned psychiatrist about then."

"Why did she go to him, Fred?" mother inquired. "If she had any inhibitions I never noticed them."

If there was a barb in this he didn't notice it. He gave up all pretension of eating and lit a cigarette.

"You saw him," he said. "He is a good-looking devil. Maybe she liked to look at him. It would be a change from looking at me."

He went home soon after that. I thought, in spite of his previous protests, that he had resented the doctor's good looks and Elinor's visits to him. And I wondered if he was trying to build up a defense against her in his own mind, to remember her as less than perfect in order to ease his tragic sense of loss.

I slept badly. I kept seeing Fred's face, and so I was late for breakfast the next morning. Yes, we still go down to breakfast. Mother believes in the smiling morning face over the coffee cups, and the only reason I had once contemplated marrying Fred was to have a tray in bed. But at least she had finished the paper, and I took it.

Tucked away on a back page, only a paragraph or two, was an item reporting that Mrs. Thompson had been shot the night before!

I couldn't believe it.

I read and reread it. She was not dead, but her condition was critical. All the police had been able to learn from the family was that she had been sitting alone on the front porch when it happened. Nobody had even heard the shot, or if they did they had thought it was the usual backfire. She had been found by her husband lying on the porch floor when he came home from a lodge meeting. That had been at eleven o'clock. She was unconscious when he found her, and the hospital reported her as being still too low to make a statement. She had been shot through the chest.

So she had known something, poor thing. Something that made her dangerous. And again I remembered Margaret, going up the steps of the little house on Charles Street. Margaret searching for Elinor's lipstick in the street, Margaret who had hated Elinor, and who was now in safe possession of Fred, of old Joe Hammond's portrait, of Elinor's silk sheets, and—I suddenly remembered—of Fred's automatic, which had lain in his desk drawer for years on end.

I think it was the automatic which finally decided me. That and Mrs. Thompson, hurt and perhaps dying. She had looked so—well, so motherly, sitting on that little porch of hers, with children's dresses drying on a line in the side yard, and her hands swollen with hard work. She had needed some money in advance, she had gone to the doctor's office to get it, and something had happened there that she either knew all the time, or had remembered later.

Anyhow I went to our local precinct station house that afternoon, and asked a man behind a high desk to tell me who was in charge. He was eating an apple, and he kept on eating it.

"What's it about?" he said, eying me indifferently.

"It's a private matter."

"He's busy."

"All right," I said. "If he's too busy to look into a murder, then I'll go downtown to Headquarters."

He looked only mildly interested.

"Who's been murdered?"

"I'll tell *him* that."

There was an officer passing, and he called him.

"Young lady here's got a murder on her mind," he said. "Might see if the captain's busy."

The captain was not busy, but he wasn't interested either. When I told him it was about Elinor Hammond, he said he understood the case was closed, and anyhow it hadn't happened in his district. As Mrs. Thompson was not in his district either, and as he plainly thought I was either out of my mind or looking for publicity, I finally gave up. The man behind the desk grinned at me when I passed him on the way out.

"Want us to call for the corpse?" he inquired.

"I wouldn't ask you to call for a dead dog," I told him bitterly.

But there was a result, after all. I drove around the rest of the afternoon, trying to decide what to do. When I got home I found mother in the hall, looking completely outraged.

"There's a policeman here to see you," she hissed. "What on earth have you done?"

"Where is he?"

"In the living room."

"I want to see him alone, mother," I said. "I haven't done anything. It's about Elinor."

"I think you're crazy," she said furiously. "It's all over. She got into trouble and killed herself. She was always headed for trouble. The first thing you know you'll be arrested yourself."

I couldn't keep her out. She followed me into the room,

and before I could speak to the detective there she told him I had been acting strangely for the past few days, and that she was going to call a doctor and put me to bed. He smiled at that. He was a capable-looking man, and he more or less brushed her off.

"Suppose we let her talk for herself," he said. "She looks quite able to. Now, Miss Baring, what's all this about a murder?"

So I told him, with mother breaking in every now and then to protest—about Elinor and the lipstick, about her appointment at her hairdresser's shortly after the time she was lying dead on the pavement, and my own conviction that Mrs. Thompson knew something she hadn't told.

"I gather you think Mrs. Hammond didn't kill herself. Is that it?"

"Does it look like it?" I demanded.

"Then who did it?"

"I think it was her sister-in-law."

Mother almost had a fit at that. She got up, saying she had heard enough nonsense, and that I was hysterical. But the detective did not move.

"Let her alone," he said gruffly. "What about this sister-in-law?"

"I found her in Doctor Barclay's office yesterday," I said. "She insisted that Elinor had fallen out the window. She said the floor was slippery, and she wanted me to try it myself." I lit a cigarette, and found to my surprise that my hands were shaking. "Maybe it sounds silly, but she knew about the lipstick. She tried to find it in the street."

But it was my next statement which really made him sit up.

"I think she was in the office the day Elinor was killed," I said. "I think the Thompson woman knew it. And I think she went out there last night and shot her."

"Shot her?" he said sharply. "Is that the woman out on Charles Street? In the hospital now?"

"Yes."

He eyed me steadily.

"Why do you think Miss Hammond shot her?" he said. "After all that's a pretty broad statement."

"Because she went there yesterday morning to talk to her. She was there an hour. I know. I followed her."

Mother started again. She couldn't imagine my behavior. I had been carefully reared. She had done her best by me. And as for Margaret, she had been in bed last night with a headache. It would be easy to verify that. The servants—

He waited patiently, and then got up. His face was expressionless.

"I have a little advice for you, Miss Baring," he said. "Leave this to us. If you're right and there's been a murder and a try at another one, that's our job. If you're wrong no harm's been done. Not yet, anyhow."

It was mother who went to bed that afternoon, while I waited at the telephone. And when he finally called me the news left me exactly where I had been before. Mrs. Thompson had recovered consciousness and made a statement. She did not know who shot her, or why, but she insisted that Margaret had visited her merely to thank her for her testimony, which had shown definitely that Elinor had either fallen or jumped out of the window. She had neither been given nor offered any money.

There was more to it, however. It appeared that Mrs. Thompson had been worried since the inquest and had called Margaret on the telephone to ask her if it was important. As a matter of fact, someone *had* entered the doctor's office while she was in the hall.

"But it was natural enough," he said. "It was the one individual nobody ever really notices. The postman."

"The postman?" I said weakly.

"Exactly. I've talked to him. He saw Mrs. Hammond in the office that morning. He remembers her all right. She had her hat off, and she was reading a magazine."

"Did he see Mrs. Thompson?"

"He didn't notice her, but she saw him all right."

"So he went out last night and shot her!"

He laughed.

"He took his family to the movies last night. And remember this, Miss Baring. That shot may have been an accident. Plenty of people are carrying guns now who never did before."

It was all very cheerio. Elinor had committed suicide and Mrs. Thompson had been shot by someone who was practicing for Hitler. Only I just didn't believe it. I believed it even less after I had a visit from Doctor Barclay that night.

I had eaten dinner alone. Mother was still in bed refusing to see me, and I felt like an orphan. I was listening to the war news on the radio and wondering if I could learn enough about nursing to get away somewhere when the parlormaid showed him in. He was apparently not sure of his welcome, for he looked uncomfortable.

"I'm sorry to butt in like this," he said. "I won't take much of your time."

"Then it's not a professional call?"

He looked surprised.

"Certainly not. Why?"

"Because my mother thinks I'm losing my mind," I said rather wildly. "Elinor Hammond is dead, so let her lie. Mrs. Thompson is shot, but why worry? Remember the papers! Remember the family name! No scandal, please. No—"

"See here," he said. "You're in pretty bad shape, aren't you? How about going to bed? I'll talk to you later."

"So I'm to go to bed!" I said nastily. "That would be nice and easy, wouldn't it? Somebody is getting away with murder. Maybe two murders. And everybody tries to hush me up. Even the police!"

That jolted him.

"You've been to the police?"

"Why not? Why shouldn't the police be told? Just because you don't want it known that someone was pushed out of your office window—"

He was angry. He hadn't sat down, and I made no move to do so. We must have looked like a pair of chickens with our feathers spread ready to fight. But he tried to control himself.

"See here," he said. "You're dealing with things you don't understand. Good God, why can't you stay out of this case?"

"There wasn't any case until I made one," I said furiously. "I don't understand. Why is everybody warning me off?" I suppose I lost control then. The very way he was watching me set me off. "How do I know you didn't do it yourself? You could have. Either you or the postman. And he was at the movies!"

"The postman!" he said, staring. "What do you mean, the postman?"

I suppose it was his astonished face which made me laugh. I laughed and laughed. I couldn't stop. Then I was crying too. I couldn't stop that either. I could hear myself practically screaming, and suddenly and without warning he slapped me in the face.

It jerked my head back and he had to catch me. But it stopped me all right. I pulled loose from him and told him to get out of the house. He didn't move, however. It didn't help to see that he had stopped looking angry, that in fact he seemed rather pleased with himself.

"That's the girl," he said. "You'd have had the neighbors in in another minute. You'd better go up to bed, and I'll send you some sleeping stuff from the drugstore."

"I wouldn't take anything you sent me on a bet," I said bitterly.

He ignored that. He redeemed my cigarette from where it was busily burning a hole in the carpet—good heavens! Mother!—and dropped it in an ashtray. Then to my fury he leaned down and patted me on the shoulder.

"Believe it or not," he said, "I didn't come here to attack you! I came to ask you not to go out alone at night, until I tell you you may." He picked up his hat. "I mean what I'm saying," he added. "Don't go out of this house alone at night, Miss Baring. Any night."

"Don't be ridiculous," I said, still raging. "Why shouldn't I go out at night?"

He was liking me less and less by the minute. I could see that.

"Because it may be dangerous," he said shortly. "And I particularly want you to keep away from the Hammond house. I mean that, and I hope you'll have sense enough to do it."

He banged the front door when he went out, and I spent the next half hour trying to smooth the burned spot in the carpet and hating him like poison. I was still angry when the telephone rang in the hall. It was Margaret!

"I suppose we have you to thank for the police coming here tonight," she said. "Why in heaven's name can't you leave us alone? We're in trouble enough, without you making things worse."

"All right," I said recklessly. "Now I'll ask you one. Why did you visit Mrs. Thompson yesterday morning? And who shot her last night?"

She did not reply. She gave a sort of gasp. Then she hung up the receiver.

It was a half hour later when the druggist's boy brought the sleeping tablets. I took them back to the kitchen and dropped them in the coal range, while Annie watched me with amazement. She was fixing mother's hot milk, I remember, and she told me that Clara, the Hammonds' cook, had been over that night.

"She says things are queer over there," she reported. "Somebody started the furnace last night, and the house was so hot this morning you couldn't live in it."

I didn't pay much attention. I was still pretty much shaken. Then I saw Annie look up, and Fred was standing on the kitchen porch, smiling his tired apologetic smile.

"May I come in?" he said. "I was taking a walk and I saw the light."

He looked better, I thought. He said Margaret was in bed, and the house was lonely. Then he asked if Annie would make him a cup of coffee.

"I don't sleep much anyhow," he said. "It's hard to get adjusted. And the house is hot. I've been getting rid of a lot of stuff. Burning it."

So that explained the furnace. I hoped Annie heard it.

I walked out with him when he left, and watched him as he started home. Then I turned up the driveway again. I was near the house when it happened. I remember the shrubbery rustling, and stopping to see what was doing it. But I never heard the shot. Something hit me on the head. I fell, and after that there was a complete blackout until I heard mother's voice. I was in my own bed, with a bandage around my head and an ache in it that made me dizzy.

"I warned her," mother was saying, in a strangled tone. "The very idea of going out when you told her not to!"

"I did my best," said a masculine voice. "But you have a very stubborn daughter, Mrs. Baring."

It was Doctor Barclay. He was standing beside the bed when I opened my eyes. I suppose I was still confused, for I remember saying feebly:

"You slapped me."

"And a lot of good it did," he retorted briskly. "Now look where you are! And you're lucky to be there."

I could see him better by that time. He looked very queer. One of his eyes was almost shut, and his collar was a wilted mess around his neck. I stared at him.

"What happened?" I asked dizzily. "You've been in a fight."

"More or less."

"And what's this thing on my head?"

"That," he said, "is what you get for disobeying orders."

I began to remember then, the scuffling in the bushes, and something knocking me down. He reached over calmly and took my pulse.

"You've got a very pretty bullet graze on the side of

your head," he said calmly. "Also I've had to shave off quite a bit of your hair." I suppose I wailed at that, for he shifted from my pulse to my hand. "Don't worry about that," he said. "It was very pretty hair, but it will grow again. At least thank God you're here!"

"Who did it? Who shot at me?"

"The postman, of course," he said, and to my rage and fury went out of the room.

I slept after that. I suppose he had given me something. Anyhow it was the next morning before I heard the rest of the story. Mother had fallen for him completely, and she wouldn't let him see me until my best silk blanket cover was on the bed, and I was surrounded by baby pillows. Even then in a hand mirror I looked dreadful, with my head bandaged and my skin a sort of yellowish gray. He didn't seem to mind, however. He came in, big and smiling, with his right eye purple and completely closed by that time and told me I looked like the wrath of heaven.

"You're not looking your best yourself," I said.

"Oh, that!" he observed, touching his eye gingerly. "Your mother put a silver knife smeared with butter on it last night. Quite a person, mother. We get along fine."

He said I was to excuse his appearance, because he hadn't been home. He had been busy all night with the police. He thought he would go there now and clean up. And with that my patience gave way completely.

"You're not moving out of this room until I know what's been going on," I stormed. "I'm running a fever right now, out of pure excitement."

He put a big hand on my forehead.

"No fever," he said. "Just your detective mind running in circles. All right. Where do I start?"

"With the postman."

So then he told me. Along in the spring Elinor had come to him with a queer story. She said she was being followed. It made her nervous. In fact, she was pretty well frightened. It seemed that the man who was watching her wherever she

went wore a postman's uniform. She would be having lunch
at a restaurant—perhaps with what she called a man friend
—and he would be outside a window. He would turn up in
all sorts of places. Of course it sounded fantastic, but she
swore it was true.

Some faint ray of intelligence came to me.

"Do you mean it was this man the Thompson woman
remembered she had seen going into your office?"

"She's already identified him. The real letter carrier
had been there earlier. He had seen Mrs. Hammond sitting
in a chair, reading a magazine. But he had gone before the
Thompson woman arrived. The one she saw was the one
who—well, the one who killed Elinor."

I think I knew before he told me. I know I felt sick.

"It was Fred, wasn't it?"

"It was Fred Hammond. Yes." He reached over and
took my hand. "Tough luck, my dear," he said. "I was worried about it. I tried to get her to go away, but you knew her.
She wouldn't do it. And then not long ago she wore a dress
at a party with the scarlet letter 'A' on it, and I suppose that
finished him."

"It's crazy," I gasped. "He adored her."

"He had an obsession about her. He loved her, yes. But
he was afraid he might lose her. Was losing her. And he was
wildly jealous of her." He looked slightly embarrassed. "I
think now he was particularly jealous of me."

"But if he really loved her—"

"The line between love and hate is pretty fine. And it's
just possible too that he felt she was never really his until—
well, until no one else could have her."

"So he killed her!"

"He killed her," he said slowly. "He knew that nobody
notices the postman, so he walked into my office and—"

He got up and went to the window. I sat up dizzily
in bed.

"But he was insane," I said. "You can't send him to the
chair."

"Nobody will send him to the chair," he said somberly.

"Just remember this, my dear. He's better off where he is. Perhaps he has found his wife by this time. I think he hoped that." He hesitated. "I was too late last night. I caught him just in time when he fired at you, but he put up a real battle. He got loose somehow and shot himself."

He went on quietly. There was no question of Fred's guilt, he said. Mrs. Thompson in the hospital had identified his photograph as that of the postman she had seen going into the office, and coming out shortly before she heard the nurse screaming. The bullet with which she had been shot had come from Fred's gun. And Margaret—poor Margaret —had been suspicious of his sanity for a long time.

"She came to see me yesterday after she learned the Thompson woman had been shot. She wanted him committed to an institution, but she got hysterical when I mentioned the police. I suppose there wasn't much of a case, anyhow. With Mrs. Thompson apparently dying and the uniform gone—"

"Gone? Gone how?"

"He'd burned it in the furnace. We found some charred buttons and things last night."

I lay still, trying to think.

"Why did he try to kill Mrs. Thompson?" I asked. "What did she know?"

"She had not only remembered seeing a postman going in and out of my office just before Miss Comings screamed. She even described him. And Margaret went home and searched the house. She found the uniform in a trunk in the attic. She knew then.

"She collapsed. She couldn't face Fred. She locked herself in her room, trying to think what to do. But she had told Fred she was going to see Mrs. Thompson that day, and she thinks perhaps he knew she had found the uniform. Something might have been disturbed. She doesn't know, nor do I. All we do know is that he left this house that night, got out his car, and tried to kill the only witness against him. Except you, of course."

"Except me!" I said.

"Except you," he repeated dryly. "I tried to warn you, you may remember! I came here and you threw me out."

"But why me? He had always liked me. Why should he try to kill me?"

"Because you wouldn't leave things alone," he said. "Because you were a danger from the minute you insisted Elinor had been murdered. And because you telephoned Margaret last night and asked her why she had visited Mrs. Thompson, and who had shot her."

"You think he was listening in?"

"I know he was listening in. He wasn't afraid of his sister. She would have died to protect him, and he knew it. But here you were, a child with a stick of dynamite, and you come out with a thing like that! That was when Margaret sent me to warn you."

I suppose I flushed.

"I'm sorry," I said guiltily. "I've been a fool all along, of course."

His one remaining eye twinkled.

"I wouldn't go as far as that," he said. "That stubbornness of yours really broke the case. Not," he added, "that I like stubborn women. Gentle and mild is my motto."

I had difficulty in getting him back to the night before. He seemed to want to forget it. But he finally admitted that he had been watching the Hammond house all evening, and that when Fred came to our kitchen door he had been just outside. Fred however had seemed quiet. He drank his coffee and lit a cigarette. And then of course I had walked out to the street with him.

"Good God," he said. "If ever I wanted to waylay anyone and beat her up—!"

However, it had looked all right at first. Fred had started down the street toward home, and he followed him behind the hedge. But just too late he lost him, and he knew he was on his way back. Fred had his revolver lifted to shoot me when he grabbed him.

Suddenly I found I was crying. It was all horrible. Elinor

at the window, and Fred behind her. Mrs. Thompson, resting after a hard day's work, and Fred shooting her. And I myself—

He got out a grimy handkerchief and dried my eyes.

"Stop it," he said. "It's all over now, and you're a very plucky young woman, Louise Baring. Don't spoil the record."

He got up rather abruptly.

"I think you've had enough of murder and sudden death," he said lightly. "What you need is quiet. I'm giving up your case, you know. There will be someone in soon to dress that head of yours."

"Why can't you do it?"

"I'm not that sort of doctor."

I looked up at him. He was haggard and tight with strain. He was dirty, he needed a shave, and that awful eye of his was getting blacker by the minute. But he was big and strong and sane. A woman would be safe with him, I thought. Any woman. Although of course she could never tell him her dreams.

"I don't see why you can't look after me," I said. "If I'm to look bald I'd prefer you to see it. After all, you did it."

He grinned. Then to my surprise he leaned down and kissed me lightly on the cheek.

"I've wanted to do that ever since you slammed that lipstick down in front of me," he said. "And now for God's sake will you stop being a detective and concentrate on growing some hair on the side of your head? Because I'm going to be right around for a considerable time."

When I looked up mother was in the doorway, beaming.

POSTICHE

Mignon G. Eberhart

Postiche: A pretentious imitation, particularly used of an inartistic addition to an otherwise perfect work of art—*Encyclopædia Britannica*

For more than fifty years, Mignon Eberhart has been one of the most respected names in mystery fiction. Her first novel, The Patient in Room 18, *was published in 1929; she has followed it with half a hundred more, as well as two plays, five short-story collections, and numerous uncollected stories. Although best known for her nonseries novels combining elements of the Gothic romance and the classic mystery* (Speak No Evil, Hunt with the Hounds, The Bayou Road), *Ms. Eberhart has also created several detective characters, the most accomplished of whom is Susan Dare, herself a writer of mysteries, who solves such baffling cases as the one posed in "Postiche."*

T he Wiggenhorn house could never have been a pleasant place: its slate roof was too heavy and dark, its turrets too many, its windows too high and too narrow. It was still less so on the cold, windy March afternoon when Susan Dare dismissed the taxi that had brought her from the train, and put her hand upon the gate.

Susan pressed the bell and thought of Jim's words to her over the telephone. "Go ahead, if you must, Susie," he'd said. "But if it looks like trouble, you get out. You take too many chances, my girl." He'd paused there, and then said in an offhand way: "Where'd you say the place is? Just outside Warrington? And what's the name of the people?" She'd told him, and had an impression that he'd written it down.

The door opened. A plump little maid took Susan's bag and invited her to enter.

The interior of the house was exactly what one would expect. There was a great deal of heavy, darkly upholstered furniture, stiff curtains which looked dusty and a musty smell tinged with camphor.

She had only a glimpse of the hall, however, for she was ushered at once into a hideous drawing room and from a jungle of armchairs a woman arose. She was a large woman, very fat, with a jolly smile, several chins, eyes that were almost hidden in folds of flesh and lightish, untidy hair. There was an open box of chocolates on the table beside her.

"Miss Dare, I suppose," she said in an asthmatic voice. "I was expecting you. I am Miss Wiggenhorn. Miriam Wiggenhorn. Do sit down. Will you have tea?"

There was no tea in sight, so Susan said no, and thought Miss Wiggenhorn looked disappointed. "Now then, Miss Dare, I daresay you want to know exactly why I asked you to come here. I heard of you, you see, from John Van Dusen, our family lawyer. I believe he is acquainted with a woman for whom you did—er—something of the kind. A Mrs. Lasher." She picked up some embroidery hoops and then paused to glance quickly at Susan over them. Or at least, so Susan thought.

"Yes."

"Yes. Well, at any rate, when things—owing to the confusion—to my own wish rather"—she floundered, threading a needle with care, and said, "So John said call in Miss Dare. Let her look around."

"Perhaps you'd better tell me just what it is about. I have only your note asking me to come. I ought to tell you that I'm not a detective, but a writer of mystery stories. And that I'm not at all sure of being able to help you."

"I think that's quite sufficient. I mean—Mrs. Lasher— Mr. Van Dusen—you see, Miss Dare, this is the trouble." She made a careful and intricate stitch, took a breath and said: "My uncle, Keller Wiggenhorn, died a few days ago. He was buried yesterday. And I want to make sure he—died a natural death."

"You mean you think he was murdered?"

"Oh, dear, no."

"Then what do you mean?"

Miriam Wiggenhorn ate a chocolate cream thoughtfully. Then she said: "I think I'd better tell you the whole story. I'll tell it briefly."

And denuded of Miss Wiggenhorn's panting breaths and hesitation it was certainly a brief enough story. Keller Wiggenhorn had been ailing for some time, owing to a serious heart weakness. Had been so ill in fact that for some three months he'd been obliged to have the care of a trained nurse. He had died suddenly, when alone. The doctor was not surprised; it was to be expected, he said. The nurse was not surprised although she regretted that she had not been with her patient when he was taken with the last and fatal attack. No one had known it even, although it had happened during the daytime. But the nurse had been out in the garden, taking her rightful air and exercise. Durrie had been in town ("Durrie?" said Susan. "My brother," said Miss Wiggenhorn. "Younger than I. We have lived with my uncle for many years.")—Durrie had been in town; the cook busy in the kitchen, and Miss Wiggenhorn herself had been in the kitchen. "Putting up pickled peaches," said Miss Wiggenhorn. "Uncle was very fond of them."

Only the maid might have known of his fatal attack, and she had not. For he had apparently merely felt faint at first and had called to the girl as she passed his door to hand him his bottle of smelling salts. The girl had done so, had asked if he wanted anything else, had been assured that he didn't. He was lying, she'd said, on a sort of couch, drawn up to the windows so he could read. He had made no complaint, seemed no worse than usual. The girl had gone on about her work downstairs.

There were no sounds. He hadn't rung the bell on the table beside him.

It was perhaps an hour after that that the maid returned and found he was dead.

Miss Wiggenhorn paused again and Susan waited. There was nothing, certainly, in the recital so far to suggest the thing that Miss Wiggenhorn had implied and then denied.

"But you see," said Miriam Wiggenhorn. "He died in great pain and struggle."

"Struggle!" said Susan sharply.

"The pillows were tossed about, his clothing disheveled, there were—marks on his throat."

It was very still. In the stillness someone walked heavily across the floor above and stopped.

"The doctor said it was all right. That with that particular trouble he was likely to gasp for breath at the last. He signed a certificate at once. Mind you, Miss Dare, I'm not saying there was murder done."

"Whom do you suspect?" said Susan bluntly.

Miriam Wiggenhorn did not reply directly. Instead she

put down her embroidery with an air of decision and turned to face Susan.

"I only want you to stay here for a few days. To consider the thing. I want him to have died naturally, of course. But I cannot forget the—look of things. The marks on his throat. The doctor says he made them himself—clutching—you see?—for air. I don't suspect anyone. There is no one to suspect. Durrie and I. A cook who has been with us for years. A maid who is—too stupid in the first place; and has no motive."

"The nurse?"

"The nurse was devoted to her patient. And he to her. She is a sweet, charming young woman. As you will see."

"Did anyone profit directly by your uncle's death?"

"You mean money and property? Yes, of course. He left his property and money—all his possessions, equally divided between Durrie and me. We were like children to him. He was only a moderately wealthy man. His will permits us to live on in exactly the same manner. There's no motive at all."

"But still you feel he was murdered?"

"I feel that I want to be sure he was not. That is all."

There were footsteps overhead again and then someone was running down the stairway in the hall beyond. Miss Wiggenhorn said: "There's Durrie now."

"Do they—your family—know why I am here?" asked Susan.

"Oh, yes," said Miriam Wiggenhorn readily, and Durrie entered the room.

He was certainly much younger than his sister; young and slender with light-brown hair that had a crisp wave which any woman might have envied, light gray-blue eyes and a handsome profile which just escaped being pretty. He looked Susan over from under thick blond eyelashes and said, "How do you do," shortly.

"Rosina's out for a walk," said Miriam. "Were you looking for her?"

"No," he said quickly. "Not at all. That is—have you seen the book I was reading?"

"What book?" asked Miriam. In the midst of the little distraction of explaining and searching Durrie looked up. "You write, don't you, Miss Dare?"

"Yes," said Susan, prepared to be modest. It wasn't necessary. He said "Humph" with definite disfavor, took up a book from another table and went away.

"Dinner's at seven," said Miss Wiggenhorn. "I'll take you to your room."

Left to herself in an unaired guest room, Susan sat down and surveyed the worn red roses of a Brussels carpet blankly.

Marks on a dead man's throat. A doctor's certificate. No motives. No murder. Yet she was there.

She rose and went to the window. Nottingham lace curtains did not obscure the depressing view of a bare, cold March garden. As she looked, however, a woman came into view, walking with her head bent against the wind. She wore a dark cape which, when the wind blew, showed glimpses of a scarlet lining, and paused at a fountain as if waiting for something—paused and looked up suddenly at the house. Despite the gathering gloom Susan could see the outline of her face, a darkly beautiful face with a rich, full mouth. Rosina, that would be. The nurse. A sweet and charming young woman, Miriam had said.

Quite suddenly another figure was beside the nurse, coming swiftly from some shrub-masked path. It was Durrie, with no hat on and the collar of his coat turned up around his ears. He spoke to the woman briefly, they both turned to look directly upward at Susan's window and almost immediately moved away. They couldn't have seen her, of course; there was no light in her room. She pulled down the shade, and rang briskly for the maid.

Miss Wiggenhorn had said, leaving her, to question and explore as she liked.

And the little maid, Susan thought, had been prepared,

for she answered her questions directly and fully and eyed her with a timorous look.

It was all exactly as Miss Wiggenhorn had already told her. The maid had heard Mr. Wiggenhorn call her, had entered the room and handed him his smelling salts.

"But didn't you think that perhaps he was having or about to have an attack?"

The maid hadn't. "He always liked to have things near him; his books, his spectacles; a glass of water; his smelling salts. I never thought anything about it."

"What did you do then?"

"I asked if there was anything else. The water glass was empty and he said to fill it and I did."

"Who found him? I mean after he was dead."

The girl's face paled a little but her eyes did not blink.

"I did. Dreadful, he looked. Everything was tossed about. Glass on the floor. Books—bottle with all the smelling salts spilled out of it. It looked as if he'd grabbed hold of the table cover and just jerked the whole thing off at once. He must have struggled—for a moment or two. I didn't hear anything at all. But then we'd shut the doors everywhere."

"Why? Was that customary?"

"I mean the doors to the back part of the house. Miss Miriam was making pickled peaches in the kitchen and the smell was all over the house. You know—vinegar and spices. So strong it was sort of sickening. The nurse said to shut the door of his bedroom."

"The nurse? What is her name?"

"Miss Hunt. Miss Rosina Hunt."

There was certainly something the girl wanted to tell —her plump face was bursting with it.

"I suppose Miss Hunt will be leaving soon?"

"She can't leave too soon," said the girl. "Not that she's not treated me well enough. But she's too bossy."

"Bossy?"

"Snappy—as if she owned the place. And stubborn!

Even with Miss Miriam. After all, it's Miss Miriam's house. Hers and Mr. Durrie's."

"Mr. Durrie is not married?"

"No, ma'am. Not him. Though he was engaged to be married once. But it didn't last long."

Susan said abruptly: "Will you show me the room in which Mr. Wiggenhorn died, please."

But at the end of a good half hour spent in that chilly, huge bedroom Susan was little wiser than when she had entered it.

In the hall she met Miriam Wiggenhorn.

"Oh, you've been in his room?"

"Yes."

"That was right—John Van Dusen will be here to dinner. If there's anything—"

"There's nothing," said Susan, "yet."

Dinner. So she was to see the lawyer who had suggested sending for her. And the nurse would be there too. Rosina.

Miriam, now in cherry silk, was in the drawing room when, half an hour later, Susan went down. With her was the lawyer, John Van Dusen, a spare, gray little man of fifty or so, who lifted his eyebrows, bowed to Susan and looked as if he were stuffed with sawdust.

And almost immediately Durrie came into the room, and then the nurse. And if the lawyer looked as if he were stuffed with sawdust, then the nurse looked as if she were charged with some high explosive. But she kept her beautiful dark eyes lowered and her red, rich mouth silent.

The dining room was dimly lighted. The food was very rich and very heavy and there was no conversation. The lawyer talked a little of politics and lifted his eyebrows a great deal; Durrie said nothing and looked at the nurse; the nurse looked at the tablecloth and Miriam looked at nobody and ate steadily.

After dinner Susan had vaguely expected a talk with the lawyer. Instead they played Parcheesi. Played it till ten o'clock.

There was somewhere in the house a clock which struck on a gasping, breathless note not unlike Miriam's panting voice. When it struck ten John Van Dusen rose, the Parcheesi board disappeared, the nurse murmured and vanished.

"Good night, Miriam. Good night, Durrie, A pleasant evening. Good night, Miss Dare." The little lawyer paused and looked at Susan as if he had just become conscious of her presence. "Oh, yes," he said. "Miss Dare. So good of you to come. Not of course that there's any—er—reason for it. It really is absurd—the whole idea. Miriam is aware of my feeling, but she insisted—"

"Now, John," panted Miriam good-naturedly, "don't blame me for this. And don't trip on the step—it's likely to be slippery. Go with him to his car, Durrie."

Durrie obeyed.

Miriam looked at Susan.

"Well, my dear," she said expectantly. "How is it going? What did you think of John? He's a dear old fellow. But timid. Very timid. Wouldn't admit a murder if he saw it with his own eyes."

"Why is the nurse still here?" asked Susan.

"Rosina? Oh, I asked her to stay on for a little. During Uncle's long illness and her extreme devotion to him we became very fond of her."

The hall door opened and closed again and they could hear Durrie locking it.

"Well—how about some cake or sandwiches before you go to sleep. No? Very well. Just ring the bell if you do want anything."

Susan was still shuddering when she reached her room; her hostess's interest in food was, to say the least, inordinate.

And it was ubiquitous. Susan tossed and turned and between times dreamed of enormous boxes of chocolate creams pursuing her. Once, quite late, a sound of some kind in the hall roused her so thoroughly that she rose and opened her door cautiously and peered into the shadows of the night-lighted hall. There was, however, nothing there.

But she was still wide-awake and tense when she heard it again. Or at least she heard a faint sound which was very like the creaking of the steps of a stairway. This time she reached the door softly and managed to open it without, she thought, being detected. And her care had its reward for she saw, coming very quietly from the landing of the stairs, the nurse. Rosina. She was wearing something long and dark and her face was hidden so that Susan saw only her thick, smooth black hair. But as she passed under the light she turned suddenly and cast a sharp strange look at Miriam Wiggenhorn's door. A look so strange and pale and fiery, so full of malevolence, that Susan felt queer and shaken long after the nurse had glided away.

But there was no reason to suspect murder. She told Miriam Wiggenhorn that the next morning.

She did not add that there was something hidden, something secret and ugly, going on in the house. She said merely that she had thus far found no reason to suspect murder.

Miss Wiggenhorn took it with bland detachment and asked her, still blandly, to stay on a few days. She would welcome proof of Keller Wiggenhorn's death being natural; she wanted Susan to have plenty of time. Susan said in that case she would like to see both the lawyer and the doctor and forestalled an offer on Miriam's part to have them summoned. She would go to their offices, said Susan firmly, and Miriam embroidered a flower and then said Durrie would take her in his car.

It was then that Susan risked a direct question about the nurse. "I saw her last night coming very quietly up the stairway. What would she be doing on the first floor so late? Do you know?"

"How late?"

"I don't know exactly. I suppose only around midnight."

Miriam Wiggenhorn pondered very briefly and offered a—to her—sound explanation.

"I suppose she had gone down to the kitchen for a glass of milk," she said. "Or for something to eat. I hope you aren't going to involve little Rosina in this, Miss Dare."

"But there's only you and your brother and Rosina who had the opportunity," said Susan brutally. "That is, if you except the cook and housemaid."

"I suppose so," said Miriam Wiggenhorn. "Well—I'll ask Durrie to take you to see John. And the doctor."

She did so. Durrie looked sullen but consented, and said, during the six-mile drive into Warrington, not one word.

And neither the doctor nor the lawyer yielded anything to Susan's inquiries. Except that the lawyer again rather nervously put the responsibility for calling Susan upon Miriam's plump shoulders.

In the end Susan, still with a silent and sullen Durrie, returned to the Wiggenhorn house no wiser than when she had left. They approached it this time along an old drive leading to a porte-cochere at a side door. Through the shrubs Susan caught glimpses of the garden, and, once, of a kind of summerhouse, except that it was much more substantial than most summerhouses are. Durrie caught her look and said: "My studio."

"Studio? Oh, you paint, then?"

"Well, yes and no. I sort of dabble around at this and that." He hesitated and then said suddenly: "Look here, Miss Dare, I don't know what on earth's got into Miriam. Uncle wasn't murdered. Why, there's no one who would want to murder Uncle. It's a perfectly senseless notion. I wish—I wish you'd tell her so and leave."

"And there were no outsiders in the house, anyway," said Susan. "Except the nurse and—"

"Rosina didn't do it! That's impossible. Why, she—she—I tell you she couldn't have done it. She thought the world of Uncle. And he of her."

"Will Rosina be leaving soon?"

"I suppose so. Just for a time. Until we can be married."

"Oh—"

"Yes."

"Did your uncle approve of your engagement?" asked Susan after a moment.

The reply was not what she expected.

"Yes," said Durrie. "He thought it was fine. Here you are, Miss Dare."

He opened the door for her. She lingered to watch as he walked around the car which he left standing in the drive and disappeared in the direction of the summerhouse.

Susan went thoughtfully into the hideous drawing room. Rosina, immaculate in her white uniform, was there reading, and she lifted her fine eyes to give Susan one long, smoldering look. She was not disposed to be communicative.

Yes, she had liked Mr. Wiggenhorn very much. Yes, it was too bad he died alone; she felt very badly about that.

"But it takes them that way. It can't be helped. But it wasn't murder," she added with sudden, vehement scorn. "If he was murdered, it was an absolutely perfect crime. So perfect that it fooled me and the doctor, and I'm not easily fooled."

Susan was very thoughtful during a dreary, silent lunch. But it was not until late afternoon that, during a solitary, slow walk up and down the damp garden paths, one small phrase out of all the things that had been said to her began to emphasize itself. Was dispelled and returned. Began to assume rather curious proportions. Under its insistency she finally let her fancy go and built up, with that as a premise, a curious fabric of murder. Or rather it built itself up, queerly, almost instantly, with the most terrifying logic.

It couldn't be. There were reasons why it couldn't be.

Yet—well, who would know? No one. Who could tell her what she must know? Come now, Susie, she could hear Jim saying: let's get down to brass tacks. How *could* it have been done?

The house was still quiet when at length she returned to it. She summoned the little housemaid to her own room again. "I want you to tell me again, exactly how you found Mr. Wiggenhorn."

The girl shut her eyes and twisted her white apron.

"Well, he was there on the couch. That's the first thing I saw, because he was all twisted—looked so queer, you know. Somehow I knew right away he was dead. I screamed and everybody—that is, Miss Wiggenhorn and cook and then the nurse—came running."

"And he had pulled off the cover of the table—"

"Oh, yes, and everything was spilled. Glass and water and—"

"Did you straighten the room?"

"Yes, ma'am. Right away. While Miss Wiggenhorn was telephoning for the doctor."

"What did you pick up?"

The girl's eyes opened widely. "Why, the—empty water glass. The bottle of smelling salts—"

"Was it open? I mean, had Mr. Wiggenhorn used it?"

"Oh, yes, the stopper was out and it had fallen on its side."

"Then you gathered up the crystals of salts that had fallen out?"

"No, ma'am," said the girl. "The bottle must have been empty. There wasn't anything in it at all. Except a sort of mist—"

"Mist!" said Susan violently.

"Well—steam. As if it had had hot water in it—you know. Only the bottle was empty."

"I see," said Susan after a moment. "What did you do with it?"

"Why, I—I put it on the table. And straightened up the table and wiped up the water that had spilled from the glass—"

"Wait. There was nothing in the glass?"

"No, ma'am. It had fallen on its side too. I took it and washed it and put it back on the table."

She waited for further questions. Finally Susan said: "Was there any unusual odor in the room?"

The girl thought and then shook her head decisively. "No, ma'am. I didn't notice anything. Not even smelling salts—but then, the bottle was empty. But we were all excited—everybody running around—putting up windows."

"Opening windows? Who?"

But she didn't know exactly. "Besides," she said, "the smell of the vinegar and spices was all over the house. Suffocating, it was."

"It must have been. Did you replace the stopper in the smelling-salts bottle?"

She was dubious. Then remembered: "Yes. When I cleaned the room the next day. It had rolled under the couch."

"Do you clean Mr. Durrie's studio?" asked Susan abruptly.

"Oh, no," said the girl. "He's got bottles and glass things in there. And he won't let me clean it. Miss Miriam does it. Only Miss Miriam and the nurse are allowed to go into the studio. And if you want smells," she added with vehemence, "that's the place to get them. He says it's chemical experiments. Me and the cook think it's dreadful."

"Oh," said Susan. I've got to go, thought Susan, blindly. I've got to leave. I've got to get out of here now. At once. Will they try to stop me? And I have no proof.

The girl was looking worried.

"What's the matter, miss? Have I done anything wrong?"

"No, no," said Susan sharply. "It's all right. Do your parents live near here?"

"Two miles away."

"You'd better go to them at once. Walk. Make some excuse. Don't tell anyone you have talked to me. But go."

"G-go"—stammered the girl looking frightened. "Now?"

Somehow, tersely, Susan convinced her and watched her scuttle anxiously downstairs. (Besides she would be a valuable witness.) And still there was no proof. And no time to be lost.

The house was silent all around her. The hall empty, but shadowy and narrow. Which was Rosina's room?

She found it after opening doors to several cold, darkened bedrooms. The nurse's red-lined cape was across a chair. Her books on a table; powder and creams and bottles quite evidently belonging to the nurse and not to Miriam, on the dressing table. In an adjoining bathroom were other things: a bathing cap, bath salts, sponge, toothpaste. She was exploring a large jar of bath powder with a cautious forefinger when there was a small rustle and Rosina herself stood in the doorway, eyes blazing.

"What are you doing in my things?"

"Searching," said Susan with false airiness.

"Searching! What for? I've nothing to conceal. I wish you'd get out of here."

"Nothing," said Susan, "would suit me better. Look here, when are you planning to be married?"

Rosina blinked.

"I don't know. Next summer. Why?"

"Why not immediately?"

"Why, I—we haven't—"

"Is there anything to prevent an immediate marriage?"

"Why—no! Certainly not!"

"Could you be married next week?"

"Y-yes. Yes, of course."

"Tomorrow?"

"Yes."

Susan permitted herself to look incredulous. "Are you sure?" she said very softly.

For a long moment the nurse's fine black eyes blazed into Susan's. Then she said furiously:

"Certainly. It's no affair of yours, but you might like to know, since you are so officious, that that is exactly what I'm going to do. I shall be married, Miss Snoopy Dare, tomorrow."

They stepped out into the hall and Rosina banged her door and, furious, went downstairs. Susan waited and then returned once more to the same room.

She looked around it again. There were remarkably few places of concealment. None, indeed, except the old-fashioned mahogany wardrobe. She looked at it with disfavor, but finally opened one of the heavy mirrored doors and stepped up into it. The few dresses offered little concealment. And there was only one way out. And Jim had said something about danger. But she didn't think of all that until she had settled herself to wait.

Not an easy wait. For the space was narrow and cramped, the air not too good in spite of the small opening she had left to enable her to see into the room, and a sense of danger, like a small red signal, became more and more marked. Danger in that muffled, orderly house. Danger— danger.

Minutes dragged on and Susan's muscles were numb and cramped. Suppose no one came. Suppose Rosina had decided on another course. But she wouldn't. And they knew, too, that Susan's own departure was imminent. Susan's eyes were blurred from staring too long and too fixedly at that crack of light. She closed them wearily.

And it was then that someone entered the room. Entered it so stealthily, so furtively that Susan felt only the faint jar of footsteps on the old floor.

Her heart pounded in her throat and her eyes were glued again to that crack.

And too late she realized that the wardrobe itself might be the objective.

Suppose the door should suddenly, silently open—suppose the very torrent of her thoughts betrayed, telepathically, her hiding place. Suppose—something passed across Susan's range of vision and obscured for an instant that crack of light.

Obscured it. And then was gone as silently, as swiftly, as it had come. But not too swiftly for recognition.

It was a long ten minutes before Susan dared move and open the door and, cautiously, emerge from her hiding place.

It was not difficult to find what she sought. The pungent odor of bath salts guided her. The jar was closed again, but it had been opened and disturbed.

She was cautious, too, in returning to her own room.

Now then, to get away. At once. Without fail.

Would they let her leave? She tossed her things in her bag and closed it; put on her coat. Knotted a yellow scarf with trembling hands and pulled her small brown hat at a jaunty angle over her light-brown hair. She looked pale and frightened. And was. But they had told her to go; at least Durrie had.

On the stairway she could hear their voices coming from the drawing room.

Susan braced herself and entered.

And she need not have braced herself for it was all very simple and easy. They agreed that if Miss Dare felt that she could do no more and wished to go, she must go. They were very grateful to her. Her advice had relieved them greatly (this only from Miriam).

It was all very easy and very simple. Except that she didn't leave.

For something was wrong with the car.

"Wrong with the car?" panted Miriam. "Why, you were driving it only this morning."

"I know," said Durrie sulkily. "The thing won't start. I don't know what's wrong. You'll have to wait till morning, I guess, Miss Dare. There's only one night train in to Chicago. It leaves at six."

"A taxi"—said Susan with stiff lips.

"Too late," said Durrie, looking at his watch. "It's five-thirty now and the roads are a fright. You can't possibly make it."

Miriam looked up from her embroidery hoops. "It looks as if you'll have to spend another night with us, Miss Dare. We are very happy, indeed, to have you."

Susan's bag dropped and her heart with it. She had a sudden, sharp pang of longing for Jim. "Very well," she said

after a moment. "But—a theater engagement—I'll telephone—"

There was an instant of complete silence. Then Miriam
said, panting: "Show her the telephone, Durrie. It's there in
the hall, Miss Dare."

They were listening, all of them, while she called Chicago and then a familiar number. But Jim was not there.
"Will you give him a message, please?" Susan said. "Tell him
Miss Dare can't keep her engagement for the theater tonight. That she's"—she hesitated and then made curious use
of a conventional phrase. "Tell him," she said, "that she's
unavoidably detained."

But if they thought the use curious they did not say so.

Jim would understand her message; they had had no
theater engagement. But there was no way of knowing
when he would return and find it.

Was there anything really wrong with the car? And
what would they say when they discovered that the little
housemaid had gone home?

They said nothing of it. Nothing at all. The cook, enormous in a white apron, served the meal. What did they
know? Somehow Susan managed to get food past a stricture
in her throat.

Later they played Parcheesi again.

"Tired, Miss Dare?" said Rosina once when Susan had
glanced surreptitiously at her watch. And Miriam, holding
dice in her fat, ringed hand, said:

"Are you perfectly sure you have nothing to tell us, Miss
Dare? Your view of Uncle's death, I mean? Does it coincide
in every way with what we know of it?"

Susan had to speak without hesitation. "I'm afraid I've
discovered nothing that wasn't already known. But I'll think
it over carefully; sometimes it takes a little while for things
to become clear in one's mind."

Miriam tossed the dice and Durrie took his turn. He said
calmly: "Is that why you sent the girl away?"

The question fell into absolute silence. Long afterward
Susan was to remember the way Rosina's strong, wide, white

hand closed upon the dice and held them rigidly. And her own swift, queer recollection of the empty room upstairs. The room where a kind old man had been cruelly murdered.

She couldn't have spoken. And Durrie, all at once white and strange, cried: "You thought you'd fasten it on Rosina. But she didn't kill him. She—"

"Durrie," said Miriam, *"don't you know that only Rosina could have done it?"*

Durrie leaped to his feet. Rosina did not move and neither did Miriam.

And in the silence they all heard the sudden squealing of the brakes of an automobile at the side of the house.

Jim, thought Susan. Oh, let it be Jim—

It was. Durrie went to the door and let him in. He gave one look at Susan and said very pleasantly that he'd come to take her home.

There was a bad moment when Miriam Wiggenhorn raised an objection.

"But you have only begun the investigation, Miss Dare. This is most distressing—most inconclusive—"

Jim said crisply: "Miss Dare will put any evidence she has into your hands in due form—"

It puzzled them a little. And in the instant of perplexity Jim thrust Susan out the door and closed it smartly behind them.

The engine of his car was running. Thirty seconds later they had turned into the public road and the Wiggenhorn house was a dark, brooding bulk behind them. "J-Jim," said Susan shakily.

"Scared?"

"Terrified—"

His profile looked forbidding. He said grimly: "I got your message. Drove like hell. What have you been stirring up?"

"Oh," said Susan. "A man was murdered, and I know who killed him. Can you remember chemistry?"

The car swerved, recovered, and Jim muttered. Susan went on:

"What was the name of that gas that's so dangerous? To breathe, I mean. It's heavier than air and if left open passes into the air. And when you transfer it from one container to another you have to be so careful not to breathe it—it burns the lungs or something."

"Wait a minute. Let me pull myself together." He lighted a cigarette and thought for a moment. "I know—you can see the fumes above the test tube. Otherwise you can't detect its presence except by smell. And if the tube is on its side all the gas escapes into the air. I'll remember it in a minute—hydrogen—"

"Hydrogen chloride," said Susan.

"Somebody die of it?"

"I think so," said Susan. "I'm sure—but somebody else can do the proving. I won't. They'll have to start with an autopsy."

Jim said: "Begin at the beginning."

Susan did. It took a long time and Jim said nothing till she had finished.

Then he said: "I begin to see the outline. Rich old man subject to heart attacks, likely to die of one, but doesn't. Somebody wants him to die at once. Hydrogen chloride is introduced into a smelling-salts bottle; bottle is green and thus no one is likely to perceive its apparent emptiness or its actual content. Maid hands man smelling salts, when he is alone. He gets a good big sniff of it before he can stop himself—that's bad, Susan. Think of the horrible pain—the shock—he dies really of the shock; his heart can't stand it. Ordinarily I think a person might live for some hours, or even days, and be conscious. But the murderer counted on that bad heart and won. It looks like a natural death. Anyway it is a successful murder. Durrie has a studio where he seems to do chemical experiments. The nurse would know something of chemistry. But the murder would have been perfect if Miriam hadn't suspected something. Which one did it?"

"It's funny," said Susan, "that you used the words 'perfect murder.' That very word is what started me thinking. Perfect. Too perfect!"

"Huh," said Jim with vehemence.

"Too perfect. No one suspected it was murder. And that was the motive, you see. Murder had to be suspected."

"Murder had to be—sorry, Susie, but I don't see."

"All right. Look at this. Durrie is in love with the nurse; wants to marry her. *His uncle didn't object.* And there was no motive at all, remember, for murder—no money motive. No question of thwarted love. No motive at all except— except that Rosina was a very willful young woman—and Miriam, no less willful, hated her."

"But Miriam approved the marriage."

"Oh, *did* she!" said Susan. "Then why were Rosina and Durrie obliged to steal meetings. In the garden at dusk. At midnight."

"How do you know Rosina had gone downstairs to see Durrie?"

"I didn't. But it's a good reason. Name a better one."

"Suppose she did," conceded Jim. "What then?"

"Miriam had ruled that house and Durrie in the smallest detail for years. She loved her rule—a previous engagement of Durrie's had been mysteriously broken off. The uncle was about to die anyway; here was a perfect plan to get rid of Rosina."

"Do you mean Miriam murdered the old man? But that doesn't make sense. She didn't gain by it."

"She did, Jim, if she could make Durrie think, in his heart, that it was murder. And that the newcomer, the nurse, was the only one who could have done it."

"You can't prove this, Susan, it's mere theory. How do you know it was Miriam?"

"You've said it yourself, Jim—there's a French term, *postiche.* It means a counterfeit, an inartistic addition to an otherwise perfect work of art. Well, the murder was perfect. *It was too perfect.* No one suspected it was murder. So Miriam had failed. Had failed unless she could get someone—

someone without official standing—like me—to look into it; perhaps to discover some little thing, not too much (she was very sure of herself), but enough to make Durrie think *it might have been murder.* And that if it was murder, only Rosina could have done it. She didn't know exactly how much she could trust me to see or not to see. I think she meant to watch—to—to gauge—me. If necessary to introduce a little evidence against the nurse, as she did. It's queer; her very words of praise for Rosina made me suspect the nurse. At first. She's very clever—Miriam Wiggenhorn."

"Then the housemaid was in danger from her—"

"The housemaid is a very valuable witness. And Miriam might have discovered that I had something of the true story from her. The real story. It wasn't just accident that Miriam was pickling peaches that afternoon, filling the house with a smell of vinegar that would mask any other smell. This isn't the season for putting up fruit. She had to pickle canned fruit. Besides there was the inartistic addition—"

"You mean her calling you and talking of murder when *nobody had suspected it was murder* shows that she thought of murder when, if she were innocent, she would have had no reason to suspect it. And that for some reason she was determined to suggest that it *was* murder."

"To suggest it anyway. The perfect murder, except for the inartistic addition. *Postiche.* And I," said Susan, "am it."

"But"—Jim paused and said in a helpless way: "All this is very nice. But angel, it's only theory. It isn't a bad idea, you know, to have proof."

"Oh, yes—proof. It's in my bag. Wrapped in a handkerchief and mixed with bath salts. But identifiable."

"What!"

"Smelling salts. When she emptied the bottle she kept the salts in case her investigation should need a little steering. Rosina, you see, has a fine temper. When I hinted there was something preventing their marriage, as if I were suspicious about it, she flounced down to tell Durrie and Miriam that she wanted it to take place at once. Durrie agreed, of course. Rosina had much the stronger will. Miriam agreed, too—and came straight upstairs to plant the clue. Nobody in the house ever used smelling salts but Keller Wiggenhorn."

"Framing her."

"Exactly. I suppose she would have tried something more open, given time."

"How did you know it was Miriam?"

"Saw her."

"From where?" demanded Jim.

"N-never mind," said Susan in a small voice.

Jim stopped the car and looked at her intently. But when he spoke it was with an air of preoccupation. "There's guilt in your voice," he said absently. "But we'll skip it. Do you know, I have a queer sort of impulse. I'd like to—"

"To what?"

"To kiss you," said Jim unexpectedly, and did so.

SUSPICION

Dorothy L. Sayers

Dorothy L. Sayers (1893–1957) is one of the most important figures in the annals of mystery fiction, not only because of her invention of Lord Peter Wimsey but because of her scholarly commentary on the genre in, among other places, her introduction to her three-volume Great Short Stories of Detection, Mystery and Horror. *From 1923 —when the first case for Lord Peter,* Whose Body?, *appeared—until 1939, she published sixteen detective novels (three in collaboration with others) and six collections of detective short stories. Although she lived another two decades, she wrote nothing more in the field after 1939; instead, she devoted her literary activities to the writing of religious books, verse, and plays. One wonders what memorable stories she might have given us during those last twenty years of her life had she not decided to forgo her fictionally criminous endeavors.*

As the atmosphere of the railway carriage thickened with tobacco smoke, Mr. Mummery became increasingly aware that his breakfast had not agreed with him.

There could have been nothing wrong with the breakfast itself. Brown bread, rich in vitamin content, as advised by the *Morning Star*'s health expert; bacon fried to a delicious crispness; eggs just nicely set; coffee made as only Mrs. Sutton knew how to make it. Mrs. Sutton had been a real find, and that was something to be thankful for. For Ethel, since her nervous breakdown in the summer, had really not been fit to wrestle with the untrained girls who had come and gone in tempestuous succession. It took very little to upset Ethel nowadays, poor child. Mr. Mummery, trying hard to ignore his growing internal discomfort, hoped he was not in for an illness. Apart from the trouble it would cause at the office, it would worry Ethel terribly, and Mr. Mummery would cheerfully have laid down his rather uninteresting little life to spare Ethel a moment's uneasiness.

He slipped a digestive tablet into his mouth—he had taken lately to carrying a few tablets about with him—and opened his paper. There did not seem to be very much news. A question had been asked in the House about Government typewriters. The Prince of Wales had smilingly opened an all-British exhibition of footwear. A further split had occurred in the Liberal party. The police were still looking for the woman who was supposed to have poisoned a family in Lincoln. Two girls had been trapped in a burning factory. A film star had obtained her fourth decree nisi.

At Paragon Station, Mr. Mummery descended and took a tram. The internal discomfort was taking the form of a definite nausea. Happily he contrived to reach his office before the worst occurred. He was seated at his desk, pale but in control of himself, when his partner came breezing in.

" 'Morning, Mummery," said Mr. Brookes in his loud tones, adding inevitably, "Cold enough for you?"

"Quite," replied Mr. Mummery. "Unpleasantly raw, in fact."

"Beastly, beastly," said Mr. Brookes. "Your bulbs all in?"

"Not quite all," confessed Mr. Mummery. "As a matter of fact I haven't been feeling—"

"Pity," interrupted his partner. "Great pity. Ought to get 'em in early. Mine were in last week. My little place will be a picture in the spring. For a town garden, that is. You're lucky, living in the country. Find it better than Hull, I expect, eh? Though we get plenty of fresh air up in the Avenues. How's the missus?"

"Thank you, she's very much better."

"Glad to hear that, very glad. Hope we shall have her about again this winter as usual. Can't do without her in the Drama Society, you know. By Jove, I shan't forget her acting last year in 'Romance.' She and young Welbeck positively brought the house down, didn't they? The Welbecks were asking after her only yesterday."

"Thank you, yes. I hope she will soon be able to take up her social activities again. But the doctor says she mustn't overdo it. No worry, he says—that's the important thing. She is to go easy and not rush about or undertake too much."

"Quite right, quite right. Worry's the devil and all. I cut out worrying years ago and look at me! Fit as a fiddle, for all I shan't see fifty again. *You're* not looking altogether the thing, by the way."

"A touch of dyspepsia," said Mr. Mummery. "Nothing much. Chill on the liver, that's what I put it down to."

"That's what it is," said Mr. Brookes, seizing his opportunity. "Is life worth living? It depends upon the liver. Ha, ha! Well now, well now—we must do a spot of work, I suppose. Where's that lease of Ferraby's?"

Mr. Mummery, who did not feel at his conversational best that morning, rather welcomed this suggestion, and for half an hour was allowed to proceed in peace with the duties of an estate agent. Presently, however, Mr. Brookes burst into speech again.

"By the way," he said abruptly, "I suppose your wife doesn't know of a good cook, does she?"

"Well, no," replied Mr. Mummery. "They aren't so easy to find nowadays. In fact, we've only just got suited ourselves. But why? Surely your old Cookie isn't leaving you?"

"Good lord, no!" Mr. Brookes laughed heartily. "It would take an earthquake to shake off old Cookie. No. It's for the Philipsons. Their girl's getting married. That's the worst of girls. I said to Philipson, 'You mind what you're doing,' I said. 'Get somebody you know something about, or you may find yourself landed with this poisoning woman—what's her name—Andrews. Don't want to be sending wreaths to your funeral yet awhile,' I said. He laughed, but it's no laughing matter and so I told him. What we pay the police for I simply don't know. Nearly a month now, and they can't seem to lay hands on the woman. All they say is, they think she's hanging about the neighbourhood and 'may seek a situation as cook.' As cook! Now I ask you!"

"You don't think she committed suicide, then?" suggested Mr. Mummery.

"Suicide my foot!" retorted Mr. Brookes coarsely. "Don't you believe it, my boy. That coat found in the river was all eyewash. *They* don't commit suicide, that sort don't."

"What sort?"

"Those arsenic maniacs. They're too damned careful of their own skins. Cunning as weasels, that's what they are. It's only to be hoped they'll manage to catch her before she tries her hand on anybody else. As I told Philipson—"

"You think Mrs. Andrews did it, then?"

"Did it? Of course she did it. It's plain as the nose on your face. Looked after her old father, and he died suddenly—left her a bit of money, too. Then she keeps house for an elderly gentleman, and *he* dies suddenly. Now there's this husband and wife—man dies and woman taken very ill, of arsenic poisoning. Cook runs away, and you ask, did she do it? I don't mind betting that when they dig up the father and the other old bird they'll find *them* bung full of arsenic, too. Once that sort gets started, they don't stop. Grows on 'em, as you might say."

"I suppose it does," said Mr. Mummery. He picked up his paper again and studied the photograph of the missing woman. "She looks harmless enough," he remarked. "Rather a nice, motherly-looking kind of woman."

"She's got a bad mouth," pronounced Mr. Brookes. He had a theory that character showed in the mouth. "I wouldn't trust that woman an inch."

As the day went on, Mr. Mummery felt better. He was rather nervous about his lunch, choosing carefully a little boiled fish and custard pudding and being particular not to rush about immediately after the meal. To his great relief, the fish and custard remained where they were put, and he was not visited by that tiresome pain which had become almost habitual in the last fortnight. By the end of the day he became quite light-hearted. The bogey of illness and doctor's bills ceased to haunt him. He bought a bunch of bronze chrysanthemums to carry home to Ethel, and it was with a feeling of pleasant anticipation that he left the train and walked up the garden path of *Mon Abri*.

He was a little dashed by not finding his wife in the sitting-room. Still clutching the bunch of chrysanthemums he pattered down the passage and pushed open the kitchen door.

Nobody was there but the cook. She was sitting at the table with her back to him, and started up almost guiltily as he approached.

"Lor', sir," she said, "you give me quite a start. I didn't hear the front door go."

"Where is Mrs. Mummery? Not feeling bad again, is she?"

"Well, sir, she's got a bit of a headache, poor lamb. I

made her lay down and took her up a nice cup o' tea at half past four. I think she's dozing nicely now."

"Dear, dear," said Mr. Mummery.

"It was turning out the dining-room done it, if you ask me," said Mrs. Sutton. " 'Now, don't you overdo yourself, ma'am,' I says to her, but you know how she is, sir. She gets that restless, she can't abear to be doing nothing."

"I know," said Mr. Mummery. "It's not your fault, Mrs. Sutton. I'm sure you look after us both admirably. I'll just run up and have a peep at her. I won't disturb her if she's asleep. By the way, what are we having for dinner?"

"Well, I *had* made a nice steak-and-kidney pie," said Mrs. Sutton, in accents suggesting that she would readily turn it into a pumpkin or a coach and four if it was not approved of.

"Oh!" said Mr. Mummery. "Pastry? Well, I—"

"You'll find it beautiful and light," protested the cook, whisking open the oven door for Mr. Mummery to see. "And it's made with butter, sir, you having said that you found lard indigestible."

"Thank you, thank you," said Mr. Mummery. "I'm sure it will be most excellent. I haven't been feeling altogether the thing just lately, and lard does not seem to suit me nowadays."

"Well, it don't suit some people, and that's a fact," agreed Mrs. Sutton. "I shouldn't wonder if you've got a bit of a chill on the liver. I'm sure this weather is enough to upset anybody."

She bustled to the table and cleared away the picture paper which she had been reading.

"Perhaps the mistress would like her dinner sent up to her?" she suggested.

Mr. Mummery said he would go and see, and tiptoed his way upstairs. Ethel was lying snuggled under the eiderdown and looked very small and fragile in the big double bed. She stirred as he came in and smiled up at him.

"Hullo, darling!" said Mr. Mummery.

"Hullo! You back? I must have been asleep. I got tired and headachy, and Mrs. Sutton packed me off upstairs."

"You've been doing too much, sweetheart," said her husband, taking her hand in his and sitting down on the edge of the bed.

"Yes—it was naughty of me. What lovely flowers, Harold. All for me?"

"All for you, Tiddleywinks," said Mr. Mummery tenderly. "Don't I deserve something for that?"

Mrs. Mummery smiled, and Mr. Mummery took his reward several times over.

"That's quite enough, you sentimental old thing," said Mrs. Mummery. "Run away, now, I'm going to get up."

"Much better go to bed, my precious, and let Mrs. Sutton send your dinner up," said her husband.

Ethel protested, but he was firm with her. If she didn't take care of herself, she wouldn't be allowed to go to the Drama Society meetings. And everybody was so anxious to have her back. The Welbecks had been asking after her and saying that they really couldn't get on without her.

"Did they?" said Ethel with some animation. "It's very sweet of them to want me. Well, perhaps I'll go to bed after all. And how has my old Hubby been all day?"

"Not too bad, not too bad."

"No more tummyaches?"

"Well, just a *little* tummyache. But it's quite gone now. Nothing for Tiddleywinks to worry about."

Mr. Mummery experienced no more distressing symptoms the next day or the next. Following the advice of the newspaper expert, he took to drinking orange juice, and was delighted with the results of the treatment. On Thursday, however, he was taken so ill in the night that Ethel was alarmed and insisted on sending for the doctor. The doctor felt his pulse and looked at his tongue and appeared to take the matter lightly. An inquiry into what he had been eating elicited the fact that dinner had consisted of pig's trotters, followed by a milk pudding, and that, before retiring, Mr. Mummery had consumed a large glass of orange juice, according to his new régime.

"There's your trouble," said Dr. Griffith cheerfully. "Orange juice is an excellent thing, and so are trotters, but not in combination. Pig and oranges together are extraordinarily bad for the liver. I don't know why they should be, but there's no doubt that they are. Now I'll send you round a little prescription and you stick to slops for a day or two and keep off pork. And don't you worry about him, Mrs. Mummery, he's as sound as a trout. *You're* the one we've got to look after. I don't want to see those black rings under the eyes, you know. Disturbed night, of course—yes. Taking your tonic regularly? That's right. Well, don't be alarmed about your hubby. We'll soon have him out and about again."

The prophecy was fulfilled, but not immediately. Mr. Mummery, though confining his diet to Benger's food, bread and milk and beef tea skilfully prepared by Mrs. Sutton and brought to his bedside by Ethel, remained very seedy all through Friday, and was only able to stagger rather shakily downstairs on Saturday afternoon. He had evidently suffered a "thorough upset." However, he was able to attend to a few papers which Brookes had sent down from the office for his signature, and to deal with the household books. Ethel was not a business woman, and Mr. Mummery always ran over the accounts with her. Having settled up with the butcher, the baker, the dairy and the coal merchant, Mr. Mummery looked up inquiringly.

"Anything more, darling?"

"Well, there's Mrs. Sutton. This is the end of her month, you know."

"So it is. Well, you're quite satisfied with her, aren't you, darling?"

"Yes, rather—aren't you? She's a good cook, and a sweet, motherly old thing, too. Don't you think it was a real brain wave of mine, engaging her like that, on the spot?"

"I do, indeed," said Mr. Mummery.

"It was a perfect providence, her turning up like that, just after that wretched Jane had gone off without even giving notice. I was in absolute *despair*. It was a little bit of a gamble, of course, taking her without any references, but naturally, if she'd been looking after a widowed mother, you couldn't expect her to give references."

"N-no," said Mr. Mummery. At the time he had felt uneasy about the matter, though he had not liked to say much because, of course, they simply had to have somebody. And the experiment had justified itself so triumphantly in practice that one couldn't say much about it now. He had once rather tentatively suggested writing to the clergyman of Mrs. Sutton's parish but, as Ethel had said, the clergyman wouldn't have been able to tell them anything about cooking, and cooking, after all, was the chief point.

Mr. Mummery counted out the month's money.

"And by the way, my dear," he said, "you might just mention to Mrs. Sutton that if she *must* read the morning paper before I come down, I should be obliged if she would fold it neatly afterwards."

"What an old fuss-box you are, darling," said his wife.

Mr. Mummery sighed. He could not explain that it was somehow important that the morning paper should come to him fresh and prim, like a virgin. Women did not feel these things.

On Sunday, Mr. Mummery felt very much better— quite his old self, in fact. He enjoyed the *News of the World* over breakfast in bed, reading the murders rather carefully. Mr. Mummery got quite a lot of pleasure out of murders— they gave him an agreeable thrill of vicarious adventure, for, naturally, they were matters quite remote from daily life in the outskirts of Hull.

He noticed that Brookes had been perfectly right. Mrs. Andrews's father and former employer had been "dug up" and had, indeed, proved to be "bung full" of arsenic.

He came downstairs for dinner—roast sirloin, with the

potatoes done under the meat and Yorkshire pudding of delicious lightness, and an apple tart to follow. After three days of invalid diet, it was delightful to savour the crisp fat and underdone lean. He ate moderately, but with a sensuous enjoyment. Ethel, on the other hand, seemed a little lacking in appetite, but then, she had never been a great meat eater. She was fastidious and, besides, she was (quite unnecessarily) afraid of getting fat.

It was a fine afternoon, and at three o'clock, when he was quite certain that the roast beef was "settling" properly, it occurred to Mr. Mummery that it would be a good thing to put the rest of those bulbs in. He slipped on his old gardening coat and wandered out to the potting shed. Here he picked up a bag of tulips and a trowel, and then, remembering that he was wearing his good trousers, decided that it would be wise to take a mat to kneel on. When had he had the mat last? He could not recollect, but he rather fancied he had put it away in the corner under the potting shelf. Stooping down, he felt about in the dark among the flower pots. Yes, there it was, but there was a tin of something in the way. He lifted the tin carefully out. Of course, yes—the remains of the weed killer.

Mr. Mummery glanced at the pink label, printed in staring letters with the legend: ARSENICAL WEED KILLER. POISON, and observed, with a mild feeling of excitement, that it was the same brand of stuff that had been associated with Mrs. Andrews's latest victim. He was rather pleased about it. It gave him a sensation of being remotely but definitely in touch with important events. Then he noticed, with surprise and a little annoyance, that the stopper had been put in quite loosely.

"However'd I come to leave it like that?" he grunted. "Shouldn't wonder if all the goodness has gone off." He removed the stopper and squinted into the can, which appeared to be half-full. Then he rammed the thing home again, giving it a sharp thump with the handle of the trowel for better security. After that he washed his hands carefully at the scullery tap, for he did not believe in taking risks.

He was a trifle disconcerted, when he came in after planting the tulips, to find visitors in the sitting-room. He was always pleased to see Mrs. Welbeck and her son, but he would rather have had warning, so that he could have scrubbed the garden mould out of his nails more thoroughly. Not that Mrs. Welbeck appeared to notice. She was a talkative woman and paid little attention to anything but her own conversation. Much to Mr. Mummery's annoyance, she chose to prattle about the Lincoln Poisoning Case. A most unsuitable subject for the tea table, thought Mr. Mummery, at the best of times. His own "upset" was vivid enough in his memory to make him queasy over the discussion of medical symptoms, and besides, this kind of talk was not good for Ethel. After all, the poisoner was still supposed to be in the neighbourhood. It was enough to make even a strong-nerved woman uneasy. A glance at Ethel showed him that she was looking quite white and tremulous. He must stop Mrs. Welbeck somehow, or there would be a repetition of one of the old, dreadful, hysterical scenes.

He broke into the conversation with violent abruptness.

"Those Forsyth cuttings, Mrs. Welbeck," he said. "Now is just about the time to take them. If you care to come down the garden I will get them for you."

He saw a relieved glance pass between Ethel and young Welbeck. Evidently the boy understood the situation and was chafing at his mother's tactlessness. Mrs. Welbeck, brought up all standing, gasped slightly and then veered off with obliging readiness on the new tack. She accompanied her host down the garden and chattered cheerfully about horticulture while he selected and trimmed the cuttings. She complimented Mr. Mummery on the immaculacy of his gravel paths. "I simply *cannot* keep the weeds down," she said.

Mr. Mummery mentioned the weed killer and praised its efficacy.

"That stuff!" Mrs. Welbeck stared at him. Then she

shuddered. "I wouldn't have it in my place for a thousand pounds," she said, with emphasis.

Mr. Mummery smiled. "Oh, we keep it well away from the house," he said. "Even if I were a careless sort of person—"

He broke off. The recollection of the loosened stopper had come to him suddenly, and it was as though, deep down in his mind, some obscure assembling of ideas had taken place. He left it at that, and went into the kitchen to fetch a newspaper to wrap up the cuttings.

Their approach to the house had evidently been seen from the sitting-room window, for when they entered, young Welbeck was already on his feet and holding Ethel's hand in the act of saying good-bye. He manœuvred his mother out of the house with tactful promptness and Mr. Mummery returned to the kitchen to clear up the newspapers he had fished out of the drawer. To clear them up and to examine them more closely. Something had struck him about them, which he wanted to verify. He turned them over very carefully, sheet by sheet. Yes—he had been right. Every portrait of Mrs. Andrews, every paragraph and line about the Lincoln Poisoning Case, had been carefully cut out.

Mr. Mummery sat down by the kitchen fire. He felt as though he needed warmth. There seemed to be a curious cold lump of something at the pit of his stomach—something that he was chary of investigating.

He tried to recall the appearance of Mrs. Andrews as shown in the newspaper photographs, but he had not a good visual memory. He remembered having remarked to Brookes that it was a "motherly" face. Then he tried counting up the time since the disappearance. Nearly a month, Brookes had said—and that was a week ago. Must be over a month now. A month. He had just paid Mrs. Sutton her month's money.

"Ethel!" was the thought that hammered at the door of his brain. At all costs, he must cope with this monstrous suspicion on his own. He must spare her any shock or anxiety. And he must be sure of his ground. To dismiss the only decent cook they had ever had out of sheer, unfounded panic, would be wanton cruelty to both women. If he did it at all, it would have to be done arbitrarily, preposterously—he could not suggest horrors to Ethel. However it was done, there would be trouble. Ethel would not understand and he dared not tell her.

But if by any chance there was anything in this ghastly doubt—how could he expose Ethel to the appalling danger of having the woman in the house a moment longer? He thought of the family at Lincoln—the husband dead, the wife escaped by a miracle with her life. Was not any shock, any risk, better than that?

Mr. Mummery felt suddenly very lonely and tired. His illness had taken it out of him.

Those illnesses—they had begun, when? Three weeks ago he had had the first attack. Yes, but then he had always been rather subject to gastric troubles. Bilious attacks. Not so violent, perhaps, as these last, but undoubted bilious attacks.

He pulled himself together and went, rather heavily, into the sitting-room. Ethel was tucked up in a corner of the chesterfield.

"Tired, darling?"

"Yes, a little."

"That woman has worn you out with talking. She oughtn't to talk so much."

"No." Her head shifted wearily in the cushions. "All about that horrible case. I don't like hearing about such things."

"Of course not. Still, when a thing like that happens in the neighbourhood, people will gossip and talk. It would be a relief if they caught the woman. One doesn't like to think—"

"I don't want to think of anything so hateful. She must be a horrible creature."

"Horrible. Brookes was saying the other day—"

"I don't want to hear what he said. I don't want to hear about it at all. I want to be quiet. I want to be quiet!"

He recognised the note of rising hysteria.

"Tiddleywinks shall be quiet. Don't worry, darling. We won't talk about horrors."

No. It would not do to talk about them.

Ethel went to bed early. It was understood that on Sundays Mr. Mummery should sit up till Mrs. Sutton came in. Ethel was a little anxious about this, but he assured her that he felt quite strong enough. In body, indeed, he did; it was his mind that felt weak and confused. He had decided to make a casual remark about the mutilated newspapers—just to see what Mrs. Sutton would say.

He allowed himself the usual indulgence of a whisky and soda as he sat waiting. At a quarter to ten he heard the familiar click of the garden gate. Footsteps passed up the gravel—squeak, squeak, to the back-door. Then the sound of the latch, the shutting of the door, the rattle of the bolts being shot home. Then a pause. Mrs. Sutton would be taking off her hat. The moment was coming.

The step sounded in the passage. The door opened. Mrs. Sutton in her neat black dress stood on the threshold. He was aware of a reluctance to face her. Then he looked up. A plump-faced woman, her eyes obscured by thick horn-rimmed spectacles. Was there, perhaps, something hard about the mouth? Or was it just that she had lost most of her front teeth?

"Would you be requiring anything tonight, sir, before I go up?"

"No thank you, Mrs. Sutton."

"I hope you are feeling better, sir." Her eager interest in his health seemed to him almost sinister, but the eyes, behind the thick glasses, were inscrutable.

"Quite better, thank you, Mrs. Sutton."

"Mrs. Mummery is not indisposed, is she, sir? Should I take her up a glass of hot milk or anything?"

"No, thank you, no." He spoke hurriedly, and fancied that she looked disappointed.

"Very well, sir. Good night, sir."

"Good night. Oh! by the way, Mrs. Sutton—"

"Yes, sir?"

"Oh, nothing," said Mr. Mummery, "nothing."

Next morning Mr. Mummery opened his paper eagerly. He would have been glad to learn that an arrest had been made over the weekend. But there was no news for him. The chairman of a trust company had blown out his brains, and the headlines were all occupied with tales about lost millions and ruined shareholders. Both in his own paper and in those he purchased on the way to the office, the Lincoln Poisoning Tragedy had been relegated to an obscure paragraph on a back page, which informed him that the police were still baffled.

The next few days were the most uncomfortable that Mr. Mummery had ever spent. He developed a habit of coming down early in the morning and prowling about the kitchen. This made Ethel nervous, but Mrs. Sutton offered no remark. She watched him tolerantly, even, he thought, with something like amusement. After all, it was ridiculous. What was the use of supervising the breakfast, when he had to be out of the house every day between half past nine and six?

At the office, Brookes rallied him on the frequency with which he rang up Ethel. Mr. Mummery paid no attention. It was reassuring to hear her voice and to know that she was safe and well.

Nothing happened, and by the following Thursday he began to think that he had been a fool. He came home late that night. Brookes had persuaded him to go with him to a little bachelor dinner for a friend who was about to get married. He left the others at eleven o'clock, however, refusing to make a night of it. The household was in bed when he got back but a note from Mrs. Sutton lay on the table, informing him that there was cocoa for him in the kitchen, ready for hotting up. He hotted it up accordingly in the little saucepan where it stood. There was just one good cupful.

He sipped it thoughtfully, standing by the kitchen stove. After the first sip, he put the cup down. Was it his fancy, or was there something queer about the taste? He sipped it again, rolling it upon his tongue. It seemed to him to have a faint tang, metallic and unpleasant. In a sudden dread he ran out to the scullery and spat the mouthful into the sink.

After this, he stood quite still for a moment or two. Then, with a curious deliberation, as though his movements had been dictated to him, he fetched an empty medicine bottle from the pantry shelf, rinsed it under the tap and tipped the contents of the cup carefully into it. He slipped the bottle into his coat pocket and moved on tiptoe to the back door. The bolts were difficult to draw without noise, but he managed it at last. Still on tiptoe, he stole across the garden to the potting shed. Stooping down, he struck a match. He knew exactly where he had left the tin of weed killer, under the shelf behind the pots at the back. Cautiously he lifted it out. The match flared up and burnt his fingers, but before he could light another his sense of touch had told him what he wanted to know. The stopper was loose again.

Panic seized Mr. Mummery, standing there in the earthy-smelling shed, in his dress suit and overcoat, holding the tin in one hand and the match box in the other. He wanted very badly to run and tell somebody what he had discovered.

Instead, he replaced the tin exactly where he had found it and went back to the house. As he crossed the garden again, he noticed a light in Mrs. Sutton's bedroom window. This terrified him more than anything which had gone before. Was she watching him? Ethel's window was dark. If she had drunk anything deadly there would be lights everywhere, movements, calls for the doctor, just as when he himself had been attacked. Attacked—that was the right word, he thought.

Still with the same odd presence of mind and precision, he went in, washed out the utensils and made a second brew of cocoa, which he left standing in the saucepan. He crept quietly to his bedroom. Ethel's voice greeted him on the threshold.

"How late you are, Harold. Naughty old boy! Have a good time?"

"Not bad. You all right, darling?"

"Quite all right. Did Mrs. Sutton leave something hot for you? She said she would."

"Yes, but I wasn't thirsty."

Ethel laughed. "Oh! it was *that* sort of party, was it?"

Mr. Mummery did not attempt any denials. He undressed and got into bed and clutched his wife to him as though defying death and hell to take her from him. Next morning he would act. He thanked God that he was not too late.

Mr. Dimthorpe, the chemist, was a great friend of Mr. Mummery's. They had often sat together in the untidy little shop on Spring Bank and exchanged views on green-fly and club-root. Mr. Mummery told his story frankly to Mr. Dimthorpe and handed over the bottle of cocoa. Mr. Dimthorpe congratulated him on his prudence and intelligence.

"I will have it ready for you by this evening," he said, "and if it's what you think it is, then we shall have a clear case on which to take action."

Mr. Mummery thanked him, and was extremely vague and inattentive at business all day. But that hardly mattered, for Mr. Brookes, who had seen the party through to a riotous end in the small hours, was in no very observant mood. At half past four, Mr. Mummery shut up his desk decisively and announced that he was off early, he had a call to make.

Mr. Dimthorpe was ready for him.

"No doubt about it," he said. "I used Marsh's test. It's a heavy dose—no wonder you tasted it. There must be four or five grains of pure arsenic in that bottle. Look, here's the mirror. You can see it for yourself."

Mr. Mummery gazed at the little glass tube with its ominous purple-black stain.

"Will you ring up the police from here?" asked the chemist.

"No," said Mr. Mummery. "No—I want to get home. God knows what's happening there. And I've only just time to catch my train."

"All right," said Mr. Dimthorpe. "Leave it to me. I'll ring them up for you."

The local train did not go fast enough for Mr. Mummery. Ethel—poisoned—dying—dead—Ethel—poisoned—dying—dead—the wheels drummed in his ears. He almost ran out of the station and along the road. A car was standing at his door. He saw it from the end of the street and broke into a gallop. It had happened already. The doctor was there. Fool, murderer that he was to have left things so late.

Then, while he was still a hundred and fifty yards off, he saw the front door open. A man came out followed by Ethel herself. The visitor got into his car and was driven away. Ethel went in again. She was safe—safe!

He could hardly control himself to hang up his hat and coat and go in looking reasonably calm. His wife had returned to the armchair by the fire and greeted him in some surprise. There were tea things on the table.

"Back early, aren't you?"

"Yes—business was slack. Somebody been to tea?"

"Yes, young Welbeck. About the arrangements for the Drama Society." She spoke briefly but with an undertone of excitement.

A qualm came over Mr. Mummery. Would a guest be any protection? His face must have shown his feelings, for Ethel stared at him in amazement.

"What's the matter, Harold, you look so queer."

"Darling," said Mr. Mummery, "there's something I want to tell you about." He sat down and took her hand in his. "Something a little unpleasant, I'm afraid—"

"Oh, ma'am!"

The cook was in the doorway.

"I beg your pardon, sir—I didn't know you was in. Will you be taking tea or can I clear away? And, oh, ma'am, there was a young man at the fishmonger's and he's just come from Grimsby and they've caught that dreadful woman—that Mrs. Andrews. Isn't it a good thing? It's worritted me dreadful to think she was going about like that, but they've caught her. Taken a job as housekeeper she had to two elderly ladies and they found the wicked poison on her. Girl as spotted her will get a reward. I been keeping my eyes open for her, but it's at Grimsby she was all the time."

Mr. Mummery clutched at the arm of his chair. It had all been a mad mistake then. He wanted to shout or cry. He wanted to apologise to this foolish, pleasant, excited woman. All a mistake.

But there had been the cocoa. Mr. Dimthorpe. Marsh's test. Five grains of arsenic. Who, then—?

He glanced around at his wife, and in her eyes he saw something that he had never seen before. . . .

HARLEQUIN'S LANE

Agatha Christie

It is difficult to think of anything laudatory to say about the work of Agatha Christie that has not already been said by any number of critics and aficionados of mystery fiction. She was, quite simply, the field's grande dame—one of the four or five most innovative writers ever to work within the form, as such novels as The Murder of Roger Ackroyd, Murder on the Orient Express, *and* And Then There Were None *eloquently attest. Her most famous detective creations, of course, are the little Belgian, Hercule Poirot, and Miss Jane Marple; but her most unusual detective is certainly Harley Quin, who appears in fourteen short stories, most of which were collected in* The Mysterious Mr. Quin *(1930). Is he, or is he not, a supernatural being—even, as has been postulated, a personification of Death itself? The Harley Quin stories are mysteries on more than one level, and it is perhaps for this reason that Mrs. Christie once called them her favorites of all her fiction. If you're unfamiliar with Quin and his decidedly human aide, Mr. Satterthwaite, you're in for quite a surprise when you take your disturbing little stroll along "Harlequin's Lane."* . . .

Mr. Satterthwaite was never quite sure what took him to stay with the Denmans. They were not of his kind—that is to say, they belonged neither to the great world, nor to the more interesting artistic circles. They were Philistines, and dull Philistines at that. Mr. Satterthwaite had met them first at Biarritz, had accepted an invitation to stay with them, had come, had been bored, and yet strangely enough had come again and yet again.

Why? He was asking himself that question on this twenty-first of June, as he sped out of London in his Rolls-Royce.

John Denman was a man of forty, a solid, well-established figure, respected in the business world. His friends were not Mr. Satterthwaite's friends, his ideas even less so. He was a man clever in his own line but devoid of imagination outside it.

Why am I doing this thing? Mr. Satterthwaite asked himself once more—and the only answer that came seemed to him so vague and so inherently preposterous that he almost put it aside. For the only reason that presented itself was the fact that one of the rooms in the house (a comfortable, well-appointed house) stirred his curiosity. That room was Mrs. Denman's own sitting room.

It was hardly an expression of her personality because, so far as Mr. Satterthwaite could judge, she had no personality. He had never met a woman so completely expressionless. She was, he knew, a Russian by birth. John Denman had been in Russia at the outbreak of the European War; he had fought with the Russian troops, had narrowly escaped with his life on the outbreak of the Revolution, and had brought this Russian girl with him, a penniless refugee. In face of strong disapproval from his parents he had married her.

Mrs. Denman's room was in no way remarkable. It was

well and solidly furnished with good Hepplewhite furniture —a trifle more masculine than feminine in atmosphere. But in it there was one incongruous item: a Chinese lacquer screen—a thing of creamy yellow and pale rose. Any museum might have been glad to own it. It was a collector's piece, rare and beautiful.

It was out of place against that solid English background. It should have been the keynote of the room with everything arranged to harmonize subtly with it. And yet Mr. Satterthwaite could not accuse the Denmans of lack of taste. Everything else in the house was in perfectly blended accord.

He shook his head. The thing, trivial though it was— puzzled him. Because of it, so he verily believed, he had come again and again to the house. It was, perhaps, a woman's fantasy—but that solution did not satisfy him as he thought of Mrs. Denman—a quiet, hard-featured woman, speaking English so correctly that no one would ever have guessed her a foreigner.

The car drew up at his destination and he got out, his mind still dwelling on the problem of the Chinese screen. The name of the Denmans' house was Ashmead, and it occupied some five acres of Melton Heath, which is thirty miles from London, stands five hundred feet above sea level, and is, for the most part, inhabited by those who have ample incomes.

The butler received Mr. Satterthwaite suavely. Mr. and Mrs. Denman were both out—at a rehearsal—they hoped Mr. Satterthwaite would make himself at home until they returned.

Mr. Satterthwaite nodded and proceeded to carry out these injunctions by stepping into the garden. After a cursory examination of the flower beds, he strolled down a shady walk and presently came to a door in the wall. It was unlocked and he passed through it and came out into a narrow lane.

Mr. Satterthwaite looked to left and right. A very

charming lane, shady and green, with high hedges—a rural lane that twisted and turned in good old-fashioned style. He remembered the stamped address: *Ashmead, Harlequin's Lane*—remembered, too, a local name for it that Mrs. Denman had once told him.

"Harlequin's Lane," he murmured to himself softly. "I wonder—"

He turned a corner.

Not at the time, but afterward, he wondered why this time he felt no surprise at meeting that elusive friend of his: Mr. Harley Quin. The two men clasped hands.

"So *you're* down here," said Mr. Satterthwaite.

"Yes," said Mr. Quin. "I'm staying in the same house as you are."

"Staying there?"

"Yes. Does it surprise you?"

"No," said Mr. Satterthwaite slowly. "Only—well, you never stay anywhere for long, do you?"

"Only as long as is necessary," said Mr. Quin gravely.

"I see," said Mr. Satterthwaite.

They walked on in silence for some minutes.

"This lane—" began Mr. Satterthwaite, and stopped.

"Belongs to me," said Mr. Quin.

"I thought it did," said Mr. Satterthwaite. "Somehow I thought it must. There's the other name for it, too, the local name. They call it the 'Lovers' Lane.' You know that?"

Mr. Quin nodded. "But surely," he said gently, "there is a 'Lovers' Lane' in every village."

"I suppose so," said Mr. Satterthwaite, and he sighed a little.

He felt suddenly rather old and out of things, a little dried-up wizened old fogey of a man. Each side of him were the hedges, very green and alive.

"Where does this lane end, I wonder?" he asked suddenly.

"It ends—*here*," said Mr. Quin.

They came round a last bend. The lane ended in a piece of waste ground, and almost at their feet a great pit opened.

In it were tin cans gleaming in the sun, and other cans that were too red with rust to gleam, old boots, fragments of newspapers, a hundred and one odds and ends that were no longer of account to anybody.

"A rubbish heap," exclaimed Mr. Satterthwaite, and breathed deeply and indignantly.

"Sometimes there are very wonderful things on a rubbish heap," said Mr. Quin.

"I know, I know," cried Mr. Satterthwaite, and quoted with just a trace of self-consciousness: " *'Bring me the two most beautiful things in the city,' said God.* You know how it goes, eh?"

Mr. Quin nodded.

Mr. Satterthwaite looked up at the ruins of a small cottage perched on the brink of the wall of cliff.

"Hardly a pretty view for a house," he remarked.

"I fancy this wasn't a rubbish heap in those days," said Mr. Quin. "I believe the Denmans lived there when they were first married. They moved into the big house when the old people died. The cottage was pulled down when they began to quarry the rock here—but nothing much was done, as you can see."

They turned and began retracing their steps.

"I suppose," said Mr. Satterthwaite, smiling, "that many couples come wandering down this lane on these warm summer evenings."

"Probably."

"Lovers," said Mr. Satterthwaite. He repeated the word thoughtfully and quite without the normal embarrassment of the Englishman. Mr. Quin had that effect upon him. "Lovers. You have done a lot for lovers, Mr. Quin."

The other bowed his head without replying.

"You have saved them from sorrow—from worse than sorrow, from death. You have been an advocate for the dead themselves."

"You are speaking of yourself—of what *you* have done —not of me."

"It is the same thing," said Mr. Satterthwaite. "You

know it is," he urged, as the other did not speak. "You have acted—through me. For some reason or other you do not act directly—yourself."

"Sometimes I do," said Mr. Quin.

His voice held a new note. In spite of himself Mr. Satterthwaite shivered a little. The afternoon, he thought, must be growing chilly. And yet the sun seemed as bright as ever.

At that moment a girl turned the corner ahead of them and came into sight. She was a very pretty girl, fair-haired and blue-eyed, wearing a pink cotton frock. Mr. Satterthwaite recognized her as Molly Stanwell, whom he had met down here before.

She waved a hand in welcome to him. "John and Anna have just gone back," she cried. "They thought you must have come, but they simply had to be at the rehearsal."

"Rehearsal of what?" inquired Mr. Satterthwaite.

"This masquerade thing—I don't quite know what you'd call it. There is singing and dancing and all sorts of things in it. Mr. Manly (do you remember him down here?), he has quite a good tenor voice, is to be Pierrot, and I am Pierrette. Two professionals are coming down for the dancing—Harlequin and Columbine, you know. And then there is a big chorus of girls. Lady Roscheimer is so keen on training village girls to sing. She's really getting the thing up for that. The music is rather lovely—but very modern—next to no tune anywhere. Claude Wickam. Perhaps you know him?"

Mr. Satterthwaite nodded, for, as has been mentioned before, it was his métier to know everybody. He knew about that aspiring genius Claude Wickam, and about Lady Roscheimer, who was fat and had a penchant for young men of the artistic persuasion. And he knew all about Sir Leopold Roscheimer, who liked his wife to be happy and, most rare among husbands, did not mind her being happy in her own way.

They found Claude Wickam at tea with the Denmans, cramming his mouth indiscriminately with anything handy, talking rapidly, and waving long white hands that had a double-jointed appearance. His short-sighted eyes peered through large horn-rimmed spectacles.

John Denman, upright, slightly florid with the faintest possible tendency to sleekness, listened with an air of bored attention. On the appearance of Mr. Satterthwaite, the musician transferred his remarks to him. Anna Denman sat behind the tea things, quiet and expressionless as usual.

Mr. Satterthwaite stole a covert glance at her. Tall, gaunt, very thin, with the skin tightly stretched over high cheekbones, black hair parted in the middle, a skin that was weather-beaten. An out-of-door woman who cared nothing for the use of cosmetics. A Dutch Doll of a woman, wooden, lifeless—and yet—

He thought, *There* should *be meaning behind that face, and yet there isn't. That's what's all wrong. Yes, all wrong.* And to Claude Wickam he said, "I beg your pardon? You were saying?"

Claude Wickam, who liked the sound of his own voice, began all over again. Russia, he said, that was the only country in the world worth being interested in. They experimented. With lives, if you like, but still they experimented. "Magnificent!" He crammed a sandwich into his mouth with one hand, and added a bite of the chocolate éclair he was waving about in the other. "Take," he said (with his mouthful), "the Russian Ballet." Remembering his hostess, he turned to her. What did *she* think of the Russian Ballet?

The question was obviously only a prelude to the important point—what Claude Wickam thought of the Russian Ballet—but her answer was unexpected and threw him completely out of his stride.

"I have never seen it."

"What?" He gazed at her open-mouthed. "But—surely—"

Her voice went on level and emotionless. "Before my marriage, I was a dancer. So now—"

"A busman's holiday," said her husband.

"Dancing." She shrugged her shoulders. "I know all the tricks of it. It does not interest me."

"Oh!"

It took but a moment for Claude to recover his aplomb.

"Talking of lives," said Mr. Satterthwaite, "and experimenting in them, the Russian nation made one costly experiment."

Claude Wickam swung round on him. "I know what you are going to say," he cried. "Kharsanova! The immortal, the only Kharsanova! You saw her dance?"

"Three times," said Mr. Satterthwaite. "Twice in Paris, once in London. I shall—not forget it."

He spoke in an almost reverent voice.

"I saw her too," said Claude Wickam. "I was ten years old. An uncle took me. God! I shall never forget it."

He threw a piece of bun fiercely into a flower bed.

"There is a statuette of her in a museum in Berlin," said Mr. Satterthwaite. "It is marvelous. That impression of fragility—as though you could break her with a flip of the thumbnail. I have seen her as Columbine, in the Swan, as the dying Nymph." He paused, shaking his head. "There was genius. It will be long years before such another is born. She was young too. Destroyed ignorantly and wantonly in the first days of the Revolution."

"Fools! Madmen! Apes!" said Claude Wickam. He choked with a mouthful of tea.

"I studied with Kharsanova," said Mrs. Denman. "I remember her well."

"She was wonderful?" said Mr. Satterthwaite.

"Yes," said Mrs. Denman quietly. "She was wonderful."

Claude Wickam departed, and John Denman drew a deep sigh of relief, at which his wife laughed.

Mr. Satterthwaite nodded. "I know what you think. But in spite of everything, the music that that boy writes *is* music."

"I suppose it is," said Denman.

"Oh! undoubtedly. How long it will be—well, that is different."

John Denman looked at him curiously. "You mean?"

"I mean that success has come early. And that is dangerous. Always dangerous." He looked across at Mr. Quin. "You
agree with me?"

"You are always right," said Mr. Quin.

"We will come upstairs to my room," said Mrs. Denman. "It is pleasant there."

She led the way, and they followed her. Mr. Satterthwaite drew a deep breath as he caught sight of the Chinese
screen. He looked up to find Mrs. Denman watching him.

"You are the man who is always right," she said, nodding her head slowly at him. "What do you make of my
screen?"

He felt that in some way the words were a challenge to
him, and he answered almost haltingly, stumbling over the
words a little. "Why, it's—it's beautiful. More, it's unique."

"You're right." Denman had come up behind him. "We
bought it early in our married life. Got it for about a tenth
of its value, but even then—well, it crippled us for over a
year. You remember, Anna?"

"Yes," said Mrs. Denman, "I remember."

"In fact, we'd no business to buy it at all—not then.
Now, of course, it's different. There was some very good
lacquer going at Christie's the other day. Just what we need
to make this room perfect. All Chinese together. Clear out
the other stuff. Would you believe it, Satterthwaite, my wife
wouldn't hear of it?"

"I like this room as it is," said Mrs. Denman.

There was a curious look on her face. Again Mr. Satterthwaite felt challenged and defeated. He looked round
him, and for the first time he noticed the absence of all
personal touch. There were no photographs, no flowers, no
knickknacks. It was not like a woman's room at all. Save for
that one incongruous factor of the Chinese screen it might
have been a sample room shown at some big furnishing
house.

He found her smiling at him.

"Listen," she said. She bent forward, and for a moment

she seemed less English, more definitely foreign. "I speak to you, for you will understand. We bought that screen with more than money—with love. For love of it, because it was beautiful and unique, we went without other things, things we needed and missed. These other Chinese pieces my husband speaks of, those we should buy with money only, we should not pay away anything of ourselves."

Her husband laughed. "Oh! have it your own way," he said, but with a trace of irritation in his voice. "But it's all wrong against this English background. This other stuff, it's good enough of its kind, genuine solid, no fake about it—but mediocre. Good plain late Hepplewhite."

She nodded. "Good, solid, genuine English," she murmured softly.

Mr. Satterthwaite stared at her. He caught a meaning behind these words. The English room—the flaming beauty of the Chinese screen— No, it was gone again.

"I met Miss Stanwell in the lane," he said conversationally. "She tells me she is going to be Pierrette in this show tonight."

"Yes," said Denman. "And she's awfully good, too."

"She has clumsy feet," said Anna.

"Nonsense," said her husband. "All women are alike, Satterthwaite. Can't bear to hear another woman praised. Molly is a very good-looking girl, and so of course every woman has to have their knife into her."

"I spoke of dancing," said Anna Denman. She sounded faintly surprised. "She is very pretty, yes, but her feet move clumsily. You cannot tell me anything else, because I know about dancing."

Mr. Satterthwaite intervened tactfully. "You have two professional dancers coming down, I understand?"

"Yes. For the ballet proper. Prince Oranoff is bringing them down in his car."

"Sergius Oranoff?"

The question came from Anna Denman. Her husband turned and looked at her.

"You know him?"

"I used to know him—in Russia."

Mr. Satterthwaite thought that John Denman looked disturbed.

"Will he know you?"

"Yes. He will know me."

She laughed—a low, almost triumphant laugh. There was nothing of the Dutch Doll about her face now. She nodded reassuringly at her husband. "Serge. So he is bringing down the two dancers. He was always interested in dancing."

"I remember."

John Denman spoke abruptly, then turned and left the room. Mr. Quin followed him. Anna Denman crossed to the telephone and asked for a number. She arrested Mr. Satterthwaite with a gesture as he was about to follow the example of the other two men.

"Can I speak to Lady Roscheimer. Oh! it is you. This is Anna Denman speaking. Has Prince Oranoff arrived yet? What? *What?* Oh! my dear! But how ghastly."

She listened for a few moments longer, then replaced the receiver. She turned to Mr. Satterthwaite.

"There has been an accident. There would be with Sergius Ivanovitch driving. Oh! he has not altered in all these years. The girl was not badly hurt, but bruised and shaken, too much to dance tonight. The man's arm is broken. Serge Ivanovitch himself is unhurt. The devil looks after his own, perhaps."

"And what about tonight's performance?"

"Exactly, my friend. Something must be done about it."

She sat thinking. Presently she looked at him. "I am a bad hostess, Mr. Satterthwaite. I do not entertain you."

"I assure you that it is not necessary. There's one thing though, Mrs. Denman, that I would very much like to know."

"Yes?"

"How did you come across Mr. Quin?"

"He is often down here," she said slowly. "I think he owns land in this part of the world."

"He does, he does. He told me so this afternoon," said Mr. Satterthwaite.

"He is—" She paused. Her eyes met Mr. Satterthwaite's. "I think you know what he is better than I do," she finished.

"I?"

"Is it not so?"

He was troubled. His neat little soul found her disturbing. He felt that she wished to force him further than he was prepared to go, that she wanted him to put into words that which he was not prepared to admit to himself.

"*You* know!" she said. "I think you know most things, Mr. Satterthwaite."

Here was incense, yet for once it failed to intoxicate him. He shook his head in unwonted humility. "What can anyone know?" he asked. "So little—so very little."

She nodded in assent. Presently she spoke again, in a queer, brooding voice, without looking at him.

"Supposing I were to tell you something—you would not laugh? No, I do not think you would laugh. Supposing, then, that to carry on one's"—she paused—"one's trade, one's profession, one were to make use of a fantasy— one were to pretend to oneself something that did not exist —that one were to imagine a certain person. It is a pretense, you understand, a make-believe—nothing more. But one day—"

"Yes?" said Mr. Satterthwaite. He was keenly interested.

"The fantasy came true! The thing one imagined—the impossible thing, the thing that could not be—was real! Is that madness? Tell me, Mr. Satterthwaite. Is that madness —or do you believe it too?"

"I—" Queer how he could not get the words put. How they seemed to stick somewhere at the back of his throat.

"Folly," said Anna Denman. "Folly."

She swept out of the room and left Mr. Satterthwaite with his confession of faith unspoken.

He came down to dinner to find Mrs. Denman entertaining a guest, a tall, dark man approaching middle age.

"Prince Oranoff—Mr. Satterthwaite."

The two men bowed. Mr. Satterthwaite had the feeling that some conversation had been broken off on his entry which would not be resumed. But there was no sense of strain. The Russian conversed easily and naturally on those subjects which were nearest to Mr. Satterthwaite's heart. He was a man of very fine artistic taste, and they soon found that they had many friends in common. John Denman joined them, and the talk became localized. Oranoff expressed regret for the accident.

"It was not my fault. I like to drive fast—yes, but I am a good driver. It was Fate—chance"—he shrugged his shoulders—"the masters of all of us."

"There speaks the Russian in you, Sergius Ivanovitch," said Mrs. Denman.

"And finds an echo in you, Anna Mikalovna," he threw back quickly.

Mr. Satterthwaite looked from one to the other of the three of them. John Denman, fair, aloof, English, and the other two, dark, thin, strangely alike. Something rose in his mind—what was it? Ah! he had it now. The first act of the *Walküre*. Sigmund and Sieglinde—so alike—and the alien Hunding. Conjectures began to stir in his brain. Was this the meaning of the presence of Mr. Quin? One thing he believed in firmly—wherever Mr. Quin showed himself, there lay drama. Was this it here—the old hackneyed three-cornered tragedy?

He was vaguely disappointed. He had hoped for better things.

"What's been arranged, Anna?" asked Denman. "The thing will have to be put off, I suppose. I heard you ringing the Roscheimers up."

She shook her head. "No—there is no need to put it off."

"But you can't do it without the ballet?"

"You certainly couldn't have a Harlequinade without Harlequin and Columbine," agreed Anna Denman dryly. "I'm going to be Columbine, John."

"You?" He was astonished—disturbed, Mr. Satterthwaite thought.

She nodded composedly. "You need not be afraid, John. I shall not disgrace you. You forget—it was my profession once."

Mr. Satterthwaite thought, *What an extraordinary thing a voice is. The things it says—and the things it leaves unsaid and means! I wish I knew—*

"Well," said John Denman grudgingly. "That solves one half of the problem. What about the other? Where will you find Harlequin?"

"I *have* found him—there!"

She gestured toward the open doorway where Mr. Quin had just appeared. He smiled back at her.

"Good Lord, Quin," said John Denman. "Do you know anything of this game? I should never have imagined it."

"Mr. Quin is vouched for by an expert," said his wife. "Mr. Satterthwaite will answer for him."

She smiled at Mr. Satterthwaite, and the little man found himself murmuring, "Oh! yes, I—I answer for Mr. Quin."

Denman turned his attention elsewhere. "You know there's to be a fancy-dress dance business afterward. Great nuisance. We'll have to rig you up, Satterthwaite."

Mr. Satterthwaite shook his head very decidedly. "My years will excuse me." A brilliant idea struck him. "A table napkin under the arm. There I am, an elderly waiter who has seen better days."

He laughed.

"An interesting profession," said Mr. Quin. "One sees so much."

"I've got to put on some fool Pierrot thing," said Denman gloomily. "It's cool anyway, that's one thing. What about you?" He looked at Oranoff.

"I have a Harlequin costume," said the Russian. His eyes wandered for a minute to his hostess's face.

Mr. Satterthwaite wondered if he was mistaken in fancying that there was just a moment of constraint.

"There might have been three of us," said Denman, with a laugh. "I've got an old Harlequin costume my wife made me when we were first married for some show or other." He paused, looking down on his broad shirt front. "I don't suppose I could get into it now."

"No," said his wife, "you couldn't get into it now." And again her voice said something more than mere words.

She glanced up at the clock. "If Molly doesn't turn up soon, we won't wait for her."

But at that moment the girl was announced. She was already wearing her Pierrette dress of white and green, and very charming she looked in it, so Mr. Satterthwaite reflected.

She was full of excitement and enthusiasm over the forthcoming performance. "I'm getting awfully nervous, though," she announced, as they drank coffee after dinner. "I know my voice will wobble, and I shall forget the words."

"Your voice is very charming," said Anna. "I should not worry about it if I were you."

"Oh! but I do. The other I don't mind about—the dancing, I mean. That's sure to go all right. I mean, you can't go very far wrong with your feet, can you?"

She appealed to Anna, but the older woman did not respond. Instead she said, "Sing something now to Mr. Satterthwaite. You will find that he will reassure you."

Molly went over to the piano. Her voice rang out, fresh and tuneful in an old Irish ballad:

"Sheila, dark Sheila, what is it that you're seeing?
What is it that you're seeing, that you're seeing in the
    fire?
'I see a lad that loves me—and I see a lad that leaves me,
    and a third lad, a Shadow Lad—and he's the lad
    that grieves me.'"

The song went on. At the end, Mr. Satterthwaite nodded vigorous approval.

"Mrs. Denman is right. Your voice is charming. Not, perhaps, very fully trained, but delightfully natural, and with that unstudied quality of youth in it."

"That's right," agreed John Denman. "You go ahead, Molly, and don't be downed by stage fright. We'd better be getting over to the Roscheimers' now."

The party separated to don cloaks. It was a glorious night and they proposed to walk over, the house being only a few hundred yards down the road.

Mr. Satterthwaite found himself by his friend.

"It's an odd thing," he said, "but that song made me think of you. *A third lad—a Shadow Lad*—there's mystery there, and wherever there's mystery I—well, think of you."

"Am I so mysterious?" smiled Mr. Quin.

Mr. Satterthwaite nodded vigorously. "Yes, indeed. Do you know, until tonight, I had no idea that you were a professional dancer."

"Really?" said Mr. Quin.

"Listen," said Mr. Satterthwaite. He hummed the love motif from the *Walküre*. "That is what has been ringing in my head all through dinner as I looked at those two."

"Which two?"

"Prince Oranoff and Mrs. Denman. Don't you see the difference in her tonight? It's as though—as though a shutter had suddenly been opened and you see the glow within."

"Yes," said Mr. Quin. "Perhaps so."

"The same old drama," said Mr. Satterthwaite. "I am right, am I not? Those two belong together. They are of the same world, think the same thoughts, dream the same dreams. One sees how it has come about. Ten years ago Denman must have been very good-looking, young, dashing, a figure of romance. And he saved her life. All quite natural. But now—what is he, after all? A good fellow—prosperous, successful—but—well, mediocre. Good honest English stuff—very much like that Hepplewhite furniture upstairs. As English—and as ordinary—as that pretty English girl with her fresh, untrained voice. Oh! You may smile, Mr. Quin, but you cannot deny what I am saying."

"I deny nothing. In what you see you are always right. And yet—"

"Yet what?"

Mr. Quin leaned forward. His dark, melancholy eyes searched those of Mr. Satterthwaite. "Have you learned so little of life?" he breathed.

He left Mr. Satterthwaite vaguely disquieted, such a prey to meditation that he found the others had started without him, owing to his delay in selecting a scarf for his neck. He went out by the garden, and through the same door as in the afternoon. The lane was bathed in moonlight, and even as he stood in the doorway, he saw a couple enlaced in each other's arms.

For a moment he thought—

And then he saw. *John Denman and Molly Stanwell.* Denman's voice came to him, hoarse and anguished.

"I can't live without you. What are we to do?"

Mr. Satterthwaite turned to go back the way he had come, but a hand stayed him. Someone else stood in the doorway beside him, someone else whose eyes had also seen.

Mr. Satterthwaite had only to catch one glimpse of her face to know how wildly astray all his conclusions had been.

Her anguished hand held him there until those other two had passed up the lane and disappeared from sight. He heard himself speaking to her, saying foolish little things meant to be comforting, and ludicrously inadequate to the agony he had divined. She only spoke once.

"Please," she said, "don't leave me."

He found that oddly touching. He was, then, of use to someone. And he went on saying those things that meant nothing at all, but which were, somehow, better than silence. They went that way to the Roscheimers'. Now and then her hand tightened on his shoulder, and he understood that she was glad of his company. She only took it away when they finally came to their destination. She stood very erect, her head held high.

"Now," she said, "I shall dance! Do not be afraid for me, my friend. I shall dance."

She left him abruptly. He was seized upon by Lady Roscheimer, much bediamonded and very full of lamentations. By her he was passed on to Claude Wickam.

"Ruined! Completely ruined. The sort of thing that always happens to me. All these country bumpkins think they can dance. I was never even consulted—"

His voice went on—went on interminably. He had found a sympathetic listener, a man who *knew*. He gave himself up to an orgy of self-pity. It only ended when the first strains of music began.

Mr. Satterthwaite came out of his dream. He was alert once more, the critic. Wickam was an unutterable ass, but he could write music—delicate gossamer stuff, intangible as a fairy web—yet with nothing of the pretty-pretty about it.

The scenery was good. Lady Roscheimer never spared expense when aiding her protégées. A glade of Arcady with lighting effects that gave it the proper atmosphere of unreality.

Two figures dancing as they had danced through time immemorial. A slender Harlequin flashing spangles in the moonlight with magic wand and masked face, a white Columbine pirouetting like some immortal dream—

Mr. Satterthwaite sat up. He had lived through this before. Yes, surely—

Now his body was far away from Lady Roscheimer's drawing room. It was in a Berlin museum gazing at a statuette of an immortal Columbine.

Harlequin and Columbine danced on. The wide world was theirs to dance in.

Moonlight—and a human figure. Pierrot wandering through the wood, singing to the moon. Pierrot who has seen Columbine and knows no rest. The immortal two vanish, but Columbine looks back. She has heard the song of a human heart.

Pierrot wandering on through the wood—darkness—his voice dies away in the distance—

The village green—dancing of village girls—pierrots and pierrettes. Molly as Pierrette. No dancer—Anna Denman was right there—but a fresh tuneful voice as she sings her song, "Pierrette dancing on the green."

A good tune—Mr. Satterthwaite nodded approval. Wickam wasn't above writing a tune when there was need for it. The majority of the village girls made him shudder, but he realized that Lady Roscheimer was determinedly philanthropical.

They press Pierrot to join the dance. He refuses. With white face he wanders on—the eternal lover seeking his ideal. Evening falls. Harlequin and Columbine, invisible, dance in and out of the unconscious throng. The place is deserted, only Pierrot, weary, falls asleep on a grassy bank. Harlequin and Columbine dance round him. He wakes and sees Columbine. He woos her in vain, pleads, beseeches—

She stands uncertain. Harlequin beckons to her to begone. But she sees him no longer. She is listening to Pierrot, to his song of love outpoured once more. She falls into his arms, and the curtain comes down.

The second act is Pierrot's cottage. Columbine sits on his hearth. She is pale, weary. She listens—for what? Pierrot sings to her—woos her back to thoughts of him once more. The evening darkens. Thunder is heard. Columbine puts aside her spinning wheel. She is eager, stirred. She listens no longer to Pierrot. It is her own music that is in the air, the music of Harlequin and Columbine. She is awake. She remembers.

A crash of thunder! Harlequin stands in the doorway. Pierrot cannot see him, but Columbine springs up with a glad laugh. Children come running, but she pushes them aside. With another crash of thunder the walls fall, and Columbine dances out into the wild night with Harlequin.

Darkness, and through it the tune that Pierrette has sung. Light comes slowly. The cottage once more. Pierrot and Pierrette, grown old and gray, sit in front of the fire in two armchairs. The music is happy, but subdued. Pierrette nods in her chair. Through the window comes a shaft of moonlight, and with it the motif of Pierrot's long-forgotten song. He stirs in his chair.

Faint music—fairy music—Harlequin and Columbine outside. The door swings open and Columbine dances in. She leans over the sleeping Pierrot, kisses him on the lips.

Crash! A peal of thunder. She is outside again. In the center of the stage is the lighted window and through it are seen the two figures of Harlequin and Columbine dancing slowly away, growing fainter and fainter. . . .

A log falls. Pierrette jumps up angrily, rushes across to the window, and pulls the blind. So it ends, on a sudden discord.

Mr. Satterthwaite sat very still among the applause and vociferations. At last he got up and made his way outside. He came upon Molly Stanwell, flushed and eager, receiving compliments. He saw John Denman, pushing and elbowing his way through the throng, his eyes alight with a new flame. Molly came toward him, but, almost unconsciously, he put her aside. It was not her he was seeking.

"My wife? Where is she?"

"I think she went out in the garden."

It was, however, Mr. Satterthwaite who found her, sitting on a stone seat under a cypress tree. When he came up to her, he did an odd thing. He knelt down and raised her hand to his lips.

"Ah!" she said. "You think I danced well?"

"You danced—as you always danced, Madame Kharsanova."

She drew in her breath sharply. "So—you have guessed."

"There is only one Kharsanova. No one could see you dance and forget. But why—why?"

"What else was possible?"

"You mean?"

She had spoken very simply. She was just as simple now.

"Oh! but you understand. You are of the world. A great dancer—she can have lovers, yes—but a husband, that is different. And he—he did not want the other. He wanted me to belong to him as—as Kharsanova could never have belonged."

"I see," said Mr. Satterthwaite. "I see. So you gave it up?"

She nodded.

"You must have loved him very much," said Mr. Satterthwaite gently.

"To make such a sacrifice?" She laughed.

"Not quite that. To make it so lightheartedly."

"Ah! yes—perhaps—you are right."

"And now?" asked Mr. Satterthwaite.

Her face grew grave. "Now?" She paused, then raised her voice and spoke into the shadows.

"Is that you, Sergius Ivanovitch?"

Prince Oranoff came out into the moonlight. He took her hand and smiled at Mr. Satterthwaite without self-consciousness.

"Ten years ago I mourned the death of Anna Kharsanova," he said simply. "She was to me as my other self. Today I have found her again. We shall part no more."

"At the end of the lane in ten minutes," said Anna. "I shall not fail you."

Oranoff nodded and went off again. The dancer turned to Mr. Satterthwaite. A smile played about her lips.

"Well—you are not satisfied, my friend?"

"Do you know," said Mr. Satterthwaite abruptly, "that your husband is looking for you?"

He saw the tremor that passed over her face, but her voice was steady enough. "Yes," she said gravely. "That may well be."

"I saw his eyes. They—" he stopped abruptly.

She was still calm.

"Yes, perhaps. For an hour. An hour's magic, born of past memories, of music, of moonlight. That is all."

"Then there is nothing that I can say?" He felt old, dispirited.

"For ten years I have lived with the man I love," said Anna Kharsanova. "Now I am going to the man who for ten years has loved me."

Mr. Satterthwaite said nothing. He had no arguments left. Besides, it really seemed the simplest solution. Only—

Only, somehow, it was not the solution he wanted. He felt her hand on his shoulder.

"I know, my friend, I know. But there is no third way. Always one looks for one thing—the lover, the perfect, the eternal lover. It is the music of Harlequin one hears. No lover ever satisfies one, for all lovers are mortal. And Harlequin is only a myth, an invisible presence—unless—"

"Yes," said Mr. Satterthwaite. "Yes?"

"Unless—his name is—Death!"

Mr. Satterthwaite shivered. She moved away from him, was swallowed up in the shadows.

He never knew quite how long he sat on there, but suddenly he started up with the feeling that he had been wasting valuable time. He hurried away, impelled in a certain direction almost in spite of himself.

As he came out into the lane he had a strange feeling of unreality. Magic—magic and moonlight. And two figures coming toward him.

Oranoff in his Harlequin dress. So he thought at first. Then as they passed him he knew his mistake. That lithe swaying figure belonged to one person only—Mr. Quin.

They went on down the lane—their feet light as though they were treading on air. Mr. Quin turned his head and looked back, and Mr. Satterthwaite had a shock, for it was not the face of Mr. Quin as he had ever seen it before. It was the face of a stranger—no, not quite a stranger. Ah! he had it now, it was the face of John Denman as it might have looked before life went too well with him! Eager, adventurous, the face at once of a boy and of a lover.

Her laugh floated down to him, clear and happy. . . . He looked after them and saw in the distance the lights of a little cottage. He gazed after them like a man in a dream.

He was rudely awakened by a hand that fell on his shoulder and he was jerked round to face Sergius Oranoff. The man looked white and distracted.

"Where is she? Where is she? She promised—and she has not come."

"Madame has just gone up the lane—alone."

It was Mrs. Denman's maid who spoke from the shadow of the door behind them. She had been waiting with her mistress's wraps.

"I was standing here and saw her pass," she added.

Mr. Satterthwaite threw one harsh word at her.

"Alone? Alone, did you say?"

The maid's eyes widened in surprise. "Yes, sir. Didn't you see her?"

Mr. Satterthwaite clutched at Oranoff. "Quickly," he muttered. "I'm—I'm afraid."

They hurried down the lane together, the Russian talking in quick, disjointed sentences.

"She is a wonderful creature. Ah! how she danced tonight. And that friend of yours. Who is he? Ah! but he is wonderful—unique. In the old days, when she danced the Columbine of Rimsky-Korsakoff, she never found the perfect Harlequin. Mordroff, Kassnine—none of them was quite perfect. She had her own little fancy. She told me of it once. Always she danced with a dream Harlequin—a man who was not really there. It was Harlequin himself, she said, who came to dance with her. It was that fancy of hers that made her Columbine so wonderful."

Mr. Satterthwaite nodded. There was only one thought in his head. "Hurry," he said. "We must be in time. Oh! we must be in time."

They came round the last corner—came to the deep pit

and to something lying in it that had not been there before, the body of a woman lying in a wonderful pose, arms flung wide and head thrown back. A dead face and body that were triumphant and beautiful in the moonlight.

Words came back to Mr. Satterthwaite dimly—Mr. Quin's words:—*"wonderful things on a rubbish heap. . . ."* He understood them now.

Oranoff was murmuring broken phrases. The tears were streaming down his face.

"I loved her. Always I loved her." He used almost the same words that had occurred to Mr. Satterthwaite earlier in the day. "We were of the same world, she and I. We had the same thoughts, the same dreams. I would have loved her always—"

"How do you know?"

The Russian stared at him—at the fretful peevishness of the tone.

"How do you know?" went on Mr. Satterthwaite. "It is what all lovers think—what all lovers say. There is only one lover—"

He turned and almost ran into Mr. Quin. In an agitated manner, Mr. Satterthwaite caught him by the arm and drew him aside.

"It was *you*," he said. "It was *you* who were with her just now?"

Mr. Quin waited a minute and then said gently, "You can put it that way, if you like."

"And the maid didn't see you?"

"The maid didn't see me."

"But *I* did. Why was that?"

"Perhaps, as a result of the price you have paid, you see things that other people—do not."

Mr. Satterthwaite looked at him uncomprehendingly for a minute or two. Then he began suddenly to quiver all over like an aspen leaf. "What is this place?" he whispered. "What is this place?"

"I told you earlier today. It is *My* lane."

"A Lovers' Lane," murmured Mr. Satterthwaite. "And people pass along it."

"Most people, sooner or later."

"And at the end of it—what do they find?"

Mr. Quin smiled. His voice was very gentle. He pointed at the ruined cottage above them. "The house of their dreams—or a rubbish heap—who shall say?"

Mr. Satterthwaite looked up at him suddenly. A wild rebellion surged over him. He felt cheated, defrauded.

"But *I*—" his voice shook. "*I* have never passed down your lane."

"And do you regret?"

Mr. Satterthwaite quailed. Mr. Quin seemed to have loomed to enormous proportions. Mr. Satterthwaite had a vista of something at once menacing and terrifying. Joy, Sorrow, Despair.

And his comfortable little soul shrank back appalled.

"Do you regret?" Mr. Quin repeated his question. There was something terrible about him.

"No," Mr. Satterthwaite stammered. "N-No."

And then suddenly he rallied.

"But I see things," he cried. "I may have been only a looker-on at Life—but I see things that other people do not. You said so yourself, Mr. Quin."

But Mr. Quin had vanished.

HIS HEART COULD BREAK

Craig Rice

Craig Rice (1908–1957) was a highly popular writer of mystery novels, short stories, radio plays, screenplays, and true-crime tales during the 1940s and 1950s. (She also ghost-wrote the criminous novels attributed to the famous stripper, Gypsy Rose Lee, and to the actor George Sanders.) She created a number of series sleuths, including the comic duo of Bingo Riggs and Handsome Kusak (The Sunday Pigeon Murders, The Thursday Turkey Murders) *and a hard-drinking, woman-chasing Chicago lawyer named John J. Malone* (Eight Faces at Three, The Wrong Murder, The Lucky Stiff). *"His Heart Could Break," in which Malone investigates a bizarre murder in the death house of a state prison, is Craig Rice at the top of her form, and that makes it very good indeed.*

"As I passed by the ol' state's prison,
Ridin' on a stream-line' train—"

John J. Malone shuddered. He wished he could get the insidious melody out of his mind—or remember the rest of the words. It had been annoying him since three o'clock that morning, when he'd heard it sung by the janitor of Joe the Angel's City Hall Bar.

It seemed like a bad omen, and it made him uncomfortable. Or maybe it was the cheap gin he'd switched to between two and four A.M. that was making him uncomfortable. Whichever it was, he felt terrible.

"I bet your client's happy today," the guard said cordially, leading the way toward the death house.

"He ought to be," Malone growled. He reminded himself that he too ought to be happy. He wasn't. Maybe it was being in a prison that depressed him. John J. Malone, criminal lawyer, didn't like prisons. He devoted his life to keeping his clients out of them.

"Then the warden told me gently—"

That song again! How did the next line go?

"Well," the guard said, "they say you've never lost a client yet." It wouldn't do any harm, he thought, to get on the good side of a smart guy like John J. Malone.

"Not yet," Malone said. He'd had a close call with this one, though.

"You sure did a wonderful job, turning up the evidence to get a new trial," the guard rattled on. Maybe Malone could get him a better appointment, with his political drag. "Your client sure felt swell when he heard about it last night, he sure did."

"That's good," Malone said noncommittally. It hadn't

been evidence that had turned the trick, though. Just a little matter of knowing some interesting facts about the judge's private life. The evidence would have to be manufactured before the trial, but that was the least of his worries. By that time, he might even find out the truth of what had happened. He hummed softly under his breath. Ah, there were the next lines!

> *"Then the warden told me gently,*
> *He seemed too young, too young to die,*
> *We cut the rope and let him down—"*

John J. Malone tried to remember the rhyme for "die." By, cry, lie, my and sigh. Then he let loose a few loud and indignant remarks about whoever had written that song, realized that he was entering the death house, and stopped, embarrassed. That particular cellblock always inspired him with the same behavior he would have shown at a high-class funeral. He took off his hat and walked softly.

And at that moment hell broke loose. Two prisoners in the block began yelling like banshees. The alarms began to sound loudly, causing the outside siren to chime in with its hideous wail. Guards were running through the corridor, and John J. Malone instinctively ran with them toward the center of disturbance, the fourth cell on the left.

Before the little lawyer got there, one of the guards had the door open. Another guard cut quickly through the bright new rope from which the prisoner was dangling, and eased the limp body down to the floor.

The racket outside was almost deafening now, but John J. Malone scarcely heard it. The guard turned the body over, and Malone recognized the very young and rather stupid face of Paul Palmer.

"He's hung himself," one of the guards said.

"With me for a lawyer?" Malone said angrily. "Hung himself—" He started to say "hell," then remembered he was in the presence of death.

"Hey," the other guard said excitedly. "He's alive. His neck's broke, but he's breathing a little."

Malone shoved the guard aside and knelt down beside the dying man. Paul Palmer's blue eyes opened slowly, with an expression of terrible bewilderment. His lips parted.

"It wouldn't break," Paul Palmer whispered. He seemed to recognize Malone, and stared at him, with a look of frightful urgency. *"It wouldn't break,"* he whispered to Malone. Then he died.

"You're damned right I'm going to sit in on the investigation," Malone said angrily. He gave Warden Garrity's wastebasket a vicious kick. "The inefficient way you run your prison has done me out of a client." Out of a fat fee, too, he reminded himself miserably. He hadn't been paid yet, and now there would be a long tussle with the lawyer handling Paul Palmer's estate, who hadn't wanted him engaged for the defense in the first place. Malone felt in his pocket, found three crumpled bills and a small handful of change. He wished now that he hadn't got into that poker game last week.

The warden's dreary office was crowded. Malone looked around, recognized an assistant warden, the prison doctor—a handsome gray-haired man named Dickson—the guards from the death house, and the guard who had been ushering him in—Bowers was his name, Malone remembered, a tall, flat-faced, gangling man.

"Imagine him hanging himself," Bowers was saying incredulously. "Just after he found out he was gonna get a new trial."

Malone had been wondering the same thing. "Maybe he didn't get my wire," he suggested coldly.

"I gave it to him myself," Bowers stated positively. "Just last night. Never saw a man so happy in my life."

Doctor Dickson cleared his throat. Everyone turned to look at him.

"Poor Palmer was mentally unstable," the doctor said

sadly. "You may recall I recommended, several days ago, that he be moved to the prison hospital. When I visited him last night he appeared hilariously—hysterically—happy. This morning, however, he was distinctly depressed."

"You mean the guy was nuts?" Warden Garrity asked hopefully.

"He was nothing of the sort," Malone said indignantly. Just let a hint get around that Paul Palmer had been of unsound mind, and he'd never collect that five thousand dollar fee from the estate. "He was saner than anyone in this room, with the possible exception of myself."

Dr. Dickson shrugged his shoulders. "I didn't suggest that he was insane. I only meant he was subject to moods."

Malone wheeled to face the doctor. "Say. Were you in the habit of visiting Palmer in his cell a couple of times a day?"

"I was," the doctor said, nodding. "He was suffering from a serious nervous condition. It was necessary to administer sedatives from time to time."

Malone snorted. "You mean he was suffering from the effect of being sober for the first time since he was sixteen."

"Put it any way you like," Dr. Dickson said pleasantly. "You remember, too, that I had a certain personal interest."

"That's right," Malone said slowly. "He was going to marry your niece."

"No one was happier than I to hear about the new trial," the doctor said. He caught Malone's eye and added, "No, I wasn't fond enough of him to smuggle in a rope. Especially when he'd just been granted a chance to clear himself."

"Look here," Warden Garrity said irritably. "I can't sit around listening to all this stuff. I've got to report the result of an investigation. Where the hell did he get that rope?"

There was a little silence, and then one of the guards said, "Maybe from the guy who was let in to see him last night."

"What guy?" the warden snapped.

"Why—" The guard paused, confused. "He had an

order from you, admitting him. His name was La Cerra."

Malone felt a sudden tingling along his spine. Georgie La Cerra was one of Max Hook's boys. What possible connection could there be between Paul Palmer, socialite, and the big gambling boss?

Warden Garrity had recognized the name too. "Oh yes," he said quickly. "That must have been it. But I doubt if we could prove it." He paused just an instant, and looked fixedly at Malone, as though daring him to speak. "The report will read that Paul Palmer obtained a rope, by means which have not yet been ascertained, and committed suicide while of unsound mind."

Malone opened his mouth and shut it again. He knew when he was licked. Temporarily licked, anyway. "For the love of mike," he said, "leave out the unsound mind."

"I'm afraid that's impossible," the warden said coldly.

Malone had kept his temper as long as he could. "All right," he said, "but I'll start an investigation that'll be a pip." He snorted. "Letting a gangster smuggle a rope in to a guy in the death house!" He glared at Dr. Dickson. "And you, foxy, with two escapes from the prison hospital in six months." He kicked the wastebasket again, this time sending it halfway across the room. "I'll show you from investigations! And I'm just the guy who can do it, too."

Dr. Dickson said quickly, "We'll substitute 'temporarily depressed' for the 'unsound mind.' "

But Malone was mad, now. He made one last, loud comment regarding the warden's personal life and probably immoral origin, and slammed the door so hard when he went out that the steel engraving of Chester A. Arthur over the warden's desk shattered to the floor.

"Mr. Malone," Bowers said in a low voice as they went down the hall, "I searched that cell, after they took the body out. Whoever smuggled in that rope smuggled in a letter, too. I found it hid in his mattress, and it wasn't there yesterday because the mattress was changed." He paused, and added, "And the rope couldn't of been there last night either, because there was no place he could of hid it."

Malone glanced at the envelope the guard held out to him—pale-gray expensive stationery, with "Paul Palmer" written across the front of it in delicate, curving handwriting.

"I haven't any money with me," the lawyer said.

Bowers shook his head. "I don't want no dough. But there's gonna be an assistant warden's job open in about three weeks."

"You'll get it," Malone said. He took the envelope and stuffed it in an inside pocket. Then he paused, frowned, and finally added, "And keep your eyes open and your mouth shut. Because there's going to be an awful stink when I prove Paul Palmer was murdered."

The pretty, black-haired girl in Malone's anteroom looked up as he opened the door. "Oh, Mr. Malone," she said quickly. "I read about it in the paper. I'm so sorry."

"Never mind, Maggie," the lawyer said. "No use crying over spilled clients." He went into his private office and shut the door.

Fate was treating him very shabbily, evidently from some obscure motive of personal spite. He'd been counting heavily on that five thousand buck fee.

He took a bottle of rye out of the filing cabinet marked "Personal," poured himself a drink, noted that there was only one more left in the bottle, and stretched out on the worn red-leather davenport to think things over.

Paul Palmer had been an amiable, stupid young drunk of good family, whose inherited wealth had been held in trust for him by an uncle considered to be the stingiest man in Chicago. The money was to be turned over to him on his thirtieth birthday—some five years off—or on the death of the uncle, Carter Brown. Silly arrangement, Malone reflected, but rich men's lawyers were always doing silly things.

Uncle Carter had cramped the young man's style considerably, but he'd managed pretty well. Then he'd met Madelaine Starr.

Malone lit a cigar and stared dreamily through the smoke. The Starrs were definitely social, but without money. A good keen eye for graft, too. Madelaine's uncle was probably making a very good thing out of that political appointment as prison doctor.

Malone sighed, wished he weren't a lawyer, and thought about Madelaine Starr. An orphan, with a tiny income which she augmented by modeling in an exclusive dress shop—a fashionable and acceptable way of making a living. She had expensive tastes. (The little lawyer could spot expensive tastes in girls a mile away.)

She'd had to be damned poor to want to marry Palmer, Malone reflected, and damned beautiful to get him. Well, she was both.

But there had been another girl, one who had to be paid off. Lillian Claire by name, and a very lovely hunk of girl, too. Lovely, and smart enough to demand a sizable piece of money for letting the Starr-Palmer nuptials go through without a scandalous fuss.

Malone shook his head sadly. It had looked bad at the trial. Paul Palmer had taken his bride-to-be nightclubbing, delivering her back to her kitchenette apartment just before twelve. He'd been a shade high, then, and by the time he'd stopped off at three or four bars, he was several shades higher. Then he'd paid a visit to Lillian Claire, who claimed later at the trial that he'd attempted—unsuccessfully—to talk her out of the large piece of cash money, and had drunk up all the whiskey in the house. She'd put him in a cab and sent him home.

No one knew just when Paul Palmer had arrived at the big, gloomy apartment he shared with Carter Brown. The manservant had the night off. It was the manservant who discovered, next morning, that Uncle Carter had been shot neatly through the forehead with Paul Palmer's gun, and that Paul Palmer had climbed into his own bed, fully dressed, and was snoring drunk.

Everything had been against him, Malone reflected sadly. Not only had the jury been composed of hardworking, poverty-stricken men who liked nothing better than to convict a rich young wastrel of murder, but worse still, they'd all been too honest to be bribed. The trial had been his most notable failure. And now, this.

But Paul Palmer would never have hanged himself. Malone was sure of it. He'd never lost hope. And now, especially, when a new trial had been granted, he'd have wanted to live.

It had been murder. But how had it been done?

Malone sat up, stretched, reached in his pocket for the pale-gray envelope Bowers had given him, and read the note through again.

> *My dearest Paul:*
>
> I'm getting this note to you this way because I'm in terrible trouble and danger. I need you—no one else can help me. I know there's to be a new trial, but even another week may be too late. Isn't there *any* way?
>
> Your own
>
> *M.*

"M," Malone decided, would be Madelaine Starr. She'd use that kind of pale-gray paper, too.

He looked at the note and frowned. If Madelaine Starr had smuggled that note to her lover, would she have smuggled in a rope by the same messenger? Or had someone else brought in the rope?

There were three people he wanted to see. Madelaine Starr was one. Lillian Claire was the second. And Max Hook was the third.

He went out into the anteroom, stopped halfway across it and said aloud, "But it's a physical impossibility. If someone smuggled that rope into Paul Palmer's cell and then Palmer hanged himself, it isn't murder. But it must have been murder." He stared at Maggie without seeing her. "Damn it, though, no one could have got into Paul Palmer's cell and hanged him."

Maggie looked at him sympathetically, familiar from long experience with her employer's processes of thought. "Keep on thinking and it'll come to you."

"Maggie, have you got any money?"

"I have ten dollars, but you can't borrow it. Besides, you haven't paid my last week's salary yet."

The little lawyer muttered something about ungrateful and heartless wenches, and flung himself out of the office.

Something had to be done about ready cash. He ran his mind over a list of prospective lenders. The only possibility was Max Hook. No, the last time he'd borrowed money from the Hook, he'd got into no end of trouble. Besides, he was going to ask another kind of favor from the gambling boss.

Malone went down Washington Street, turned the corner, went into Joe the Angel's City Hall Bar, and cornered its proprietor at the far end of the room.

"Cash a hundred dollar check for me, and hold it until a week from—" Malone made a rapid mental calculation— "Thursday?"

"Sure," Joe the Angel said. "Happy to do you a favor." He got out ten ten-dollar bills while Malone wrote the check. "Want I should take your bar bill out of this?"

Malone shook his head. "I'll pay next week. And add a double rye to it."

As he set down the empty glass, he heard the colored janitor's voice coming faintly from the back room.

"They hanged him for the thing you done,
*   You knew it was a sin,*
*   You didn't know his heart could break—"*

The voice stopped suddenly. For a moment Malone considered calling for the singer and asking to hear the whole thing, all the way through. No, there wasn't time for it now. Later, perhaps. He went out on the street, humming the tune.

What was it Paul Palmer had whispered in that last moment? *"It wouldn't break!"* Malone scowled. He had a curious feeling that there was some connection between those words and the words of that damned song. Or was it his Irish imagination, tripping him up again? *"You didn't know his heart could break."* But it was Paul Palmer's neck that had been broken.

Malone hailed a taxi and told the driver to take him to the swank Lake Shore Drive apartment-hotel where Max Hook lived.

The gambling boss was big in two ways. He took in a cut from every crooked gambling device in Cook County, and most of the honest ones. And he was a mountain of flesh, over six feet tall and three times too fat for his height. His pink head was completely bald and he had the expression of a pleased cherub.

His living room was a masterpiece of the gilt-and-brocade school of interior decoration, marred only by a huge, battle-scarred rolltop desk in one corner. Max Hook swung around from the desk to smile cordially at the lawyer.

"How delightful to see you! What will you have to drink?"

"Rye," Malone said, "and it's nice to see you too. Only this isn't exactly a social call."

He knew better, though, than to get down to business before the drinks had arrived. (Max Hook stuck to pink champagne.) That wasn't the way Max Hook liked to do things. But when the rye was down, and the gambling boss had lighted a slender, tinted (and, Malone suspected, perfumed) cigarette in a rose-quartz holder, he plunged right in.

"I suppose you read in the papers about what happened to my client, Palmer," he said.

"I never read the papers," Max Hook told him, "but one of my boys informed me. Tragic, wasn't it?"

"Tragic is no name for it," Malone said bitterly. "He hadn't paid me a dime."

Max Hook's eyebrows lifted. "So?" Automatically he reached for the green metal box in the left-hand drawer. "How much do you need?"

"No, no," Malone said hastily, "that isn't it. I just want to know if one of your boys—Little Georgie La Cerra—smuggled the rope in to him. That's all."

Max Hook looked surprised, and a little hurt. "My dear Malone," he said at last, "why do you imagine he'd do such a thing?"

"For money," Malone said promptly, "if he did do it. I don't care, I just want to know."

"You can take my word for it," Max Hook said, "he did nothing of the kind. He did deliver a note from a certain young lady to Mr. Palmer, at my request—a bit of a nuisance, too, getting hold of that admittance order signed by the warden. I assure you, though, there was no rope. I give you my word, and you know I'm an honest man."

"Well, I was just asking," Malone said. One thing about the big gangster, he always told the truth. If he said Little Georgie La Cerra hadn't smuggled in that rope, then Little Georgie hadn't. Nor was there any chance that Little Georgie had engaged in private enterprises on the side. As Max Hook often remarked, he liked to keep a careful watch on his boys. "One thing more, though," the lawyer said, "if you don't mind. Why did the young lady come to you to get her note delivered?"

Max Hook shrugged his enormous shoulders. "We have a certain—business connection. To be exact, she owes me a large sum of money. Like most extremely mercenary people she loves gambling, but she is not particularly lucky. When she told me that the only chance for that money to be paid was for the note to be delivered, naturally I obliged."

"Naturally," Malone agreed. "You didn't happen to know what was in the note, did you?"

Max Hook was shocked. "My dear Malone! You don't think I read other people's personal mail!"

No, Malone reflected, Max Hook probably didn't. And not having read the note, the big gambler probably wouldn't know what kind of "terrible trouble and danger" Madelaine Starr was in. He decided to ask, though, just to be on the safe side.

"Trouble?" Max Hook repeated after him. "No, outside of having her fiancé condemned to death, I don't know of any trouble she's in."

Malone shrugged his shoulders at the reproof, rose and walked to the door. Then he paused, suddenly. "Listen, Max. Do you know the words to a tune that goes like this?" He hummed a bit of it.

Max Hook frowned, then nodded. "Mmm—I know the tune. An entertainer at one of my places used to sing it." He thought hard, and finally came up with a few lines.

"He was leaning against the prison bars,
Dressed up in his new prison clothes—"

"Sorry," Max Hook said at last, "that's all I remember. I guess those two lines stuck in my head because they reminded me of the first time I was in jail."

Outside in the taxi, Malone sang the two lines over a couple of times. If he kept on, eventually he'd have the whole song. But Paul Palmer hadn't been leaning against the prison bars. He'd been hanging from the water pipe.

Damn and double damn that song!

It was well past eight o'clock, and he'd had no dinner, but he didn't feel hungry. He had a grim suspicion that he wouldn't feel hungry until he'd settled this business. When the cab paused for the next red light, he flipped a coin to decide whether he'd call first on Madelaine Starr or Lillian Claire, and Madelaine won.

He stepped out of the cab in front of the small apartment building on Walton Place, paid the driver, and started across the sidewalk just as a tall, white-haired man emerged from the door. Malone recognized Orlo Featherstone, the lawyer handling Paul Palmer's estate, considered ducking out of sight, realized there wasn't time, and finally managed to look as pleased as he was surprised.

"I was just going to offer Miss Starr my condolences," he said.

"I'd leave her undisturbed, if I were you," Orlo Featherstone said coldly. He had only one conception of what a lawyer should be, and Malone wasn't anything like it. "I only called myself because I am, so to speak and in a sense, a second father to her."

If anyone else had said that, Malone thought, it would have called for an answer. From Orlo Featherstone, it sounded natural. He nodded sympathetically and said, "Then I won't bother her." He tossed away a ragged cigar and said, "Tragic affair, wasn't it?"

Orlo Featherstone unbent at least half a degree. "Distinctly so. Personally, I cannot imagine Paul Palmer doing such a thing. When I visited him yesterday, he seemed quite cheerful and full of hope."

"You—visited him yesterday?" Malone asked casually. He drew a cigar from his pocket and began unwrapping it with exquisite care.

"Yes," Featherstone said, "about the will. He had to sign it, you know. Fortunate for her," he indicated Madelaine Starr with a gesture toward the building, "that he did so. He left her everything, of course."

"Of course," Malone said. He lighted his cigar on the second try. "You don't think Paul Palmer could have been murdered, do you?"

"Murdered!" Orlo Featherstone repeated, as though it was an obscene word. "Absurd! No Palmer has ever been murdered."

Malone watched him climb into a shiny 1928 Rolls-Royce, then started walking briskly toward State Street. The big limousine passed him just as he reached the corner; it turned north on State Street and stopped. Malone paused by the newsstand long enough to see Mr. Orlo Featherstone get out and cross the sidewalk to the corner drugstore. After a moment's thought he followed and paused at the cigar counter, from where he could see clearly into the adjacent telephone booth.

Orlo Featherstone, in the booth, consulted a little notebook. Then he took down the receiver, dropped a nickel in the slot, and began dialing. Malone watched carefully. D-E-L–9-6-0— It was Lillian Claire's number.

The little lawyer cursed all soundproof phone booths, and headed for a bar on the opposite corner. He felt definitely unnerved.

After a double rye, and halfway through a second one, he came to the heartening conclusion that when he visited Lillian Claire, later in the evening, he'd be able to coax from her the reason why Orlo Featherstone, of all people, had telephoned her, just after leaving the late Paul Palmer's fiancée. A third rye braced him for his call on the fiancée herself.

Riding up in the self-service elevator to her apartment, another heartening thought came to him. If Madelaine Starr was going to inherit all the Palmer dough—then it might not be such a trick to collect his five thousand bucks. He might even be able to collect it by a week from Thursday.

And he reminded himself, as she opened the door, this was going to be one time when he wouldn't be a sucker for a pretty face.

Madelaine Starr's apartment was tiny, but tasteful. Almost too tasteful, Malone thought. Everything in it was cheap, but perfectly correct and in exactly the right place, even to the Van Gogh print over the midget fireplace. Madelaine Starr was in exactly the right taste, too.

She was a tall girl, with a figure that still made Malone blink, in spite of the times he'd admired it in the courtroom. Her bronze-brown hair was smooth and well-brushed, her pale face was calm and composed. Serene, polished, suave. Malone had a private idea that if he made a pass at her, she wouldn't scream. She was wearing black rayon house-pajamas. He wondered if they were her idea of mourning.

Malone got the necessary condolences and trite remarks out of the way fast, and then said, "What kind of terrible trouble and danger are you in, Miss Starr?"

That startled her. She wasn't able to come up with anything more original than "What do you mean?"

"I mean what you wrote in your note to Paul Palmer," the lawyer said.

She looked at the floor and said, "I hoped it had been destroyed."

"It will be," Malone said gallantly, "if you say so."

"Oh," she said. "Do you have it with you?"

"No," Malone lied. "It's in my office safe. But I'll go back there and burn it." He didn't add when.

"It really didn't have anything to do with his death, you know," she said.

Malone said, "Of course not. You didn't send him the rope too, did you?"

She stared at him. "How awful of you."

"I'm sorry," Malone said contritely.

She relaxed. "I'm sorry too. I didn't mean to snap at you. I'm a little unnerved, naturally." She paused. "May I offer you a drink?"

"You may," Malone said, "and I'll take it."

He watched her while she mixed a lot of scotch and a little soda in two glasses, wondering how soon after her fiancé's death he could safely ask her for a date. Maybe she wouldn't say yes to a broken-down criminal lawyer, though. He took the drink, downed half of it, and said to himself indignantly, "Who's broken-down?"

"Oh, Mr. Malone," she breathed, "you don't believe my note had anything to do with it?"

"Of course not," Malone said. "That note would have made him want to live, and get out of jail." He considered bringing up the matter of his five thousand dollar fee, and then decided this was not the time. "Nice that you'll be able to pay back what you owe Max Hook. He's a bad man to owe money to."

She looked at him sharply and said nothing. Malone finished his drink, and walked to the door.

"One thing, though," he said, hand on the knob. "This —terrible trouble and danger you're in. You'd better tell me. Because I might be able to help, you know."

"Oh, no," she said. She was standing very close to him, and her perfume began to mingle dangerously with the rye and scotch in his brain. "I'm afraid not." He had a definite impression that she was thinking fast. "No one can help, now." She looked away, delicately. "You know—a girl— alone in the world—"

Malone felt his cheeks reddening. He opened the door and said, "Oh." Just plain oh.

"Just a minute," she said quickly. "Why did you ask all these questions?"

"Because," Malone said, just as quickly, "I thought the answers might be useful—in case Paul Palmer was murdered."

That, he told himself, riding down the self-service elevator, would give her something to think about.

He hailed a cab and gave the address of the apartment building where Lillian Claire lived, on Goethe Street. In the lobby of the building he paused long enough to call a certain well-known politician at his home and make sure that he was there. It would be just as well not to run into that particular politician at Lillian Claire's apartment, since he was paying for it.

It was a nice apartment, too, Malone decided, as the slim mulatto maid ushered him in. Big, soft modernistic divans and chairs, paneled mirrors, and a built-in bar. Not half as nice, though, as Lillian Claire herself.

She was a cuddly little thing, small, and a bit on the plump side, with curly blond hair and a deceptively simple stare. She said, "Oh, Mr. Malone, I've always wanted a chance to get acquainted with you." Malone had a pleasant feeling that if he tickled her, just a little, she'd giggle.

She mixed him a drink, lighted his cigar, sat close to him on the biggest and most luxurious divan, and said, "Tell me, how on earth did Paul Palmer get that rope?"

"I don't know," Malone said. "Did you send it to him, baked in a cake?"

She looked at him reprovingly. "You don't think I wanted him to kill himself and let that awful woman inherit all that money?"

Malone said, "She isn't so awful. But this is tough on you, though. Now you'll never be able to sue him."

"I never intended to," she said. "I didn't want to be paid off. I just thought it might scare her away from him."

Malone put down his glass, she hopped up and refilled it. "Were you in love with him?" he said.

"Don't be silly." She curled up beside him again. "I liked him. He was much too nice to have someone like that marry him for his money."

Malone nodded slowly. The room was beginning to swim—not unpleasantly—before his eyes. Maybe he should have eaten dinner after all.

"Just the same," he said, "you didn't think that idea up all by yourself. Somebody put you up to asking for money."

She pulled away from him a little—not too much. "That's perfect nonsense," she said unconvincingly.

"All right," Malone said agreeably. "Tell me just one thing—"

"I'll tell you this one thing," she said. "Paul never murdered his uncle. I don't know who did, but it wasn't Paul. Because I took him home that night. He came to see me, yes. But I didn't put him in a cab and send him home. I took him home, and got him to his own room. Nobody saw me. It was late—almost daylight." She paused and lit a cigarette. "I peeked into his uncle's room to make sure I hadn't been seen, and his uncle was dead. I never told anybody because I didn't want to get mixed up in it worse than I was already."

Malone sat bolt upright. "Fine thing," he said, indignantly and a bit thickly. "You could have alibied him and you let him be convicted."

"Why bother?" she said serenely. "I knew he had you for a lawyer. Why would he need an alibi?"

Malone shoved her back against the cushions of the davenport and glared at her. "A'right," he said. "But that wasn't the thing I was gonna ask. Why did old man Featherstone call you up tonight?"

Her shoulders stiffened under his hands. "He just asked me for a dinner date," she said.

"You're a liar," Malone said, not unpleasantly. He ran an experimental finger along her ribs. She did giggle. Then he kissed her.

All this time spent, Malone told himself reprovingly, and you haven't learned one thing worth the effort. Paul Palmer hadn't killed his uncle. But he'd been sure of that all along, and anyway it wouldn't do any good now. Madelaine Starr needed money, and now she was going to inherit a lot of it. Orlo Featherstone was on friendly terms with Lillian Claire.

The little lawyer leaned his elbows on the table and rested his head on his hands. At three o'clock in the morning, Joe the Angel's was a desolate and almost deserted place. He knew now, definitely, that he should have eaten dinner. Nothing, he decided, would cure the way he felt except a quick drink, a long sleep, or sudden death.

He would probably never learn who had killed Paul Palmer's uncle, or why. He would probably never learn what had happened to Paul Palmer. After all, the man had hanged himself. No one else could have got into that cell. It wasn't murder to give a man enough rope to hang himself with.

No, he would probably never learn what had happened to Paul Palmer, and he probably would never collect that five thousand dollar fee. But there was one thing that he could do. He'd learn the words of that song.

He called for a drink, the janitor, and the janitor's guitar. Then he sat back and listened.

> *"As I passed by the ol' State's prison,*
> *Ridin' on a steam-line' train—"*

It was a long, rambling ballad, requiring two drinks for the janitor and two more for Malone. The lawyer listened, remembering a line here and there.

> *"When they hanged him in the mornin',*
>   *His last words were for you,*
> *Then the sheriff took his shiny knife*
>   *An' cut that ol' rope through."*

A sad story, Malone reflected, finishing the second drink. Personally, he'd have preferred "My Wild Irish Rose" right now. But he yelled to Joe for another drink, and went on listening.

> *"They hanged him for the thing you done,*
>   *You knew it was a sin,*
> *How well you knew his heart could break,*
>   *Lady, why did you turn him in—"*

The little lawyer jumped to his feet. That was the line he'd been trying to remember! And what had Paul Palmer whispered? *"It wouldn't break."*

Malone knew, now.

He dived behind the bar, opened the cash drawer, and scooped out a handful of telephone slugs.

"You're drunk," Joe the Angel said indignantly.

"That may be," Malone said happily, "and it's a good idea too. But I know what I'm doing."

He got one of the slugs into the phone on the third try, dialed Orlo Featherstone's number, and waited till the elderly lawyer got out of bed and answered the phone.

It took ten minutes, and several more phone slugs to convince Featherstone that it was necessary to get Madelaine Starr out of bed and make the three-hour drive to the State's prison, right now. It took another ten minutes to wake up Lillian Claire and induce her to join the party. Then he placed a long-distance call to the sheriff of Statesville County and invited him to drop in at the prison and pick up a murderer.

Malone strode to the door. As he reached it, Joe the Angel hailed him.

"I forgot," he said, "I got sumpin' for you." Joe the Angel rummaged back of the cash register and brought out a long envelope. "That cute secretary of yours was looking for you all over town to give you this. Finally she left it with me. She knew you'd get here sooner or later."

Malone said, "Thanks," took the envelope, glanced at it, and winced. "First National Bank." Registered mail. He knew he was overdrawn, but—

Oh, well, maybe there was still a chance to get that five thousand bucks.

The drive to Statesville wasn't so bad, in spite of the fact that Orlo Featherstone snored most of the way. Lillian snuggled up against Malone's left shoulder like a kitten, and with his right hand he held Madelaine Starr's hand under the auto robe. But the arrival, a bit before seven A.M., was depressing. The prison looked its worst in the early morning, under a light fog.

Besides, the little lawyer wasn't happy over what he had to do.

Warden Garrity's office was even more depressing. There was the warden, eyeing Malone coldly and belligerently, and Madelaine Starr and her uncle, Dr. Dickson, looking a bit annoyed. Orlo Featherstone was frankly skeptical. The sheriff of Statesville County was sleepy and bored, Lillian Claire was sleepy and suspicious. Even the guard, Bowers, looked bewildered.

And all these people, Malone realized, were waiting for him to pull a rabbit out of his whiskers.

He pulled it out fast. "Paul Palmer was murdered," he said flatly. Warden Garrity looked faintly amused. "A bunch of pixies crawled in his cell and tied the rope around his neck?"

"No," Malone said, lighting a cigar. "This murderer made one try—murder by frame-up. He killed Paul Palmer's uncle for two reasons, one of them being to send Paul Palmer to the chair. It nearly worked. Then I got him a new trial. So another method had to be tried, fast, and that one did work."

"You're insane," Orlo Featherstone said. "Palmer hanged himself."

"I'm not insane," Malone said indignantly, "I'm drunk. There's a distinction. And Paul Palmer hanged himself because he thought he wouldn't die, and could escape from prison." He looked at Bowers and said, "Watch all these people, someone may make a move."

Lillian Claire said, "I don't get it."

"You will," Malone promised. He kept a watchful eye on Bowers and began talking fast. "The whole thing was arranged by someone who was mercenary and owed money. Someone who knew Paul Palmer would be too drunk to know what had happened the night his uncle was killed, and who was close enough to him to have a key to the apartment. That person went in and killed the uncle with Paul Palmer's gun. And, as that person had planned, Paul Palmer was tried and convicted and would have been electrocuted, if he hadn't had a damn smart lawyer."

He flung his cigar into the cuspidor and went on, "Then Paul Palmer was granted a new trial. So the mercenary person who wanted Paul Palmer's death convinced him that he had to break out of prison, and another person showed him how the escape could be arranged—by pretending to hang himself, and being moved to the prison hospital— *watch her, Bowers!*"

Madelaine Starr had flung herself at Dr. Dickson. "Damn you," she screamed, her face white. "I knew you'd break down and talk. But you'll never talk again—"

There were three shots. One from the little gun Madelaine had carried in her pocket, and two from Bowers's service revolver.

Then the room was quite still.

Malone walked slowly across the room, looked down at the two bodies, and shook his head sadly. "Maybe it's just as well," he said. "They'd probably have hired another defense lawyer anyway."

"This is all very fine," the Statesville County sheriff said. "But I still don't see how you figured it. Have another beer?"

"Thanks," Malone said. "It was easy. A song tipped me off. Know this?" He hummed a few measures.

"Oh, sure," the sheriff said. "The name of it is 'The Statesville Prison.' " He sang the first four verses.

"Well, I'll be double-damned," Malone said. The bartender put the two glasses of beer on the table. "Bring me a double gin for a chaser," the lawyer told him.

"Me too," the sheriff said. "What does the song have to do with it, Malone?"

Malone said, "It was the crank on the adding machine, pal. Know what I mean? You put down a lot of stuff to add up and nothing happens, and then somebody turns the crank and it all adds up to what you want to know. See how simple it is?"

"I don't," the sheriff said, "but go on."

"I had all the facts," Malone said, "I knew everything I needed to know, but I couldn't add it up. I needed one thing, that one thing." He spoke almost reverently, downing his gin. "Paul Palmer said *'It wouldn't break'*—just before he died. And he looked terribly surprised. For a long time, I didn't know what he meant. Then I heard that song again, and I did know." He sang a few lines. *"The sheriff took his shiny knife, and cut that ol' rope through."* Then he finished his beer, and sang on, *"They hanged him for the thing you done, you knew it was a sin. You didn't know his heart could break, Lady, why did you turn him in?"* He ended on a blue note.

"Very pretty," the sheriff said. "Only I heard it, *'You knew that his poor heart could break.'* "

"Same thing," Malone said, waving a hand. "Only, that song was what turned the crank on the adding machine. When I heard it again, I knew what Palmer meant by *'It wouldn't break.'* "

"His heart?" the sheriff said helpfully.

"No," Malone said, "the rope."

He waved at the bartender and said, "Two more of the same." Then to the sheriff, "He expected the rope to break.

He thought it would be artfully frayed so that he would drop to the floor unharmed. Then he could have been moved to the prison hospital—from which there had been two escapes in the past six months. He had to escape, you see, because his sweetheart had written him that she was in terrible trouble and danger—the same sweetheart whose evidence had helped convict him at the trial.

"Madelaine Starr wanted his money," Malone went on, "but she didn't want Paul. So her murder of his uncle served two purposes. It released Paul's money, and it framed him. Using poor old innocent Orlo Featherstone, she planted in Lillian Claire's head the idea of holding up Paul for money, so Paul would be faced with a need for ready cash. Everything worked fine, until I gummixed up the whole works by getting my client a new trial."

"Your client shouldn't of had such a smart lawyer," the sheriff said, over his beer glass.

Malone tossed aside the compliment with a shrug of his cigar. "Maybe he should of had a better one. Anyway, she and her uncle, Dr. Dickson, fixed it all up. She sent that note to Paul, so he'd think he had to break out of the clink. Then her uncle, Dickson, told Paul he'd arrange the escape, with the rope trick. To the world, it would have looked as though Paul Palmer had committed suicide in a fit of depression. Only he did have a good lawyer, and he lived long enough to say *'It wouldn't break.'* "

Malone looked into his empty glass and lapsed into a melancholy silence.

The phone rang—someone hijacked a truck over on the Springfield Road—and the sheriff was called away. Left by himself, Malone cried a little into his beer. Lillian Claire had gone back to Chicago with Orlo Featherstone, who really had called her up for a date, and no other reason.

Malone reminded himself he hadn't had any sleep, his head was splitting, and what was left of Joe the Angel's hundred dollars would just take him back to Chicago. And there was that letter from the bank, probably threatening a summons. He took it out of his pocket and sighed as he tore it open.

"Might as well face realities," Malone said to the bartender. "And bring me another double gin."

He drank the gin, tore open the envelope, and took out a certified check for five thousand dollars, with a note from the bank to the effect that Paul Palmer had directed its payment. It was dated the day before his death.

Malone waltzed to the door, waltzed back to pay the bartender and kiss him good-bye.

"Do you feel all right?" the bartender asked anxiously.

"All right!" Malone said. "I'm a new man!"

What was more, he'd just remembered the rest of that song. He sang it, happily, as he went up the street toward the railroad station.

> *"As I passed by the ol' State's prison,*
> *Ridin' on a stream-line' train*
> *I waved my hand, and said out loud,*
> *I'm never comin' back again,*
> *I'm never comin' back a—gain!"*

CHINOISERIE

Helen McCloy

Chinoiserie, *according to* Webster's Dictionary, *means "a style in art reflecting Chinese qualities or motifs"; and "Chinoiserie" is just that—a piece of intricately made literary art set in Victorian China, rich in imagery and suspense, which tells the tale of the disappearance of Olga Kyrilovna in the heart of Old Pekin. It is one of Helen McCloy's finest stories, and that is high praise indeed. During her forty years as a writer, critic, and editor, Ms. McCloy has published many novels and short stories of considerable merit and wide critical acclaim. She is the creator of the first psychiatrist detective, Dr. Basil Willing, and was the first mystery writer to use psychiatry in solving fictional crimes* (The Goblin Market, Through a Glass, Darkly, Two-Thirds of a Ghost). *She has written a number of first-rate psychological thrillers as well, among these* Before I Die *(1963) and* A Change of Heart *(1973).*

This is the story of Olga Kyrilovna and how she disappeared in the heart of Old Pekin.

Not Peiping, with its American drugstore on Hatamen Street. Pekin, capital of the Manchu Empire. Didn't you know that I used to be language clerk at the legation there? Long ago. Long before the Boxer Uprising. Oh, yes, I was young. So young I was in love with Olga Kyrilovna . . . Will you pour the brandy for me? My hand's grown shaky the last few years. . . .

When the nine great gates of the Tartar City swung to at sunset, we were locked for the night inside a walled, medieval citadel, reached by camel over the Gobi or by boat up the Pei-ho, defended by bow and arrow and a painted representation of cannon. An Arabian Nights' city where the nine gate towers on the forty-foot walls were just ninety-nine feet high so they would not impede the flight of air spirits. Where palace eunuchs kept harems of their own to "save face." Where musicians were blinded because the use of the eye destroys the subtlety of the ear. Where physicians prescribed powdered jade and tigers' claws for anemia brought on by malnutrition. Where mining operations were dangerous because they opened the veins of the Earth Dragon. Where felons were slowly sliced to death and beggars were found frozen to death in the streets every morning in the winter.

It was into this world of fantasy and fear that Olga Kyrilovna vanished as completely as if she had dissolved into one of the air spirits or ridden away on one of the invisible dragons that our Chinese servants saw in the atmosphere all around us.

It happened the night of a New Year's Eve ball at the Japanese Legation.

When I reached the Russian Legation for dinner, a Cossack of the Escort took me into a room that was once a Tartar general's audience hall. Two dozen candle flames hardly pierced the bleak dusk. The fire in the brick stove barely dulled the cutting edge of a North China winter. I chafed my hands, thinking myself alone. Someone stirred and sighed in the shadows. It was she.

Olga Kyrilovna . . . How can I make you see her as I saw her that evening? She was pale in her white dress against walls of tarnished gilt and rusted vermilion. Two smooth, shining wings of light brown hair. An oval face, pure in line, delicate in color. And, of course, unspoiled by modern cosmetics. Her eyes were blue. Dreaming eyes. She seemed to live and move in a waking dream, remote from the enforced intimacies of our narrow society. More than one man had tried vainly to wake her from that dream. The piquancy of her situation provoked men like Lucien de l'Orges, the French Chargé.

She was just seventeen, fresh from the convent of Smolny. Volgorughi had been Russian Minister in China for many years. After his last trip to Petersburg, he had brought Olga back to Pekin as his bride, and . . . Well, he was three times her age.

That evening she spoke first. "Monsieur Charley . . ."

Even at official meetings the American Minister called me "Charley." Most Europeans assumed it was my last name.

"I'm glad you are here," she went on in French, our only common language. "I was beginning to feel lonely. And afraid."

"Afraid?" I repeated stupidly. "Of what?"

A door opened. Candle flames shied and the startled shadows leaped up the walls. Volgorughi spoke from the doorway, coolly. "Olga, we are having sherry in the study. . . . Oh!" His voice warmed. "Monsieur Charley, I didn't see you. Good evening."

I followed Olga's filmy skirts into the study, conscious of Volgorughi's sharp glance as he stood aside to let me pass.

He always seemed rather formidable. In spite of his grizzled hair, he had the leanness of a young man and the carriage of a soldier. But he had the weary eyes of an old man. And the dry, shriveled hands, always cold to the touch, even in summer. A young man's imagination shrank from any mental image of those hands caressing Olga. . . .

In the smaller room it was warmer and brighter. Glasses of sherry and vodka had been pushed aside to make space on the table for a painting on silk. Brown, frail, desiccated as a dead leaf, the silk looked hundreds of years old. Yet the ponies painted on its fragile surface in faded pigments were the same lively Mongol ponies we still used for race meetings outside the city walls.

"The Chinese have no understanding of art," drawled Lucien de l'Orges. "Chinese porcelain is beginning to enjoy a certain vogue in Europe, but Chinese painters are impossible. In landscape they show objects on a flat surface, without perspective, as if the artist were looking down on the earth from a balloon. In portraits they draw the human face without shadows or thickness as untutored children do. The Chinese artist hasn't enough skill to imitate nature accurately."

Lucien was baiting Volgorughi. "Pekin temper" was as much a feature of our lives as "Pekin throat." We got on each other's nerves like a storm-stayed house party. An unbalanced party where men outnumbered women six to one.

Volgorughi kept his temper. "The Chinese artist doesn't care to 'imitate' nature. He prefers to suggest or symbolize what he sees."

"But Chinese art is heathen!" This was Sybil Carstairs, wife of the English Inspector-General of Maritime Customs. "How can heathen art equal art inspired by Christian morals?"

Her husband's objection was more practical: "You're wastin' money, Volgorughi. Two hundred Shanghai taels for a daub that will never fetch sixpence in any European market!"

Incredible? No. This was before Hirth and Fenollosa

made Chinese painting fashionable in the West. Years later I saw a fragment from Volgorughi's collection sold in the famous *Salle Six* of the Hôtel Drouot. While the *commissaire-priseur* was bawling, *"On demande quatre cent mille francs,"* I was seeing Olga again, pale in a white dress against a wall of gilt and vermilion in the light of shivering candle flames. . . .

Volgorughi turned to her just then. "Olga, my dear, you haven't any sherry." He smiled as he held out a glass. The brown wine turned to gold in the candlelight as she lifted it to her lips with an almost childish obedience.

I had not noticed little Kiada, the Japanese Minister, bending over the painting. Now he turned sleepy slant-eyes on Volgorughi and spoke blandly. "This is the work of Han Kan, greatest of horse painters. It must be the finest painting of the T'ang Dynasty now in existence."

"You think so, Count?" Volgorughi was amused. He seemed to be yielding to an irresistible temptation as he went on. "What would you say if I told you I knew of a T'ang painting infinitely finer—a landscape scroll by Wang Wei himself?"

Kiada's eyes lost their sleepy look. He had all his nation's respect for Chinese art, tinctured with jealousy of the older culture. "One hears rumors now and then that these fabulous masterpieces still exist, hidden away in the treasure chests of great Chinese families. But I have never seen an original Wang Wei."

"Who, or what, is Wang Wei?" Sybil sounded petulant.

Kiada lifted his glass of sherry to the light. "Madame, Wang Wei could place scenery extending to ten thousand *li* upon the small surface of a fan. He could paint cats that would keep any house free from mice. When his hour came to Pass Above, he did not die. He merely stepped through a painted doorway in one of his own landscapes and was never seen again. All these things indicate that his brush was guided by a god."

Volgorughi leaned across the table, looking at Kiada.

"What would you say if I told you that I had just added a Wang Wei to my collection?"

Kiada showed even, white teeth. "Nothing but respect for your Excellency's judgment could prevent my insisting that it was a copy by some lesser artist of the Yüän Dynasty—possible Chao Mēng Fu. An original Wang Wei could not be bought for money."

"Indeed?" Volgorughi unlocked a cabinet with a key he carried on his watch chain. He took something out and tossed it on the table like a man throwing down a challenge. It was a cylinder in an embroidered satin cover. Kiada peeled the cover and we saw a scroll on a roller of old milk-jade.

It was a broad ribbon of silk, once white, now ripened with great age to a mellow brown. A foot wide, sixteen feet long, painted lengthwise to show the course of a river. As it unrolled a stream of pure lapis, jade and turquoise hues flowed before my enchanted eyes, almost like a moving picture. Born in a bubbling spring, fed by waterfalls, the river wound its way among groves of tender, green bamboo, parks with dappled deer peeping through slender pine trees, cottages with curly roofs nestling among round hills, verdant meadows, fantastic cliffs, strange wind-distorted trees, rushes, wild geese and at last, a foam-flecked sea.

Kiada's face was a study. He whispered brokenly, "I can hear the wind sing in the rushes. I can hear the wail of the wild geese. Of Wang Wei truly is it written—his pictures were unspoken poems."

"And the color!" cried Volgorughi, ecstasy in his eyes.

Lucien's sly voice murmured in my ear. "A younger man, married to Olga Kyrilovna, would have no time for painting, Chinese or otherwise."

Volgorughi had Kiada by the arm. "This is no copy by Chao Mēng Fu! Look at that inscription on the margin. Can you read it?"

Kiada glanced—then stared. There was more than suspicion in the look he turned on Volgorughi. There was fear.

"I must beg your Excellency to excuse me. I do not read Chinese."

We were interrupted by a commotion in the compound. A gaunt Cossack, in full-skirted coat and sheepskin cap, was coming through the gate carrying astride his shoulders a young man, elegantly slim, in an officer's uniform. The Cossack knelt on the ground. The rider slipped lightly from his unconventional mount. He sauntered past the window and a moment later he was entering the study with a nonchalance just this side of insolence. To my amazement I saw that he carried a whip which he handed with his gloves to the Chinese boy who opened the door.

"Princess, your servant. Excellency, my apologies. I believe I'm late."

Volgorughi returned the greeting with the condescension of a Western Russian for an Eastern Russian—a former officer of *Chevaliers Gardes* for an obscure colonel of Oussurian Cossacks. Sometimes I wondered why such a bold adventurer as Alexei Andreitch Liakoff had been appointed Russian Military Attaché in Pekin. He was born in Tobolsk, where there is Tartar blood. His oblique eyes, high cheekbones and sallow, hairless skin lent color to his impudent claim of descent from Genghis Khan.

"Are Russian officers in the habit of using their men as saddle horses?" I muttered to Carstairs.

Alexei's quick ear caught the words. "It may become a habit with me." He seemed to relish my discomfiture. "I don't like Mongol ponies. A Cossack is just as surefooted. And much more docile."

Olga Kyrilovna roused herself to play hostess. "Sherry, Colonel Liakoff? Or vodka?"

"Vodka, if her Excellency pleases." Alexei's voice softened as he spoke to Olga. His eyes dwelt on her face gravely as he took the glass from her hand.

The ghost of mockery touched Volgorughi's lips. He despised vodka as a peasant's drink.

Alexei approached the table to set down his empty

glass. For the first time, his glance fell on the painting by Wang Wei. His glass crashed on the marble floor.

"You read Chinese, don't you?" Volgorughi spoke austerely. "Perhaps you can translate this inscription?"

Alexei put both hands wide apart on the table and leaned on them studying the ideographs. " 'Wang Wei.' And a date. The same as our A.D. 740."

"And the rest?" insisted Volgorughi.

Alexei looked at him. "Your Excellency really wishes me to read this? Aloud?"

"By all means."

Alexei went on. *"At an odd moment in summer I came across this painting of a river course by Wang Wei. Under its influence I sketched a spray of peach blossom on the margin as an expression of my sympathy for the artist and his profound and mysterious work. The Words of the Emperor. Written in the Lai Ching summerhouse, 1746."*

Kaida had been frightened when he looked at that inscription. Alexei was angry. Why I did not know.

Carstairs broke the silence. "I don't see anything mysterious about a picture of a river!"

"Everything about this picture is—mysterious." Kiada glanced at Volgorughi. "May one inquire how your Excellency obtained this incomparable masterpiece?"

"From a peddler in the Chinese City." Volgorughi's tone forbade further questions. Just then his Number One Boy announced dinner.

There was the usual confusion when we started for the ball at the Japanese Legation. Mongol ponies had to be blindfolded before they would let men in European dress mount and even then they were skittish. For this reason it was the custom for men to walk and for women to drive in hooded Pekin carts. But Sybil Carstairs always defied this convention, exclaiming, "Why should I be bumped black and blue in a springless cart just because I am a woman?" She and her husband were setting out on foot when Olga's little cart clattered into the compound driven by a Chinese groom. Kiada had gone on ahead to welcome his early guests. Volgorughi lifted Olga into the cart. She was quite helpless in a Siberian cloak of blue fox paws and clumsy Mongol socks of white felt over her dancing slippers. Her head drooped against Volgorughi's shoulder drowsily as he put her down in the cart. He drew the fur cloak around her in a gesture that seemed tenderly possessive. She lifted languid eyes.

"Isn't Lady Carstairs driving with me?"

"My dear, you know she never drives in a Pekin cart. You are not afraid?" Volgorughi smiled. "You will be quite safe, Olga Kyrilovna. I promise you that."

Her answering smile wavered. Then the hood hid her face from view as the cart rattled through the gateway.

Volgorughi and Lucien walked close behind Olga's cart. Alexei and I followed more slowly. Our Chinese lantern boys ran ahead of us in the darkness to light our way like the linkmen of medieval London. Streetlamps in Pekin were lighted only once a month—when the General of the Nine Gates made his rounds of inspection.

The lantern light danced down a long, empty lane winding between high, blank walls. A stinging Siberian wind threw splinters of sleet in my face. We hadn't the macadamized roads of the Treaty Ports. The frozen mud was hard and slippery as glass. I tried to keep to a ridge that ran down the middle of the road. My foot slipped and I stumbled down the slope into a foul gutter of sewage frozen solid. The lanterns turned a corner. I was alone with the black night and the icy wind.

I groped my way along the gutter, one hand against the wall. No stars, no moon, no lighted windows, no other pedestrians. My boot met something soft that yielded and squirmed. My voice croaked a question in Mandarin: "Is this the way to the Japanese Legation?" The answer came in singsong Cantonese. I understood only one word: "Alms . . ."

Like heaven itself, I saw a distant flicker of light coming

nearer. Like saints standing in the glow of their own halos I recognized Alexei and our lantern boys. "What happened?" Alexei's voice was taut. "I came back as soon as I missed you."

"Nothing. I fell. I was just asking this . . ."

Words died on my lips. Lantern light revealed the blunted lion-face, the eyeless sockets, the obscene, white stumps for hands—"mere corruption, swaddled man-wise." A leper. And I had been about to touch him.

Alexei's gaze followed mine to the beggar, hunched against the wall. "She is one of the worst I've ever seen."

"She?"

"I think it's a woman. Or, shall I say, it was a woman?" Alexei laughed harshly. "Shall we go on?"

We rounded the next corner before I recovered my voice. "These beggars aren't all as wretched as they seem, are they?"

"What put that idea into your head, Charley?"

"Something that happened last summer. We were in a market lane of the Chinese City—Sybil Carstairs and Olga Kyrilovna, Lucien and I. A beggar, squatting in the gutter, stared at us as if he had never seen Western men before. He looked like any other beggar—filthy, naked to the waist, with tattered blue trousers below. But his hands were toying with a little image carved in turquoise matrix. It looked old and valuable."

"He may have stolen it."

"It wasn't as simple as that," I retorted. "A man in silk rode up on a mule leading a white pony with a silver embroidered saddle. He called the beggar 'elder brother' and invited him to mount the pony. Then the two rode off together."

Alexei's black eyes glittered like jet beads in the lantern light. "Was the beggar the older of the two?"

"No. That's the queer part. The beggar was young. The man who called him 'elder brother' was old and dignified. . . . Some beggars at home have savings accounts. I suppose the same sort of thing could happen here."

Again Alexei laughed harshly. "Hold on to that idea, Charley, if it makes you feel more comfortable."

We came to a gate where lanterns clustered like a cloud of fireflies. A piano tinkled. In the compound, lantern boys were gathering outside the windows of a ballroom, tittering as they watched barbarian demons "jump" to Western music.

Characteristically, the Japanese Legation was the only European house in Pekin. Candle flames and crystal prisms. Wall mirrors and a polished parquet floor. The waltz from *Traviata*. The glitter of diamonds and gold braid. Punch *à la Romaine*.

"Where is Princess Volgorughi?" I asked Sybil Carstairs.

"Didn't she come with you and Colonel Liakoff?"

"No. Her cart followed you. We came afterward."

"Perhaps she's in the supper room." Sybil whirled off with little Kiada.

Volgorughi was standing in the doorway of the supper room with Lucien and Carstairs. "She'll be here in a moment," Carstairs was saying.

Alexei spoke over my shoulder. "Charley and I have just arrived. We did not pass her Excellency's cart on the way."

"Perhaps she turned back," said Lucien.

"In that case she would have passed us," returned Alexei. "Who was with her?"

Volgorughi's voice came out in a hoarse whisper. "Her groom and lantern boy. Both Chinese. But Kiada and the Carstairses were just ahead of her; Monsieur de l'Orges and I, just behind her."

"Not all the way," amended Lucien. "We took a wrong turning and got separated from each other in the dark. That was when we lost sight of her."

"My fault." Volgorughi's mouth twisted bitterly. "I was leading the way. And it was I who told her she would be— safe."

Again we breasted the wind to follow lanterns skimming before us like will o' the wisps. Vainly we strained our eyes through glancing lights and broken shadows. We met no one. We saw nothing. Not even a footprint or wheel rut on that frozen ground. Once something moaned in the void beyond the lights. It was only the leper.

At the gate of the Russian Legation, the Cossack guard sprang to attention. Volgorughi rapped out a few words in Russian. I knew enough to understand the man's reply. "The *baryna* has not returned, excellency. There has been no sign of her or her cart."

Volgorughi was shouting. Voices, footfalls, lights filled the compound. Alexei struck his forehead with his clenched hand. "Fool that I am! The leper!"

He walked so fast I could hardly keep up with him. The lantern boys were running. A Cossack came striding after us. Alexei halted at the top of the ridge. The leper had not moved. He spoke sharply in Mandarin. "Have you seen a cart?" No answer. "When she asked me for alms, she spoke Cantonese," I told him. He repeated his question in Cantonese. Both Volgorughi and Alexei spoke the southern dialects. All the rest of us were content to stammer Mandarin.

Still no answer. The Cossack stepped down into the gutter. His great boot prodded the shapeless thing that lay there. It toppled sidewise.

Alexei moved down the slope. "Lights!" The lanterns shuddered and came nearer. The handle of a knife protruded from the leper's left breast.

Alexei forced himself to drop on one knee beside that obscene corpse. He studied it intently, without touching it.

"Murdered . . . There are many knives like that in the Chinese City. Anyone might have used it—Chinese or European." He rose, brushing his knee with his gloved hand.

"Why?" I ventured.

"She couldn't see." His voice was judicious. "She must have heard—something."

"But what?"

Alexei's Asiatic face was inscrutable in the light from the paper lanterns.

* * *

Police? Extraterritorial law courts? That was Treaty Port stuff. Like pidgin English. We had only a few legation guards. No gunboats. No telegraph. No railway. The flying machine was a crank's daydream. Even cranks hadn't dreamed of a wireless telegraphy. . . . Dawn came. We were still searching. Olga Kyrilovna, her cart and pony, her groom and lantern boy, had all vanished without a trace as if they had never existed.

As character witnesses, the Chinese were baffling. "The Princess's groom was a Manchu of good character," Volgorughi's Number One Boy told us. "But her lantern boy was a Cantonese with a great crime on his conscience. He caued his mother's death when he was born which the Ancients always considered Unfilial."

At noon some of us met in the smoking room of the Pekin Club. "It's curious there's been no demand for ransom," I said.

"Bandits? Within the city walls?" Carstairs was skeptical. "Russia has never hesitated to use *agents provocateurs*. They say she's going to build a railway across Siberia. I don't believe it's practical. But you never can tell what those mad Russians will do. She'll need Manchuria. And she'll need a pretext for taking it. Why not the abduction of the Russian Minister's wife?"

Kiada shook his head. "Princess Volgorughi will not be found until 'The River' is restored to its companion pictures, 'The Lake,' 'The Sea' and 'The Cloud.' "

"What do you mean?"

Kiada answered me patiently as an adult explaining the obvious to a backward child. "It is known that Wang Wei painted this series of pictures entitled 'Four Forms of Water.' Volgorughi has only one of them—'The River.' The separation of one painting from others in a series divinely inspired is displeasing to the artist."

"But Wang Wei has been dead more than a thousand years!"

"It is always dangerous to displease those who have

Passed Above. An artist as steeped in ancient mysteries as the pious Wang Wei has power over men long after he has become a Guest On High. Wang Wei will shape the course of our lives into any pattern he pleases in order to bring those four paintings together again. I knew this last night when I first saw 'The River' and—I was afraid."

"I wonder how Volgorughi did get that painting?" mused Carstairs. "I hope he didn't forget the little formality of payment."

"He's not a thief!" I protested.

"No. But he's a collector. All collectors are mad. Especially Russian collectors. It's like gambling or opium."

Lucien smiled unpleasantly. "Art! Ghosts! Politics! Why go so far afield? Olga Kyrilovna was a young bride. And Volgorughi is—old. Such marriages are arranged by families, we all know. Women, as Balzac said, are the dupes of the social system. When they consent to marriage, they have not enough experience to know what they are consenting to. Olga Kyrilovna found herself in a trap. She has escaped, as young wives have escaped from time immemorial, by taking a lover. Now they've run off together. *Sabine a tout donné, sa beauté de colombe, et son amour . . .*"

"Monsieur de l'Orges."

We all started. Alexei was standing in the doorway. His eyes commanded the room. "What you say is impossible. Do I make myself clear?"

"Of course, Alexei. I—I was only joking." Lucien sounded piteous.

But Alexei had no pity. "A difference of taste in jokes has broken many friendships. . . . Charley, will you come back to the Russian Legation with me?"

The Tartar general's audience hall had never seemed more shabby. Volgorughi sat staring at the garish wall of red and gilt. He was wearing an overcoat, carrying hat and gloves.

"News, Excellency?" queried Alexei.

Volgorughi shook his head without looking up. "I've

been to the *Tsungli Yamên*." He spoke like a somnambulist.
"The usual thing. Green tea. Melon seeds. A cold stone pavilion. Mandarins who giggle behind satin sleeves. I asked for
an audience with the Emperor himself. It was offered—on
the usual terms. I had to refuse—as usual. By the time a
gunboat gets to the mouth of the Pei-ho, they may agree to
open another seaport to Russian trade by way of reparation,
but—I shall never see Olga Kyrilovna again. Sometimes I
think our governments keep us here in the hope that something will happen to give them a pretext for sending troops
into China. . . ."

We all felt that. The *Tsungli Yamên,* or Foreign Office,
calmly assumed that our legations were vassal missions to
the Emperor, like those from Tibet. The Emperor would not
receive us unless we acknowledged his sovereignty by kow-
towing, the forehead to strike the floor audibly nine times.
Even if we had wished to go through this interesting performance for the sake of peace and trade, our governments
would not let us compromise their sovereignty. But they
kept us there, where we had no official standing, where our
very existence was doubted. "It may be there are as many
countries in the West as England, France, Germany and
Russia," one mandarin had informed me. "But the others
you mention—Austria, Sweden, Spain and America—they
are all lies invented to intimidate the Chinese."

Alexei was not a man to give up easily. "Excellency, I
shall find her."

Volgorughi lifted his head. "How?"

Alexei shouted. The study door opened. An old man in
workman's dress came in with a young Chinese. I knew the
old man as Antoine Billot, one of the Swiss clockmakers who
were the only Western tradesmen allowed in Pekin.

"Charley," said Alexei, "tell Antoine about the fingering
piece you saw in the hands of a beggar last summer."

"It was turquoise matrix, carved to represent two nude
figures embracing. The vein of brown in the stone colored
their heads and spotted the back of the smaller figure."

"I have seen such a fingering piece," said Antoine. "In the Palace of Whirring Phoenixes. It is in that portion of the Chinese City known as the Graveyard of the Wu family, in the Lane of Azure Thunder."

"It is the Beileh Tsai Heng who lives there," put in Antoine's Chinese apprentice. "Often have we repaired his French clocks. Very fine clocks of Limoges enamel sent to the Emperor Kang Hsi by Louis XIV. The Beileh's grandmother was the Discerning Concubine of the Emperor Tao Kwang."

"An old man?" asked Alexei.

"The Beileh has not yet attained the years of serenity. Though the name Heng means 'Steadfast,' he is impetuous as a startled dragon. He memorialized the late Emperor for permission to live in a secluded portion of the Chinese City so that he could devote his leisure to ingenious arts and pleasures."

I looked at Alexei. "You think the beggar who stared at us was a servant of this Prince?"

"No. Your beggar was the Prince himself. 'Elder Brother' is the correct form for addressing a Manchu prince of the third generation."

"It is the latest fad among our young princes of Pekin," explained the apprentice, "to haunt the highways and taverns dressed as beggars, sharing the sad life of the people for a few hours. They vie with each other to see which can look the most dirty and disreputable. But each one has some little habit of luxury that he cannot give up, even for the sake of disguise. A favorite ring, a precious fan, an antique fingering piece. That is how you can tell them from the real beggars."

Alexei turned to me. "When a taste for the exquisite becomes so refined that it recoils upon itself and turns into its opposite—a taste for the ugly—we call that decadence. Prince Heng is decadent—bored, curious, irresponsible, ever in search of a new sensation." Alexei turned back to the apprentice. "Could the Beileh be tempted with money?"

"Who could offer him anything he does not already

possess?" intoned the young Chinese. "His revered father amassed one hundred thousand myriad snow-white taels of silver from unofficial sources during his benevolent reign as Governor of Kwantung. In the Palace of Whirring Phoenixes even the washbowls and spitting basins are curiously wrought of fine jade and pure gold, for this prince loves everything that is rare and strange."

Alexei hesitated before his next question. "Does the Beileh possess any valuable paintings?"

"His paintings are few but priceless. Four landscape scrolls from the divine brush of the illustrious Wang Wei."

Volgorughi started to his feet. "What's this?"

"You may go, Antoine." Alexei waited until the door had closed. "Isn't it obvious, sir? Your Wang Wei scroll was stolen."

Volgorughi sank back in his chair. "But—I bought it. From a peddler in the Chinese City. I didn't ask his name."

"How could a nameless peddler acquire such a painting from such a prince honestly?" argued Alexei. "Your peddler was a thief or a receiver. Such paintings have religious as well as artistic value to the Chinese. They are heirlooms, never sold even by private families who need the money. Last night the moment I saw the marginal note written by the Emperor Ch'ien Lung I knew the picture must have been stolen from the Imperial Collection. I was disturbed because I knew that meant trouble for us if it were known you had the painting. That's why I didn't want to read the inscription aloud. It's easy to see what happened. The thief was captured and tortured until he told Heng you had the painting. Heng saw Olga Kyrilovna with Charley and Lucien in the Chinese City last summer. He must have heard then that she was your wife. When he found you had the painting, he ordered her abduction. Now he is holding her as hostage for the return of the painting. All this cannot be coincidence."

Volgorughi buried his face in his hands. "What can we do?"

"With your permission, Excellency, I shall go into the Chinese City tonight and return the painting to Heng. I shall bring back Olga Kyrilovna—if she is still alive."

Volgorughi rose, shoulders bent, chin sunk on his chest. "I shall go with you, Alexei Andreitch."

"Your Excellency forgets that special circumstances make it possible for me to go into the Chinese City after dark when no other European can do so with safety. Alone I have some chance of success. With you to protect, it would be impossible."

"You will need a Cossack escort."

"That would strip the legation of guards. And it would antagonize Heng. Olga Kyrilovna might be harmed before I could reach her. I prefer to go alone."

Volgorughi sighed. "Report to me as soon as you get back. . . . You are waiting for something?"

"The painting, Excellency."

Volgorughi walked with a shuffling step into the study. He came back with the scroll in its case. "Take it. I never want to see it again."

At the door I looked back. Volgorughi was slumped in his seat, a figure of utter loneliness and despair.

Alexei glanced at me as we crossed the compound. "Something is puzzling you, Charley. What is it?"

"If this Beileh Heng is holding Olga Kyrilovna as a hostage for the painting, he wants you to know that he has abducted her. He has nothing to conceal. Then why was the leper murdered if not to conceal something?"

Alexei led the way into a room of his own furnished with military severity. "I'm glad Volgorughi didn't think of that question, Charley. It has been troubling me too."

"And the answer?"

"Perhaps I shall find it in the Palace of Whirring Phoenixes. Perhaps it will lead me back to one of the men who dined with us yesterday evening. Except for the Carstairses, we were all separated from each other at one time or another in those dark streets—even you and I. . . ."

Alexei was opening a cedar chest. He took out a magnificent robe of wadded satin in prismatic blues and greens. When he had slipped it on he turned to face me. The Tartar cast of his oblique eyes and sallow skin was more pronounced than I had ever realized. Had I passed him wearing this costume in the Chinese City I should have taken him for a Manchu or a Mongol.

He smiled. "Now will you believe I have the blood of Temudjin Genghis Khan in my veins?"

"You've done this before!"

His smile grew sardonic. "Do you understand why I am the only European who can go into the Chinese City after dark?"

My response was utterly illogical. "Alexei, take me with you tonight!"

He studied my face. "You were fond of Olga Kyrilovna, weren't you?"

"Is there no way?" I begged.

"Only one way. And it's not safe. You could wear the overalls of a workman and carry the tools of a clockmaker. And stay close to me, ostensibly your Chinese employer."

"If Antoine Billot will lend me his clothes and tools . . ."

"That can be arranged." Alexei was fitting a jeweled nail shield over his little finger.

"Well? Is there any other objection?"

"Only this." He looked up at me intently. His pale face and black eyes were striking against the kingfisher blues and greens of his satin robe. "We are going to find something ugly at the core of this business, Charley. You are younger than I and—will you forgive me if I say you are rather innocent? Your idea of life in Pekin is a series of dances and dinners, race meetings outside the walls in spring, charades at the English Legation in winter, snipe shooting at Hai Ten in the fall. Your government doesn't maintain an Intelligence Service here. So you can have no idea of the struggle that goes on under the surface of this pleasant social life.

Imperialist ambitions and intrigues, the alliance between politics and trade, even the opium trade—what do you know of all that? Sometimes I think you don't even know much about the amusements men like Lucien find in the Chinese City. . . . Life is only pleasant on the surface, Charley. And now we're going below the surface. Respectability is as artificial as the clothes we wear. What it hides is as ugly as our naked bodies and animal functions. Whatever happens tonight, I want you to remember this: under every suit of clothes, broadcloth or rags, there is the same sort of animal."

"What are you hinting at?"

"There are various possibilities. You said Heng stared at your party as if he had never seen Western men before. Are you sure he wasn't staring at Olga Kyrilovna as if he had never seen a Western woman before?"

"But our women are physically repulsive to Chinese!"

"In most cases. But the Chinese are not animated types. They are individuals, as we are. Taste is subjective and arbitrary. Individual taste can be eccentric. Isn't it possible that there are among them, as among us, men who have romantic fancies for the exotic? Or sensual fancies for the experimental? I cannot get those words of Antoine's apprentice out of my mind: *This prince loves everything that is rare and strange. . . .*"

A red sun was dipping behind the Western Hills when we passed out a southern gate of the Tartar City. In a moment all nine gates would swing shut and we would be locked out of our legations until tomorrow's dawn. It was not a pleasant feeling. I had seen the head of a consul rot on a pike in the sun. That was what happened to barbarian demons who went where they were not wanted outside the Treaty Ports.

The Chinese City was a wilderness of twisting lanes, shops, taverns, theaters, tea houses, opium dens and brothels. Long ago conquering Manchu Tartars had driven conquered Chinese outside the walls of Pekin proper, or the Tartar City, to this sprawling suburb where the conquered

catered to the corruption of the conqueror. The Chinese
City came to life at nightfall when the Tartar City slept
behind its walls. Here and there yellow light shone through
blue dusk from a broken gateway. Now and then we caught
the chink of porcelain cups or the whine of a *yuehkin* guitar.

Alexei seemed to know every turn of the way. At last I
saw why he was Russian Military Attaché at Pekin. Who else
would learn so much about China and its people as this bold
adventurer who could pass for a Manchu in Chinese robes?
When we were snipe shooting together, he seemed to know
the Pei-chih-li Plain as if he carried a military map of the
district in his head. Years afterward, when the Tsar's men
took Port Arthur, everyone learned about Russian Intelligence in China. I learned that evening. And I found myself
looking at Alexei in his Chinese dress as if he had suddenly
become a stranger. What did I know of this man whom I had
met so casually at legation parties? Was he ruthless enough
to stab a beggar already dying of leprosy? Had he had any
reason for doing so?

We turned into a narrower lane—a mere crack between high walls. Alexei whispered, "The Lane of Azure
Thunder."

A green-tiled roof above the dun-colored wall pro-
claimed the dwelling of a prince. Alexei paused before a
gate painted vermilion. He spoke Cantonese to the gatekeeper. I understood only two words—"Wang Wei." There
were some moments of waiting. Then the gate creaked open
and we were ushered through that drab wall into a wonder-
land of fantastic parks and lacquered pavilions blooming
with all the colors of Sung porcelain.

I was unprepared for the splendor of the audience hall.
The old palaces we rented for legations were melancholy
places, decaying and abandoned by their owners. But here
rose, green and gold rioted against a background of dull
ebony panels, tortured by a cunning chisel into grotesquely
writhing shapes. There were hangings of salmon satin embroidered with threads of gold and pale green, images of

birds and flowers carved in jade and coral and malachite. The slender rafters were painted a poisonously bright jade green and on them tiny lotus buds were carved and gilded. There was a rich rustle of satin and the Beileh Heng walked slowly into the room.

Could this stately figure be the same rude fellow I had last seen squatting in the gutter, half naked in the rags of a beggar? He moved with the deliberate grace of the grave religious dancers in the Confucian temples. His robe was lustrous purple—the "myrtle-red" prescribed for princes of the third generation by the Board of Rites. It swung below the paler mandarin jacket in sculptured folds, stiff with a sable lining revealed by two slits at either side. Watered in the satin were the Eight Famous Horses of the Emperor Mu Wang galloping over the Waves of Eternity. His cuffs were curved like horseshoes in honor of the cavalry that set the Manchu Tartars on the throne. Had that cavalry ridden west instead of south, Alexei himself might have owed allegiance to this prince. Though one was Chinese and one Russian, both were Tartar.

Heng's boots of purple satin looked Russian. So did his round cap faced with a band of sable. His skin was a dull ivory, not as yellow as the southern Chinese. His cheeks were lean; his glance searching and hungry. He looked like a purebred descendant of the "wolf-eyed, lantern-jawed Manchus" of the Chinese chronicles. A conqueror who would take whatever he wanted, but who had learned from the conquered Chinese to want only the precious and fanciful . . .

Something else caught my eye. There was no mistake. This was the beggar. For pale against his purple robe gleamed the fingering piece of turquoise matrix which his thin, neurotic fingers caressed incessantly.

No ceremonial tea was served. We were being received as enemies during a truce. But Alexei bowed profoundly and spoke with all the roundabout extravagance of mandarin politeness.

"An obscure design of Destiny has brought the property of your Highness, a venerable landscape scroll painted by the devout Wang Wei, into the custody of the Russian Minister. Though I appear Chinese in this garb, know that I am Russian and my minister has sent me in all haste and humility to restore this inestimable masterpiece to its rightful owner."

Heng's eyes were fixed on a point above our heads for, Chinese or barbarian, we were inferiors, unworthy of his gaze. His lips scarcely moved. "When you have produced the scroll, I shall know whether you speak truth or falsehood."

"All your Highness's words are unspotted pearls of perpetual wisdom." Alexei stripped the embroidered case from the jade roller. Like a living thing, the painted silk slipped out of his grasp and unwound itself at the Beileh's feet.

Once again a faery stream of lapis, jade and turquoise hues unrolled before my enchanted eyes. Kiada was right. I could hear the wind sing in the rushes and the wail of the wild geese, faint and far, a vibration trembling on the outer edge of the physical threshold for sound.

The hand that held the fingering piece was suddenly still. Only the Beileh's eyeballs moved, following the course of Wang Wei's river from its bubbling spring to its foam-flecked sea. Under his cultivated stolidity, I saw fear and, more strangely, sorrow.

At last he spoke. "This painting I inherited from my august ancestor, the ever-glorious Emperor Ch'ien Lung, who left his words and seal upon the margin. How has it come into your possession?"

Alexei bowed again. "I shall be grateful for an opportunity to answer that question if your Highness will first condescend to explain to my mean intelligence how the scroll came to leave the Palace of Whirring Phoenixes?"

"Outside Barbarian, you are treading on a tiger's tail when you speak with such insolence to an Imperial Clansman. I try to make allowances for you because you come of an inferior race, the Hairy Ones, without manners or music, unversed in the Six Fine Arts and the Five Classics. Know then that it is not your place to ask questions or mine to answer them. You may follow me, at a distance of nine paces, for I have something to show you."

He looked neither to right nor left as he walked soberly through the audience hall, his hands tucked inside his sleeves. At the door he lifted one hand to loosen the clasp of his mandarin jacket, and it slid from his shoulders. Before it had time to touch the ground, an officer of the Coral Button sprang out of the shadows to catch it reverently. The Beileh did not appear conscious of this officer's presence. Yet he had let the jacket fall without an instant's hesitation. He knew that wherever he went at any time there would always be someone ready to catch anything he let fall before it was soiled or damaged.

We followed him into a garden, black and white in the moonlight. We passed a pool spanned by a crescent bridge. Its arc of stone matched the arc of its reflection in the ice-coated water, completing a circle that was half reality, half illusion. We came to another pavilion, its roof curling up at each corner, light filtering through its doorway. Again we heard the shrill plaint of a guitar. We rounded a devil-screen of gold lacquer and the thin sound ended on a high, feline note.

I blinked against a blaze of lights. Like a flight of particolored butterflies, a crowd of girls fluttered away from us, tottering on tiny, mutilated feet. One who sat apart from the rest rose with dignity. A Manchu princess, as I saw by her unbound feet and undaunted eyes. Her hair was piled high in the lacquered coils of the Black Cloud Coiffure. She wore hairpins, earrings, bracelets and tall heels of acid-green jade. Her gown of sea-green silk was sewn with silver thread worked in the Pekin stitch to represent the Silver Crested Love Birds of Conjugal Peace. But when she turned her face, I saw the sour lines and sagging pouches of middle age.

Princess Heng's gaze slid over us with subtle contempt

and came to rest upon the Beileh with irony. "My pleasure in receiving you is boundless and would find suitable expression in appropriate compliments were the occasion more auspicious. As it is, I pray you will forgive me if I do not linger in the fragrant groves of polite dalliance, but merely inquire why your Highness has seen fit to introduce two male strangers, one a barbarian, into the sanctity of the Inner Chamber?"

Heng answered impassively. "Even the Holy Duke of Yen neglected the forms of courtesy when he was pursued by a tiger."

A glint of malice sparkled in the eyes of the Beileh's Principal Old Woman. "Your Highness finds his present situation equivalent to being pursued by a tiger? To my inadequate understanding that appears the natural consequence of departing from established custom by attempting to introduce a barbarian woman into the Inner Chamber."

Heng sighed. "If the presence of these far-traveled strangers distresses you and my Small Old Women you have permission to retire."

Princess Heng's jade bangles clashed with the chilly ring of ice in a glass as she moved toward the door. The Small Old Women, all girls in their teens, shimmered and rustled after the Manchu princess, who despised them both as concubines and as Chinese.

Heng led us through another door.

"Olga!"

The passion in Alexei's voice was a shock to me. In my presence he had always addressed her as "Excellency" or "Princess." . . . She might have been asleep as she lay there on her blue fox cloak, her eyes closed, her pale face at peace, her slight hands relaxed in the folds of her white tulle skirt. But the touch of her hands was ice and faintly from her parted lips came the sweet sickish odor of opium.

Alexei turned on Heng. "If you had not stolen her, she would not have died!"

"Stolen?" It was the first word that had pierced Heng's

reserve. "Imperial Clansmen do not steal women. I saw this far-traveled woman in a market lane of the Chinese City last summer. I coveted her. But I did not steal her. I offered money for her, decently and honorably, in accord with precepts of morality laid down by the Ancients. Money was refused. Months passed. I could not forget the woman with faded eyes. I offered one of my most precious possessions. It was accepted. The painting was her price. But the other did not keep his side of the bargain. For she was dead when I lifted her out of her cart."

The lights were spinning before my eyes. "Alexei, what is this? Volgorughi would not . . ."

Alexei's look stopped me.

"You . . ." Words tumbled from my lips. "There was a lover. And you were he. And Volgorughi found out. And he watched you together and bided his time, nursing his hatred and planning his revenge like a work of art. And finally he punished you both cruelly by selling her to Heng. Volgorughi knew that Olga would drive alone last night. Volgorughi had lived so long in the East that he had absorbed the Eastern idea of women as well as the Eastern taste in painting. The opium must have been in the sherry he gave her. She was already drowsy when he lifted her into the cart. No doubt he had planned to give her only a soporific dose that would facilitate her abduction. But at the last moment he commuted her sentence to death and let her have the full, lethal dose. He gave her good-bye tenderly because he knew he would never see her again. He promised her she would be safe because death is, in one sense, safety—the negation of pain, fear and struggle. . . .

"There was no peddler who sold him the painting. That was his only lie. He didn't prevent your coming here tonight because he wanted you to know. That was your punishment. And he saw that you could make no use of your knowledge now. Who will believe that Olga Kyrilovna, dead of a Chinese poison in the Chinese City, was killed by her own husband? Some Chinese will be suspected—Heng himself, or his jealous wife, or the men who carry out his orders. No European would take Heng's story seriously unless it were supported by at least one disinterested witness. That was why the leper had to die last night, while Volgorughi was separated from Lucien through a wrong turning that was Volgorughi's fault. The leper must have overheard some word of warning or instruction from Volgorughi to Olga's lantern boy that revealed the whole secret. That word was spoken in Cantonese. Olga's lantern boy was Cantonese. Volgorughi spoke that dialect. The leper knew no other tongue. And Lucien, the only person who walked with Volgorughi, was as ignorant of Cantonese as all the rest of us, save you."

Heng spoke sadly in his own tongue. "The treachery of the Russian Minister in sending this woman to me dead deserves vengeance. But one thing induces me to spare him. He did not act by his own volition. He was a blind tool in the skillful hand of the merciless Wang Wei. Through this woman's death 'The River' has been restored to its companion pictures, 'The Lake,' 'The Sea' and 'The Cloud.' And I, who separated the pictures so impiously, have had my own share of suffering as a punishment. . . ."

. . . Yes, I'll have another brandy. One more glass. Olga? She was buried in the little Russian Orthodox cemetery at Pekin. Volgorughi was recalled. The breath of scandal clung to his name the rest of his life. The Boxer Uprising finally gave the West its pretext for sending troops into China. That purple-satin epicurean, the Beileh Heng, was forced to clean sewers by German troops during the occupation and committed suicide from mortification. The gay young bloods of Pekin who had amused themselves by playing beggars found themselves beggars in earnest when the looting was over. Railways brought Western businessmen to Pekin and before long it was as modern as Chicago.

Alexei? He became attentive to the wife of the new French Minister, a woman with dyed hair who kept a Pekinese sleeve dog in her bedroom. I discovered the distraction that can be found in study of the early Chinese poets. When I left the service, I lost track of Alexei. During the Russian Revolution, I often wondered if he were still living. Did he join the Reds, as some Cossack officers did? Or was he one of the Whites who settled in Harbin or Port Arthur? He would have been a very old man then, but I think he could have managed. He spoke so many Chinese dialects. . . .

The scroll? Any good reference book will tell you that there are no Wang Wei scrolls in existence today, though there are some admirable copies. One, by Chao Mēng Fu, in the British Museum, shows the course of a river. Scholars have described this copy in almost the same words I have used tonight to describe the original. But they are not the same. I went to see the copy. I was disappointed. I could no longer hear the song of the wind in the rushes or the wail of the wild geese. Was the change in the painting? Or in me?

GOOD-BYE, MISS LIZZIE BORDEN

Lillian de la Torre

Lillian de la Torre is the author of true-crime books (Elizabeth Is Missing, *1945;* Villainy Detected, *1947;* The Heir of Douglas, *1952;* The Truth About Belle Gunness, *1955) as well as a superior detective series featuring Dr. Samuel Johnson. The twenty-six stories about the eighteenth-century lexicographer appeared originally in* Ellery Queen's Mystery Magazine *and were collected in* Dr. Sam: Johnson, Detector *(1946) and* The Detections of Dr. Sam: Johnson *(1960). In her one-act play,* Good-bye, Miss Lizzie Borden *(1948), Miss de la Torre combines her interests in the theater and true crime to offer a unique solution to the famous Fall River, Massachusetts, axe murders.*

O n a sweltering hot day in August, 1892, in a dingy old house in Fall River, Massachusetts, somebody committed murder—the most famous of American murders. Somebody struck down Mr. and Mrs. Andrew Jackson Borden with an axe. The police investigated Mr. Borden's brother-in-law and his maid-of-all-work and his old-maid daughters, Emma and Lizzie. They arrested Lizzie, and put her on trial for her life. Miss Emma stood by her sister loyally, went on the stand on her behalf, and was largely instrumental in getting her acquitted. After the acquittal, the two sisters went back to the murder house and shut themselves up in it together. Then one day Miss Emma left. She never came back. The sisters never saw one another again. What happened? What happened between those two old maids, shut up together in that bloodstained house, that made it impossible for them ever again to look one another in the face?

Good-bye, Miss Lizzie Borden, a sinister play in one act, takes place at the scene of the crime on the anniversary of the murders, and fictitiously portrays the showdown which places one of the sisters in deadly peril and parts the two forever.

SCENE: *A sitting room in a house on Second Street, Fall River, Massachusetts. The room is sparsely furnished with black horsehair and walnut furniture. Prominent against the left wall is a sinister-looking black sofa with a gloomy Bible print, framed in black wood, hanging above it. In the right wall is a single window, un-screened, open, with dark heavy drapes pulled back. In the back wall, center, is a large open fireplace of dark wood and brick. Right of the fireplace the staircase comes down to a landing two steps high. The outside door opens onto the landing. Left is the kitchen door, open, but covered by closed portières. Above the fireplace is a picture of Sutter's Fort garishly painted on a log. A round table in the center is covered with a fringed tapestry tablecloth, and flanked by a straight chair placed primly on each side.*

TIME: August 4, 1893; afternoon.

(As the curtain rises, MISS EMMA BORDEN *comes furtively down the stairs. She is 43 years old, drab and characterless. One can see that her life has been one long story of being pushed around by other people. She wears dressy black and carries a small grip. She sets the grip down by the outside door, muttering to herself.)*

EMMA Grip . . . Lunch . . . *(She locates it on the center table)* Gloves . . . *(On the mantel)* Umbrella . . . *(By the door in the umbrella stand)* Ticket . . . *(She sets her purse on the center table and opens it to check this item. Just then she hears a noise on the stairs, and whirls guiltily, hiding her purse behind her. It is* MAGGIE, *a positive, sturdy young Irishwoman, dressed for the street in shirtwaist and skirt.)*

MAGGIE *(Quietly but urgently)* Hurry up, Miss Emma, she's moving about up there, best be going in time.

EMMA *(Moving Right, toward the stairs, as if to listen)* Oh, dear. *(She begins picking up her things.* MAGGIE *fetches a bundle from where she has hidden it behind the portières over the kitchen door.* EMMA *sees it)* Why, Maggie —your bundle—where are *you* going?

MAGGIE I'm leaving.

EMMA *(Wailing)* Oh, Maggie!

MAGGIE I can't help it, I'm leaving. I can't stand it another minute.

EMMA Oh, dear, they all leave. What are we to do?

MAGGIE I'm sorry, Miss Emma, I've only stayed this long

for your sake. I couldn't bear to leave you alone with (*glancing up*) her.

EMMA   Thank you, Maggie.

MAGGIE   But now you'll be gone off to Fairhaven on your little vacation, and she'll have another servant in the kitchen, maybe, before you come back.

EMMA   Oh, dear, Maggie, how can she get another servant?

MAGGIE   (*Setting down her bag on the straight chair Left*) I can't stand it, Miss Emma, I never feel alone in this house. I'm cleaning about, thinking no evil, and then I get a shiver between me shoulder blades, and I turn around, and there *she* is—perfectly still—just looking at me—with that look she's had since the trial. . . . It's more than a person can stand. I'm leaving.

EMMA   (*Touching her arm as she reaches for the bundle again*) I know. She's always spying. She knows every move we make.

MAGGIE   (*Leaving the bundle and crossing to the window Right*) And never a party nor a shindig, no callers, not a friend to drop in of an evening—it's like a house of death.

EMMA   (*Somberly, drawn Left toward the sofa*) It *is* a house of death. I can't stand it any more than you can. (*Turning to* MAGGIE, *above table*) That's why I'm going down to Fairhaven. I can't stay cooped up with *her* any longer.

MAGGIE   (*To her above table*) Then you see what I mean.

EMMA   Oh, Maggie, why didn't you say something?

MAGGIE   I was afraid to say anything. I was afraid to tell her I wanted to leave. But when *you* decided to go away for a while . . . I can't stay alone with *her*—I'm leaving this minute.

(*She takes her bag and turns to go, but at the stair-foot checks herself to listen.*)

EMMA   What is she doing?

MAGGIE   Just moving around . . .

EMMA   Better hurry. . . . Good-bye, Maggie.

MAGGIE   Good-bye, Miss Emma. Don't miss your train.

EMMA   (*Looks at chatelaine watch*) I won't. I'll go right away. I have a half-hour yet, and anyway, 'tisn't as if there wasn't another one soon after.

MAGGIE   Well, I know you, Miss Emma, don't miss 'em *both*.

(*There is a sound from upstairs. Both women freeze for an instant, listening. Then* MAGGIE *goes quickly to the door. As she opens it a woman comes up the step and confronts her. This is* NELLIE CUTTS, *a brisk, hearty creature of indeterminate age, dressed in mannish clothes, a severe black skirt, shirtwaist with stiff collar and tie, a straw boater on her pompadour.*)

NELLIE   Is Miss Lizzie Borden in?

MAGGIE   Miss Borden is out. (*She pushes her back and closes the door on both of them.* MISS EMMA *gets her umbrella from the stand and starts to check her traps again, talking to herself.*)

EMMA   Oh, dear, why can't they leave us in peace? Where's my gloves? What time is it? (*The bell peals violently*) Maggie! Oh, she's gone. (*Bell again, very determined*) Oh, dear, Lizzie will come down. (*Bell again, still more determined*) Oh, dear, who is it, who is it?

(*She opens the door. The same woman immediately puts her foot in the door.*)

NELLIE   Miss Borden?

EMMA   Oh, no, you can't come in, we don't see anybody. . . .

NELLIE   Of course I'll come in. (*She pushes past* EMMA, *not rudely, but irresistibly, and stands up Center above table surveying the room coolly*) So this is the scene of the crime. Corpse found there—(*advancing to the sofa Left*) blood splattered all over the walls . . . Had 'em redone, haven't you? Picked a nice jolly color, too, didn't you? This is the picture that had forty-six blood spots on it? (*Picking at the frame*) They tell me there were eighty-seven spatters of blood in a space no larger than a palm-leaf fan (*Sketching with her hand*) right here. . . . (*During this harangue* EMMA *is irresolute. She goes to the stair-foot as if to call* LIZZIE, *loses her courage, comes back to the sitting room, up Center,* NELLIE *advancing to her upstage Center*) You're Miss Lizzie Borden, I presume? (EMMA *shakes her head, but* NELLIE *goes right on unheeding*) I must say you're not what I expected. Out West where I come from, when a woman's tough she's tough. Now, Miss Lizzie, I'm here to . . .

EMMA   (*Making herself heard*) I'm not Miss Lizzie, I'm Miss Emma.

NELLIE   Oh, the sister. That accounts for it. Well, Miss Emma, this is the anniversary of the Second Street murders, isn't it? It's just a year since the murder of Mr. and Mrs. Andrew J. Borden by . . .

EMMA   (*Cutting in*) Since my father and my stepmother— died. We don't talk about it.

NELLIE   I missed your sister's trial. Some old girl, they tell me.

EMMA   She was acquitted. We don't talk about it.

NELLIE   Of course not. But the public is interested, you know. Now I'm from Sacramento, California, Miss Emma—greatest town on earth, pick up gold right in the streets—I represent the *Sacramento Record*, and I'm here to get some impressions for my paper—Second Street revisited, and all that . . .

EMMA   (*Recoiling down Right*) Oh, dear, you're one of those nasty female reporters. Lizzie hates reporters. I know she won't listen to you for a moment.

NELLIE   (*Looking around for inspiration*) Of course not, of course she won't. (*She finds it*) Say, isn't that a picture of Sutter's Fort on the wall? (*Approaching it upstage Center*)

EMMA   (*Approaching it also with an affectionate smile*) Yes, artistic, isn't it? Uncle Morse brought it back from the goldfields. It's all he brought back. He painted it himself.

NELLIE   Brought it back from the goldfields, did he, eh? Now isn't that a coincidence? I'm from those goldfields myself. Morse, Morse . . . ? Say, is your Uncle Morse an old codger, sixtyish, maybe, with—uh . . . (*Fishing*)

EMMA   (*Eager*)—a droopy moustache—

NELLIE   (*Pouncing on it*) That's it, a droopy moustache— and sort of . . . (*She sketches a figure of indeterminate shape and size*)

EMMA   . . . tall and thin? My goodness, do you know Uncle Morse?

NELLIE   I should say I do! Knew him well in Sacramento. Put her there, Miss Emma. Any niece of Old Man Morse is a friend of mine!

EMMA   (*Shaking hands*) How do you do, Miss . . . ?

NELLIE   Nellie Cutts. Just call me Nellie. Now as I was saying, Miss Emma, I represent the *Sacramento Record,* and I'm on a roving commission to report how things are in the East. And say, this Borden story's got everything! New England old maid, Sunday-school teacher and all that—up and kills half the family with an axe! Interview with Miss Lizzie Borden twelve months after! Great stuff! They'll eat it up in Sacramento!

EMMA   Oh, dear, I know Lizzie won't see you. (*Consulting her watch*) Really, Miss, I have to go now.

NELLIE   (*Blocking her way up Center*) Now just a moment, Miss Emma, how about a word from *you?* (*Ready with pencil and flimsy copy-paper*) Here, I'll have to have something to lean on—this box'll do— (*Taking up the shoebox of lunch from the center table*) How does it feel, now tell me, Miss Emma, to live day in and day out within sight of the very bloodstains, as you might say. . . . (EMMA'S *hand goes to her mouth in a characteristic gesture, pressing it as if to keep it from trembling. She is drawn to the couch Left and stares haunted at the wall above it.*) How does it feel to take three meals a day with the woman who—was tried for the crime?

EMMA   (*To herself*) I've stood it as long as I can. That's why I'm going to Fairhaven. I can be alone in Fairhaven.

NELLIE   Of course, you must have found the last year very trying to the nerves. I suppose Miss Lizzie must be very difficult to live with?

EMMA   (*Looking upward*) Ssh. She's always listening and spying. She's down on you when you least expect it. (*Looks at watch*) Oh, dear, I mustn't miss the 3:37.

NELLIE   (*Intercepts her as she moves toward door up Right*) You won't miss it.

(*They compare watches, during which a rattling of fence posts is heard outside, and then a childish voice chanting:*)

LITTLE GIRL   Lizzie Borden took an axe
And gave her mother forty whacks,
And when she saw what she had done
She gave her father forty-one.

(*Both women react immediately.* MISS EMMA *rushes out the door. The reporter seizes her papers and box and rushes to the window, taking the chant down hastily. It is repeated.* NELLIE *scribbles furiously. The last line is broken off by a cry of pain from the child.*)

NELLIE   (*Crossing down Left, reading*) Oh, this is a classic! "Lizzie Borden took an axe, And gave her mother forty whacks—(*Reenter* EMMA. *She holds the side of her face, as if in pain. The reporter reads on*) And when she saw what she had done, She gave her father forty-one."

EMMA   (*Up Center, with an anxious gaze upward*) Oh, do be quiet. Lizzie hears every word you say down here; her room is right up there.

NELLIE   (*Looking up*) Right up there, eh? But she wasn't up there when her father was being murdered, was she? (*Crossing to window Right and looking out*) She was out there in the barn eating pears—she says.

EMMA   Yes, she was. Oh, I have to be going. (*Approaching the door*)

NELLIE   Now, Miss Emma, just sit down a minute, please. . . . (*Seating her by the table Right*)

EMMA   (*Protesting ineffectually*) But I have to be going. . . .

NELLIE   (*Above table*) Is it true that on the morning of the murders the breakfast consisted of bananas, cookies, and cold mutton soup?

EMMA   I don't know, I wasn't here. I was in Fairhaven.

NELLIE   (*Shaking her head*) Cold mutton soup! In August! No wonder somebody committed murder! Well, now, Miss Emma, your stepmother was found upstairs (*She moves up Right to the stair-foot and looks up*) with her head battered in with an axe?

EMMA   That's right.

NELLIE (*Crossing to sofa Left*) And your father's body was on the sofa here, like this. . . . (*She illustrates by stretching herself out on it, feet to ground.*)

EMMA (*Crying out*) Don't!

NELLIE (*Sitting up*) Miss Lizzie spread the alarm. The front door was triple-locked, and Miss Lizzie was watching the side door—so *she* says. . . . (*Crossing to window Right*) She was watching from the upper barn window—just standing there eating a pear and looking out—she *says*. (*Above* EMMA'S *chair, Right*) How could anyone from outside have done it? How could they escape right under Miss Lizzie's eyes? *If* Miss Lizzie wasn't lying.

EMMA (*Stiffly*) My sister was acquitted.

NELLIE (*To herself, gazing out window*) Beats me how they acquitted her.

EMMA Blood.

NELLIE Hey?

EMMA Blood. The air was full of blood. You said yourself there were bloodstains all over the wall. Whoever did it was covered with blood. (*She stops. Her hand goes to her mouth.*)

NELLIE Well, what of it?

EMMA The whole world saw Lizzie within ten minutes of the crime, and she hadn't a spot of blood on her. What could they do but acquit her?

NELLIE (*Close to* EMMA, *Left, above table*) Tell me, Miss Emma, did *you* look carefully at Miss Lizzie to see if there was any blood on her? Her hair, perhaps? Or her shoes?

EMMA Certainly not! My own sister! Besides, I didn't see Lizzie till I got back from Fairhaven that night. . . . Fairhaven! My train! (*Rising*) You'll have to excuse me now. . . .

NELLIE   (*Seating her firmly with a hand on her shoulder*) Maybe she used an apron, one of those big coverall aprons. . . .

EMMA   They never found one. . . .

NELLIE   Easy enough to hide a thing like that in your own house. They never found the axe, either, did they?

EMMA   No, they never found the axe. I've often wondered where the axe got to.

NELLIE   But they searched the house?

EMMA   Oh, yes, they searched the house.

NELLIE   (*Breaking down Right and scuffing at a place in the carpet*) Did they take up the carpet?

EMMA   Yes, they did.

NELLIE   (*Moving to the fireplace up Center*) Did they search the chimney?

EMMA   Of course they did.

NELLIE   (*Exploring the fireplace from Right to Left*) did they open the flue?

EMMA   Of course not; we couldn't have them tearing up the house.

NELLIE   (*Poking and prodding*) I'd tear it up. Might be a sliding panel or something.

EMMA   Oh, Lizzie wouldn't have it. Everything's Lizzie's now. That is, of course, it's half mine, but Lizzie takes care of everything for me.

NELLIE   (*Wiping sooty fingers*) Now, Miss Emma, you'll have to excuse me; there's a question I have to ask. (*She seats herself Left of the table and prepares to take notes with papers and shoebox which she has left on the table*) Is there any insanity in your family?

EMMA   (*Indignant*) Certainly not. That's the first thing they started asking. They asked ever so many questions about Uncle Morse. . . .

NELLIE   He arrived for a visit, didn't he, just the day before the murders?

EMMA   Yes, he did. They were horrid about Uncle Morse. They kept asking people if he was quite right in his head. Just because he doesn't work steady anyplace, and just sort of drifts around and visits people. Anybody pleasures himself in New England, folks say he's a mite tetched. It made me terribly angry. Uncle Morse is as sane as I am.

NELLIE   Where was Uncle Morse the morning of the murders?

EMMA   Visiting around. They had to admit it. He had a perfect alibi. It was just humiliating, the way they snooped around after everybody. "Did Uncle Morse visit you on Thursday morning? Did you see Miss Emma Borden in Fairhaven?" Imagine asking about me all over Fairhaven! They got sent about their business, I guess. Of course, I was right there in my room the whole time, but Uncle Morse was moving around; that made it harder. They certainly asked a lot of questions about Uncle Morse before they decided to arrest Lizzie.

NELLIE   (*Leaning across the table, confidentially*) And say, Miss Emma, tell me about the kitten.

EMMA   (*Hand to mouth*) Oh, dear.

NELLIE   They say the kitten was found down cellar dead. It had been killed with an axe.

EMMA   The kitten was the hardest. I cried for a week. It brought on my neuralgia. I like kittens. (*With a frightened look toward the stairs, then across the table to* NELLIE, *confidentially*) Lizzie never cried at all. It was Lizzie's kitten. Lizzie's a hard woman.

NELLIE   (*Rising*) Well, now, Miss Emma, let's get back to the fatal day. Mrs. Borden is lying in her blood upstairs. (*Referring upward*) The servant is downstairs.

She hears Mr. Borden at the front door trying to get in. She goes to let him in. (*Going toward the door up Right*) She finds the door is triple-locked. She lets him in, and upstairs on the landing (*looking up the stairs*) she hears a horrible gloating laugh. The murderer is standing up there, Miss Emma, within sight of her first victim, and as she sees her second victim walk into her trap, she laughs. What a moment!

EMMA It wasn't Lizzie. Lizzie was downstairs.

NELLIE (*Coming to her Right of chair*) She changed her story, Miss Emma. First she said she was downstairs—then she said she was upstairs—she was certainly lying. Well now (*satisfied with the effect on* EMMA) in comes Mr. Borden and lies down for a nap, right here on the sofa. (*Approaching it and looking at him*) The murderer covers herself with something (*she begins to act it out*) and creeps up on the old man with the axe (*taking the poker from the fireplace*) from behind, like this—and brings down the axe again and again— (EMMA *jumps to her feet, crying out and covering her face with her hands, backing off Right.* NELLIE *approaches her upstage Center*) Was it Miss Lizzie? Was it?

EMMA (*Confronting her up Center*) No! No, no, no! It wasn't Lizzie! It wasn't!

(MISS LIZZIE BORDEN *sweeps aside the portières. She is a stout, not unpleasant-looking woman, clothed in a drab cotton housedress. She is very composed and quiet.*)

LIZZIE Emma. (*Thunderstruck pause*) You talk too much, Emma.

EMMA Oh, Lizzie, this is different, this lady is a friend of Uncle Morse.

(*The reporter makes as if to acknowledge the introduction, but* LIZZIE *crosses to* EMMA *without looking at her.*)

LIZZIE   Go upstairs, Emma. (EMMA *pauses as if to defy her*) I said go upstairs, Emma.

EMMA   (*Giving ground*) All right, Lizzie.

(LIZZIE *turns to* NELLIE.)

LIZZIE   Now, then, Miss, I'll take that poker. (NELLIE *hesitates stubbornly. As their glances lock,* EMMA, *pausing at the foot of the stairs, gets up her courage, snatches up her purse and bolts out the door.* LIZZIE, *as the reporter yields the poker, hears the door close. She takes an angry step after her sister, then shrugs and replaces the poker*) She won't get far.

NELLIE   Hey, what's that?

LIZZIE   Nothing. Now look here . . .

NELLIE   (*Cutting in*) I represent the *Sacramento Record*, Miss Lizzie. . . .

LIZZIE   (*Coming down to her Left*) Friend of Uncle Morse, eh? What color hair has the old man got?

NELLIE   (*Choosing instantly*) Gray . . . (*At Lizzie's look of triumph she amends hastily*) What there is of it . . .

LIZZIE   There's lots of it, and it's bright white. You never saw Uncle Morse in your life. Good day, Miss.

(*Defeated, the reporter slowly crosses downstage, and approaches the door, up Right. When she is almost there she pauses, gets up her courage, and comes back, upstage, to Right Center.*)

NELLIE   But, Miss Borden—my paper wants an interview.

LIZZIE   (*Advancing on her up Center*) I don't give interviews.

NELLIE   Just one question, Miss Lizzie—the bloodstained apron—where did it get to?

LIZZIE   (*Edging her toward the door*) I have nothing to say.

NELLIE (*Giving ground*) And the bloody axe? Why wasn't the fireplace searched? (*On the landing, one last try*) If you'd just say a word for my paper . . .

LIZZIE (*Final*) Good day, Miss! (*The door closes on her. Immediately the bell peals. Grimly*) Oh, no, you don't!

(NELLIE'S *head comes in at the window.*)

NELLIE Your evening paper came, Miss Lizzie. (LIZZIE *whirls to face her.* NELLIE *grins at her surprise. She scales the paper into the room at* LIZZIE'S *feet.* LIZZIE *glares at her, and begins to stoop for the paper*) Goodbye, Miss Lizzie.

(LIZZIE *straightens. The reporter waves, and disappears.* LIZZIE *picks up the paper and sets it on the table, absently. She stands thinking for a moment, looks toward the fireplace, frowns, shakes her head, looks toward the window, then again toward the fireplace. Suddenly she seems to make a decision. She pulls the portières over the window, then goes to the fireplace. With the poker she forces open the secret panel, then thrusts in her arm to the elbow and begins groping for something. While she is absorbed in the task the door opens and* MISS EMMA *comes in. She gets far enough into the room to see what* LIZZIE *is doing. At the same moment* LIZZIE *drags out a bundle of cloth by one end. It unrolls, and a small hand axe or hatchet spills out on the hearth.* LIZZIE *turns to pick it up, and confronts her sister.*)

EMMA (*Dry throat*) I missed my train.

LIZZIE (*Grimly*) Too bad.

EMMA I stopped at the corner to get out my handkerchief, and I heard the train tooting for the crossing. I missed it. . . . (*Her voice dies away as she stares at the axe, taking it in slowly. Her hand goes to her face in the neuralgia gesture.*)

LIZZIE   Lock the door, Emma.

(EMMA *locks the door and pockets the key.* LIZZIE *carries the axe and the apron to the table.* EMMA *comes down and stands by* LIZZIE, *Right, above the table. Both sisters stare at the mute evidence of guilt.*)

EMMA   Lizzie—your apron—and the axe—they were in the chimney all the time. . . .

LIZZIE   (*Backing off up Left, staring at the things with loathing*) Yes, Emma.

EMMA   You, Lizzie—you hid them there—after . . .

LIZZIE   (*Coming down Left*) Yes, Emma. I was afraid Maggie would come down any minute. I hid them in the chimney.

EMMA   (*Inspecting the panel*) I always wondered where they got to. I wondered how they could search and search and never find them.

LIZZIE   Father kept money behind that panel. He never knew I knew, and once he—was dead—nobody knew about it but me.

EMMA   Why did you do it?

LIZZIE   There's a way, isn't there, to tell who has been handling—a weapon?

EMMA   (*Coming down to the table, Right*) I don't know; you've always been the clever one. (*She unrolls the blood-splashed apron and looks at it vaguely*) I don't see any marks.

LIZZIE   (*Approaching her above the table and staring at the apron in her turn.* EMMA *drops it and backs away from it up Right*) I don't either, but they say the police can. A Frenchman wrote a book about it. Besides (*confronting* EMMA *deliberately up Right*) you had brought the axe from Fairhaven; it had the store mark etched on the head.

(EMMA *has been staring at the blood on the apron, her hand to her mouth. Now she slowly raises her head and looks full at* LIZZIE.)

EMMA   Why, Lizzie—you knew—all the time. . . .

LIZZIE   I saw you. (*She crosses to the window, Right, and stares off*) I saw you from the upper barn window. You came out the side door and stood looking around. I saw your face. (*She shudders*) That was all I needed. You ran to the street, and I came in and found Father. (*Turning toward the room*) It was my apron, and the blood on it . . . You needn't have used *my* apron, Emma.

EMMA   (*Reasonably*) It was the handiest, Lizzie.

LIZZIE   And you had brought the axe from Fairhaven. I only had a minute. I hid them in Father's hidey-hole. They were safe there until that (*angry*) newspaper snooper began to get ideas.

EMMA   (*Curiously*) Why did you hide them, Lizzie?

LIZZIE   (*Approaching her Right Center*) What else could I do? I hated her too, Emma.

EMMA   (*Breaking down Left*) You don't remember Mother as I do. You couldn't have hated Mrs. Borden as I did.

LIZZIE   (*Remembers*) I didn't. But Father—Emma, why Father?

EMMA   After what he did to Mother, marrying that woman so soon after? You were always soft over Father, Lizzie.

LIZZIE   (*Sits Right of table, passing her hand over her face*) It's a relief, rather. Time after time I've wanted to ask you about things—when they were examining and cross-examining me and keeping after me—I wanted so badly to know the truth, so I would know what to say. But I never dared ask you—they had spies about me all the time. I made so many mistakes. When they asked if I had seen anybody leave the house, I was on my guard not to mention you. I said, "No, nobody." "Then," says they, "there couldn't have been a stranger did it—so it must have been Miss Lizzie!" I ought to have said that I did see the murderer leaving, a big bearded man with a bloody axe. But I wasn't used to lying.

EMMA   I told the truth, I did hate Mrs. Borden worse than you did. But they wouldn't believe me, they thought I was lying to cover you.

LIZZIE   I had to lie about the laugh. I had to change my story and say I was up there laughing. Otherwise they would have started asking. Who *was* laughing? Whose laugh sounds like Lizzie's?

EMMA   There's only one answer—Emma's.

LIZZIE   I haven't laughed since.

EMMA   Neither have I.

LIZZIE   I haven't laughed since I found my kitten dead. I should have guessed, after the kitten. I ought to have been better on my guard.

EMMA   (*Coming down to her above table*) Having to kill the kitten was the hardest. It brought on my neuralgia. I cried for a week over the kitten.

LIZZIE   I know you did. How could I have supposed that you did it?

EMMA   That's why I cried, because I had to do it.

LIZZIE   (*Rising abruptly and coming down Left*) I was afraid at first they would find out you had been away from Fairhaven.

EMMA   I prayed for guidance, Lizzie. All the time I was at Fairhaven, I stayed in my room and prayed for guidance.

LIZZIE   (*Turning on her testily*) What has that got to do with it?

EMMA Don't you see? When the answer came to me, I just got the axe out of the shed and started for Fall River. They thought I was still in my room, I guess, praying for guidance. They didn't know I had had my answer.

LIZZIE What a risk you ran!

EMMA Oh, no, Lizzie, no risk at all. The Lord told me what to do, and He protected me. Nobody recognized me. The Lord protected me.

LIZZIE (*Grimly, coming to her above table*) I protected you.

EMMA Why? Why did you hide the axe? Why did you let them arrest you? (*Cunningly*) You could have had all Father's money for yourself if they had found out about me. (*Retrospective*) I used to think about that, sometimes, when the lawyers were telling the jury to find you guilty. I would think, maybe they'll take Lizzie, and I'll have all the money for myself. Why did you protect me, Lizzie?

LIZZIE I don't know. Because I've always protected you, I suppose. Because I enjoyed having the laugh on everybody, maybe.

EMMA I never guessed. You had the laugh on me, didn't you, Lizzie?

LIZZIE Didn't you know I knew?

EMMA I had no idea. I thought the Lord had arranged it. Why didn't you tell me?

LIZZIE With police spies all around?

EMMA What would you have done, Lizzie, if they had found you guilty?

LIZZIE (*Crossing to the window, reflectively*) I don't know. Gone through with it, I guess. I'd have gone through with it before I'd have given in to them.

EMMA I guess you would. You were always a wicked stubborn little piece.

LIZZIE   (*Facing out the window, as if facing the world*) I'd get sick of it, the jail, the reporters, the examining and re-examining, I'd get sick of it, and tired to the bone, and I'd think, I've had enough, I'll tell them now. And then that prosecutor would come along with his pious face like a public statue, and the very thought of giving in and admitting I'd lied would make my gorge rise, and I'd say to myself, I'll face it down, they shan't break me. And (*over her shoulder, with grim triumph*) they didn't.

EMMA   No, they didn't.

LIZZIE   And besides, it would have been giving in for nothing; they wouldn't have believed me.

EMMA   I suppose they wouldn't.

LIZZIE   (*Facing her coolly*) I used to wonder, Emma—if they had found me guilty, what would you have done?

EMMA   I used to wonder, too. But I'd have had guidance, when the time came. I didn't let it worry me.

LIZZIE   (*Nettled*) Oh, you didn't let it worry you! You let me go through it—sit out there in court day after day —pilloried—the crowd hating me . . .

EMMA   I know, Lizzie.

LIZZIE   (*Approaching her angrily*) How do you know? (*Moving down Left, remembering*) How do you know what I went through? The crowds staring at you, thinking you did it—the women who hiss you at the courtroom door—they hate you—they want to see you dead. What do you know about it?

EMMA   (*Following her up, intensely*) What do *you* know about it, Lizzie? You had the easy part. You didn't have to do it. I thought it would be like chopping wood. It isn't. (*She fingers the back of the Left chair*) Wood splits. Flesh . . . (*She fixes her eyes on* LIZZIE'S *arm, and reaches to touch it.* LIZZIE *shrinks*) Flesh strikes back. It stops you. You feel the resistance all the way up to your elbow. And wood doesn't bleed. Blood . . . (*She crosses Left to stand in front of the sofa and stare at the wall where the bloodstains were*) Blood doesn't flow, Lizzie. It flies. It jumps at you. The air is red with it. (*Her hand goes to her face in the neuralgia gesture.*)

LIZZIE   (*Crossing down Right in revulsion*) I know. I saw the walls.

EMMA   You don't know. You don't know anything. You didn't have to do it. (*She lifts her head suddenly*) Listen! (LIZZIE, *following her gaze, goes toward the stair and listens. She hears nothing and turns to* EMMA *in apprehension*) Listen! There she is—Mrs. Borden—going up the stairs. I'll have to hurry. . . . I'll need the axe. . . .

LIZZIE   (*Appalled*) I've known it, I've watched you night and day for a year, knowing this would come. . . . (EMMA *gets the axe and starts for the stairs.* LIZZIE *blocks her above the table. Firmly, as to a child*) Mrs. Borden's gone, Emma, she's been gone for a year.

EMMA   She's upstairs—don't stop me. (*She rounds the table Left and starts to cross downstage.*)

LIZZIE   (*Blocking her down Right*) Put down the axe, Emma, and come with me.

EMMA   (*Suspiciously*) Now? Where?

LIZZIE   Just across the street to see Dr. Bowen.

EMMA   So you can put me away. So you can shut me up. I'll not be shut up, Lizzie. It wasn't meant I should be shut up.

LIZZIE   (*Patiently*) Just come and see Dr. Bowen.

EMMA   (*Backing away up Center*) He'll put me away. I'll not have it, Lizzie. I'll die first. (*She looks at the axe*)

But I don't have to die, do I? Nobody knows but you. No, I'm not the one to die. . . . (*She has reached the kitchen door, up Left. Suddenly she turns and locks it.*)

LIZZIE (*Testily, without fear*) What nonsense is this, Emma? (EMMA *does not answer. She comes down to the table and starts tying on the apron. Disturbed*) Emma! What are you doing?

EMMA (*Quietly*) I'm putting on my apron. I just explained to you, Lizzie. Blood spatters. You don't want me to spoil my best dress, do you? (*She picks up the axe again.*)

LIZZIE (*Going to her, firmly and earnestly*) Emma, listen to me. You have to go to Fairhaven. You'll miss your train, Emma.

EMMA (*Still in an expressionless voice, reasonably*) It won't take long. It's over in a minute, Lizzie.

LIZZIE (*Beginning to be alarmed, retreats Left around table and puts the Left chair between them*) Emma! Think what you're doing! You can't escape twice.

EMMA (*Following her*) Oh, yes, I can. I do what I have to do, and the rest takes care of itself. I don't want to, Lizzie, you must understand that.

LIZZIE (*Giving ground*) Then wait, Emma, wait—be sure it's what you have to do.

EMMA Oh, it is. I knew as soon as I saw the axe. What else did you keep it for? I knew there was to be another just as soon as I saw the axe.

LIZZIE I kept it to protect you, Emma. Think, Emma . . . !

EMMA (*Crying out in anguish*) Oh, Lizzie, don't talk, it only makes it harder.

(*She lifts the axe.* LIZZIE, *at bay against the murder couch, braces herself. The front doorbell peals sharply.* EMMA *turns her head for an instant, and* LIZZIE *wrenches the axe from her hand. The reporter sticks her head between the portières over the window.* LIZZIE, *hiding the axe behind her, steps forward quickly to cover* EMMA.)

NELLIE   Say, Miss Lizzie, can't you change your mind and give me a statement, now that Miss Emma's gone? (LIZZIE'S *involuntary glance points to* EMMA, *standing motionless, her back turned.*) Oh, there you are, Miss Emma, you missed your train after all, did you?

LIZZIE   (*Her authority restored*) Take that thing off, Emma, and open the front door.

NELLIE   (*Waving her hand cheerfully*) Good for you, Miss Lizzie. (*She withdraws her head.* EMMA *takes off the apron and stuffs it behind a sofa cushion.* LIZZIE *fakes upstage Left, watching her.* EMMA *crosses up slowly. She pauses as if to assert herself, but* LIZZIE *makes a threatening step toward her, and she crosses and unlocks the door up Right. As* EMMA *turns the key,* LIZZIE *realizes that she is still holding the axe concealed in a fold of her skirt. She has barely time to conceal it in the folded newspaper on the table when* NELLIE CUTTS *barges in.* EMMA *drifts down Right by window*) Now this is real nice of you, Miss Lizzie. (LIZZIE *draws a handkerchief from her sleeve and wipes her brow and the palms of her hands*) Hot day—hope we have rain. What's the forecast? What's the paper say? (*Reaching for it*)

LIZZIE   (*Quickly*) Fair and warmer. (*Her finger, pointing to the forecast, holds the paper firmly down.*)

NELLIE   (*Reading*) Fair and *cooler.* (*She gives* LIZZIE *a quick look.*)

LIZZIE   Now, then, young woman, be quick.

NELLIE   I'll take only a few minutes of your time. (*She takes out pencil and copy-paper*) Tell me, Miss Lizzie —I've been thinking about the murder weapon. It was never found. What's your opinion? Where did it get to?

LIZZIE   I think the murderer carried it away with him.

(NELLIE *tries to note this reply, but the paper is too flimsy.*)

NELLIE   Say, I'll have to have something to lean on. Where's that box? Here, the newspaper will do. (*Reaching for it*)

(LIZZIE *sits down quickly in the Left chair, leaning her elbow on the paper and her chin on her hand.*)

LIZZIE   Emma, get your friend a book. (EMMA *fetches a book from the mantel,* LIZZIE *talking fast the while*) An axe isn't an easy thing to hide, is it? Such an odd shape, and heavy too. Of course you could burn the handle, but what would you do with the head?

NELLIE   (*Accepting the book from* EMMA *and making a note*) Say, I never thought of that. (EMMA *drifts back down Right.*)

LIZZIE   All in all, I'm convinced that the murderer carried off his weapon with him. Well, thank you very much.

NELLIE   Say, Miss Lizzie, I'm not nearly through.

LIZZIE   (*Rising*) I have nothing more to say. (*Crossing down Right and speaking directly to* EMMA) Miss Emma is leaving now. You can walk with her to the station.

NELLIE   Well . . . (*Putting up her paper and pencil*) Say, isn't this the Providence *Journal*? I'll just take a look at it. . . . (*She has picked it up from the table while talking.* LIZZIE, *her attention fixed on* EMMA, *is too far away to stop her. The axe falls with a clatter in front of the table.* EMMA's *eyes fix. She circles Left of table, her eyes on the axe, and bends slowly to pick it up.*)

LIZZIE (*Sharply*) Emma! Don't miss your train!

EMMA (*Confused, hand to mouth*) Oh, dear, I mustn't miss my train.

LIZZIE (*Pushing her firmly toward the door*) Here's your purse. And your grip . . .

(EMMA *accepts the things and opens the door. On the threshold she stops and turns back. She stands on the landing, and takes in the room slowly, item by item. Then she looks directly at* LIZZIE, *standing Left of the step.*)

EMMA I'll send for my things, Lizzie.

LIZZIE Very well, Emma.

EMMA Good-bye, Lizzie.

(*She goes. The door closes.* LIZZIE *stands motionless, back to audience.*)

LIZZIE Good-bye, Emma.

NELLIE Send for her things—say, isn't she coming back?

LIZZIE (*Over her shoulder*) What did you say?

NELLIE Isn't she coming back?

LIZZIE (*Looking after* EMMA) No. She isn't coming back.

NELLIE (*Looking at the axe, on the floor below the table*) Whole thing torn wide open, eh? Say, Miss Lizzie, now will you give me a statement?

LIZZIE Certainly not.

NELLIE Miss Emma thinks now you killed them, doesn't she? *Did* you, Miss Lizzie? Did you kill them?

LIZZIE (*Wearily, no expression*) No, I didn't kill them.

NELLIE (*Crowding her*) Come along, Miss Lizzie, give me the straight tip. You've been acquitted, you can't be tried again. Go ahead, spill it.

LIZZIE (*Coming down Right*) I didn't do it.

NELLIE Then who did it? It was somebody in this house. There's the murder weapon. If you didn't do it, who did? Maggie? Miss Emma? (**LIZZIE** *stiffens, but says nothing.* **NELLIE** *snaps her fingers*) Miss Emma! That's it! I see it all! What a sensation! They can't try Miss Lizzie Borden again—but they can try Miss Emma! And I'll be in the thick of it! I see the headlines! Miss Emma Borden unmasked! Reporter bares murder weapon! Miss Emma's marks on deadly axe! Slayer of two condemned to die! Miss Lizzie's martyrdom in vain! It's the sensation of the century! Miss Emma Borden! Why didn't I see it before!

LIZZIE Stop talking such rubbish, young woman, and get out that pencil of yours. I'll make a statement. I did it.

NELLIE (*Delighted, descending on* **LIZZIE**) You killed them? You killed them both? With the axe?

LIZZIE (*Crossing away from her down Left*) I killed them. I killed them both. With the axe.

NELLIE Why? Why did you kill them?

LIZZIE (*Turning on her, sick of the whole thing—ferociously*) I don't like cold mutton soup!

NELLIE (*Walking Right, taking it down.*) Chiggers, what a scoop!

LIZZIE (*Coolly*) 'Tisn't such a scoop.

NELLIE It isn't? Why not?

LIZZIE 'Tisn't a scoop if you can't print it (*striding to her*) and I'll sue you if you print it. I've been acquitted in open court—I'm innocent, and don't you forget it. You print a word of this, and you'll hear from me. I've got a quarter of a million dollars, my girl, and I'll spend every cent of it, if I have to, to defend my good name.

NELLIE (*Jaw to jaw, contemptuously*) Good name! Everybody in Fall River knows you did it. You just admitted it yourself.

LIZZIE Never mind what they know. Never you mind what I just admitted. Just *you* keep your tongue between your teeth. You're not going to print that story, so you can just tear up those notes of yours.

(*She turns away contemptuously. Her foot touches the axe on the floor, and she automatically picks it up.*)

NELLIE (*Defiantly*) I certainly will not tear it up. I have a duty to my paper . . .

LIZZIE (*Turning on her, axe in hand, authoritatively*) I said tear it up.

(LIZZIE *is used to being obeyed, but this time the results rather surprise her.* NELLIE *catches sight of the axe and begins to back toward the door, tearing the notes the while*)

NELLIE Of course, Miss Lizzie, glad to oblige you. Thank you, Miss Lizzie. I'm just going, Miss Lizzie . . . (*She reaches the door, pauses a moment on the step, and looks at* LIZZIE *with horror*) No wonder Miss Emma isn't coming back! Good-bye, Miss Lizzie Borden!

(LIZZIE *is left by the table with the axe in her hand. She lifts it, looks at it with loathing, and is about to set it down when from outside comes the rattle of palings and the same childish voice is heard chanting:*)

LITTLE GIRL Lizzie Borden took an axe
And gave her mother forty whacks
And when she saw what she had done
She gave her father forty-one.

(LIZZIE's *grip on the axe tightens in anger as she listens, and she draws the axe elbow high. When the quatrain is finished she lets the axe strike into the wood in a gesture of hopelessness, letting it fall without force into the wood of the table. She works it loose, and again lets it fall. Suddenly she brings the axe around in a full circle and crashes it savagely into the table as the curtain falls.)*

McGOWNEY'S MIRACLE

Margaret Millar

With the publication of her first novel, The Invisible Worm, *in 1941, Margaret Millar immediately established herself as an important writer of mystery and suspense fiction. Such subsequent novels as* Wall of Eyes, Beast in View, How Like an Angel, The Fiend, *and* Beyond This Point Are Monsters *have enhanced that reputation. Many discerning readers, writers, and critics consider her work to be, at the very least, the equal in literary merit of that of her more famous husband, Kenneth Millar (Ross Macdonald). She has published only a trio of short stories, but each is a gem, and "McGowney's Miracle," the tale of an undertaker and his second wife, is perhaps the most finely polished of the three.*

When I finally found him, it was by accident. He was waiting for a cable car on Powell Street, a dignified little man about sixty, in a black topcoat and a gray fedora. He stood apart from the crowd, aloof but friendly, his hands clasped just below his chest, like a minister about to bless a batch of heathen. I knew he wasn't a minister.

A sheet of fog hung over San Francisco, blurring the lights and muffling the clang of the cable cars.

I stepped up behind McGowney and said, "Good evening."

There was no recognition in his eyes, no hesitation in his voice. "Why, good evening, sir." He turned with a little smile. "It is kind of you to greet a stranger so pleasantly."

For a moment, I was almost ready to believe I'd made a mistake. There are on record many cases of perfect doubles, and what's more, I hadn't seen McGowney since the beginning of July. But there was one important thing McGowney couldn't conceal: his voice still carried the throaty accents of the funeral parlor.

He tipped his hat and began walking briskly up Powell Street toward the hill, his topcoat flapping around his skinny legs like broken wings.

In the middle of the block, he turned to see if I was following him. I was. He walked on, shaking his head from side to side as if genuinely puzzled by my interest in him. At the next corner, he stopped in front of a department store and waited for me, leaning against the window, his hands in his pockets.

When I approached, he looked up at me, frowning. "I don't know why you're following me, young man, but—"

"Why don't you ask me, McGowney?"

But he didn't ask. He just repeated his own name,

"McGowney," in a surprised voice, as if he hadn't heard it for a long time.

I said, "I'm Eric Meecham, Mrs. Keating's lawyer. We've met before."

"I've met a great many people. Some I recall, some I do not."

"I'm sure you recall Mrs. Keating. You conducted her funeral last July."

"Of course, of course. A great lady, a very great lady. Her demise saddened the hearts of all who had the privilege of her acquaintance, all who tasted the sweetness of her smile—"

"Come off it, McGowney. Mrs. Keating was a sharp-tongued virago without a friend in this world."

He turned away from me, but I could see the reflection of his face in the window, strained and anxious.

"You're a long way from home, McGowney."

"This is my home now."

"You left Arbana very suddenly."

"To me it was not sudden. I had been planning to leave for twenty years, and when the time came, I left. It was summer then, but all I could think of was the winter coming on and everything dying. I had had enough of death."

"Mrs. Keating was your last—client?"

"She was."

"Her coffin was exhumed last week."

A cable car charged up the hill like a drunken rocking horse, its sides bulging with passengers. Without warning, McGowney darted out into the street and sprinted up the hill after the car. In spite of his age, he could have made it, but the car was so crowded there wasn't a single space for him to get a handhold. He stopped running and stood motionless in the center of the street, staring after the car as it plunged and reared up the hill. Oblivious to the honks and shouts of motorists, he walked slowly back to the curb where I was waiting.

"You can't run away, McGowney."

He glanced at me wearily, without speaking. Then he took out a half-soiled handkerchief and wiped the moisture from his forehead.

"The exhumation can't be much of a surprise to you," I said. "You wrote me the anonymous letter suggesting it. It was postmarked Berkeley. That's why I'm here in this area."

"I wrote you no letter," he said.

"The information it contained could have come only from you."

"No. Somebody else knew as much about it as I did."

"Who?"

"My—wife."

"Your wife." It was the most unexpected answer he could have given me. Mrs. McGowney had died, along with her only daughter, in the flu epidemic after World War I. The story is the kind that still goes the rounds in a town like Arbana, even after thirty-five years: McGowney, unemployed after his discharge from the army, had had no funds to pay for the double funeral, and when the undertaker offered him an apprenticeship to work off the debt, McGowney accepted. It was common knowledge that after his wife's death he never so much as looked at another woman, except, of course, in the line of duty.

I said, "So you've married again."

"Yes."

"When?"

"Six months ago."

"Right after you left Arbana."

"Yes."

"You didn't lose much time starting a new life for yourself."

"I couldn't afford to. I'm not young."

"Did you marry a local woman?"

"Yes."

I didn't realize until later that he had taken "local" to mean Arbana, not San Francisco as I had intended.

I said, "You think your wife wrote me that anonymous letter?"

"Yes."

The streetlights went on, and I realized it was getting late and cold. McGowney pulled up his coat collar and put on a pair of ill-fitting white cotton gloves. I had seen him wearing gloves like that before; they were as much a part of his professional equipment as his throaty voice and his vast store of sentimental aphorisms.

He caught me staring at the gloves and said, with a trace of apology, "Money is a little tight these days. My wife is knitting me a pair of woolen gloves for my birthday."

"You're not working?"

"No."

"It shouldn't be hard for a man of your experience to find a job in your particular field." I was pretty sure he hadn't even applied for one. During the past few days, I had contacted nearly every mortician within the Bay area; McGowney had not been to any of them.

"I don't want a job in my particular field," McGowney said.

"It's the only thing you're trained for."

"Yes. But I no longer believe in death."

He spoke with simple earnestness, as if he had said, I no longer play blackjack, or I no longer eat salted peanuts.

Death, blackjack, or salted peanuts—I was not prepared to argue with McGowney about any of them, so I said, "My car's in the garage at the Canterbury Hotel. We'll walk over and get it, and I'll drive you home."

We started toward Sutter Street. The stream of shoppers had been augmented by a flow of white-collar workers, but all the people and the noise and the confusion left McGowney untouched. He moved sedately along beside me, smiling a little to himself, like a man who has developed the faculty of walking out on the world from time to time and going to live on some remote and happy island of his own. I wondered where McGowney's island was and who lived there with him. I knew only one thing for sure: on McGowney's island there was no death.

He said suddenly, "It must have been very difficult."

"What was?"

"The exhumation. The ground gets so hard back East in the wintertime. I presume you didn't attend, Mr. Meecham?"

"You presume wrong."

"My, that's no place for an amateur."

For my money, it was no place for anyone. The cemetery had been white with snow that had fallen during the night. Dawn had been breaking, if you could call that meager, grudging light a dawn. The simple granite headstone had read: ELEANOR REGINA KEATING, OCTOBER 3, 1899– JUNE 30, 1953. A BLESSED ONE FROM US IS GONE, A VOICE WE LOVED IS STILL.

The blessed one had been gone, all right. Two hours later, when the coffin was pulled up and opened, the smell that rose from it was not the smell of death, but the smell of newspapers rotted with dampness and stones gray-greened with mildew.

I said, "You know what we found, don't you, McGowney?"

"Naturally. I directed the funeral."

"You accept sole responsibility for burying an empty coffin?"

"Not sole responsibility, no."

"Who was in with you? And why?"

He merely shook his head.

As we waited for a traffic light, I studied McGowney's face, trying to estimate the degree of his sanity. There seemed to be no logic behind his actions. Mrs. Keating had died quite unmysteriously of a heart attack and had been buried, according to her instructions to me, in a closed coffin. The doctor who had signed the death certificate was indisputably honest. He had happened to be in Mrs. Keating's house at the time, attending to her older daughter,

Mary, who had had a cold. He had examined Mrs. Keating, pronounced her dead, and sent for McGowney. Two days later I had escorted Mary, still sniffling (whether from grief or the same cold, I don't know), to the funeral. McGowney, as usual, said and did all the correct things.

Except one. He neglected to put Mrs. Keating's body in the coffin.

Time had passed. No one had particularly mourned Mrs. Keating. She had been an unhappy woman, mentally and morally superior to her husband, who had been killed during a drinking spree in New Orleans, and to her two daughters, who resembled their father. I had been Mrs. Keating's lawyer for three years. I had enjoyed talking to her; she had had a quick mind and a sharp sense of humor. But as in the case of many wealthy people who have been cheated of the privilege of work and the satisfactions it brings, she had been a bored and lonely woman who carried despair on her shoulder like a pet parakeet and fed it from time to time on scraps from her bitter memories.

Right after Mrs. Keating's funeral, McGowney had sold his business and left town. No one in Arbana had connected the two events until the anonymous letter arrived from Berkeley shortly before Mrs. Keating's will was awaiting admission into probate. The letter, addressed to me, had suggested the exhumation and stated the will must be declared invalid since there was no proof of death. I could think of no reason why McGowney's new wife wrote the letter, unless she had tired of him and had chosen a roundabout method of getting rid of him.

The traffic light changed, and McGowney and I crossed the street and waited under the hotel marquee while the doorman sent for my car. I didn't look at McGowney, but I could feel him watching me intently.

"You think I'm mad, eh, Meecham?"

It wasn't a question I was prepared to answer. I tried to look noncommittal.

"I don't pretend to be entirely normal, Meecham. Do you?"

"I try."

McGowney's hand, in its ill-fitting glove, reached over and touched my arm, and I forced myself not to slap it away. It perched on my coat sleeve like a wounded pigeon. "But suppose you had an abnormal experience."

"Like you?"

"Like me. It was a shock, a great shock, even though I had always had the feeling that someday it would happen. I was on the watch for it every time I had a new case. It was always in my mind. You might even say I *willed* it."

Two trickles of sweat oozed down behind my ears into my collar. "What did you will, McGowney?"

"I willed her to live again."

I became aware the doorman was signaling to me. My car was at the curb with the engine running.

I climbed in behind the wheel, and McGowney followed me into the car with obvious reluctance, as if he was already regretting what he'd told me.

"You don't believe me," he said as we pulled away from the curb.

"I'm a lawyer. I deal in facts."

"A fact is what happens, isn't it?"

"Close enough."

"Well, this happened."

"She came back to life?"

"Yes."

"By the power of your will alone?"

He stirred restlessly in the seat beside me. "I gave her oxygen and adrenaline."

"Have you done this with other clients of yours?"

"Many times, yes."

"Is this procedure usual among members of your profession?"

"For me it was usual," McGowney said earnestly. "I've always wanted to be a doctor. I was in the Medical Corps during the war, and I picked up a little knowledge here and there."

"Enough to perform miracles?"

"It was not my knowledge that brought her back to life. It was my will. She had lost the will to live, but I had enough for both of us."

If it is true that only a thin line separates sanity and madness, McGowney crossed and recrossed that line a dozen times within an hour, jumping over it and back again, like a child skipping rope.

"You understand now, Meecham? She had lost all desire. I saw it happening to her. We never spoke—I doubt she even knew my name—but for years I watched her pass my office on her morning walk. I saw the change come over her, the dullness of her eyes and the way she walked. I knew she was going to die. One day when she was passing by, I went out to tell her, to warn her. But when she saw me, she ran. I think she realized what I was going to say."

He was telling the truth, according to his lights. Mrs. Keating had mentioned the incident to me last spring. I recalled her words: "A funny thing occurred this morning, Meecham. As I was walking past the undertaking parlor, that odd little man rushed out and almost scared the life out of me. . . ."

In view of what subsequently happened, this was a giant among ironies. As we drove toward the Bay Bridge and Berkeley, McGowney told me his story.

It was midday at the end of June, and the little back room McGowney used as a lab was hot and humid after a morning rain.

Mrs. Keating woke up as if from a long and troubled sleep. Her hands twitched, her mouth moved in distress, a pulse began to beat in her temple. Tears squeezed out from between her closed lids and slithered past the tips of her ears into the folds of her hair.

McGowney bent over her, quivering with excitement. "Mrs. Keating! Mrs. Keating! You are alive!"

"Oh—God."

"A miracle has just happened!"

"Leave me alone. I'm tired."

"You are alive, you are *alive*!"

Slowly she opened her eyes and looked up at him. "You officious little wretch, what have you done?"

McGowney stepped back, stunned and shaken. "But —but you are alive. It's happened. My miracle has happened."

"Alive. Miracle." She mouthed the words as if they were lumps of alum. "You meddling idiot."

"I— But I—"

"Pour me a glass of water. My throat is parched."

He was trembling so violently he could hardly get the water out of the cooler. This was his miracle. He had hoped and waited for it all his life, and now it had exploded in his face like an April-fool cigar.

He gave her the water and sat down heavily in a chair, watching her while she drank very slowly, as if in her short recess from life her muscles had already begun to forget their function.

"Why did you do it?" Mrs. Keating crushed the paper cup in her fist as if it were McGowney himself. "Who asked you for a miracle, anyway?"

"But I— Well, the fact is—"

"The fact is, you're a blooming meddler, that's what the fact is, McGowney."

"Yes, ma'am."

"Now what are you going to do?"

"Well, I—I hadn't thought."

"Then you'd better start right now."

"Yes, ma'am." He stared down at the floor, his head hot with misery, his limbs cold with disappointment. "First, I had better call the doctor."

"You'll call no one, McGowney."

"But your family—they'll want to know right away that—"

"They are not going to know."

"But—"

"No one is going to know, McGowney. No one at all. Is that clear?"

"Yes."

"Now sit down and be quiet and let me think."

He sat down and was quiet. He had no desire to move or to speak. Never had he felt so futile and depressed.

"I suppose," Mrs. Keating said grimly, "you expect me to be grateful to you."

McGowney shook his head.

"If you do, you must be crazy." She paused and looked at him thoughtfully.

"You are a little crazy, aren't you, McGowney?"

"There are those who think so," he said, with some truth. "I don't agree."

"You wouldn't."

"Can't afford to, ma'am."

The windows of the room were closed and no street sounds penetrated the heavy frosted glass, but from the corridor outside the door came the sudden tap of footsteps on tile.

McGowney bolted across the room and locked the door and stood against it.

"Mr. McGowney? You in there?"

McGowney looked at Mrs. Keating. Her face had turned chalky, and she had one hand clasped to her throat.

"Mr. McGowney?"

"Yes, Jim."

"You're wanted on the telephone."

"I—can't come right now, Jim. Take a message."

"She wants to talk to you personally. It's the Keating girl, about the time and cost of the funeral arrangements."

"Tell her I'll call her back later."

"All right." There was a pause. "You feeling okay, Mr. McGowney?"

"Yes."

"You sound kind of funny."

"I'm fine, Jim. Absolutely first-rate."

"Okay. Just thought I'd ask."

The footsteps tapped back down the tile corridor.

"Mary loses no time." Mrs. Keating spoke through dry, stiff lips. "She wants me safely underground so she can marry her electrician. Well, your duty is clear, McGowney."

"What is it?"

"Put me there."

McGowney stood propped against the door like a wooden soldier. "You mean, b-b-bury you?"

"Me, or a reasonable facsimile."

"That I couldn't do, Mrs. Keating. It wouldn't be ethical."

"It's every bit as ethical as performing unsolicited miracles."

"You don't understand the problems."

"Such as?"

"For one thing, your family and friends. They'll want to see you lying in— What I mean is, it's customary to put the body on view."

"I can handle that part of it all right."

"How?"

"Get me a pen and some paper."

McGowney didn't argue, because he knew he was at fault. It was his miracle; he'd have to take the consequences.

Mrs. Keating predated the letter by three weeks, and wrote the following:

To whom it may concern, not that it should concern anybody except myself:

I am giving these instructions to Mr. McGowney concerning my funeral arrangements. Inasmuch as I have valued privacy during my life, I want no intrusion on it after my death. I am instructing Mr. McGowney to close my coffin immediately and to see it stays closed, in spite of any mawkish pleas from my survivors.

Elinor Regina Keating

She folded the paper twice and handed it to McGowney. "You are to show this to Mary and Joan and to Mr. Meecham, my lawyer." She paused, looking very pleased with herself. "Well. This is getting to be quite exciting, eh, McGowney?"

"Quite," McGowney said listlessly.

"As a matter of fact, it's given me an appetite. I don't suppose there's a kitchen connected with this place?"

"No."

"Then you'd better get me something from the corner drugstore. A couple of tuna-salad sandwiches, on wheat, with plenty of coffee. Lunch," she added with a satiric little smile, "will have to be on you. I forgot my handbag."

"Money," McGowney said. *"Money."*

"What about it?"

"What will happen to your money?"

"I made a will some time ago."

"But *you*, what will you live on?"

"Perhaps," Mrs. Keating said dryly, "you'd better perform another miracle."

When he returned from the drugstore with her lunch, Mrs. Keating ate and drank with obvious enjoyment. She offered McGowney a part of the second sandwich, but he was too disheartened to eat. His miracle, which had started out as a great golden bubble, had turned into an iron ball chained to his leg.

Somehow he got through the day. Leaving Mrs. Keating in the lab with some old magazines and a bag of apples, McGowney went about his business. He talked to Mary and Joan Keating in person and to Meecham on the telephone. He gave his assistant, Jim Wagner, the rest of the afternoon off, and when Jim had gone, he filled Mrs. Keating's coffin (the de luxe white-and-bronze model Mary had chosen out of the catalogue) with rocks packed in newspapers, until it was precisely the right weight.

McGowney was a small man, unaccustomed to physical exertion, and by the time he had finished, his body was throbbing with weariness.

It was at this point Mary Keating telephoned to say she and Joan had been thinking the matter over, and since Mrs. Keating had always inclined toward thrift, it was decided she would never rest at ease in such an ostentatious affair as the white and bronze. The plain gray would be far more appropriate, as well as cheaper.

"You should," McGowney said coldly, "have let me know sooner."

"We just decided a second ago."

"It's too late to change now."

"I don't see why."

"There are—certain technicalities."

"Well, really, Mr. McGowney. If you're not willing to put yourself out a little, maybe we should take our business somewhere else."

"No! You can't do that—I mean, it wouldn't be proper, Miss Keating."

"It's a free country."

"Wait a minute. Suppose I give you a special price on the white and bronze."

"How special?"

"Say, twenty-five percent off?"

There was a whispered conference at the other end of the line, and then Mary said, "It's still a lot of money."

"Thirty-five."

"Well, that seems more *like* it," Mary said, and hung up.

The door of McGowney's office opened, and Mrs. Keating crossed the room, wearing a grim little smile.

McGowney looked at her helplessly. "You shouldn't be out here, ma'am. You'd better go back and—"

"I heard the telephone ring, and I thought it might be Mary."

"It wasn't."

"Yes, it was, McGowney. I heard every word."

"Well," McGowney cleared his throat. "Well. You shouldn't have listened."

"Oh, I'm not surprised. Or hurt. You needn't be sorry for me. I haven't felt so good in years. You know why?"

"No, ma'am."

"Because I don't have to go home. I'm free. Free as a bird." She reached over and touched his coat sleeve. "I don't have to go home, do I?"

"I guess not."

"You'll never tell anyone?"

"No."

"You're a very good man, McGowney."

"I have never thought I wasn't," McGowney said simply.

When darkness fell, McGowney got his car out of the garage and brought it around to the ambulance entrance behind his office.

"You'd better hide in the backseat," he said, "until we get out of town."

"Where are we going?"

"I thought I'd drive you into Detroit, and from there you can catch a bus or a train."

"To where?"

"To anywhere. You're free as a bird." She got into the backseat, shivering in spite of the mildness of the night, and McGowney covered her with a blanket.

"McGowney."

"Yes, ma'am?"

"I felt freer when I was locked in your little lab."

"You're a bit frightened now, that's all. Freedom is a mighty big thing."

He turned the car toward the highway. Half an hour later, when the city's lights had disappeared, he stopped the car, and Mrs. Keating got into the front seat with the blanket wrapped around her shoulders, Indian style. In the gloom of oncoming headlights, her face looked a little troubled. McGowney felt duty bound to cheer her up, since he was reponsible for her being there in the first place.

"There are," he said firmly, "wonderful places to be seen."

"Are there?"

"California, that's the spot I'd pick. Flowers all year round, never an end to them." He hesitated. "I've saved a bit throughout the years. I always thought someday I'd sell the business and retire to California."

"What's to prevent you?"

"I couldn't face the idea, of, well, of being alone out there without friends or a family of some kind. Have you ever been to California?"

"I spent a couple of summers in San Francisco."

"Did you like it?"

"Very much."

"I'd like it, too, I'm sure of that." He cleared his throat. "Being alone, though, that I wouldn't like. Are you warm enough?"

"Yes, thanks."

"Birds—well, birds don't have such a happy time of it that I can see."

"No?"

"All that freedom and not knowing what to do with it except fly around. A life like that couldn't suit a mature woman like yourself, Mrs. Keating."

"Perhaps not."

"What I mean is—"

"I know what you mean, McGowney."

"You—you do?"

"Of course."

McGowney flushed. "It's—well, it's very unexpected, isn't it?"

"Not to me."

"But I never thought of it until half an hour ago."

"I did. Women are more foresighted in these matters."

McGowney was silent a moment. "This hasn't been a very romantic proposal. I ought to say something a bit on the sentimental side."

"Go ahead."

He gripped the steering wheel hard. "I think I love you, ma'am."

"You didn't have to say that," she replied sharply. "I'm not a foolish young girl to be taken in by words. At my age, I don't expect love. I don't want to—"

"But you are loved," McGowney declared.

"I don't believe it."

"Eventually you will."

"Is this another of your miracles, McGowney?"

"This is the important one."

It was the first time in Mrs. Keating's life she had been told she was loved. She sat beside McGowney in awed silence, her hands folded on her lap, like a little girl in Sunday school.

McGowney left her at a hotel in Detroit and went home to hold her funeral.

Two weeks later they were married by a justice of the peace in a little town outside Chicago. On the long and leisurely trip west in McGowney's car, neither of them talked much about the past or worried about the future. McGowney had sold his business, but he'd been in too much of a hurry to wait for a decent price, and so his funds were limited. But he never mentioned this to his bride.

By the time they reached San Francisco, they had gone through quite a lot of McGowney's capital. A large portion of the remainder went toward the purchase of the little house in Berkeley.

By late fall, they were almost broke, and McGowney got a job as a shoe clerk in a department store. A week later, along with his first paycheck, he received his notice of dismissal.

That night at dinner he told Eleanor about it, pretending it was all a joke, and inventing a couple of anecdotes to make her laugh.

She listened, grave and unamused. "So that's what you've been doing all week. Selling shoes."

"Yes."

"You didn't tell me we needed money that badly."

"We'll be all right. I can easily get another job."

"Doing what?"

"What I've always done."

She reached across the table and touched his hand. "You don't want to be a mortician again."

"I don't mind."

"You always hated it."

"I *don't mind,* I tell you."

She rose decisively.

"Eleanor, what are you going to do?"

"Write a letter," she said with a sigh.

"Eleanor, don't do anything drastic."

"We have had a lot of happiness. It couldn't last forever. Don't be greedy."

The meaning of her words pierced McGowney's brain. "You're going to let someone know you're alive?"

"No. I couldn't face that, not just yet. I'm merely going to show them I'm not dead so they can't divide up my estate."

"But why?"

"As my husband, you're entitled to a share of it if anything happens to me."

"Nothing will ever happen to you. We agreed about that, didn't we?"

"Yes, McGowney. We agreed."

"We no longer believe in death."

"I will address the letter to Meecham," she said.

"So she wrote the letter." McGowney's voice was weary. "For my sake. You know the rest, Meecham."

"Not quite," I said.

"What else do you want to know?"

"The ending."

"The ending." McGowney stirred in the seat beside me and let out his breath in a sigh. "I don't believe in endings."

I turned right at the next traffic light, as McGowney directed. A sign on the lamppost said LINDEN AVENUE.

Three blocks south was a small green-and-white house, its eaves dripping with fog.

I parked my car in front of it and got out, pleasantly excited at the idea of seeing Mrs. Keating again. McGowney sat motionless, staring straight ahead of him, until I opened the car door.

"Come on, McGowney."

"Eh? Oh. All right. All right."

He stepped out on the sidewalk so awkwardly he almost fell. I took his arm. "Is anything wrong?"

"No."

We went up the porch steps.

"There are no lights on," McGowney said. "Eleanor must be at the store. Or over at the neighbor's. We have some very nice neighbors."

The front door was not locked. We went inside and McGowney turned on the lights in the hall and the sitting room to the right.

The woman I had known as Mrs. Keating was sitting in a wing chair in front of the fireplace, her head bent forward as if she were in deep thought. Her knitting had fallen on the floor, and I saw it was a half-finished glove in bright colors. McGowney's birthday present.

In silence, McGowney reached down and picked up the glove and put it on a table. Then he touched his wife gently on the forehead. I knew from the way his hand flinched that her skin was as cold as the ashes in the grate.

I said, "I'll get a doctor."

"No."

"She's dead?"

He didn't bother to answer. He was looking down at his

wife with a coaxing expression. "Eleanor dear, you must wake up. We have a visitor."

"McGowney, for God's sake—"

"I think you'd better leave now, Mr. Meecham," he said in a firm, clear voice. "I have work to do."

He took off his coat and rolled up his sleeves.

ST. PATRICK'S DAY IN THE MORNING

Charlotte Armstrong

Poet, dramatist, and novelist Charlotte Armstrong (1905–1969) was born in an iron-mining town in Michigan's Upper Peninsula—a place whose isolation undoubtedly was a stimulus to her natural imagination. After moving to New York in the early 1920s, she worked as a fashion reporter, then published poetry in The New Yorker. *Her plays,* The Happiest Days *and* Ring Around Elizabeth, *were produced on Broadway but with notable lack of success, running a total of seventeen days. It was with mystery fiction that Ms. Armstrong found her métier; her fourth novel,* The Unsuspected, *was widely praised, and* A Dram of Poison *won the Mystery Writers of America Edgar for Best Novel of 1956. In her novels and short stories—of which "St. Patrick's Day in the Morning" is a particularly fine example—Ms. Armstrong repeatedly proves critic Anthony Boucher's contention that she was "one of the few authentic spell-casting witches of modern times."*

Very carefully, in a state of fearful pleasure, he put all the pieces of paper in order. One copy of the manuscript he put into an envelope and addressed it. The other copies he put into an empty suitcase. Then he called an airline and was lucky. A seat for New York in the morning. Morning? What morning? St. Patrick's Day in the morning.

He had been out of this world. But now he stretched, breathed, blinked, and put out feelers for what is known as reality.

See now. He was Mitchel Brown, playwright (God willing), and he had finished the job of revision he had come home to Los Angeles to do. Wowee! Finished!

The hour was a quarter after one in the morning and therefore already the seventeenth of March. The place was his ground-floor apartment, and it was a mess: smoky, dirty, disorderly. . . . Oh, well, first things had come first. His back was aching, his eyes were burning, his head was light. He would have to clean up, eat, sleep, bathe, shave, dress, pack. But first . . .

He slammed a row of airmail stamps on the envelope and went out. The street was dark and deserted. A few cars sat lumpishly along the curbs. The manuscript thumped down into the mailbox—safe in the bosom of the Postal Service. Now, even if he, the plane, and the other copies perished . . .

Mitch laughed at himself and turned the corner, feeling suddenly let down, depressed, and forlorn.

The Parrakeet Bar and Grill, he noted gratefully, was still open. He walked the one block and went in. The Bar ran all the way along one wall and the Grill, consisting of eight booths, ran all the way along the other. The narrow room was dim and felt empty. Mitch groped for a stool.

"Hi, Toby. Business slow?"

"Hi, Mr. Brown." The bartender seemed glad to see him. He was a small man with a crest of dark hair, a blue chin and a blue tinge to the whites of his eyes. "This late on a weeknight, I'm never crowded."

"The kitchen's gone home, eh?" Mitch said. The kitchen was not the heart of this establishment.

"That's right, Mr. Brown. You want any food, you better go elsewhere."

"A drink will do me," said Mitch with a sigh. "*I* can go home and scramble yet another egg."

Toby turned to his bottles. When he turned back with Mitch's usual, he said in an anxious whine, "Fact is, I got to close up pretty soon and I don't know what to do."

"What do you mean, what to do?"

"Look at her." Toby's gaze passed over Mitch's left shoulder.

Mitch glanced behind him and was startled to see there was a woman sitting in one of the booths. Or perhaps one could say lying, since her fair hatless head was down on the red-checked tablecloth. Mitch turned again and wagged inquiring eyebrows.

"Out like a light," said Toby in a hoarse whisper. "Listen, I don't want to call the cops. Thing like that, not so good for the place. But I got a kid sick and my wife is all wore out and I wanted to get home."

"You try black coffee?"

"Sure, I tried." Toby's shoulders despaired.

"How'd she get this way?"

"Not here," said Toby quickly. "Don't see how. So help me, a coupla drinks hit her like that. Trouble is, she's not a bum. You can see that. So what should I do?"

"Put her in a taxi," said Mitch blithely. "Just ship her where she belongs. Why not? She'll have something on her for identity."

"I don't want to mess around with her pocketbook," Toby said fearfully.

"Hm. Well, let's see . . ." Mitch got off the stool. His

drink had gone down and bounced lightly and he was feeling cheerful and friendly toward all the world. Furthermore, he felt *very* intelligent and he understood that he had been born to understand everybody.

Toby came too, and they lifted the woman's torso.

Her face was slack in drunken sleep; but even so it was not an ugly face. It was not young; neither was it old. Her clothing was expensive. No, she wasn't a tramp.

Then she opened her eyes and said in a refined voice, "I beg your pardon."

She was not exactly conscious; still this was encouraging. The two men got her to her feet. With their support she could stand. In fact, she could walk. Mitch ran his left arm through the handle of her expensive-looking handbag. The two of them walked her to the door.

"The air maybe?" said the bartender hopefully.

"Right," said Mitch. "Listen, there's a cab stand next to the movie theater. By the time we walk her over there . . ."

Toby said shrilly. "I got to lock up. I got to take care of the place."

"Go ahead," said Mitch, standing in the sweet night air with the strange woman heavy in his arms, "I've got her."

He heard the lock click behind him as he set off on the sidewalk, the woman putting one foot ahead of the other willingly enough. Musing on the peculiar and surprising qualities of "reality," Mitch had guided her halfway along the block before he recognized the fact that the bartender had taken him literally and was not coming along at all.

Oh, well. Mitch was not annoyed. On the contrary, he felt filled with compassion for all human beings. This woman was human and, therefore, frail. He was glad to try to help her to some place of her own.

The neighborhood business section was deserted. They were moving in an empty world. When Mitch had struggled all the way to the next corner, he could see ahead that there were no cabs near the theater. At this time of night the theater was dead and dark, as he should have known. He guessed he hadn't quite been meshed with the gears of ordinary time.

Anyhow, he couldn't turn her over to a handy cab driver. Nor to the police, since there were no policemen around either. There was nothing but pavement, those few lumps of metal left at the curb for the night, and no traffic.

Mitch wouldn't have hailed a motorist anyway. Most motorists were suspicious and afraid. So he did the only thing he could—he kept walking.

He guided her automatic steps around the corner and down the street, for surely, he thought, if he kept her walking she would begin to be conscious and he could then ask her what *she* wanted him to do about her. This he felt was the right thing. Perhaps he could get out his own car . . .

But the air was not having the desired effect. She began to stumble. Her weight slumped against him. Mitch found he was almost carrying her. Then he discovered that he was standing, holding her upright with both arms, directly in front of his own building. Obviously, the only thing to do was take her inside, where he could investigate her identity and telephone for a taxi.

The apartment had not tidied itself up during his absence. He let her weight go and she sagged down on his sofa. He guided her blond head to a pillow. There she lay, out like a light, a perfect stranger. To straighten the body and make it look more comfortable, he lifted the lower part of the legs. One of her shoes—beautiful shoes in a fine green leather, with a high spike heel and a small brass buckle—one of them came off.

Mitch took hold of the other shoe and also removed it. Full of cosmic thoughts about females and heels, he put her shoes on his desk and slipped her handbag off his arm. It was the same fine green leather.

It did feel sneaky to be rifling the property of a strange woman. Still, it had to be done.

Her name, on the driver's license, was Natalie Maxwell.

Her address was in Santa Barbara. Mitch whistled. That knocked over his scheme of sending her home in a cab, since her home was a hundred miles away. Then he found a letter addressed to Mrs. Julius Maxwell and Mitch whistled again. So she was married!

Furthermore, she was married to somebody whose name was familiar. Julius Maxwell. All that came to Mitch's musing memory was an aroma of money. She probably wasn't broke, then. He peered into her wallet and saw a few bills. Not many. So he riffled her checkbook and whistled for the third time. Well! No penniless waif, this one.

Mitch ran his hand through his hair and considered his predicament. Here he was, harboring a wealthy matron from Santa Barbara who had passed out from liquor. What was he going to do with her?

There was nothing in the bag to tell him where she was staying locally. The letter was woman's chatter from someone in San Francisco.

So what to do?

Well, he might phone the police and dump her on them. This he could not quite imagine. Or, he could phone the residence of Julius Maxwell, in Santa Barbara, and if her husband were there, ask for instructions; or, if he were not there, surely Mitch could ask somebody where Mrs. Maxwell was staying in Los Angeles, and dump her *there*. All this went through his mind and was rejected.

Why cause another human being humiliation and trouble? He didn't think she was ill. Just stinko. Sooner or later the fumes would wear away and she would come to herself. Meantime, she was perfectly safe, right where she was. Heaven knew he had no evil thoughts.

Also, he—Mitchel Brown, playwright, artist, apostle of compassion—*he* was no bourgeois to conform, cravenly fearing for his reputation if he were to do what is "not done." Was he, being what he was, to put this human being into a jam with the Law, or even with her own husband? When this human being, for some human reason, had simply imbibed a little too much alcohol? He couldn't do it.

Okay. He had been dragooned by his mood and by the perfidious desertion of Toby the bartender into acting the Samaritan. Why not be the *good* Samaritan, then? Give her a break.

This pleased him. It felt lucky to him. Give her a break. God knows we all need them, he thought piously.

So Mitch scribbled a note. *Dear Mrs. Maxwell: Use my phone if you like. Or be my guest, as long as you need to be.*

He signed it, went into his bedroom, got a light blanket, and spread it over her. She was snoring faintly. He studied her face a moment more. He put the note on the rug under her shoes where she would be sure to see it. Then he went into his bedroom, closed the door, and went to bed.

Mitchel Brown woke up on St. Patrick's Day, early in the morning, absolutely ravenous. He had forgotten to eat anything. Now he remembered. New York! Catch plane! Pack!

He started for his kitchen and at the bedroom door remembered the lady. So he turned and put a robe on before emerging.

He needn't have bothered. She was gone. Her shoes were gone. Her bag was gone. His note was gone. In fact, there was no trace of her at all.

He did *not* wonder whether he had been dreaming. So she had come to and fled. Hm, without even a "Thank you"? Oh, well, panic, he supposed. Ah, human frailty! Mitch shrugged. But he had things to do and not enough time to do them in.

He went into a spell of demon housekeeping, threw everything perishable out of his refrigerator, everything dirty into the laundry bag, everything wearable into his suitcase. He caught the plane by a whisker.

Once on it he began to suffer. He reread his manuscript in his mind's eye and squirmed with doubt. He tried to nap and could not, and then, suddenly, he could . . . and then he was in New York and God was willing and his producer was still hot and eager . . .

Six weeks later Mitchel Brown, playwright, got off the plane in Los Angeles. He had a play on Broadway. The verdict was *comme ci, comme ça.* Time, box office, word of mouth . . . personally he could bear no more. He wasn't licked, but he knew he would be unless he got home and got to work on something else and that, soon.

He had been out of this world all this time, for when one has a play in rehearsal, earthquake, major catastrophe, declaration of war mean nothing. Nothing whatever.

He got to his apartment about five A.M. and kicked aside the pile of newspapers he had forgotten to stop. The place smelled stale and wasn't really clean, but no matter. He opened all the windows, mixed himself a highball, and sat down with the last paper on the heap to catch up with the way the Western world had wagged since he had left it. International affairs he had glanced over, the last week in the East. Local affairs, of course, were completely unknown to him.

The latest murder, hm . . . Los Angeles papers are always hopeful that a murder is going to turn out to be a big one, so any and every murder gets off with a bang. This one didn't look promising. A mere brawl, he judged. Would die down in a couple of days.

He skimmed the second page where all the older murders were followed up. He had missed two or three. Some woman knifed by an ex-husband. Some man shot in his own hall. Run-of-the-mill. Mitch yawned. He would get out his car, go somewhere for a decent meal, he decided. Tomorrow, back to the salt mines.

At 6:30 P.M. he walked into his favorite restaurant, ordered a drink, settled to contemplate the menu.

She came in quietly about ten minutes later and sat down by herself at a table directly across from Mitch. The first thing he noted, with the tail of his eye, was her shoes.

He had seen them before. Yes, and held them—held them in his hands.

His eyes traveled higher and there was Mrs. Julius Maxwell. (Natalie was her given name, he remembered.) It was not only Mrs. Julius Maxwell in the flesh, but Mrs. Julius Maxwell *in the very same clothing she had worn before!* The same green suit, the same pale blouse, and no hat. She was a lady, well groomed, prosperous, pretty and poised—and now perfectly sober.

Mitch kept his head cocked and his eyes on her, waiting for her to feel his stare and respond to it. Her eyes came to his in a moment, but they were cool and empty of recognition.

Well, of course, he thought. How would she know me? She never *saw* me. He glanced away, feeling amused, then glanced back. Natalie Maxwell was ordering. She sat back, relaxed, and her gaze slipped past him again, returned briefly to note his interest, then went away, indicating none on her part.

Mitch could not help feeling that this was not fair. He got up and crossed to her. "How do you do, Mrs. Maxwell?" he said pleasantly. "I am glad you are feeling better."

"I beg your pardon?" she said. He remembered that he had heard her say this, and only this, once before.

"I'm Mitchel Brown." He waited, smiling down at her.

"I don't believe . . ." she murmured in genteel puzzlement. She had a nice straight nose and, although she was looking up at him, she seemed to be looking down that nose.

"I'm sure you remember the name," Mitch said. "It was the sixteenth of March. No, it was Saint Patrick's Day in the morning, actually."

"I don't quite . . ."

Was she stupid or what? Mitch said, with a bit of a sting in the tone, "Did you have much of a hangover?"

"I'm very *sorry*," she said with a little exasperated laugh, "but I really don't know what you are talking about."

"Oh, come now, Natalie," said Mitch, beginning to feel miffed, "it was my apartment."

"What?" she said.

"My apartment that you passed out in—here in Los Angeles."

"I am afraid you are making a mistake," she said distantly.

Mitch did not think so.

"Aren't you Mrs. Julius Maxwell?"

"Yes, I am."

"From Santa Barbara?"

"Why, yes, I am." She was frowning a little.

"Then the apartment you woke up in, on Saint Patrick's Day in the morning, was *my* apartment," said Mitch huffily, "and why the amnesia?"

"What is this?" said a male voice.

Mitch swiveled his head and knew at once that here was Mr. Julius Maxwell. He saw a medium-sized, taut-muscled, middle-aged man with a thatch of salt-and-pepper hair and fierce black eyes under heavy black brows. Everything about this man blazoned aggression and possession. He reeked of push and power, of *I* and *Mine*.

Mitchel Brown, playwright, artist, and apostle of compassion, drew his own forces together, as if he folded in some wings.

"Julius," said the blond woman, "this man knows my name. He keeps talking about Saint Patrick's Day in the morning."

"Oh, he does?" said her husband.

"He says I was in his apartment, here in Los Angeles."

To Mitch Brown came a notion that would explain all this. Obviously, Natalie's husband had never found out where Natalie had been that night. So Natalie had to pretend she didn't know Mitch, because *she* knew, as he did not, that Julius Maxwell was nearby and would appear. But something in the woman's manner did not quite fit this theory. She didn't seem to be concerned enough. She looked straight ahead and her bewilderment was perfunctory.

Still, he thought he should be gallant. "I must have made a mistake," he said. "But the resemblance is remarkable. Perhaps you have a double, ma'am?"

He thought this was handsome of him and that it gave her a way out.

"A double?" said Julius Maxwell nastily. "Who uses my wife's *name*?"

Well, of course, if the man was going to be intelligent about it, that tore it. "Sorry," said Mitch lightly.

"Sit down and tell me about it," said Maxwell commandingly. "Mr. . . . er . . . ?"

"Brown," said Mitch shortly. He was of a mind to turn on his heel and go away. But he glanced at Natalie. She had opened her handbag and found her compact. This stuck him as either offensively nonchalant or pathetically trusting. Or what? Curiosity rose in Mitch—and he sat down.

"Why, I happened into a bar where a lady had had too much to drink," he said, as if this were nothing unusual. "I volunteered to put her in a taxi but there was no taxi. I wound up leaving her passed out on my sofa. In the morning she was gone. That's all there is to the story."

"This was on Saint Patrick's Day?" said Maxwell intently.

"In the small hours. In the morning."

"Then the lady was not my wife. My wife was with me in Santa Barbara at our home that night."

"With you?" said Mitch carefully, feeling a bit of shock.

"Certainly." Maxwell's tone was belligerent.

Mitch was beginning to wonder. The woman had powdered her nose and sat looking as if she couldn't care less. "Not simply in the same building," Mitch inquired, "as you may have assumed?"

"Not simply in the same building," said Julius Maxwell, "and no assumption. She was *with* me, *speaking* to me, *touching* me, if you like." His black eyes were hostile.

Oh, ho, thought Mitch, then you are a liar, too. Now what *is* all this? He did not care for this Maxwell at all.

"Perhaps I have mistaken her for another lady," he said

smoothly. "But isn't it strange that she is wearing exactly the same clothes now that she was wearing on Saint Patrick's Day?"

(Try that one on for size, Mitch thought smugly.)

Julius said ominously, "Do you know who I am?"

"I have heard your name," said Mitch.

"You know that I am an influential man?"

"Oh, yes," said Mitch pleasantly. "In fact, I can smell the money from here."

"How much do you want to forget that you saw my wife in Los Angeles that night?"

Mitch's brows went up.

"On Saint Patrick's Day in the morning," added Julius sneeringly.

Mitch felt his feathers ruffling, his temper flaring. "Why? What is it worth?" he said.

They locked gazes. It was ridiculous. Mitch felt as if he had strayed into a Class B movie. Then Maxwell rose from the table. "Excuse me." He lashed Mitch with a sharp look which seemed to be saying, "Stay," as if Mitch were a dog. Then he strode off.

Mitch, alone with the blond woman, said to her quickly, "What do you want me to do or say?"

He was looking at her hand, long-fingered, pink-nailed, limp on the table. It did not clench. It did not even move. "I don't understand," she said in a mechanical way.

"Okay," said Mitch disgustedly. "I came here for dinner and I see no profit in this discussion, so please excuse me."

He got up, crossed over to his own table, and ordered his meal.

Julius Maxwell returned in a few moments and stood looking at Mitch with a triumphant light in his eyes. Mitch waved the wand of reason over the very human activity of his own glands. It was necessary for Mitch's self-respect that he dine here, as he had planned to do, and that he remain unperturbed by these strange people.

His steak had come when a man walked into the room

and up to Maxwell's table. There was an exchange of words. Julius rose. Both men came over to Mitch.

Julius said, "This is the fellow, Lieutenant."

Mitch found that the stranger was slipping into the seat beside him and Julius was slipping in beside him on his other hand. He rejected a feeling of being trapped. "What's all this?" he inquired mildly, patting his lips with his napkin.

"Name's Prince," said the stranger. "Los Angeles Police Department. Mr. Maxwell tells me you are saying something about Mrs. Maxwell's being here in town on the night of the sixteenth of March and the morning of the seventeenth?"

Mitch sipped from his water glass, watchful and wary.

Julius Maxwell said, "This man was trying to blackmail me with a crazy story."

"I was *what*!" Mitch exploded.

The police lieutenant, or whoever he was, had a long lean face, slightly crooked at the bottom, and he had very tired eyelids. He said, "Your story figured to destroy her alibi?"

"Her alibi for *what*?" Mitch leaned back.

"Oh, come off that, Brown," said Julius Maxwell, "or whatever your name is. You knew my wife from having seen her picture in the newspaper."

Mitch's brain was racing. "I haven't seen the papers for six weeks," he said aggressively.

Julius Maxwell's black eyes were bright with that triumphant shine. "Now that," he said flatly, "is impossible."

"Oh, is it?" said Mitch rather gently. His role of apostle of compassion was fast fading out. Mitch was now a human clashing with another human and he knew he had to look out for himself. He could feel his wings retracting into his spine. "Alibi for what?" he insisted, looking at the policeman intently.

The policeman sighed. "You want it from me? Okay. On the sixteenth of last March, late in the evening," he droned, "a man named Joseph Carlisle was shot to death in his own front hall." (Mitch, ears pricked up, remembered the paragraph he had seen just tonight.) "Lived in a canyon, Hollywood Hills," the Lieutenant continued. "Winding road, lonely spot. Looked like somebody rang his bell, he answered, they talked in the hall. It was his own gun that he kept in a table there. Whoever shot him closed the front door, which locked it, and threw the gun in the shrubbery. Then beat it. Wasn't seen—by anybody."

"And what has this got to do with Mrs. Maxwell?" Mitch asked.

"Mrs. Maxwell used to be married to this Carlisle," said the policeman. "We had to check her out. She has this alibi."

"I see," said Mitch.

"Mrs. Maxwell," said Julius through his teeth, "was with me in our home in Santa Barbara that evening and all that night."

Mitch saw. He saw that either Maxwell was trying to save his wife from the embarrassment of suspicion or . . . that compassion was a fine thing but it can get a well-meaning person into trouble. And a few drinks might hit a murderess very hard and very fast. Mitch *knew*, that whatever else Maxwell said, he was lying in his teeth about this alibi. Because the woman, still sitting across this restaurant, was the very same woman whom Mitch Brown had taken in, had given a break.

But nobody was giving Mitch Brown any break. And why all this nonsense about blackmail? Mitch, with his wings folded tight away, said to the Lieutenant, "Suppose I tell you my story." And he did so, coldly, briefly.

Afterward, Maxwell laughed. "You believe that? You believe that he would take a drunken woman home with him—and close the door?"

In his breast Mitch Brown felt the smoulder of dislike burst into a flame of hatred.

"No, no," said Maxwell. "What must have happened was this. He spotted my wife here. Oh, he'd read the papers —don't you believe that he hadn't. He knew she had been married to Joe Carlisle. So, spur of the moment, he tried out his little lie. Might be some profit in it—who knows? Listen to this: when I asked him how much he wanted to keep this story to himself, he asked *me* how much it was worth."

Mitch chewed his lip. "You've got a bad ear for dialogue," he said. "That is not exactly what I said. Nor is it the sense of what I said."

"Oh, oh," said Maxwell, smiling.

The Lieutenant was pursing noncommittal lips.

Mitch spoke to him. "Who else gives Mrs. Maxwell her alibi?"

"Servants," said the Lieutenant gloomily.

"Servants?" said Mitch brightly.

"It's only natural," the Lieutenant said, even more gloomily.

"Right," said Mitch Brown. "You mean it is probable that when a man and his wife are at home together only the servants will see them there. But it isn't so probable that a stranger will take in a drunken woman, and leave her to heaven . . . simply because he feels like giving a human being a break. So this is a study in probability, is it?"

The Lieutenant's mouth moved and Mitch said quickly, "But you want the facts, eh? Okay. The only thing for us to do is go and talk to the bartender."

"That seems to be it," said the Lieutenant promptly. "Right."

Maxwell said, "Right. Wait for us."

He rose and went to fetch his wife. Mitch stood beside the Lieutenant. "Fingerprints?" he murmured. The Lieutenant shrugged. Under those weary eyelids, Mitch judged, the eyes were human. "She has a car? Was the car out?" The Lieutenant shrugged again. "Who else would shoot this Carlisle? Any enemies?"

"Who hasn't?" the Lieutenant said. "We better check with this bartender."

The four of them went in the Lieutenant's car. The Parrakeet Bar and Grill was doing well this evening. It looked brighter and more prosperous. Toby the bartender was there. "Hi, Mr. Brown," he said. "Long time no see."

"I've been back East. Tell this man, Toby, what happened around one thirty on the morning of March seventeenth."

"Huh?" said Toby. The flesh of his cheeks seemed to go flatter. His eye went duller. Suddenly Mitch knew what was going to happen.

"You see this man or this lady in here between one, two o'clock in the morning last March seventeenth?" said the Lieutenant and added, "I'm Lieutenant Prince, L.A.P.D."

"No, sir," said Toby. "I know Mr. Brown, of course. He comes in now and again, see? Lives around here. A writer, he is. But I don't remember I ever seen this lady before."

"What about Brown? Was he in here that night or that morning?"

"I don't think so," said Toby. "That's the night, now that I think back—yeah, my kid was sick and I shut the place up earlier than usual. Ask my wife," said Toby the bartender with the fixed righteous gaze of the liar.

Lieutenant Prince turned his long face, his sad eyelids, on Mitch Brown.

Mitch Brown was grinning. "Oh, no!" he said. "Not the old Paris Exposition gag!" He leaned on the bar and emitted silent laughter.

"What are you talking about?" Lieutenant Prince said sourly. "You give me corroboration for this story you're telling. Who can tell me about it? Who saw you and this lady that night?"

"Nobody. Nobody," said Mitch genially. "The streets were empty. Nobody was around. Well! I wouldn't have believed it! The old Paris Exposition gag!"

The Lieutenant made an exasperated sound.

Mitch said gaily, "Don't you remember that one? There's this girl and her mother. They go to a Paris hotel. Separate rooms. Girl wakes up in the morning, no mother. Nobody ever saw any mother. No mother's name on the

register. No room's got the mother's number. Wait. No—
that wasn't it. There *was* a room, but the wallpaper was
different."

Julius Maxwell said, "A writer"—as if that explained
everything.

"Why don't we all sit down," said Mitch cheerfully,
"and tell each other stories?"

His suggestion was accepted. Natalie Maxwell slipped
into a booth first; she was blond, expensive, protected . . . and
numb. (Is she doped up with tranquilizers or what? Mitch
wondered.) Her husband sat on her right and the policeman
sat on her left. Mitch slid in the other side of the Law and
faced his adversary.

Mitch Brown's mood was by no means as jaunty as his
words had implied. He didn't like the idea of being the
victim of the old Paris Exposition gag. But he was not rattled
or panicky. On the contrary, his mind began to reconnoiter
the enemy. Julius Maxwell, flamboyantly successful—Mitch
savored the flavor of the man's reputation. The buccaneer
type, ruthless and bold. Julius Maxwell—with money like a
club in his hand. Going to make a fool out of Mitchel Brown.
Also, there was the little matter of justice. Or mercy.

Mitch felt his wings begin to rustle again.

He said to the woman, gently, "Would you care for
something? A highball?"

"I don't drink," said Natalie primly. Her lashes came
down. Her tongue touched her lips.

Mitch Brown ran his tongue over his upper lip, very
thoughtfully.

Julius Maxwell's energy was barely contained in this
place. "Never mind the refreshments," he said. "Get to it.
This young man, whoever he is, spotted my wife and knew
her from the publicity. He knows I am a rich man. So he
thought he'd try a big lie. For the sake of the nuisance value,
he thought I'd pay *something*. Well, an opportunist," said
Julius with a nasty smile, "I can understand."

"I doubt if you understand *me*," said Mitch quietly.

"I'm sure you don't realize how old hat that Paris Exposition story is."

"What has any Paris Exposition got to do with it?" snapped Julius. "Now look here, Lieutenant Prince. Can I prosecute this man?"

"You can't prove extortion," said the Lieutenant gloomily. "You should have let him take the money, with witnesses."

"He couldn't do that," said Mitch, "because he knows the thought of money never crossed my mind."

The Lieutenant's eyes closed all the way in great weariness. They opened again and it was apparent that he believed nothing and nobody, yet. "Want to get this straight. Now you say, Mr. Maxwell—"

Julius said, "I say that my wife was at home that evening and all night, as the servants also say, and as the authorities know. So this man is a liar. Who can say why? It is plain that he can't bring anyone or anything to corroborate this yarn he is telling. The bartender denies it. And, if you ask me, the most ridiculous thing he says is his claim that he hasn't read the newspapers for six weeks. Shows you the fantastic kind of mind he's got."

The Lieutenant, without comment, turned to Mitch. "And you say—"

"I say," said Mitch, "that I have been in New York City since the seventeenth of March, attending rehearsals of my play and its opening night."

"A playwriter," said Julius.

"A play*wright*," corrected Mitch. "I guess you don't know what that is. For one thing, it is a person committed to trying to understand human beings. Oddly enough, even you." Mitch leaned over the table. "You are the bold buccaneer, so I've heard. You've pirated money out of the world and now you think money can buy whatever you want. Suppose *I* tell *your* story?"

Julius Maxwell now had a faint sneering smile, but Mitch noted that Natalie had her eyes open. Perhaps her ears were open too. Mitch plunged on.

"Your wife drove down here and shot her ex," he said brutally. (Natalie did not even wince.) "Well, now . . ." Mitch's imagination began to function, from long practice. "I suppose that Natalie felt bad enough, upset enough, maybe even sorry enough, to need a drink and to take too many drinks until she forgot her troubles." Natalie was looking at him. "But when she woke up in my apartment she ran—ran to her car which she must have had. Ran home. Ah, well, what else could she do?" Mitch mused aloud. "She had done this awful thing. Somebody would have to help her."

(Was Natalie holding her breath?)

"Who would help her?" Mitch said sharply. "*You* would, Maxwell. Why? I'll tell you why. You are not the type to want any wife of yours and the accent is on *yours*—to die in a gas chamber for murder. She'd done something stupid. You bawled her out, I imagine, for the stupidity of it. But you told her not to worry. She was yours, so you would fix it. Money can buy anything. She must do exactly as you say, and then she could forget it." Mitch hesitated. "Did you think she *could* forget it?" he murmured.

Nobody moved or spoke, so Mitch went on. "Well, you got to work. You bribed the servants. Bribed Toby, here. And you checked all around and discovered that there was only one other person who could reveal that she really had no alibi. That was a playwright. Oh, you checked on me too. Sure you did. You knew very well where I was and what I was doing. You found out the day and the hour I was due back in Los Angeles."

Lieutenant Prince snorted. "Sounds nuts," he broke in. "You say he's been bribing everybody? Why didn't he bribe *you*?"

Mitch turned a glazed eye on him. "Trouble was, I *hadn't* read the papers. I didn't know that I knew. So how could he bribe me? He put me down for an idiot," said Mitch. "For what sane person doesn't read the paper for six weeks? And then he thought of a way."

Mitch addressed himself to Maxwell. "You had some

hireling watching my apartment. And you and Natalie were ready and waiting, and quite nearby." Mitch sensed the policeman's shrug coming and he added quickly, "Otherwise, how come the very first day I'm in town I run into Natalie, and Natalie in exactly the same clothes?"

"Who says they're the same," said Maxwell smoothly, "except you?"

"She came into the restaurant," said Mitch, "alone."

"Since I had a phone call to make . . ."

"Alone," Mitch persisted, ignoring the interruption, "and why? To encourage me to come over and speak to her. That's why the same clothes—to make sure I'd recognize her again. After she pulls the blank on me, Maxwell moves in. You, knowing how deep you've bribed your defenses behind you, press me into the position of looking like an opportunist—possibly like an extortionist. "Brown's a writer,' you say to yourself. Which is 'a nut,' in your book. 'Nobody is going to believe a word *he* says.' You'll discredit me. You'll rig a little scene. You'll call a real policeman for a witness."

"Why?" croaked the Lieutenant.

Mitch was startled. "Why what?"

"Why cook all this up and call *me*?"

"Simple," Mitch said. "What if I had finally read the papers and recognized her name? What if *I* had come to *you*? What am I then? A good citizen. Isn't that so? This way, he's made it look as if I came to *them*. Making me look like an opportunist. And he's the good citizen who called you in."

Air came out of the Lieutenant, signifying nothing.

"What a wacky scheme!" Mitch said it first. (Damn it, it *was* wacky. It wasn't going to sound probable.) "How unrealistic you are!" he taunted desperately.

Maxwell sat there smugly. "You've got the imagination, all right," he said with a wry smile. "Wild one."

Then the policeman surprised them both. "Wait a minute, Brown. You're saying that Maxwell *knows* his wife is the killer. That he's acting as accessory after the fact? You *mean* to say that?"

Mitch hesitated.

Maxwell said, "He hasn't thought it out. Listen, he is just spinning a yarn, Lieutenant. He was challenged to do it. He's proving that he's clever. And that he is—for fiction. Call it a good try."

Mitch saw his way pointed out for him.

"Or, possibly," said Maxwell after a moment, "he was only trying to pick up a good-looking woman." Maxwell showed his teeth in a smile.

Mitch understood—he was being shown how to save face. It was very seductive. Not only that, he was aware that if he went along, the power, the money, the influence here, there, and everywhere, would work to Mitchel Brown's commercial advantage.

So he said slowly, "I *know* that he is a liar. I *believe* that he is an accessory after the fact. Yes, that's what I mean to say."

Julius Maxwell's face darkened, "Prove it," he snapped. "Because if you just *tell* it, I will have legal recourse, and I will have your skin. I don't sit still to be called a liar."

Mitch looked up and said with an air of pure detached curiosity, "What ever made you think that *I* would?"

"Look, give me *something,*" said the Lieutenant with sudden anger, "give me something to go on."

Maxwell said contemptuously, "He can't. It's all moonshine."

Mitch was scrambling for something that would help him. "I never thought of a car," he murmured. "But I should have guessed from the shoes she wears, that she hadn't walked here. I don't suppose she has walked much since she married so much money."

Mitch knew that Maxwell was swelling up with rage, or simulated rage. But he thought that Natalie was listening. It came to him, with conviction, that in spite of everything she *was* a human being.

So he looked at her and said, "Why did you leave this Joe Carlisle, I wonder? What kind of man was he? Did you quarrel? Did you hate him? How did he still have the power to hurt you that much?"

She looked at him, lips parted, eyes bright, startled. Her husband was on the point of getting up and hitting someone, and Mitch knew whom.

Lieutenant Prince said, "Sit down, Maxwell." He said to Mitch, "And you, hold onto your tongue. Don't analyze me any characters. Or emote me any motives. She's got an alibi unless you can break it, and evidence is what the law requires."

"But what about *my* motive for lying?" Mitch demanded. "Money? That's ridiculous!" He stopped, staring. Natalie Maxwell had opened her bag, taken out a lipstick. Murder, prison . . . she paints her mouth. Slander, blackmail . . . she paints her mouth. How probable was that?

"Give me proof," the Lieutenant said angrily.

"In a minute," Mitch said, as his heart bounced upward. He leaned back. "Let me pursue the theme of money. I imagine Natalie's got whatever money can buy. Her living is paid for. She has charge accounts."

Maxwell said, "Let's go. He's rambling now."

The Lieutenant began to push at Mitch's thigh, nudging him out of the booth.

"Know what I *can* prove?" Mitch said.

"What?" said the Lieutenant.

"That I was working in my apartment all that day and into the night on the sixteenth, seventeenth of March. Those walls are cardboard and I am a nuisance—well known in the building."

"So you were working," said the policeman. "What of it?"

"I wasn't in Santa Barbara," said Mitch cheerfully. He reached over and plucked up Natalie's handbag, the green one that matched the shoes.

"Now just a minute," Maxwell growled.

"See if her checkbook is in there," said Mitch, pushing the bag at the Lieutenant. "It's a fat one. Her name's printed on it, and all that. I don't think she has much occasion to write checks. It may be the same one."

The Lieutenant had his hands on the bag, but he looked unenlightened.

"Look at it. It's evidence," Mitch said.

The Lieutenant's hands moved and Maxwell said, "I'm not sure you have the right . . ." But the policeman's weary lids came up, only briefly, and Maxwell was silent.

The Lieutenant took out a checkbook. "It's fat," he said. "Starts February twenty-first. What of it?"

Mitch Brown leaned his head on the red leatherette and kept his eyes high. "Nobody on earth . . . unless Natalie remembers, which I doubt . . . but nobody *else* on earth can know what the balance on her check stubs was on Saint Patrick's Day in the morning. Even her bank couldn't know. *But what if I know?* How could I? Because *I looked,* while she was snoring on my sofa and I had to find out who she was and how I could help her and whether she needed any money."

The Lieutenant's hand riffled the stubs. "Well?"

"Shall I name it for you? To the penny?" Mitch was sweating. "Four thousand six hundred and fourteen dollars, and sixty-one cents," he said slowly and carefully.

"Right," snapped the Lieutenant and his eyes came up, wide-open and baleful on Julius Maxwell.

But Mitch Brown was not heeding and felt no triumph. "Natalie," he said, "I'm sorry. I wanted to give you a break. I didn't know what the trouble was. I wish you could have told me."

Her newly reddened lips were trembling.

"Not so I could buy off the consequences," Mitch said. "I'd have called the police. But I *would* have listened."

Natalie put her blond head down on the red-checked tablecloth where it had once rested before. "I didn't mean to do it," she sobbed. "But he kept at me, Joe did. Until I couldn't take any more."

Julius Maxwell, who had been thinking about evidence, said too late, "Shut up!"

The Lieutenant went for the phone.

Mitch sat there, quiet now. The woman was weeping. Maxwell said in a cold, severe way, "Natalie, if you . . ." He drew away from contamination. He was going to pretend ignorance.

But she cried out, "*You* shut up! *You* shut up! I've told you and told you and you never even tried to understand. You said, give Joe a thousand dollars. He'd go away. You said that's all he wanted. You wouldn't even listen to what I was going through, and Joe talking, talking, about our baby that was dead . . . starved, Joe said, because she had no mother. *My* baby," she shrieked, "that *you* wouldn't have, because she wasn't yours."

Now her pink-painted fingernails clawed at her scalp and the rings on her fingers were tangled in her hair. "I'm sorry," she wept. "I never meant to make the gun go off. I just wanted to stop him. I just couldn't take any more. He was killing me . . . driving me crazy . . . and money wouldn't stop him."

Mitch's heart was heavy for her. "Didn't you know what *matters*?" he barked at Maxwell. "Did you think it was mink, diamonds—that stuff?"

"The child died," said Julius Maxwell, "of natural causes."

"*Yes,* he thought it was mink," screamed Natalie. "And oh, my God . . . it *was*! I know that now. So he said he would fix it—but he can't fix what I know, and I hope to die."

Then she lay silent, as if already dead, across the red-checked tablecloth.

Julius Maxwell's face was losing color, as the policeman came back and murmured, "Have to wait." But the Lieutenant was uneasy. "Say, Brown," he said, "you can remember a row of six figures for six weeks? You a mathematical genius or something? You got what they call a photographic memory?"

Mitch felt his brain stir. He said lightly, "It stuck in my mind. First place, it repeats. You see that? Four six one, four six one. To me that's an awful lot of money."

"To me too," the Lieutenant said. "Everybody in here heard what she said, I guess."

"Sure, heard her confess and implicate him as the accessory. Take a look at Toby, for instance. *He's* had it. There's going to be plenty of evidence."

The Lieutenant looked down upon the ruin of the Maxwells. "Guess so," he said tightly.

Later that night Mitch Brown was sitting up to a strange bar. He said to the strange bartender, "Say, you ever know that the seventeenth of March is *not* Saint Patrick's birthday?"

"What d'ya know?" the bartender murmured politely.

"Nope. It's the day he died," said Mitch. "I write, see? So I read. Bits of information like that stick in my mind. I've got no memory for figures and yet . . . Know the year Saint Patrick died? It was the year 461."

"That so?" said the bartender.

"You take four sixty-one twice and put the decimal in the right place. Of course that's not very *believable,*" Mitch said, "although it really happened—on Saint Patrick's Day in the morning. How come I knew—me a person who doesn't always read the newspaper—the year Saint Patrick died? Well, a fellow doesn't want to be made a fool of, does he? And probable is probable and improbable is improbable —but it's all we've got to go on sometimes. But I'll tell *you* something," Mitch pounded the bar. "Money couldn't have bought it."

The bartender said soothingly, "I guess not, Mac."

THE POSSIBILITY OF EVIL

Shirley Jackson

Shirley Jackson (1919–1965) was a superior crafts-woman who was equally at home writing adult novels and nonfiction books, juveniles, plays, and short stories. Her 1949 collection The Lottery—*and its title story—is a classic of macabre fiction, as is her novel* The Haunting of Hill House *(1959).* And We Have Always Lived in the Castle *(1962) is felt by many to be one of the great modern tales of murder. "The Possibility of Evil" was her last story, having been first published posthumously in 1965, and is also one of her finest—as evidenced by the fact that the Mystery Writers of America awarded it the Edgar for Best Short Story of that year. Not only is it memorable "for its delicate treatment of a crime and its origins," as critic Anthony Boucher wrote, "but for the consummate skill with which the author manages to reveal, in the last sentence, that the title has not two, but three possible meanings."*

Miss Adela Strangeworth came daintily along Main Street on her way to the grocery. The sun was shining, the air was fresh and clear after the night's heavy rain, and everything in Miss Strangeworth's little town looked washed and bright. Miss Strangeworth took deep breaths and thought that there was nothing in the world like a fragrant summer day.

She knew everyone in town, of course; she was fond of telling strangers—tourists who sometimes passed through the town and stopped to admire Miss Strangeworth's roses —that she had never spent more than a day outside this town in all her long life. She was seventy-one, Miss Strangeworth told the tourists, with a pretty little dimple showing by her lip, and she sometimes found herself thinking that the town belonged to her. "My grandfather built the first house on Pleasant Street," she would say, opening her blue eyes wide with the wonder of it. "This house, right here. My family has lived here for better than a hundred years. My grandmother planted these roses, and my mother tended them, just as I do. I've watched my town grow; I can remember when Mr. Lewis, Senior, opened the grocery store, and the year the river flooded out the shanties on the low road, and the excitement when some young folks wanted to move the park over to the space in front of where the new post office is today. They wanted to put up a statue of Ethan Allen"—Miss Strangeworth would frown a little and sound stern—"but it should have been a statue of my grandfather. There wouldn't have been a town here at all if it hadn't been for my grandfather and the lumber mill."

Miss Strangeworth never gave away any of her roses, although the tourists often asked her. The roses belonged on Pleasant Street, and it bothered Miss Strangeworth to think of people wanting to carry them away, to take them into strange towns and down strange streets. When the new minister came, and the ladies were gathering flowers to decorate the church, Miss Strangeworth sent over a great basket of gladioli; when she picked the roses at all, she set them in bowls and vases around the inside of the house her grandfather had built.

Walking down Main Street on a summer morning, Miss Strangeworth had to stop every minute or so to say good morning to someone or to ask after someone's health. When she came into the grocery, half a dozen people turned away from the shelves and the counters to wave at her or call out good morning.

"And good morning to you, too, Mr. Lewis," Miss Strangeworth said at last. The Lewis family had been in the town almost as long as the Strangeworths; but the day young Lewis left high school and went to work in the grocery, Miss Strangeworth had stopped calling him Tommy and started calling him Mr. Lewis, and he had stopped calling her Addie and started calling her Miss Strangeworth. They had been in high school together, and had gone to picnics together, and to high-school dances and basketball games; but now Mr. Lewis was behind the counter in the grocery, and Miss Strangeworth was living alone in the Strangeworth house on Pleasant Street.

"Good morning," Mr. Lewis said, and added politely, "Lovely day."

"It is a very nice day," Miss Strangeworth said, as though she had only just decided that it would do after all. "I would like a chop, please, Mr. Lewis, a small, lean veal chop. Are those strawberries from Arthur Parker's garden? They're early this year."

"He brought them in this morning," Mr. Lewis said.

"I shall have a box," Miss Strangeworth said. Mr. Lewis looked worried, she thought, and for a minute she hesitated, but then she decided that he surely could not be worried over the strawberries. He looked very tired indeed. He was usually so chipper, Miss Strangeworth thought, and almost commented, but it was far too personal a subject to be introduced to Mr. Lewis, the grocer, so she only said, "and a can of cat food and, I think, a tomato."

Silently, Mr. Lewis assembled her order on the counter, and waited. Miss Strangeworth looked at him curiously and then said, "It's Tuesday, Mr. Lewis. You forgot to remind me."

"Did I? Sorry."

"Imagine your forgetting that I always buy my tea on Tuesday," Miss Strangeworth said gently. "A quarter pound of tea, please, Mr. Lewis."

"Is that all, Miss Strangeworth?"

"Yes, thank you, Mr. Lewis. Such a lovely day, isn't it?"

"Lovely," Mr. Lewis said.

Miss Strangeworth moved slightly to make room for Mrs. Harper at the counter. "Morning, Adela," Mrs. Harper said, and Miss Strangeworth said, "Good morning, Martha."

"Lovely day," Mrs. Harper said, and Miss Strangeworth said, "Yes, lovely," and Mr. Lewis, under Mrs. Harper's glance, nodded.

"Ran out of sugar for my cake frosting," Mrs. Harper explained. Her hand shook slightly as she opened her pocketbook. Miss Strangeworth wondered, glancing at her quickly, if she had been taking proper care of herself. Martha Harper was not as young as she used to be, Miss Strangeworth thought. She probably could use a good strong tonic.

"Martha," she said, "you don't look well."

"I'm perfectly all right," Mrs. Harper said shortly. She handed her money to Mr. Lewis, took her change and her sugar, and went out without speaking again. Looking after her, Miss Strangeworth shook her head slightly. Martha definitely did *not* look well.

Carrying her little bag of groceries, Miss Strangeworth came out of the store into the bright sunlight and stopped to smile down on the Crane baby. Don and Helen Crane were really the two most infatuated young parents she had ever known, she thought indulgently, looking at the delicately embroidered baby cap and the lace-edged carriage cover.

"That little girl is going to grow up expecting luxury all her life," she said to Helen Crane.

Helen laughed. "That's the way we want her to feel," she said. "Like a princess."

"A princess can see a lot of trouble sometimes," Miss Strangeworth said dryly. "How old is Her Highness now?"

"Six months next Tuesday," Helen Crane said, looking down with rapt wonder at her child. "I've been worrying, though, about her. Don't you think she ought to move around more? Try to sit up, for instance?"

"For plain and fancy worrying," Miss Strangeworth said, amused, "give me a new mother every time."

"She just seems—slow," Helen Crane said.

"Nonsense. All babies are different. Some of them develop much more quickly than others."

"That's what my mother says." Helen Crane laughed, looking a little bit ashamed.

"I suppose you've got young Don all upset about the fact that his daughter is already six months old and hasn't yet begun to learn to dance?"

"I haven't mentioned it to him. I suppose she's just so precious that I worry about her all the time."

"Well, apologize to her right now," Miss Strangeworth said. "*She* is probably worrying about why you keep jumping around all the time." Smiling to herself and shaking her old head, she went on down the sunny street, stopping once to ask little Billy Moore why he wasn't out riding in his daddy's shiny new car, and talking for a few minutes outside the library with Miss Chandler, the librarian, about the new novels to be ordered and paid for by the annual library appropriation. Miss Chandler seemed absentminded and very much as though she were thinking about something else. Miss Strangeworth noticed that Miss Chandler had not taken much trouble with her hair that morning, and sighed. Miss Strangeworth hated sloppiness.

Many people seemed disturbed recently, Miss Strangeworth thought. Only yesterday the Stewarts' fifteen-year-old Linda had run crying down her own front walk and all the way to school, not caring who saw her. People around town thought she might have had a fight with the Harris boy, but they showed up together at the soda shop after school as usual, both of them looking grim and bleak. Trouble at home, people concluded, and sighed over the problems of trying to raise kids right these days.

From halfway down the block Miss Strangeworth could catch the heavy scent of her roses, and she moved a little more quickly. The perfume of roses meant home, and home meant the Strangeworth House on Pleasant Street. Miss Strangeworth stopped at her own front gate, as she always did, and looked with deep pleasure at her house, with the red and pink and white roses massed along the narrow lawn, and the rambler going up along the porch; and the neat, the unbelievably trim lines of the house itself, with its slimness and its washed white look. Every window sparkled, every curtain hung stiff and straight, and even the stones of the front walk were swept and clear. People around town wondered how old Miss Strangeworth managed to keep the house looking the way it did, and there was a legend about a tourist once mistaking it for the local museum and going all through the place without finding out about his mistake. But the town was proud of Miss Strangeworth and her roses and her house. They had all grown together.

Miss Strangeworth went up her front steps, unlocked her front door with her key, and went into the kitchen to put away her groceries. She debated about having a cup of tea and then decided that it was too close to midday dinnertime; she would not have the appetite for her little chop if she had tea now. Instead she went into the light, lovely sitting room, which still glowed from the hands of her mother and her grandmother, who had covered the chairs with bright chintz and hung the curtains. All the furniture was spare and shining, and the round hooked rugs on the floor had been the work of Miss Strangeworth's grandmother and her mother. Miss Strangeworth had put a bowl of her red roses on the low table before the window, and the room was full of their scent.

Miss Strangeworth went to the narrow desk in the corner and unlocked it with her key. She never knew when she might feel like writing letters, so she kept her notepaper inside and the desk locked. Miss Strangeworth's usual stationery was heavy and cream-colored, with STRANGE-WORTH HOUSE engraved across the top, but, when she felt like writing her other letters, Miss Strangeworth used a pad of various-colored paper bought from the local newspaper shop. It was almost a town joke, that colored paper, layered in pink and green and blue and yellow; everyone in town bought it and used it for odd, informal notes and shopping lists. It was usual to remark, upon receiving a note written on a blue page, that so-and-so would be needing a new pad soon—here she was, down to the blue already. Everyone used the matching envelopes for tucking away recipes, or keeping odd little things in, or even to hold cookies in the school lunchboxes. Mr. Lewis sometimes gave them to the children for carrying home penny candy.

Although Miss Strangeworth's desk held a trimmed quill pen which had belonged to her grandfather, and a gold-frosted fountain pen which had belonged to her father, Miss Strangeworth always used a dull stub of pencil when she wrote her letters, and she printed them in a childish block print. After thinking for a minute, although she had been phrasing the letter in the back of her mind all the way home, she wrote on a pink sheet: DIDN'T YOU EVER SEE AN IDIOT CHILD BEFORE? SOME PEOPLE JUST SHOULDN'T HAVE CHILDREN SHOULD THEY?

She was pleased with the letter. She was fond of doing things exactly right. When she made a mistake, as she sometimes did, or when the letters were not spaced nicely on the page, she had to take the discarded page to the kitchen stove and burn it at once. Miss Strangeworth never delayed when things had to be done.

After thinking for a minute, she decided that she would like to write another letter, perhaps to go to Mrs. Harper, to follow up the ones she had already mailed. She selected a green sheet this time and wrote quickly: HAVE YOU FOUND OUT YET WHAT THEY WERE ALL LAUGHING ABOUT AFTER YOU LEFT THE BRIDGE CLUB ON THURSDAY? OR IS THE WIFE REALLY ALWAYS THE LAST ONE TO KNOW?

Miss Strangeworth never concerned herself with facts; her letters all dealt with the more negotiable stuff of suspicion. Mr. Lewis would never have imagined for a minute that his grandson might be lifting petty cash from the store register if he had not had one of Miss Strangeworth's letters. Miss Chandler, the librarian, and Linda Stewart's parents would have gone unsuspectingly ahead with their lives, never aware of possible evil lurking nearby, if Miss Strangeworth had not sent letters opening their eyes. Miss Strangeworth would have been genuinely shocked if there *had* been anything between Linda Stewart and the Harris boy, but, as long as evil existed unchecked in the world, it was Miss Strangeworth's duty to keep her town alert to it. It was far more sensible for Miss Chandler to wonder what Mr. Shelley's first wife had really died of than to take a chance on not knowing. There were so many wicked people in the world and only one Strangeworth left in the town. Besides, Miss Strangeworth liked writing her letters.

She addressed an envelope to Don Crane after a moment's thought, wondering curiously if he would show the letter to his wife, and using a pink envelope to match the pink paper. Then she addressed a second envelope, green, to Mrs. Harper. Then an idea came to her and she selected a blue sheet and wrote: YOU NEVER KNOW ABOUT DOCTORS. REMEMBER THEY'RE ONLY HUMAN AND NEED MONEY LIKE THE REST OF US. SUPPOSE THE KNIFE SLIPPED ACCIDENTALLY. WOULD DR. BURNS GET HIS FEE AND A LITTLE EXTRA FROM THAT NEPHEW OF YOURS?

She addressed the blue envelope to old Mrs. Foster, who was having an operation next month. She had thought of writing one more letter, to the head of the school board, asking how a chemistry teacher like Billy Moore's father could afford a new convertible, but, all at once, she was tired of writing letters. The three she had done would do for one day. She could write more tomorrow; it was not as though they all had to be done at once.

She had been writing her letters—sometimes two or three every day for a week, sometimes no more than one in a month—for the past year. She never got any answers, of course, because she never signed her name. If she had been asked, she would have said that her name, Adela Strangeworth, a name honored in the town for so many years, did not belong on such trash. The town where she lived had to be kept clean and sweet, but people everywhere were lustful and evil and degraded, and needed to be watched; the world was so large, and there was only one Strangeworth left in it. Miss Strangeworth sighed, locked her desk, and put the letters into her big black leather pocketbook, to be mailed when she took her evening walk.

She broiled her little chop nicely, and had a sliced tomato and a good cup of tea ready when she sat down to her midday dinner at the table in her dining room, which could be opened to seat twenty-two, with a second table, if necessary, in the hall. Sitting in the warm sunlight that came through the tall windows of the dining room, seeing her roses massed outside, handling the heavy, old silverware and the fine, translucent china, Miss Strangeworth was pleased; she would not have cared to be doing anything else. People must live graciously, after all, she thought, and sipped her tea. Afterward, when her plate and cup and saucer were washed and dried and put back onto the shelves where they belonged, and her silverware was back in the mahogany silver chest, Miss Strangeworth went up the graceful staircase and into her bedroom, which was the front room overlooking the roses, and had been her mother's and her grandmother's. Their Crown Derby dresser set and furs had been kept here, their fans and silver-backed brushes and their own bowls of roses; Miss Strangeworth kept a bowl of white roses on the bed table.

She drew the shades, took the rose satin spread from the bed, slipped out of her dress and her shoes, and lay down tiredly. She knew that no doorbell or phone would ring; no one in town would dare to disturb Miss Strangeworth during her afternoon nap. She slept, deep in the rich smell of roses.

After her nap she worked in her garden for a little while, sparing herself because of the heat; then she came in to her supper. She ate asparagus from her own garden, with sweet-butter sauce and a soft-boiled egg, and, while she had her supper, she listened to a late-evening news broadcast and then to a program of classical music on her small radio. After her dishes were done and her kitchen set in order, she took up her hat—Miss Strangeworth's hats were proverbial in the town; people believed that she had inherited them from her mother and her grandmother—and, locking the front door of her house behind her, set off on her evening walk, pocketbook under her arm. She nodded to Linda Stewart's father, who was washing his car in the pleasantly cool evening. She thought that he looked troubled.

There was only one place in town where she could mail her letters, and that was the new post office, shiny with red brick and silver letters. Although Miss Strangeworth had never given the matter any particular thought, she had always made a point of mailing her letters very secretly; it would, of course, not have been wise to let anyone see her mail them. Consequently, she timed her walk so she could reach the post office just as darkness was starting to dim the outlines of the trees and the shapes of people's faces, although no one could ever mistake Miss Strangeworth, with her dainty walk and her rustling skirts.

There was always a group of young people around the post office, the very youngest roller-skating upon its driveway, which went all the way around the building and was the only smooth road in town; and the slightly older ones already knowing how to gather in small groups and chatter and laugh and make great, excited plans for going across the street to the soda shop in a minute or two. Miss Strangeworth had never had any self-consciousness before the children. She did not feel that any of them were staring at her unduly or longing to laugh at her; it would have been most reprehensible for their parents to permit their children to mock Miss Strangeworth of Pleasant Street. Most of the children stood back respectfully as Miss Strangeworth passed, silenced briefly in her presence, and some of the older children greeted her, saying soberly, "Hello, Miss Strangeworth."

Miss Strangeworth smiled at them and quickly went on. It had been a long time since she had known the name of every child in town. The mail slot was in the door of the post office. The children stood away as Miss Strangeworth approached it, seemingly surprised that anyone should want to use the post office after it had been officially closed up for the night and turned over to the children. Miss Strangeworth stood by the door, opening her black pocketbook to take out the letters, and heard a voice which she knew at once to be Linda Stewart's. Poor little Linda was crying again, and Miss Strangeworth listened carefully. This was, after all, her town, and these were her people; if one of them was in trouble she ought to know about it.

"I can't tell you, Dave," Linda was saying—so she *was* talking to the Harris boy, as Miss Strangeworth had supposed—"I just *can't*. It's just *nasty*."

"But why won't your father let me come around anymore? What on earth did I do?"

"I can't tell you. I just wouldn't tell you for *any*thing. You've got to have a dirty, dirty mind for things like that."

"But something's happened. You've been crying and crying, and your father is all upset. Why can't *I* know about it, too? Aren't I like one of the family?"

"Not anymore, Dave, not anymore. You're not to come

near our house again; my father said so. He said he'd horse-whip you. That's all I can tell you: You're not to come near our house anymore."

"But I didn't *do* anything."

"Just the same, my father said . . ."

Miss Strangeworth sighed and turned away. There was so much evil in people. Even in a charming little town like this one, there was still so much evil in people.

She slipped her letters into the slot, and two of them fell inside. The third caught on the edge and fell outside, onto the ground at Miss Strangeworth's feet. She did not notice it because she was wondering whether a letter to the Harris boy's father might not be of some service in wiping out this potential badness. Wearily Miss Strangeworth turned to go home to her quiet bed in her lovely house, and never heard the Harris boy calling to her to say that she had dropped something.

"Old lady Strangeworth's getting deaf," he said, looking after her and holding in his hand the letter he had picked up.

"Well, who cares?" Linda said. "Who cares anymore, anyway?"

"It's for Don Crane," the Harris boy said, "this letter. She dropped a letter addressed to Don Crane. Might as well take it on over. We pass his house anyway." He laughed. "Maybe it's got a check or something in it and he'd be just as glad to get it tonight instead of tomorrow."

"Catch old lady Strangeworth sending anybody a check," Linda said. "Throw it in the post office. Why do anyone a favor?" She sniffled. "Doesn't seem to me anybody around here cares about us," she said. "Why should we care about them?"

"I'll take it over anyway," the Harris boy said. "Maybe it's good news for them. Maybe they need something happy tonight, too. Like us."

Sadly, holding hands, they wandered off down the dark street, the Harris boy carrying Miss Strangeworth's pink envelope in his hand.

* * *

Miss Strangeworth awakened the next morning with a feeling of intense happiness, and for a minute wondered why, and then remembered that this morning three people would open her letters. Harsh, perhaps, at first, but wickedness was never easily banished, and a clean heart was a scoured heart. She washed her soft old face and brushed her teeth, still sound in spite of her seventy-one years, and dressed herself carefully in her sweet, soft clothes and buttoned shoes. Then, coming downstairs and reflecting that perhaps a little waffle would be agreeable for breakfast in the sunny dining room, she found the mail on the hall floor and bent to pick it up. A bill, the morning paper, a letter in a green envelope that looked oddly familiar. Miss Strangeworth stood perfectly still for a minute, looking down at the green envelope with the penciled printing, and thought: It looks like one of my letters. Was one of my letters sent back? No, because no one would know where to send it. How did this get here?

Miss Strangeworth was a Strangeworth of Pleasant Street. Her hand did not shake as she opened the envelope and unfolded the sheet of green paper inside. She began to cry silently for the wickedness of the world when she read the words: LOOK OUT AT WHAT USED TO BE YOUR ROSES.

THE SNAIL-WATCHER

Patricia Highsmith

*American expatriate Patricia Highsmith met with in-
stant success with her first novel,* Strangers on a Train
*(1950), and the story of two murderers who exchange vic-
tims and thus provide one another with alibis was made into
a film by Alfred Hitchcock in 1951. Ms. Highsmith's subsequent novels have received great critical acclaim, notably*
Two Faces of January, *which was awarded the British Crime
Writers Association award for best foreign novel in 1964,
and* The Talented Mr. Ripley, *which received the Grand
Prix de Littérature Policière as best foreign mystery translated into French in 1957. Her finely characterized novels
and stories often explore the relationships of persons bound
together by a crime. In "The Snail-Watcher" we see a man
whose esoteric but seemingly harmless hobby takes a sudden, horrible turn.*

When Mr. Peter Knoppert began to make a hobby of snail-watching, he had no idea that his handful of specimens would become hundreds in no time. Only two months after the original snails were carried up to the Knoppert study, some thirty glass tanks and bowls, all teeming with snails, lined the walls, rested on the desk and windowsills, and were beginning even to cover the floor. Mrs. Knoppert disapproved strongly, and would no longer enter the room. It smelled, she said, and besides she had once stepped on a snail by accident, a horrible sensation she would never forget. But the more his wife and friends deplored his unusual and vaguely repellent pastime, the more pleasure Mr. Knoppert seemed to find in it.

"I never cared for nature before in my life," Mr. Knoppert often remarked—he was a partner in a brokerage firm, a man who had devoted all his life to the science of finance —"but snails have opened my eyes to the beauty of the animal world."

If his friends commented that snails were not really animals, and their slimy habitats hardly the best example of the beauty of nature, Mr. Knoppert would tell them with a superior smile that they simply didn't know all that he knew about snails.

And it was true. Mr. Knoppert had witnessed an exhibition that was not described, certainly not adequately described, in any encyclopedia or zoology book that he had been able to find. Mr. Knoppert had wandered into the kitchen one evening for a bite of something before dinner, and had happened to notice that a couple of snails in the china bowl on the drainboard were behaving very oddly. Standing more or less on their tails, they were weaving before each other for all the world like a pair of snakes hypnotized by a flute player. A moment later, their faces came together in a kiss of voluptuous intensity. Mr. Knoppert bent closer and studied them from all angles. Something else was happening: a protuberance like an ear was appearing on the right side of the head of both snails. His instinct told him that he was watching a sexual activity of some sort.

The cook came in and said something to him, but Mr. Knoppert silenced her with an impatient wave of his hand. He couldn't take his eyes from the enchanted little creatures in the bowl.

When the earlike excrescences were precisely together rim to rim, a whitish rod like another small tentacle shot out from one ear and arched over toward the ear of the other snail. Mr. Knoppert's first surmise was dashed when a tentacle sallied from the other snail, too. Most peculiar, he thought. The two tentacles withdrew, then came forth again, and as if they had found some invisible mark, remained fixed in either snail. Mr. Knoppert peered intently closer. So did the cook.

"Did you ever see anything like this?" Mr. Knoppert asked.

"No. They must be fighting," the cook said indifferently and went away. That was a sample of the ignorance on the subject of snails that he was later to discover everywhere.

Mr. Knoppert continued to observe the pair of snails off and on for more than an hour, until first the ears, then the rods, withdrew, and the snails themselves relaxed their attitudes and paid no further attention to each other. But by that time, a different pair of snails had begun a flirtation, and were slowly rearing themselves to get into position for kissing. Mr. Knoppert told the cook that the snails were not to be served that evening. He took the bowl of them up to his study. And snails were never again served in the Knoppert household.

That night, he searched his encyclopedias and a few general science books he happened to possess, but there was absolutely nothing on snails' breeding habits, though the oyster's dull reproductive cycle was described in detail. Perhaps it hadn't been a mating he had seen after all, Mr. Knoppert decided after a day or two. His wife, Edna, told him either to eat the snails or get rid of them—it was at this time that she stepped upon a snail that had crawled out onto the floor—and Mr. Knoppert might have, if he hadn't come across a sentence in Darwin's *Origin of Species* on a page given to gastropoda. The sentence was in French, a language Mr. Knoppert did not know, but the word *sensualité* made him tense like a bloodhound that has suddenly found the scent. He was in the public library at the time, and laboriously he translated the sentence with the aid of a French-English dictionary. It was a statement of less than a hundred words, saying that snails manifested a sensuality in their mating that was not to be found elsewhere in the animal kingdom. That was all. It was from the notebooks of Henri Fabre. Obviously Darwin had decided not to translate it for the average reader, but to leave it in its original language for the scholarly few who really cared. Mr. Knoppert considered himself one of the scholarly few now, and his round, pink face beamed with self-esteem.

He had learned that his snails were the freshwater type that laid their eggs in sand or earth, so he put moist earth and a little saucer of water into a big washbowl and transferred his snails into it. Then he waited for something to happen. Not even another mating happened. He picked up the snails one by one and looked at them, without seeing anything suggestive of pregnancy. But one snail he couldn't pick up. The shell might have been glued to the earth. Mr. Knoppert suspected the snail had buried its head in the ground to die. Two more days went by, and on the morning of the third, Mr. Knoppert found a spot of crumbly earth where the snail had been. Curious, he investigated the crumbles with a match stem, and to his delight discovered a pit full of shiny new eggs. Snail eggs! He hadn't been wrong. Mr. Knoppert called his wife and the cook to look at them. The eggs looked very much like big caviar, only they were white instead of black or red.

"Well, naturally they have to breed some way," was his wife's comment. Mr. Knoppert couldn't understand her lack of interest. He had to go and look at the eggs every hour that he was at home. He looked at them every morning to see if any change had taken place, and the eggs were his last thought every night before he went to bed. Moreover, another snail was now digging a pit. And another pair of snails was mating! The first batch of eggs turned a grayish color, and minuscule spirals of shells became discernible on one side of each egg. Mr. Knoppert's anticipation rose to a higher pitch. At last a morning arrived—the eighteenth after laying, according to Mr. Knoppert's careful count— when he looked down into the egg pit and saw the first tiny moving head, the first stubby little antennae uncertainly exploring the nest. Mr. Knoppert was as happy as the father of a new child. Every one of the seventy or more eggs in the pit came miraculously to life. He had seen the entire reproductive cycle evolve to a successful conclusion. And the fact that no one, at least no one that he knew of, was acquainted with a fraction of what he knew, lent his knowledge a thrill of discovery, the piquancy of the esoteric. Mr. Knoppert made notes on successive matings and egg hatchings. He narrated snail biology to fascinated, more often shocked friends and guests, until his wife squirmed with embarrassment.

"But where is it going to stop, Peter? If they keep on reproducing at this rate, they'll take over the house!" his wife told him after fifteen or twenty pits had hatched.

"There's no stopping nature," he replied good-humoredly. "They've only taken over the study. There's plenty of room there."

So more and more glass tanks and bowls were moved in. Mr. Knoppert went to the market and chose several of the more lively-looking snails, and also a pair he found mating, unobserved by the rest of the world. More and more egg pits appeared in the dirt floors of the tanks, and out of each pit crept finally from seventy to ninety baby snails, transparent as dewdrops, gliding up rather than down the strips of fresh lettuce that Mr. Knoppert was quick to give all the pits as edible ladders for the climb. Matings went on so often that he no longer bothered to watch them. A mating could last twenty-four hours. But the thrill of seeing the white caviar become shells and start to move—that never diminished however often he witnessed it.

His colleagues in the brokerage office noticed a new zest for life in Peter Knoppert. He became more daring in his moves, more brilliant in his calculations, became in fact a little vicious in his schemes, but he brought money in for his company. By unanimous vote, his basic salary was raised from forty to sixty thousand dollars per year. When anyone congratulated him on his achievements, Mr. Knoppert gave all the credit to his snails and the beneficial relaxation he derived from watching them.

He spent all his evenings with his snails in the room that was no longer a study but a kind of aquarium. He loved to strew the tanks with fresh lettuce and pieces of boiled potato and beet, then turn on the sprinkler system that he had installed in the tanks to simulate natural rainfall. Then all the snails would liven up and begin eating, mating, or merely gliding through the shallow water with obvious pleasure. Mr. Knoppert often let a snail crawl onto his forefinger—he fancied his snails enjoyed this human contact —and he would feed it a piece of lettuce by hand, would observe the snail from all sides, finding as much aesthetic satisfaction as another man might from contemplating a Japanese print.

By now, Mr. Knoppert did not allow anyone to set foot in his study. Too many snails had the habit of crawling around on the floor, of going to sleep glued to chair bottoms and to the backs of books on the shelves. Snails spent much of their time sleeping, especially the older snails. But there were enough less indolent snails who preferred lovemaking. Mr. Knoppert estimated that about a dozen pairs of snails must be kissing all the time. And certainly there was a multitude of baby and adolescent snails. They were impossible to count. But Mr. Knoppert did count the snails sleeping and creeping on the ceiling alone, and arrived at something between eleven and twelve hundred. The tanks, the bowls, the underside of his desk and the bookshelves must surely have held fifty times that number. Mr. Knoppert meant to scrape the snails off the ceiling one day soon. Some of them had been up there for weeks, and he was afraid they were not taking in enough nourishment. But of late he had been a little too busy, and too much in need of the tranquillity that he got simply from sitting in the study in his favorite chair.

During the month of June he was so busy he often worked late into the evening at his office. Reports were piling in for the end of the fiscal year. He made calculations, spotted a half-dozen possibilities of gain, and reserved the most daring, the least obvious moves for his private operations. By this time next year, he thought, he should be three or four times as well off as now. He saw his bank account multiplying as easily and rapidly as his snails. He told his wife this, and she was overjoyed. She even forgave him the ruination of the study, and the stale, fishy smell that was spreading throughout the whole upstairs.

"Still, I do wish you'd take a look just to see if anything's happening, Peter," she said to him rather anxiously one morning. "A tank might have overturned or something, and I woudn't want the rug to be spoiled. You haven't been in the study for nearly a week, have you?"

Mr. Knoppert hadn't been in for nearly two weeks. He didn't tell his wife that the rug was pretty much gone already. "I'll go up tonight," he said.

But it was three more days before he found time. He went in one evening just before bedtime and was surprised to find the floor quite covered with snails, with three or four layers of snails. He had difficulty closing the door without mashing any. The dense clusters of snails in the corners made the room look positively round, as if he stood inside some huge, conglomerate stone. Mr. Knoppert cracked his knuckles and gazed around him in astonishment. They had not only covered every surface, but thousands of snails hung down into the room from the chandelier in a grotesque clump.

Mr. Knoppert felt for the back of a chair to steady himself. He felt only a lot of shells under his hand. He had to smile a little: there were snails in the chair seat, piled up on one another, like a lumpy cushion. He really must do something about the ceiling, and immediately. He took an umbrella from the corner, brushed some of the snails off it, and cleared a place on his desk to stand. The umbrella point tore the wallpaper, and then the weight of the snails pulled down a long strip that hung almost to the floor. Mr. Knoppert felt frustrated and angry. The sprinklers would make them move. He pulled the lever.

The sprinklers came on in all the tanks, and the seething activity of the entire room increased at once. Mr. Knoppert slid his feet along the floor, through tumbling snail shells that made a sound like pebbles on a beach, and directed a couple of the sprinklers at the ceiling. This was a mistake, he saw at once. The softened paper began to tear, and he dodged one slowly falling mass only to be hit by a swinging festoon of snails, really hit quite a stunning blow on the side of the head. He went down on one knee, dazed. He should open a window, he thought, the air was stifling. And there were snails crawling over his shoes and up his trouser legs. He shook his feet irritably. He was just going to the door, intending to call for one of the servants to help him, when the chandelier fell on him. Mr. Knoppert sat down heavily on the floor. He saw now that he couldn't possibly get a window open, because the snails were fastened thick and deep over the windowsills. For a moment, he felt he couldn't get up, felt as if he were suffocating. It was not only the musty smell of the room, but everywhere he looked long wallpaper strips covered with snails blocked his vision as if he were in a prison.

"Edna!" he called, and was amazed at the muffled,

ineffectual sound of his voice. The room might have been soundproof.

He crawled to the door, heedless of the sea of snails he crushed under hands and knees. He could not get the door open. There were so many snails on it, crossing and recrossing the crack of the door on all four sides, they actually resisted his strength.

"Edna!" A snail crawled into his mouth. He spat it out in disgust. Mr. Knoppert tried to brush the snails off his arms. But for every hundred he dislodged, four hundred seemed to slide upon him and fasten to him again, as if they deliberately sought him out as the only comparatively snailfree surface in the room. There were snails crawling over his eyes. Then just as he staggered to his feet, something else hit him—Mr. Knoppert couldn't even see what. He was fainting! At any rate, he was on the floor. His arms felt like leaden weights as he tried to reach his nostrils, his eyes, to free them from the sealing, murderous snail bodies.

"Help!" He swallowed a snail. Choking, he widened his mouth for air and felt a snail crawl over his lips onto his tongue. He was in hell! He could feel them gliding over his legs like a glutinous river, pinning his legs to the floor. "Ugh!" Mr. Knoppert's breath came in feeble gasps. His vision grew black, a horrible, undulating black. He could not breathe at all, because he could not reach his nostrils, could not move his hands. Then through the slit of one eye, he saw directly in front of him, only inches away, what had been, he knew, the rubber plant that stood in its pot near the door. A pair of snails were quietly making love in it. And right beside them, tiny snails as pure as dewdrops were emerging from a pit like an infinite army into their widening world.

THE LOCKED ROOM

Celia Fremlin

Celia Fremlin is well known both in this country and in her native England for her quietly haunting tales of horror and suspense. Among her novels is The Hours Before Dawn, *which was the recipient of the Mystery Writers of America Edgar as the Best Novel of 1959. Some of the finest of her short stories, including the little nightmare which follows, can be found in her collection* Don't Go to Sleep in the Dark *(1970). "The Locked Room," in fact, may well be the best of all her short fiction.*

A door banged in the empty flat upstairs.

Margaret felt her fingers tighten on the covers of her library book, but she refused to look up. As long as she could keep her eyes running backward and forward along the lines of print, she could tell herself that she hadn't given in to her fear—to this ridiculous, unreasoning fear that had so inexplicably laid hold of her this evening.

What was there to be afraid of, anyway? Simply that the upstairs flat had been empty all this week, and that Henry was on duty tonight? But she had often been alone before —if you could call it alone, with Robin and Peter in bed in the very next room. Two little boys of six and eight sound asleep in bed can't really be called company, but still . . .

Leonora hesitated, wondering which way she should turn.

Margaret realized that she was still reading the same sentence, over and over again, and she shut the book with an angry little slam. What *was* the matter with her? Was it that murder in the papers—some woman strangled by a poor wretch who had been ill-treated in his childhood? He had a grudge against women, or something—Margaret hadn't followed it very carefully—had locked himself in an empty room in this woman's house, and then, in the middle of the night, had crept out . . .

All very horrid, of course; but then one was always reading of murders in the papers—anyway, they'd probably caught him by now. Now, what had she better do to put these silly ideas out of her head once and for all?

Go upstairs, of course. Go upstairs to the empty flat, look briskly through all the rooms, shut firmly whichever door it was that was banging, and come down again, her mind set at rest. Simple.

She put her book down on the little polished table at her

side. But why was she putting it down so softly, so cautiously? Margaret shook herself irritably. There wasn't the slightest need to be quiet. Nothing ever seemed to wake the boys once they were properly off, and poor deaf old Mrs. Palmer on the ground floor certainly wouldn't be troubled.

Just to convince herself, she picked the book up again and dropped it noisily on the table. Then, with a firm step, she walked out to the landing.

The once gracious staircase of the old house curved down into complete blackness. For a moment Margaret was taken aback. Even though old Mrs. Palmer was often in bed before ten, she always left the hall light on for the other tenants—perhaps, too, for her own sake, from a deaf woman's natural anxiety not to be shut away in darkness as well as silence.

Margaret stood for a moment, puzzled. Then she remembered. Of course; the poor old thing had gone off this morning on one of her rare visits to a married niece. Tonight the downstairs flat was empty too.

Margaret was annoyed to feel her palms growing sticky as she gripped the top of the banisters, peering down into the darkness. What on earth difference did it make whether Mrs. Palmer was there or not? Even if she was there, she would have been asleep by now, deep, deep in her world of silence, far out of reach of any human voice . . . of any screams . . .

Snap out of it, girl! Margaret scolded herself. This is what comes of reading mystery stories in the evening instead of catching up with the ironing as I meant to! She turned sharply round and walked across the landing to the other staircase—the dusty, narrower staircase that led to the empty flat above.

The hall stairs were in bad enough repair, goodness knew, but these were worse. As Margaret turned the bend which cut her off from the light of her own landing, she could feel the rotten plaster crumbling under her hands as she felt her way up in the darkness.

The pitter-patter of plaster crumbs falling onto the stairboards was a familiar enough sound to Margaret after six months in this decrepit old house; but all the same she wished the little noise would stop. It seemed to make her more nervous—to get in the way of something. And it was only then that she realized how intently her ears were strained to hear some sound from the empty rooms overhead.

But what sound? Margaret stood on the top landing listening for a moment before she reached out for the light switch.

Bother! The owners, who in all these months had never raised a finger to repair rotting plaster, broken locks, and split window frames, had nevertheless bestirred themselves in less than a week to switch off the electric light supply to the vacant flat! Now she would have to explore the place in the dark.

She felt her way along the wall to the first of the four doors that she knew opened onto this landing. It opened easily; and Margaret again silently cursed the owners. If only they'd take the trouble to fix locks on their own property she would have been spared all this—the top flat would have been properly locked up the moment the Davidsons left, and then there would have been no possibility of anyone lurking there. Her annoyance strengthened her, and she flung the door wide open.

Empty, of course. Accustomed as her eyes were to the complete blackness of the landing, the room seemed to be quite brightly lit by the dim square of the window, and she could see at a glance into every empty corner.

The next room was empty too, and the next, except for the twisted, shadowy bulk of the antique gas cooker which Mrs. Davidson so often declared had "gone funny on her," and might she boil up a kettle on the slightly newer cooker in Margaret's flat?

But the fourth door *was* locked. Nothing surprising in that, Margaret told herself, turning the shaky china knob this way and that without success. Not surprising at all. All the rooms ought to have been locked like this—probably this was the only one which *would* lock, and the owners had lazily hoped for the best about the others. A perfectly natural explanation: no need to turn the handle so stealthily . . .

To prove the point, Margaret gave the knob a brisk rattle, and it came off in her hand. Just like this house! she was thinking, and heard the corresponding knob on the other side of the door fall to the floor with a report like a pistol in the silence of the night.

But what was *that?* It might have been the echo of the bang, of course, in the empty room. Or—yes, of course, that must be it! Margaret let her breath go in a sigh of relief. That scraping, tapping noise—that was exactly the noise a china knob would make, rolling lopsidedly across the bare boards. Wasn't it?

Yes, of course it was. Margaret was surprised to find how quickly she had got back to her own flat—to her lighted sitting-room—to her own fireside, her heart beating annoyingly, and the dirty china knob still in her hand.

Leonora hesitated, wondering which way she should turn.

Margaret pushed the book away with a gesture of irritation. She had thought that by facing her fear—by going up to the empty flat, looking in all the rooms and shutting the doors firmly so that they couldn't bang, she would have regained her peace of mind. Yet here she was, sitting just as before, her heart thumping, her ears straining for she did not know what.

What *is* it all about? she asked herself. Has anything happened today to make me feel nervous? Have I subconsciously noticed anyone suspicious lurking about outside? God knows it's a queer enough neighbourhood! And leaning her chin on her hands, her thick black curls falling forward onto her damp forehead, she thought over the day.

Absolutely nothing out of the ordinary. Henry had gone

to work as usual. The boys had been got off to school with the usual amount of clatter and argument—Peter unable to find his Wellingtons, and Robin announcing, at the very last moment, just as they were starting down the steps, that his teacher had said they were all to bring a cardboard box four inches wide and a long thin piece of string.

Then had followed the morning battle for cleanliness against the obstinate old house. The paintwork that collapsed into dry rot if you wiped it too thoroughly. The cobwebs that brought bits of plaster down with them when you got at them with a broom. . . .

They weren't going to be here much longer, that was one thing, reflected Margaret. They would be moving to the country soon after Christmas, and it hadn't seemed worthwhile to look for anywhere else to live for such a short time. Besides, if they *had* to live in a flat with two lively small boys, this ramshackle old place offered some advantages. Among all this decay no one was going to notice sticky fingermarks and more chipped paint; no one was going to complain about what games the children played in the neglected garden, overgrown with brambles and willow herb. No one minded their boots, and the boots of their numerous small friends, clattering up and down the stairs.

Margaret smiled as she thought of the odd assortment of friends her sons had managed to collect during their six months here. Such a queer mixture of children in a neighbourhood like this, ranging from real little street toughs to the bespectacled son of a divorced but celebrated professor. Always in and out of the house—Margaret couldn't put a name to half of them. That crowd this afternoon, for instance—who *were* they all?

Margaret wrinkled her brows, trying to remember. Alan, of course, the freckle-faced mischief from the paper shop at the corner. And Raymond—the fair, sly boy that Henry said she shouldn't let the children play with—but what could you do? And William—stodgy, mouse-coloured William—who simply came to eat her cakes, it seemed to

Margaret, for he never played at anything in particular with the others.

Oh, and there had been another one today—a new one, for whom Margaret had felt an immediate revulsion. About eight or nine he must have been, very small, for his age and yet strangely mature, with a sharp, shrewd light in his pale, red-rimmed eyes. He had a coarse mop of ill-cut ginger hair and the palest of pale eyebrows and eyelashes, almost invisible in his pale, pinched face. And he was painfully thin.

In spite of her dislike, Margaret had been touched by the thinness—and puzzled, too—real undernourishment is so rare in children nowadays. She had pressed on him cakes and bread and jam, but he had not eaten anything—indeed, he seemed scarcely aware that anything was being offered him—and in the end Margaret had given up and let the others demolish the provisions with their usual speed.

Margaret shivered, suddenly cold, and leaned forward to put more coal on the fire. The memory of this queer, ginger-haired child had somehow made her feel uneasy all over again. She wished she'd made more effort to find out who he was and where he came from, but the boys were always so vague about that sort of thing.

"What, Mummy?" Peter had said when she had asked him about the child that evening; "Mummy, you said *I* could have the next corn-flake packet, and now Robin . . ."

"Yes, yes, darling, but listen. Who was that little ginger-haired boy you brought home from school today?"

"Who did?" interrupted Robin helpfully.

"Well—Peter, I suppose. Or do *you* know him, Robin? Perhaps he's *your* friend?"

"Who is?"

Margaret had sighed. "The little ginger-haired boy. The one who hardly ate anything at tea."

"*I* didn't hardly eat anything, either," remarked Robin smugly.

"Ooo—you story!" broke in Peter indignantly. "I saw you myself, you had three cakes, and . . ."

Margaret had given it up, and determined to ask the child himself if he ever turned up again.

And, strangely enough, as she had gone across their own landing to put on the boys' bath, she thought she caught a glimpse of the little creature in the hall below, darting past the foot of the stairs. But she couldn't be sure; dusk always fell early in that dim, derelict hall, and the whole thing might have been a trick of the light. Anyway, when she had gone to the back door and called into the damp autumn twilight, there had been no answer, and nothing stirred among the rank, overgrown shrubs and weeds.

Margaret picked up her book again, slightly reassured. All this could quite reasonably explain her nervousness tonight. She was feeling guilty, that's what it must be. There was something peculiar about the child, and she should have made more effort to find out about him. Perhaps he needed help—after all, there *were* cases of child cruelty and neglect even nowadays. Tomorrow she would really go into the matter, and then there would be nothing more to worry about.

Leonora hesitated, wondering which way she should turn.

Sometimes, on waking from a deep sleep, one knows with absolute certainty that something has wakened one, but without knowing what. Margaret knew, with just this certainty, that something had made her raise her eyes from the book. She listened—listened as she had listened before that night—to the deep pulsing in her ears, to the tiny flickering murmur of the coals. Nothing more.

But wasn't there? What was that, then, that faint, faint shuffle on the landing outside? Shuffle, shuffle, soft as an autumn leaf drifting—shuffle shuffle—pad pad . . . silently the door swung open and there stood Robin, blinking, half asleep.

Margaret let out her breath in a gasp of relief.

"Robin! Whatever's the matter? Why aren't you asleep?"

Robin blinked at her owlishly, his eyes large and round as they always were when just wakened from sleep.

"I don't like that little boy in my bed," he observed.

"What little boy? Whatever are you talking about, Robin?"

"That little boy. He's horrid. He pinches me. And he's muddling the blankets. On purpose."

"Darling, you're dreaming! Come along and let's see!"

Taking the child's hand, Margaret led him back into his own room and switched on the light.

There was Peter, rosily asleep with his mouth open as usual; and there was Robin's little bed, empty, and with the clothes tumbled this way and that as if he had tossed about a lot in his sleep.

This confirmed Margaret's opinion that he had had a nightmare. After all, what was more likely after her cross-questioning about the mysterious little visitor that evening? In spite of his apparent inattention, Robin had no doubt sensed something of the anxiety and distaste behind her questions, and it was the most likely thing in the world that he would dream about it when he went to bed.

However, to reassure the child, Margaret embarked on a thorough search of the little room. Under both the beds they looked, into the clothes closet, behind the curtains— even, at Robin's insistence, into the impossibly narrow space behind the chest of drawers.

"He was such a *thin* little boy, you see, Mummy," Robin explained, and the phrase gave Margaret a nasty little pang of uneasiness. The hungry, too-old little face seemed to hover before her for a moment, its eyes full of ancient, malicious knowledge. She blinked it away, shut the lid of the brick box (what an absurd place to look!), and bundled Robin firmly back to bed.

"And do you promise I won't dream it again?" asked Robin anxiously, and Margaret promised. This was the standard formula after Robin's nightmares. It had always worked before.

Nearly twelve o'clock. There was nothing whatever to stay up for, but somehow Margaret couldn't bring herself to go to bed. She reached out towards her library book, but felt that she could not face Leonora's indecision again, and instead picked up yesterday's evening paper. She would look for something cheerful to read before she went to bed. The autumn fashions, perhaps—or would it be the spring ones they'd be writing about in October? It was all very confusing nowadays.

But it wasn't the autumn fashions she found herself reading—or the spring ones. It was the blurred photograph of the wanted man that caught her eye—a man in his fifties perhaps—from such a bad picture it was difficult to tell. A picture of the murdered woman, too—a Mrs. Harriet somebody—and a description of her . . .

Margaret's attention suddenly became riveted and she read the report from beginning to end, hardly daring to breathe. This man, at large somewhere in London tonight, had escaped from a mental institution where he had been sent some years ago for strangling another woman in somewhat similar circumstances to this Mrs. Harriet . . .

Margaret felt her limbs grow rigid. Both women had been the mothers of small boys . . . both had lived in tall derelict houses converted into flats . . . both had had black hair done in tight curls . . . Margaret fingered her hairstyle with damp, trembling fingers, and tried not to read any more, but her eyes seemed glued to the page. Why had the man not been hanged that first time?

There followed the story of his childhood—a story of real Dickensian horror. Brought up in a tall ruined old house by a stepmother who had starved him, thrashed him, shut him in dark rooms where she told him clawed fiends were waiting . . . her black, shining curls had quivered over his childhood like the insignia of torture and death. The prison doctors had learned all this from him after the first murder —and had learned, too, how the sight of a black-haired woman going up the steps of just such a derelict house as he remembered had brought back his terror and misery with such vividness that "I didn't just *feel* like a little boy again —I *was* a little boy . . . that was my house . . . that was *her*" — that was the only way he could describe it. And he had crept into the house, locked himself in one of the empty rooms until the dead silence of the night, and then crept out, with a child's enormity of terror and hatred in his heart, and with a man's strength in his fingers. . . .

Margaret closed her eyes for a second, and then opened them again to read the description of the murderer: "About fifty years of age, medium height, ginger hair growing grey, eyebrows and eyelashes almost invisible . . ." With every word the face leaped before her more vividly—not the face of the ageing, unknown man, but the little malevolent face she had seen that afternoon—the ill-cut ginger hair, the little red-rimmed eyes filled with the twisted malice of an old and bitter man . . .

"I didn't just *feel* like a little boy again, I *was* a little boy . . ." The words beat through Margaret's brain, over and over again.

She thrust the paper away from her. Don't be so fanciful and absurd, she told herself. After all, if I *really* think anything's wrong all I've got to do is call the police. There's the telephone just there in the hall.

She walked slowly to the door and out onto the landing, and stood there in her little island of light with darkness above and below. She tried to go on telling herself what nonsense it all was, how ridiculous she was being. But now she dared not let any more words come into her mind, not any words at all. For she was listening—listening as civilized human beings rarely have need to listen—listening as an animal listens in the murderous blackness of the forest. Not just with the ears—rather with the whole body. Every organ, every nerve is alert, pricked up, so that, in the end, it is impossible to say through which sense the message comes, and comes with absolute certainty: Danger is near. Danger is on the move.

For there was no sound. Margaret was certain of that. No sound to tell her that something was stirring in the locked room upstairs—that dark, empty room so like the locked room where once a little boy had gone half mad with terror at the thought of the clawed fiends. The clawed fiends who had lost their terrors through the years and become his friends and allies, for now at last he was a clawed fiend himself.

Still Margaret heard no sound. No sound to tell that the door of the empty room was being unlocked, silently, and with consummate skill, from the inside. No shuffle of footsteps across the dusty upstairs landing. No creak from the ancient, rickety steps of that top flight of stairs.

And in the end it was not Margaret's straining ears at all which caught the first hint of the oncoming creature—it was her eyes. They seemed to have been riveted on that shadowy bend in the banisters for so long that when she saw the hand at last, long and tapering, like five snakes coiled round the rail, she could have imagined it had been there all the time, flickering in and out and dancing before her eyes.

But not the face. No, that couldn't have been there before. Not anywhere, in all the world, could there have been a face like that—a face so distorted, so alight with hate that it seemed almost luminous as it leered out of the blackness, as it seemed to glide down towards her a foot or two above the banister . . .

There was a sound now—a quick pattering of feet, horribly light and soft, like a child's, as they bore the heavy adult shape down the stairs, the white, curled fingers reaching out towards her . . .

A little frightened cry at Margaret's elbow freed her from her paralysis. A little white face, a tangle of ginger hair . . . and an instinct stronger that that of self-preservation gripped her. In a second she was on her knees, her arms round the small trembling body; she felt the little creature's shaking terror subsiding into a great peace as she held him against her breast.

That dropping on her knees was her salvation. In that

very second her assailant lunged, tripped over her suddenly lowered body, and pitched headlong down the stairs behind her. Crash upon crash as he fell from step to step, and then silence. Absolute silence.

Then a new clamour arose:

"Mummy! Mummy! Who . . . ? What . . . ?"—a tangle of small legs and arms, and in a moment her arms seemed to be full of little boys. She collected her wits and looked down at them. Only two of them, of course, her own two, their familiar dark heads pressed against her, their frightened questions clamouring in her ears . . .

And when the police came, and Henry came, and the dead man was taken away, there was so much to tell. So much to explain. It could all be explained quite easily, of course (as Henry pointed out), with only a little stretching of coincidence.

The little ginger-headed boy must come from somewhere in the neighbourhood—no doubt he could be traced, and if necessary helped in some way. Margaret's obsession about him would explain Robin's dream; it would also explain why, in that moment of terror, she imagined the strange child had rushed into her arms. Really, of course, it must have been one of her own boys.

And yet, Margaret could never forget the smile on the face of the dead man as he lay crumpled at the foot of the stairs. They say that the faces of the dead can set in all sorts of incongruous expressions, but it seemed to Margaret that the smile had not been the smile of a grown man at all; it had been the smile of a little boy who has felt the comfort of a mother's arms at last.

THE FALL OF A COIN

Ruth Rendell

A Londoner and former journalist, Ruth Rendell is perhaps best known for her series of novels featuring Chief Inspector Wexford of the village of Kingsmarkham. In addition, she has written many short stories and other novels, the most recent of which is Master of the Moor. *Ms. Rendell's honors include the British Crime Writers Association Current Crime Silver Cup for best crime novel of 1976, the Gold Dagger for best crime novel of 1975, and the Mystery Writers of America Edgar for Best Short Story of 1974. In "The Fall of a Coin" Ms. Rendell gives us a sensitive portrait of a couple trapped in a nightmarish marriage as it draws near its inevitable, horrible conclusion.*

The manageress of the hotel took them up two flights of stairs to their room. There was no lift. There was no central heating either and, though April, it was very cold.

"A bit small, isn't it?" said Nina Armadale.

"It's a double room and I'm afraid it's all we had left."

"I suppose I'll have to be thankful it hasn't got a double bed," said Nina.

Her husband winced at that, which pleased her. She went over to the window and looked down into a narrow alley bounded by brick walls. The cathedral clock struck five. Nina imagined what that would be like chiming every hour throughout the night, and maybe every quarter as well, and was glad she had brought her sleeping pills.

The manageress was still making excuses for the lack of accommodation. "You see, there's this big wedding in the cathedral tomorrow. Sir William Tarrant's daughter. There'll be five hundred guests and most of them are putting up in the town."

"We're going to it," said James Armadale. "That's why we're here."

"Then you'll appreciate the problem. Now the bathroom's just down the passage, turn right and it's the third door on the left. Dinner at seven-thirty and breakfast from eight till nine. Oh, and I'd better show Mrs. Armadale how to work the gas fire."

"Don't bother," said Nina, enraged. "I can work a gas fire." She was struggling with the wardrobe door, which at first wouldn't open, and when opened refused to close.

The manageress watched her, apparently decided it was hopeless to assist, and said to James, "I really meant about working the gas *meter*. There's a coin-in-the-slot meter—it takes fivepence pieces—and we really find it the best way for guests to manage."

James squatted on the floor beside her and studied the grey metal box. It was an old-fashioned gas meter with brass fittings of the kind he hadn't seen since he had been a student living in a furnished room. A guage with a red arrow marker indicated the amount of gas paid for, and at present it showed empty. So if you turned the dial on the gas fire to "on" no gas would come from the meter unless you had previously fed it with one or more fivepence pieces. But what was the purpose of that brass handle? There were differences between this contraption and the one he'd had in his college days. Maybe, while his had been for the old toxic coal gas, this had been converted for the supply of natural gas. He looked enquiringly at the manageress, and asked her.

"No, we're still waiting for natural in this part of the country and when it comes the old meters will have to go."

"What's the handle for?"

"You turn it to the left like this, insert your coin in the slot, and then turn it to the right. Have you got fivepence on you?"

James hadn't. Nina had stopped listening, he was glad to see. Perhaps when the inevitable quarrel started, as it would as soon as the woman had gone, it would turn upon the awfulness of going to this wedding, for which he could hardly be blamed, instead of the squalid arrangements in the hotel, for which he could.

"Never mind," the manageress was saying. "You can't go wrong, it's very simple. When you've put your fivepence in, you just turn the handle to the right as far as it will go and you hear the coin fall. Then you can switch on the fire and light the gas. Is that clear?"

James said it was quite clear, thanks very much, and immediately the manageress had left the room. Nina, who wasted no time, said, "Can you tell me one good reason why we couldn't have come here tomorrow?"

"I could tell you several," said James, getting up from the floor, turning his back on that antediluvian thing and

the gas fire which looked as if it hadn't given out a therm
of heat for about thirty years. "The principal one is that I
didn't fancy driving a hundred and fifty miles in a morning
coat and top hat."

"Didn't fancy driving with your usual Saturday morning hangover, you mean."

"Let's not start a row, Nina. Let's have a bit of peace
for just one evening. Sir William is my company chairman.
I have to take it as an honour that we were asked to this
wedding, and if we have an uncomfortable evening and
night because of it, that can't be helped. It's part of the
job."

"Just how pompous can you get?" said Nina with what
in a less attractive woman would have been called a snarl.
"I wonder what Sir William-Bloody-Tarrant would say if he
could see his sales director after he's got a bottle of whisky
inside him."

"He doesn't see me," said James, lighting a cigarette,
and adding because she hadn't yet broken his spirit, "That's
your privilege."

"*Privilege!*" Nina, who had been furiously unpacking
her case and throwing clothes onto one of the beds, now
stopped doing this because it sapped some of the energy she
needed for quarrelling. She sat down on the bed and
snapped, "Give me a cigarette. You've no manners, have
you? Do you know how uncouth you are? This place'll suit
you fine, it's just up to your mark, gas meters and a loo about
five hundred yards away. That won't bother you as long as
there's a bar. I'll be able to have the *privilege* of sharing my
bedroom with a disgusting soak." She drew breath like a
swimmer and plunged on. "Do you realise we haven't slept
in the same room for two years? Didn't think of that, did you,
when you left booking up till the last minute? Or maybe—
yes, that was it, my God!—maybe you did think of it. Oh, I
know you so well, James Armadale. You thought being in
here with me, undressing with me, would work the miracle.
I'd come round. I'd—what's the expression?—*resume mari-*

tal relations. You got them to give us this—this cell on purpose. You bloody fixed it!"

"No," said James. He said it quietly and rather feebly because he had experienced such a strong inner recoil that he could hardly speak at all.

"You liar! D'you think I've forgotten the fuss you made when I got you to sleep in the spare room? D'you think I've forgotten about that woman, that Frances? I'll never forget and I'll never forgive you. So don't think I'm going to let bygones by bygones when you try pawing me about when the bar closes."

"I shan't do that," said James, reflecting that in a quarter of an hour the bar would be opening. "I shall never again try what you so charmingly describe as pawing you about."

"No, because you know you wouldn't get anywhere. You know you'd get a slap round the face you wouldn't forget in a hurry."

"Nina," he said, "let's stop this. It's hypothetical, it won't happen. If we are going to go on living together—and I suppose we are, though God knows why—can't we try to live in peace?"

She flushed and said in a thick sullen voice, "You should have thought of that before you were unfaithful to me with that woman."

"That," he said, "was three years ago, *three years.* I don't want to provoke you and we've been into this enough times, but you know very well why I was unfaithful to you. I'm only thirty-five, I'm still young. I couldn't stand being permitted *marital relations*—pawing you about, if you like that better—about six times a year. Do I have to go over it all again?"

"Not on my account. It won't make any difference to me what excuses you make." The smoke in the tiny room made her cough and, opening the window, she inhaled the damp, cold air. "You asked me," she said, turning round, "why we have to go on living together. I'll tell you why. Because you married me. I've got a right to you and I'll

never divorce you. You've got me till death parts us. Till
death, James. Right?"

He didn't answer. An icy blast had come into the room
when she had opened the window, and he felt in his pocket.
"If you're going to stay in here till dinner," he said, "you'll
want the gas fire on. Have you got any fivepence pieces? I
haven't, unless I can get some change."

"Oh, you'll get some all right. In the bar. And just for
your information, I haven't brought any money with me.
That's *your* privilege."

When he had left her alone, she sat in the cold room for
some minutes, staring at the brick wall. Till death parts us,
she had told him, and she meant it. She would never leave
him and he must never be allowed to leave her, but she
hoped he would die. It wasn't her fault she was frigid. She
had always supposed he understood. She had supposed her
good looks and her capacity as housewife and hostess com-
pensated for a revulsion she couldn't help. And it wasn't just
against him, but against all men, any man. He had seemed
to accept it and to be happy with her. In her sexless way, she
had loved him. And then, when he had seemed happier and
more at ease than at any time in their marriage, when he
had ceased to make those painful demands and had become
so sweet to her, so generous with presents, he had suddenly
and without shame confessed it. She wouldn't mind, he had
told her, he knew that. She wouldn't resent his finding elsewhere what she so evidently disliked giving him. While he
provided for her and spent nearly all his leisure with her and
respected her as his wife, she should be relieved, disliking
sex as she did, that he had found someone else.

He had said it was the pent-up energy caused by her
repressions that made her fly at him, beat at him with her
hands, scream at him words he didn't know she knew. To
her dying day she would remember his astonishment. He
had genuinely thought she wouldn't mind. And it had taken
weeks of nagging and screaming and threats to make him
agree to give Frances up. She had driven him out of her

bedroom and settled into the bitter, unremitting vendetta she would keep up till death parted them. Even now, he didn't understand how agonisingly he had hurt her. But there were no more women and he had begun to drink. He was drinking now, she thought, and by nine o'clock he would be stretched out, dead drunk on that bed separated by only eighteen inches from her own.

The room was too cold to sit in any longer. She tried the gas fire, turning on the switch to "full," but the match she held to it refused to ignite it, and presently she made her way downstairs and into a little lounge where there was a coal fire and people were watching television.

They met again at the dinner table.

James Armadale had drunk getting on for half a pint of whisky, and now, to go with the brown Windsor soup and hotted-up roast lamb, he ordered a bottle of burgundy.

"Just as a matter of idle curiosity," said Nina, "why do you drink so much?"

"To drown my sorrows," said James. "The classic reason. Happens to be true in my case. Would you like some wine?"

"I'd better have a glass, hadn't I, otherwise you'll drink the whole bottle."

The dining room was full and most of the other diners were middle-aged or elderly. Many of them, he supposed, would be wedding guests like themselves. He could see that their arrival had been noted and that at the surrounding tables their appearance was being favourably commented upon. It afforded him a thin, wry amusement to think that they would be judged a handsome, well-suited and perhaps happy couple.

"Nina," he said, "we can't go on like this. It's not fair on either of us. We're destroying ourselves and each other. We have to talk about what we're going to do."

"Pick your moments, don't you? I'm not going to talk about it in a public place."

She had spoken in a low, subdued voice, quite different from her hectoring tone in their bedroom, and she shot quick, nervous glances at the neighbouring tables.

"It's because this is a public place that I think we stand a better chance of talking about it reasonably. When we're alone you get hysterical and then neither of us can be rational. If we talk about it now, I think I know you well enough to say you won't scream at me."

"I could walk out though, couldn't I? Besides, you're drunk."

"I am not drunk. Frankly, I probably shall be in an hour's time and that's another reason why we ought to talk here and now. Look, Nina, you don't love me, you've said so often enough, and whatever crazy ideas you have about my having designs on you, I don't love you either. We've been into the reasons for that so many times that I don't need to go into them now, but can't we come to some sort of amicable arrangement to split up?"

"So that you can have all the women you want? So that you can bring that bitch into my house?"

"No," he said, "you can have the house. The court would probably award you a third of my income, but I'll give you more if you want. I'd give you half." He had nearly added, "to be rid of you," but he bit off the words as being too provocative. His speech was already thickening and slurring.

It was disconcerting—though this was what he had wanted—to hear how inhibition made her voice soft and kept her face controlled. The words she used were the same, though. He had heard them a thousand times before. "If you leave me, I'll follow you. I'll go to your office and tell them all about it. I'll sit on your doorstep. I won't be abandoned. I'd rather die. I won't be a divorced woman just because you've got tired of me."

"If you go on like this," he said thickly, "you'll find yourself a widow. Will you like that?"

Had they been alone, she would have screamed the

affirmative at him. Because they weren't, she gave him a thin, sharp, and concentrated smile, a smile which an observer might have taken for amusement at some married couple's private joke. "Yes," she said, "I'd like to be a widow, *your* widow. Drink yourself to death, why don't you? That's what you have to do if you want to be rid of me."

The waitress came to their table. James ordered a double brandy and "coffee for my wife." He knew he would never be rid of her. He wasn't the sort of man who can stand public disruption of his life, scenes at work, molestation, the involvement of friends and employers. It must be, he knew, an amicable split or none at all. And since she would never see reason, never understand or forgive, he must soldier on. With the help of this, he thought, as the brandy spread its dim, cloudy euphoria through his brain. He drained his glass quickly, muttered an "excuse me" to her for the benefit of listeners, and left the dining room.

Nina returned to the television lounge. There was a play on whose theme was a marital situation that almost paralleled her own. The old ladies with their knitting and the old men with their after-dinner cigars watched it apathetically. She thought she might take the car and go somewhere for a drive. It didn't much matter where, anywhere would do that was far enough from this hotel and James and that cathedral clock whose chimes split the hours into fifteen-minute segments with long brazen peals. There must be somewhere in this town where one could get a decent cup of coffee, some cinema maybe where they weren't showing a film about marriage or what people, she thought shudderingly, called sexual relationships. She went upstairs to get the car keys and some money.

James was fast asleep. He had taken off his tie and his shoes, but otherwise he was fully dressed, lying on his back and snoring. Stupid of him not to get under the covers. He'd freeze. Maybe he'd die of exposure. Well, she wasn't going to cover him up, but she'd close the window for when she came in. The car keys were in his jacket pocket, mixed up with a lot of loose change. The feel of his warm body through the material made her shiver. His breath smelt of spirits and he was sweating in spite of the cold. Among the change were two fivepence pieces. She'd take one of those and keep it till the morning to feed that gas meter. It would be horrible dressing for that wedding in here at zero temperature. Why not feed it now so that it would be ready for the morning, ready to turn the gas fire on and give her some heat when she came in at midnight, come to that?

The room was faintly illuminated by the yellow light from the street lamp in the alley. She crouched down in front of the gas fire, and noticed she hadn't turned the dial to "off" after her match had failed to ignite the jets. It wouldn't do to feed that meter now with the dial turned to "full" and have fivepence worth of old-fashioned toxic gas flood the room. Not with the window tight shut and not a crack round that heavy old door. Slowly she put her hand out to turn off the dial.

Her fingers touched it. Her hand remained still, poised. She heard her heart begin to thud softly in the silence as the idea in all its brilliant awfulness took hold of her. Wouldn't do . . . ? Was she mad? It wouldn't do to feed that meter now with the gas-fire dial turned to "full"? What would do as well, as efficiently, as finally? She withdrew her hand and clasped it in the other to steady it.

Rising to her feet, she contemplated her sleeping husband. The sweat was standing on his pale forehead now. He snored as rhythmically, as stertorously, as her own heart beat. A widow, she thought, alone and free in her own unshared house. Not divorced, despised, disowned, laughed at by judges and solicitors for her crippling frigidity, not mocked by that Frances and her successors, but a widow whom all the world would pity and respect. Comfortably-off too, if not rich, with an income from James's life assurance and very likely a pension from Sir William Tarrant.

James wouldn't wake up till midnight. No, that was

wrong. He wouldn't *have* wakened up till midnight. What she meant was he wouldn't wake up at all.

The dial on the gas fire was still on, full on. She took the fivepence coin and tiptoed over to the meter. Nothing would wake him but still she tiptoed. The window was tight shut, with nothing beyond it but that alley, that glistening lamp, and the towering wall of the cathedral.

She studied the meter, kneeling down. It was the first time in her sheltered, cosseted, snug life that she had ever actually seen a coin-in-the-slot gas meter. But if morons like hotel servants and the sort of people who would stay in a place like this could work it, she could. There was the slot where the coin went in, there the gauge whose red arrow showed empty. All you had to do, presumably, was slip in the coin, fiddle about with that handle, and then, if the gas-fire dial was on, toxic coal gas—the kind of gas that had killed thousands in the past, careless old people, suicides, accident-prone fools—would rapidly begin to seep out of the unlighted jets in the fire. James wouldn't smell it. Drink paralysed him into an unconsciousness as deep as that which her own sleeping tablets brought to her.

Nina was certain it wouldn't matter that she hadn't attended closely to the manageress's instructions. What had she said? Turn the handle to the left, insert the coin, turn it to the right. She hesitated for a moment, just long enough for brief fractured memories to cross her mind—James when they were first married, James patient and self-denying on their honeymoon, James promising that her coldness didn't matter, that with time and love . . . James confessing with a defiant smirk, throwing Frances's name at her, James going on a three-day bender because she couldn't pretend the wound he'd given her was just a surface scratch, James drunk night after night after night. . . .

She didn't hesitate for long.

She got her coat, put the car keys in her handbag. Then she knelt down again between the gas fire and the meter. First she checked that the dial, which was small and almost at ground level, was set at "full." She took hold of the brass handle on the meter and turned it to the left. The coin slot was now fully exposed and open. She pressed in the five-pence piece and flicked the handle to the right. There was no need to wait for the warning smell, oniony, acrid, of the escaping gas. Without looking back, she walked swiftly from the room, closing the door behind her.

The cathedral clock chimed the last quarter before nine.

When the bar closed at eleven-thirty, the crowd of people coming upstairs and chattering in loud voices would have awakened even the deepest sleeper. They woke James. He didn't move for some time but lay there with his eyes open till he heard the clock chime midnight. When the last stroke died away he reached out and turned on the bedside lamp. The light was like knives going into his head, and he groaned. But he felt like this most nights at midnight and there was no use making a fuss. Who would hear or care if he did? Nina was evidently still downstairs in that lounge. It was too much to hope she might stay there all night out of fear of being alone with him. No, she'd be up now the television had closed down and she'd start berating him for his drunkenness and his infidelity—not that there had been any since Frances—and they would lie there bickering and smarting until grey light mingled with that yellow light, and the cathedral clock told them it was dawn.

And yet she had been so sweet once, so pathetic and desperate in her sad failure. It had never occurred to him to blame her, though his body suffered. And his own solution, honestly confessed, might have worked so well for all three of them if she had been rational. He wondered vaguely, for the thousandth time, why he had been such a fool as to confess, when, with a little deception, he might be happier now than at any time in his marriage. But he was in no fit state to think. Where had that woman said the bathroom was? Turn right down the passage and the third door on the left. He lay there till the clock struck the quarter before he felt he couldn't last out any longer and he'd have to find it.

The cold air in the passage—God, it was more like January than April—steadied him a little and made his head bang and throb. He must be crazy to go on like this. What the hell was he doing, turning himself into an alcoholic at thirty-five? Because there were no two ways about it, he was an alcoholic all right, a drunk. And if he stayed with Nina he'd be a dead alcoholic by forty. But how can you leave a woman who won't leave you? Give up his job, run away, go to the ends of the earth. . . . It wasn't unusual for him to have wild thoughts like this at midnight, but when the morning came he knew he would just soldier on.

He stayed in the bathroom for about ten minutes. Coming back along the passage, he heard footsteps on the stairs, and knowing he must look horrible and smell horribly of liquor, he retreated behind the open door of what proved to be a broom cupboard. But it was only his wife. She approached their room door slowly as if she were bracing herself to face something—himself, probably, he thought. Had she really that much loathing of him that she had to draw in her breath and clench her hands before confronting him? She was very pale. She looked ill and frightened, and when she had opened the door and gone inside he heard her give a kind of shrill gasp that was almost a shriek.

He followed her into the room, and when she turned and saw him he thought she was going to faint. She had been pale before, but now she turned paper white. Once, when he had still loved her and had hoped he might teach her to love him, he would have been concerned. But now he didn't care, and all he said was, "Been watching something nasty on the T.V.?"

She didn't answer him. She sat down on her bed and put her head into her hands. James undressed and got into bed. Presently Nina got up and began taking her clothes off slowly and mechanically. His head and body had begun to twitch as they did when he was recovering from the effects of a drinking bout. It left him wide awake. He wouldn't sleep again for hours. He watched her curiously but dispassionately, for he had long ago ceased to derive the slightest pleasure or excitement from seeing her undress. What intrigued him now was that, though she was evidently in some sort of state of shock, her hands shaking, she still couldn't discard those modest subterfuges of hers, her way of turning her back when she stepped out of her dress, of pulling her nightgown over her head before she took off her underclothes.

She put on her dressing gown and went to the bathroom. When she came back her face was greasy where she had cleaned off the make-up and she was shivering.

"You'd better take a sleeping tablet," he said.

"I've already taken one in the bathroom. I wanted a bath but there wasn't any hot water." Getting into bed, she exclaimed in her normal fierce way, "Nothing works in this damned place! Nothing goes right!"

"Put out the light and go to sleep. Anyone would think you'd got to spend the rest of your life here instead of just one night."

She made no reply. They never said good night to each other. When she had put her light out the room wasn't really dark because a street lamp was still lit in the alley outside. He had seldom felt less like sleep, and now he was aware of a sensation he hadn't expected because he hadn't thought about it. He didn't want to share a bedroom with her.

That cold modesty, which had once been enticing, now repelled him. He raised himself on one elbow and peered at her. She lay in the defensive attitude of a woman who fears assault, flat on her stomach, her arms folded under her head. Although the sleeping pill had taken effect and she was deeply asleep, her body seemed stiff, prepared to galvanise into violence at a touch. She smelt cold. A sour saltiness emanated from her as if there were sea water in her veins instead of blood. He thought of real women with warm blood, women who awoke from sleep when their husbands' faces neared theirs, who never recoiled but smiled and put out their arms. Forever she would keep him from them until the drink or time made him as frozen as she.

Suddenly he knew he couldn't stay in that room. He might do something dreadful, beat her up perhaps or even kill her. And much as he wanted to be rid of her, spend no more time with her, no more money on her, the notion of killing her was as absurd as it was grotesque. It was unthinkable. But he couldn't stay here.

He got up and put on his dressing gown. He'd go to that lounge where she'd watched television, take a blanket, and spend the rest of the night there. She wouldn't wake till nine and by then he'd be back, ready to dress for that wedding. Funny, really, their going to a wedding, to watch someone else getting into the same boat. But it wouldn't be the same boat, for if office gossip was to be relied on, Sir William's daughter had already opened her warm arms to many men. . . .

The cathedral clock struck one. By nine the room would be icy and they'd need that gas fire. Why not put a fivepence piece in the meter now so that the fire would work when he wanted it?

The fire itself lay in shadow but the meter was clearly illuminated by the street lamp. James knelt down, trying to remember the instructions of the manageress. Better try it out first before he put his coin in, his only fivepence coin. Strange, that. He could have sworn he'd had two when he first went to bed.

What had that woman said? Turn the handle to the left, insert the coin, turn the handle to the right. . . . No, turn it to the right as far as it will go until *you hear the coin fall.* Keeping hold of his coin—he didn't want to waste it if what Nina said was true and nothing worked in this place—he turned the handle to the left, then hard to the right as far as it would go.

Inside the meter a coin fell with a small dull clang. The

red arrow marker on the gauge, which had stood at empty, moved along to register payment. Good. He was glad he hadn't wasted his money. The previous guest must have put a coin in and failed to turn the handle until it fell. So Nina had been wrong about things not working. Still, it wasn't unusual for her to get the wrong idea, not unusual at all. . . .

Gas would come through now once the dial was switched on. James checked that the window was shut to keep out the cold, gave a last look at the sleeping, heavily sedated woman, and went out of the room, closing the door behind him.

DOUBLE JEOPARDY

Susan Dunlap

Born in New York City in 1943, Susan Dunlap is the author of two novels, Karma *and* As a Favor, *as well as numerous short stories in the suspense field. "Double Jeopardy" was her first published work, appearing in* Ellery Queen's Mystery Magazine *in 1978 under the title "Death Threat." A social worker before embarking on her writing career, Ms. Dunlap has a penetrating insight into the darker side of human behavior—as shown by this story of the strange relationship between two sisters.*

Don't give me excuses. Do it right, damn it! What do you think I'm paying you for?" Wynne slammed down the phone.

I stood in the doorway, still amazed at my sister's authority, despite the fact that she had controlled situations for nearly forty years.

Even now, lying in the hospital, she continued to play the executive. But, after all, she was the first woman in the state to have become senior vice president of a major corporation. I wondered if it was Warren or some other harried assistant who had felt the sting of her tongue this time.

As she looked at me her expression changed from irritation to concern. "Lynne, why are you lurking in the doorway? You're shaking. Come in and tell me what's the matter."

I walked in, a bit unsteadily, and sat on the plastic chair next to the bed. "It happened again."

"What this time?"

I took a deep breath, holding my hands one on top of the other on my lap, trying to calm myself enough to be coherent.

The room was bare—hospital-green curtains pulled back against hospital-green walls. The flowers and plant arrangements had been sent to Wynne's apartment when she had first taken sick leave months ago, but by the time I arrived in the city, they were long dead. Funny how I hesitated to change anything in her apartment, where I, for however long it might be, was only a guest.

Wynne sat propped up on the hospital bed, her hair black and shining, with not a hint of gray.

I looked at her face, at the deceptively fragile smile that had always been strong. Our features were so similar, almost

exact, yet no one had ever mixed us up. And Wynne's compact body had always looked forceful where mine had
merely seemed small.

She'd changed suddenly when she'd become ill. It was
as if her underpinnings had been jerked loose, and she had
sped past me on the way to old age.

"Lynne, I'm really worried about you," she said with an
anxiety in her voice I hadn't heard in ages. "What happened?"

"Another shot. It just missed my head. If I hadn't stumbled . . ." My hands were shaking.

Wynne leaned forward and reached out with her hands
to my own, steadying mine with her own calm. "Have you
notified the police?"

"They're no help. They take a report and then—nothing. I don't think they believe me. Another hysterical middle-aged woman."

Wynne nodded. "Let's just go through the thing again.
I'm used to handling problems—gives me something to
think about when I'm on the dialysis machine."

It sounded cold, but that was the way she was now.
We'd been apart since college, and emotionally longer
than that. Really, I could hardly claim to know her anymore. Our twin-ness had never had that special affinity—
secret baby language, intuitively shared joys and appre-
hensions. In us, the physical resemblance had merely
served to point out our very different traits. I had wound
up teaching in our home-town grammar school; she, more
determined and ambitious, had made her way up in the
world of business.

"So?" she said impatiently.

"Someone shot at me three times. If I weren't always
tripping and turning my ankle . . ."

"And you have no idea who it might be?"

"None. Who would want to kill me? Why? Really, what
difference would it make if I died? Who would care?"

"It would matter to me." She pressed my hands, then

drew away. "You're all I have. I wouldn't have asked you to come if you weren't vital to me."

I bit my lip. "There are things . . . I want to say before . . ." But I couldn't say "you die," and Wynne, for all her lack of sentimentality, didn't seem to be able to supply the words for me.

Instead I said, "Wynne, you shouldn't cut yourself off like this."

"I have you. I need someone away from the company."

"But why? Why not let Warren come?"

"No." She spat out the words. "I can't let him see me like this."

She looked all right to me. Better than I was likely to look if I didn't find out who was shooting at me.

Wynne must have divined my thoughts, for she said irritably, "You don't show someone who's after your job how sick you are. I've never told any of them that I'm on the dialysis machine." She shook her head as if to dismiss the unacceptable thought. "I told them it was just one kidney that failed, that I was having it removed." Her face moved into a tenuous smile. "I know all the details from your own operation. So don't say that you never did anything for me."

I didn't know how to answer. Could Wynne really hide the fact that she was dying? Warren had been her assistant for ten years. He had taken over her job as acting senior vice president. I had assumed they were friends, but I guess I didn't understand the nature of friendship in business.

Brusquely, Wynne gestured for me to go on.

Swallowing my annoyance, I reminded myself that she was used to giving orders and now she had no one but me to boss around.

But before I could answer, a nurse came in and with an air of authority that dwarfed even Wynne's, motioned me away as she drew the green curtain in a half oval around the bed.

I walked to the window and looked out, but I didn't want to see the parking lot again. I didn't want to search each bush, behind every car, looking for a sniper. Instead, I turned back toward the room—this small private room, so very impersonal. Even Wynne, with all her power, hadn't the ability to stamp any image of herself onto it. It was merely a holding cell for the dying.

"Just another minute," the nurse called out.

I nodded, realizing as I did so that she couldn't see me behind the curtain.

I wondered if this room held the same horror for Wynne as it did for me. Or more? Or different? Would I ever see this mind-numbing green without thinking of the day I arrived in the city, unnerved by Wynne's sudden insistence that I come, after years of increasingly perfunctory letters. That first day. I sat down and she said she was dying. No, wait, not dying. She had never used that word. It was her doctor who said "dying."

It had been bright and clear that day, too. The sunlight had been cut by the venetian blinds so that pale ribbons sliced across the green wall. And when he told me, the light merged with the green and that numbing green shone and the wall seemed to jump out at me and I couldn't focus, couldn't think about anything but the wall.

Time softens things, but that moment remained hard and bright and brittle.

"Lynne, you keep staring off in the distance. Are you sure you're all right?" The nurse was gone. Wynne was looking at me, her lips turned up in the hint of a smile, but her eyes serious. "Are you still seeing the doctor?"

"Doctor? You mean the psychiatrist at home?"

"Yes."

"Wynne, I wasn't seeing him because I was crazy. It was just therapy. I needed some perspective."

"On?"

"Us," I answered. She looked truly surprised, and I couldn't help but feel stung to realize once more that she,

who had influenced every part of my life, was so unaffected
by me.

"You were saying, before the nurse came for my spit
and polish, who might want to kill you? It's so hard to
believe."

I shifted my mind gratefully. Still, where to begin? I was
too ordinary—a middle-aged first-grade teacher—to make
enemies. If it had been Wynne . . .

"Well," she said, tightening her lips, "we'll have to examine the possibilities."

I shook my head. "I don't have any money, no insurance
other than the teachers' association policy."

"And that goes to Michael?"

"Yes, but Michael's not going to come all the way from
Los Angeles to shoot his mother so he can inherit two thousand dollars and a clapboard house."

"I didn't mean that." She looked momentarily confused, and hurt. "I was just listing the possibilities. You have
to do that. You can't let sentiment stand in the way of your
goal. I had to learn that long ago. There are plenty of people
who have wanted me out of the way."

"But they weren't trying to *murder* you!"

She shrugged. And she watched me.

"Wynne, I'm the one they're trying to kill. No
one would kill you now. What would be the point? I
mean . . ."

Her face turned white.

"Wynne, we don't have much time! Either of us. Maybe
we can't find out who's shooting at me, but at least we can
feel like sisters." I paused, then went on. "When you asked
me to come here, after all these years, I thought you wanted
to close the gap between us." I smiled, heard my voice
breaking. "Frankly, I was surprised it mattered to you. It
was a shock to realize how much it mattered to me. I . . ."

Her eyes were moist. She looked away. But when she
turned back there was no sign of the emotion that had
passed.

Startled, I began awkwardly brushing at my hair with my hand, rather than reaching toward my sister, as I'd instinctively wanted to do. I forced my attention back to the question under consideration. Suppose no one did know Wynne was dying. Warren at least had been kept in the dark, or so Wynne thought. I was beginning to wonder if she had accepted it herself. "You're not working," I said. "You don't have any connection with the company now. How could *you* be a threat to anyone?"

The lines in her face hardened. "I know things. When I get out of here, I'm going back. I'll see who's been out to get me. I'll take care of them! I'm too valuable for the company to just forget."

"You what!" I stared at the green wall. Wynne had shoved the death threat to me aside, finding it of less importance than interoffice grudges. I looked at her, wondering what we really meant to each other. In many ways we were so alike. I felt so helpless in the face of her bitterness.

"Who particularly," I asked, "would want to kill *you*?"

"Me?"

"I mean who might mistake me for you? An old lover?"

She half smiled, surprised. "What do you know about me?"

"Only what you've wanted me to know, like always. The lover was just a guess. After all, you're forty years old and single. There must have been men, maybe married . . ."

"You make it all rather melodramatic." She continued to look amused.

"Shooting is melodramatic!"

She didn't reply.

"What about Warren?" I persisted. "Would he kill to keep your job? Would he mistake me for you?"

She looked at me in amazement, as if the possibility were too fantastic to believe. "Lynne, anyone—Warren in particular—who would take the trouble and risk involved in murder, would be a bit more careful than that."

"Maybe they don't know you have an identical twin?"

She sighed, her jaw settling back in a tired frown. "They know. When you've held as important a position as I have, believe me, they know." She paused, then added, "But if you really think that someone is mistaking you for me, maybe you should move out of my apartment. Take a hotel room. I'll pay for it, of course."

I shook my head.

Fingering the phone, she said, "Lynne, you haven't made much of a case for this death threat. I don't want to sound unsympathetic, but the truth is that you've always leaned on me. Are you sure that this death thing isn't just a reaction to my own condition? It does happen in twins."

"I think not," I snapped, finally exasperated. "I've been through years of therapy. Our bodies may be identical, but my mind is all my own."

She sat silent.

The awkwardness grew. "Listen, Wynne, I know you've got business to take care of. I interrupted your phone call when I came in. I'll see you tomorrow."

She nodded, a tiredness showing in her eyes. But I wasn't out of the room before she picked up the phone.

As I walked down the hall, I thought again, what an amazing person she was. Dying from kidney failure, and she was still barking at subordinates. I wondered about Warren—did he allow her to run things from her hospital room? Did he believe Wynne's story about her condition? Could he think I was she, coming in for treatment? Not likely. If Warren were anything like Wynne, by now he would have a solid grip on the vice presidency. He would have removed any trace of Wynne, and she'd have to fight *him* for the job.

Still, I stopped by the door, afraid to go out.

If Wynne wasn't giving orders to Warren or some other subordinate, whom was she yelling at? "What do you think I'm paying you for?" she had demanded.

She wasn't paying anyone at the company. She wasn't paying any expenses—I was handling those. There was nothing she needed.

Or was there?

My hand went around back to my remaining kidney.

MY NEIGHBOR, AY

Joyce Harrington

Joyce Harrington began her writing career in a most impressive way when her first published short story, "The Purple Shroud," won the Mystery Writers of America Edgar for Best Short Story in the mystery field during 1972. Since then she has gone on to publish many fine stories dealing with the conflicts and dangers of contemporary society, a theme which is thoroughly explored in "My Neighbor, Ay." Ms. Harrington's excellent first novel, No One Knows My Name, *was published in 1980.*

I t all started the day the old man on the top floor next door emptied his spittoon out the window and the wind was blowing from the east. It wasn't what you might call an elegant antique of a spittoon. More like an old coffee can, and I caught the flash of tin up there in the fifth-floor walkup out of the corner of my eye as I was crouched over my tenderly cherished Christian Dior rosebush inspecting for aphids with a banana peel at the ready.

My wife, Brenda, who was flaked out on the garden chaise in her green bikini promoting a city suntan, caught more than a flash of tin.

"Rats! It's raining," she muttered before she opened her eyes. When she finally did get them open and adjusted to bright blue sky and dazzling August sunshine and a case of instant full-length freckles, she screamed.

"What is it? Damn, what is it? Who did that?"

She scrambled off the chaise and the freckles began to slither in streaky rivulets toward her belly button and down her incredibly long and slender legs. A few dripped off her chin and fell into her well-proportioned cleavage.

"It's not tea leaves, honey."

I must confess that the sight of lissome, fastidious Brenda spattered from head to toe with secondhand chewing tobacco brought out the snide side of my character, and I had difficulty gulping down a fit of guffaws. For my pains I was rewarded with a fit of hiccups.

"Will you stop that stupid noise and *DO SOME-THING!*" she shrieked. Have you ever seen anyone turn red with rage all over? That was Brenda. Bright pink actually, overlaid with lengthening stripes and scattered specks of mahogany, the whole girl trembling and angrier than I'd ever seen her.

I turned away, ostensibly to deposit my banana peel at

428

the foot of Christian Dior, and managed to subdue the grin
that was quirking at the corners of my mouth. It crossed my
mind that someone had once told me tobacco, like banana
peel, was good for roses, but I couldn't remember why. It
definitely wasn't good for Brenda.

"A shower, perhaps?" I hiccupped. "I'll scrub your
back."

"A shower! A disinfecting is what I need! Don't just
stand there. Call the police!"

"What'll I tell them? My wife has been spat on whole-
sale? I'll get you some paper towels." I started for the
kitchen door.

"Don't leave me here like this. Do something! If you
won't call the police, I will. I will, I will, I will!" Tears were
beginning to add to the mess on Brenda's face and the
shocked rigidity was leaving her outflung arms. She was
making an awful lot of noise.

"Do you want to stay like that so the police can see the
evidence?" I grabbed the real-estate section of the Sunday
Times and began tentative mopping-up operations, at the
same time trying to steer her indoors.

"Stop that, you nit! You're just making it worse."

She was right. Heads were beginning to appear at the
rear windows of the surrounding brownstones. Brenda came
to her senses long enough to realize that she was the star of
this backyard melodrama, and then fled howling to the bathroom.

"I'll speak to Guttierez," I called after her.

When the shower had been drumming satisfactorily for at
least five minutes and I had subdued my hiccups, I put on
a clean shirt and a stern manner and marched next door.
Guttierez owned this next-door brownstone, outwardly an
identical twin of ours, and lived in the basement apartment
with his silent, round-faced, brown-eyed wife, and four not-
so-silent young sons. Upstairs, Guttierez rented rooms. The
house was a mini-U.N. and the sounds that flowed out

through the open windows were the normal sounds of people living loudly in Spanish, Haitian French, West Indian
lilted English, with an occasional bright thread of Pakistani
or Chinese. It was microcosmic Brooklyn in the summer of
the brownstone generation.

I rang the bell. Somewhere inside a buzzer zapped and
there was instant quiet. I waited a few moments. Then a
flowered plastic curtain at the barred basement window
twitched. I hit the buzzer again. Pretty soon an inner door
rattled, an outer door rattled, and a miniature Guttierez
materialized inside the iron gate of the basement entrance.

"Hi," I said masterfully.

Young Guttierez masterfully non-replied and stared absolutely without blinking for a year-long minute before I
tried again. This was really a job for Brenda who used to
boast of having read *El Cid* in the original during her
Hunter College days. I sighed and spoke again.

"Um, hi there. Is your father home?"

Reinforcements arrived in the shape of an even smaller
and more solemn Guttierez sporting a T-shirt lettered
PUERTO RICO ENCANTA. Double-barreled silence for another minute, then the curtain twitched again. I was about
to leave, defeated by this one-sided confrontation, when the
two small brown bodies erupted into noise and action. They
pounded away back into their lair squealing, *"Mamá, Mamá
venga! Mira, Mamá, un hombre!"*

The squeals receded into a distant interior chattering,
and I stood with my nose pressed to the iron grille, trying
to decide whether it was worthwhile waiting around for
someone over the age of five to come to the door. My whole
attention was riveted through those open inner doors, listening to the rapid incomprehensible chatter, breathing in the
fumes of something cooking vaguely connected in my sen-
sory apparatus with Brenda's superb *paella,* and hoping for
the sound of adult footsteps to head in my direction.

My concentration on the Guttierez interior was such
that I failed to notice the adult footsteps coming up behind

me. I whirled at the sound of the voice and almost fell into the lidless garbage can beside the door.

" 'Ello, 'ello. What you wan' here?"

I suspected Guttierez of being slightly deaf. He always spoke in a modified roar. In the circumstances it was a bit unnerving, and I felt like the notorious neighborhood mailbox burglar caught in the act. Add to this the fact that although Guttierez and I were about the same height, I was standing one step down in the entrance to his castle. He towered over me with a six-pack of beer in each hand. It was difficult to remember that as Guttierez always roared, he always glowered even when playing stickball with his kids, and I had no desire to get beaned with the *cerveza fría*.

"Hello there. Um, I was just looking for you. Nice day, isn't it?"

I'm ashamed to say that my voice came out somewhat higher than its normal range, and suspicion flamed all over Guttierez's face. He took a firmer grip on his six-packs.

"You lookin' for me? What you wan'?"

"Well, Mr. Guttierez, I'm Jack Rollins. I live next door, you know?"

I got my voice back down into its normal range, but I was having difficulty getting to the point. I scrambled up out of the entryway and felt a little better facing Guttierez at eye level.

"*Sí*, I know. What you wan'?"

He was obviously impatient to get inside to whatever was cooking that smelled so good. Whispers and giggles came from behind the twitching curtain, and I caught an occasional *"americano"* between the giggles.

"Well, Mr. Guttierez, the old man on the top floor, you know?"

"*Sí?*"

"Well, he throws things out the window."

"*Sí?*"

"Well, he empties his spittoon out the window."

"*Sí?* What is this 'spittoon'?"

I sighed, inaudibly I hoped, and tried again.

"Well, he chews tobacco, you know? And he spits it in a can. And then he throws it out the window."

"Oh, *sí*! He is one filthy old man, him."

I squared my shoulders and prepared to do battle for my wife's honor. The guy's machismo was beginning to rub off on me.

"Well, see here, Guttierez. It's got to stop. It landed on my wife today."

"Oh, *lástima*! You wife! She with the bathing suit? In the backyard?"

It was the first time I had ever seen Guttierez smile. He was grinning. He was positively leering.

"That's right. My wife. And I want something done about it." I hoped I was scowling at least as fiercely as Guttierez normally did.

"What you wan' to do? You wan' to fight him? He is *muy viejo*, very old. An' he have one leg. You wan' to fight him?"

"No, I don't want to fight him! He's your tenant. You should speak to him. Tell him it's against the law to throw things out the window. Tell him I'll call the police."

"You called police?" Guttierez was beginning to bristle and his grin vanished.

"No, not yet. But if he does it one more time I will. You tell him that."

"Okay. I tell him. No more out the window."

A young Guttierez, who had been lurking just inside the gate throughout our exchange, now opened the gate and took the beer from his father's hands. Guttierez went through the gate, and as he turned to close it he grinned once more.

"Tell you wife she is very pretty."

The gate slammed and the chatter and giggles reached a crescendo.

Back in my own renovated townhouse, I settled into my black-leather Eames chair and sought solace with the Sunday *Times* crossword puzzle. The shower was still splashing, so I was safe from vengeance until Brenda got her hair dry. Before attacking square one across I sat back and admired for perhaps the hundredth time the restored beauty of my front parlor.

Brenda and I had scraped and Red Deviled and polished the woodwork, plastered and spackled and painted, replaced missing bits of molding. We had labored mightily and with love, and the result was a gleaming, pristine Victorian mansion with all mod cons, a duplex apartment upstairs which rented at a price that paid the mortgage, and our own lower duplex with garden. Our piece of the city.

I shook my head over Brenda's rage, decided it was justified, and clicked my ballpoint pen into action. The air conditioner hummed gently, producing just the right amount of refrigeration, and I lost myself in the wiles of the puzzle which bore the theme of "The Last Resort." I puzzled away for perhaps twenty minutes and was somewhat nearer sleeping than waking when Brenda stalked into the room.

"Well?" she demanded. The shower had cleaned her up but had not cooled her off.

"Ah, what's a ten-letter word for African animal ending in 'u'?"

"Lesser kudu. What happened?" Brenda was always very good at natural history.

"Thanks. Aren't you cold?" She had exchanged her spattered green bikini for a pair of shocking-pink short shorts and a purple scarf intricately tied to allow maximum bare skin and freedom of motion.

"No, I'm not cold. It's ninety-two degrees outside. Did you call the police?"

"Well, no. It's very cool in here. The air conditioner is on high." I settled deeper into my chair to give the impression of extreme comfort and immovability.

"If you didn't call the police, what did you do?"

"Well, I spoke to Guttierez. You aren't going outside

again, are you? Like that?" I knew I was doing this all wrong. Brenda wasn't the sort of girl you could safely practice machismo on.

"Oh course I am. It's my backyard, isn't it? What did Guttierez say?"

"He said you were very pretty. He asked if I wanted to fight the old guy."

"Oh, damn, you're impossible!" She dropped onto the blue-velvet Victorian chaise longue which was her pride and joy, and she almost laughed. "Did you ever get to the point?"

"Oh, yes. Point Number One, Guttierez will speak to the old guy. And Point Number Two, your sunbathing gives great visual pleasure to the surrounding natives. Does Mrs. G. ever sunbathe?"

"Of course not. She's always pregnant. There's a steak for the barbecue. Shall I light the fire now?"

During the week following "L'Affaire Tabac" the heat wave was still melting Madison Avenue. Brenda and I shuttled between our air-conditioned jobs and our air-conditioned bedroom, ducking in and out of air-conditioned restaurants along the way. Neither one of us felt much like cooking or even eating with the thermometer pushing 100 day after day, and the humidity making my best Brooks Brothers young-executive-on-the-rise wash-and-wear blue-and-white stripe look like a much worn and seldom washed suit of the latest in limp dishrag.

The management of the aggressive young ad agency where Brenda wrote copy had considered going on a four-day week for the summer, but had decided that there were too many Goliaths abroad on the Avenue to leave the slingshots unmanned (or unwomanned) for even one day. So Brenda hammered away at producing bright, clever words designed to sell bras and all-in-ones to the overfed female population of the nation, while I sweltered and accounted for the bookkeeping vagaries of an endless roster of small-business clients of the mammoth accounting firm where I C.P.A.'d. We both regretted our decision to save our vaction time for a January ski tour of Europe.

If we noticed Guttierez and company at all it was only in passing on the evening drag from subway to cool haven. A clutter of brown humanity, stoop-sitting, hoping for a breeze from the bay or even from the Gowanus Canal, and tossing Malta Hatuey cans languidly toward the garbage cans and just missing. Occasionally we heard a guitar and plaintive island songs, and saw the kids trundling second-hand plastic tricycles up and down the sidewalk. Mrs. Guttierez had tried to brighten the small front yard with a few marigolds, but the heat and pounding children's feet had left only a few yellow tatters among the Popsicle wrappers on the packed earth.

We passed without acknowledgment, either of overtures toward mutual understanding or mutual hostility. It was too darned hot.

One night, though, we were forced to take notice.

The heat had lifted slightly and the air was electric with premonitions of a storm. Despite the threat of rain Brenda and I decided to take a chance on Shakespeare in the Park. We did it in style: Brasserie box lunches (pâté, *ratatouille*, cold chicken) and chilled champagne (New York State) while waiting in line; a rather fine *Macbeth* with distant thunder obligingly produced on cue by the great Stage Manager in the Catskills; and afterward a taxi home across the Brooklyn Bridge with the lights of our town, ships in the Narrows, the Verrazano Bridge crowning the evening with the spectacle which never palled.

We pulled up outside our house and paid off the driver, adding a generous happy-time tip. A gale-force wind was blowing off the bay and up our street, bending the newly planted plane trees into fragile arcs. Above the clatter of the frantic leaves and the din of the wind playing Frisbee with the garbage-can lids, the roar of Guttierez was heard. The stoop-sitters were energized, plugged in to the crackling atmosphere. The children, not yet in bed, huddled smear-faced and wide-eyed on the top step.

Mrs. Guttierez wept loudly in the arms of a broad full-bellied Indian-faced woman who shrieked imprecations to the tops of houses. Armed with a saw-toothed bread knife, Guttierez bellowed and stabbed the air. The opposition, small, thin, dark, and very drunk, whirled a baseball bat above his head with both hands. The two men circled each other on the sidewalk, slow-footed, eyes aglint with the adrenaline of battle, searching for the deadly opportunity and shouting macho insults at each other.

Brenda stared, breath held, her body stiff with shock and rooted to the pavement.

"Inside!" I shouted. "Get inside!"

She didn't move. She didn't hear. She was hypnotized.

"My God!" she breathed at last. "They'll kill each other."

The wind plastered her long hair across her face, and a single fat raindrop fell on my hand as I tried to drag her away.

"Get into the house, Brenda." I spoke as calmly as I could. "The rain will stop it."

Her fascination broke abruptly, and she whirled on me, her eyes wild with near-hysteria.

"Police!" she screamed. "They'll kill each other! Call the police! I'll do it!"

She bolted for the entrance to our fortress and began scrabbling in her purse for keys. I had mine ready, but the seconds necessary for manipulating the double locks seemed like hours with Brenda shivering impatiently behind me and the shouts and weeping continuing unabated on the sidewalk.

I flung the gate open and Brenda charged through, rattling the double doors and racing down the hall to the telephone. I went back for another look at the combatants. They were still circling, still brandishing their weapons, still shouting. There was not another soul to be seen on the block —no late dog-walkers, no midnight loiterers at the corner bodega, no curious heads at windows.

Lightning flashed somewhere over Staten Island, coming closer, and raindrops spattered the sidewalk. I felt fairly
sure that Guttierez and enemy would continue their Mexi-
can standoff until the deluge, then put down their arma-
ments and go inside for another beer. But you never could
tell. When the thunder rolled I went inside and relocked the
double locks.

Brenda, at the kitchen phone, was just concluding her
conversation with 911. In a tight, edgy voice she gave her
name and address.

"Please hurry," she added. "I'm afraid they'll kill each
other."

I could imagine the laconic voice on the other end of
the wire giving assurance that law and order were on the
way, lady. Brenda hung up the phone and dug a cigarette
out of her bag, lighting it at the gas range.

"Jack." She slumped in the telephone chair and surveyed the chrome and terra cotta tile, electronic oven and
massive freezer, the ranks of custom-built walnut cabinets.

"Jack, we've done all this, and it's beautiful. I love it."
She dragged deeply on her cigarette. "But I want out. I don't
want to live next door to *THAT* anymore."

"Where do you want to go, honey?" I began to massage
her tight shoulders, her rigid neck. But she pulled away.

"How do I know? The damn suburbs. Westchester!
Nyack! Bloody Australia! The farther the better."

"Brennie, you know you'd hate the suburbs. Those guys
are just showing off for their women. They're enjoying every
minute of it, and nobody's going to get hurt."

I had some small faith in my words and the flamboyant
nature of our neighbors. Still, it was unnerving and not very
neighborly to come home to brandished bread knives and
baseball bats.

Brenda brooded unhappily.

"Come on, honey." I took her hand. "Let's go be spectators and see how long it takes the police to get here."

We took up stations at the darkened front-parlor window to find that one patrol car had already arrived, while another was flashing its way up the street.

"Well," I commented. "Nobody can say the fuzz doesn't respond in this neighborhood."

Guttierez, leaning indolently against the front fender of the police car, was answering the young officer's questions with expressions of sublime innocence and gestures of incredulity.

"Who, me?!!!" seemed to be the substance of his replies.

Mrs. Guttierez and the bread knife had disappeared. One child remained on the sidewalk, idly swinging the baseball bat. The small thin man and the Indian-looking woman leaned against the railing sipping from cans of liquid clothed in brown paper bags.

The wind had died. The trees stood expectantly, their leaves hanging limp and exhausted. A flash of lightning lit the scene in blue-white relief, and the rain crashed down.

The young policeman ducked inside his car with a final admonition to Guttierez, who nodded, tried to shake hands, then dashed for his house, picking up the boy and the baseball bat on the run. He was joined by the paper-bag drinkers, the woman laughing widely from her round jiggling belly and raising her face to the downpour. I could see her gold teeth.

After a few moments the police cars drove away, undoubtedly to respond to another crisis on another block. We watched the rain punish the empty street.

"Come on, Brennie." I hugged her. "It's bedtime."

We never found out what the argument had been about, but the next evening when we came home from work we found our backyard thoroughly inundated with garbage. There seemed to be about a ton of assorted chicken bones with fragments of yellow rice clinging stickily, dozens of the ubiquitous Malta Hatuey cans, watermelon rind and orange peel, coffee grounds, tea bags, and, yes, even the tobacco chewer of the fifth floor was represented.

"They must have taken up a collection." I tried to laugh, but it didn't come off very well. "What do you think, Brenda? The police again?"

Brenda seemed to have shrunk. Her eyes glazed over as she viewed the unexpected landfill.

"No, Jack," she said quietly. "I think the shovel and hose."

Our neighbors remained invisible and inaudible during the cleanup operation. Brenda remained silent and tight-lipped, wielding her shovel with a tense energy which augured ill for the dispensers of the odiferous revenge. Side by side we shoveled and hosed. All my attempts to point up the ridiculous side of the great kitchen-midden caper fell decidedly flat.

"You should maybe get her recipe for *arroz con pollo.*"

Brenda shoveled.

"We could toss it all back with a little contribution of our own. Make it a real classy garbage war. *Coq au vin* bones, congealed quiche, rind of brie, and shell of clam. Just think how we could expand their horizons."

Brenda swept, and looked determined.

"This may be the answer to the city's disposal problem. Just keep tossing it back and forth. You keep it one day, I'll keep it the next."

"Just shut up and shovel!"

Brenda had the hose in her hand. I shut up and shoveled.

An hour and many plastic bags later Brenda was once again showering away rage and refuse. The refuse would go down the drain. The rage I was not too sure about. Brenda's usual form was an explosion of mildly profane wrath, followed by tremulous laughter or at the very least a self-conscious smirk. This was different. This was cold fury, silent and calculating. Brenda was up to something. And I didn't like it.

I made her a drink, gin and tonic in equal proportions with two wedges of lime, and took it into the bathroom.

440   MY NEIGHBOR, AY

"Hey, Bren. Here's a drink."

"Thanks." Steam billowed out of the shower and frosted the mahogany-framed mirror over the sink. I wrote BREN & JACK 4EVER inside a lopsided heart.

"How about dinner at Gage and Tollner's?"

"No, thanks."

"How about dinner at Peter Luger's?"

"No."

"How about dinner?"

"I've lost my appetite."

Brenda without an appetite was like bagels without cream cheese. Unnatural. And for her to turn down a Peter Luger steak was worse than unnatural.

The shower shut off abruptly and Brenda emerged dripping, a pale bikini shape outlined against rosy sunburn.

"Dry you off, lady?"

"Just hand me that towel."

She snatched the towel from the rack before I could reach it, dried off in a frenzy of flapping terrycloth, and slid into her no-nonsense button-to-the-chin nightgown.

"If you can bear to think about food, there must be something in the fridge. I'm going to bed."

Sweating drink in hand, she long-legged it into the bedroom. I followed.

"Great idea. I could use a little nap myself. And then we can go to Peter Luger's."

Brenda whirled on me, sloshing her drink all over herself and the red shag bedroom rug.

"Beat it, Jack. Just bug off. I'm getting in that bed. And I'm going to drink this drink. Or what's left of it. And then I'm going to sleep sleep sleep! And I hope I never wake up! I want to be alone. Understand?"

"Okay, Garbo. Okay. All right. Pleasant dreams."

I slouched downstairs to the kitchen where I found sufficient material for a hero sandwich which, along with a couple of beers and my newest old Teddy Wilson records, induced a state of hopeful nirvana. Tomorrow would be better.

When I tiptoed into the bedroom around midnight, Brenda was asleep, asleep, asleep.

Tomorrow came right on schedule, and Brenda woke up. But refused to get out of bed. I brought her coffee, but she still refused to budge.

"Call the office around nine-thirty, Jack. Tell them I'm sick. I *am* sick." She buried her face in the pillow and moaned, unconvincingly.

"It's Friday. You can't call in sick on Friday."

"Oh, yes, I can. Anyway you're going to do it for me. Tell them I've got scurvy, beri-beri, jungle rot, anything. Garbage poisoning, that's what I've really got. Please, Jack. I really need a day off to pull myself together after last night. I'll be all right. I promise. Tell them I have a bad case of hives."

"Look, Brenda, you'd be better off to go to work and forget all about last night. It's over. Let it end."

"Hives, dear. In fact, I think I feel one blossoming on my left kneecap right now."

She sat up and scratched energetically and then piled all the pillows together into a cosy sickbed nest. Smiling and sipping coffee, she seemed altogether more like a normal Brenda. Last night's cold and silent fury must have been dissipated by ten hours of sleep on an empty stomach.

"Well," I wavered. "I hate to leave you like this."

"Don't worry. I just want to spend the day in bed with a good book. Haven't done that in a long time."

She settled in more snugly and pulled the covers up to her chin. She looked helpless and vulnerable, even though I knew better, and I really did hate to leave her.

"Shall I bring you something to eat?"

"No, thanks. I'll get up and boil an egg in a little while."

I guess that's what convinced me that all would be well. Soft-boiled eggs were convalescent food for Brenda. Whenever she was recovering from any kind of upset, physical or emotional, soft-boiled eggs appeared on the menu, and disappeared as soon as things were back to normal.

"Well." I knotted my tie. "I guess I'd better be going."

"All right, dear. Don't forget to call in for me. And don't worry." She was already thumbing through a magazine.

"You won't—uh—I mean, you'll stay away from—" I still was not entirely convinced that Brenda's intentions ran solely to bed rest and literature. "You won't start anything with Guttierez, will you?"

"No, dear. I won't start anything. I promise."

I left.

I spent a usual kind of Friday closing out the previous month's books in the super mod offices of a team of graphic designers. The bookkeeper, a minuscule and meticulous Japanese girl, drew graphically perfect numbers and persistently covered up her errors by adding or subtracting a totally fictitious petty-cash amount at the end of each month. Each month Sumi and I engaged in a polite skirmish in which errors were routed, the books balanced, and I laid down anew the simple rules of double entry. Each month Sumi accepted my edicts with apologetic and suitably flattering awe, and I felt like a samurai of the statistics. Until the next month.

I tried to reach Brenda several times during the day but each time the line was busy.

By midafternoon I had settled Sumi's accounts and decided to knock off the rest of the day. It was one of those rare summer days in New York. The unsmogged sky was actually blue and gentle breezes meandered along the cross streets. The storm of the night before had washed away heat, humidity, and dog droppings and as I walked the six blocks to the Grand Central subway station, the city and its people gleamed as dwellers in an iridescent and fantastic mirage.

The subway put an end to fantasy with its congealed heat and the smell of generations of doomed hot dogs sweating out their grease on eternally rotating grills. On the train, sparsely populated with Alexander's shopping bags and noisy groups of day-camp kids, I welcomed the dank wind that swirled through the cars and wondered if this might not be a good weekend to take advantage of an open invitation to visit friends on Fire Island. There was plenty of time to catch an evening ferry, and two days of beach-ratting in congenial company would bring Brenda out of the garbage dumps.

She met me at the door suppressing manic laughter. Her eyes gave her away. Wild and triumphant, they sparkled with discharged venom. She grabbed my arm and before I could unload my attaché case or broach my Fire Island plan she dragged me to the window.

"Look, Jack." She was almost incoherent. "The gas company. It's the gas company."

"Well, sure. It's the gas company." It was not unusual to see a blue and yellow gas-company truck parked outside. I failed to comprehend Brenda's elation over this one.

"Oh, Jack! You don't get it. It's too fantastic! I reported a gas leak!"

I turned to sniff the air.

"Where is it? In the kitchen?" I headed for the stairs. "Did they find it yet?"

"No, dummy. You still don't get it. Next door. I reported a gas leak next door. And exposed wiring. And fire hazards in the halls. The fire inspectors have already been there. I'm still waiting for the housing department. You know, illegal rooming house. He doesn't have a license. Overcrowding and rats. Plumbing violations, sewer smells. Rent gouging. Everything. Everything I could think of. I even called the Mayor's office, but he was off inspecting snowplows."

"In August?" I was stupefied. No adequate comment came to mind, and I stared out the window as two purposeful men in gas-company uniforms emerged from next door. "They're leaving now."

"Okay. Now what's next?" Brenda paced excitedly up

and down the living room. "Child abuse! That's it. I'm sure
he beats his kids. Where do you report child abuse?"

"Brenda! Knock it off. That's harassment. It's illegal. He
could sue you, for God's sake."

"Harassment! What do you call garbage in our back-
yard? I'll sue *him*. I'll put him out of business. I'll close down
that rat trap. Where's the phone book?"

Brenda's erratic pacing and arm waving came dangerously close to putting my blue Tiffany table lamp out of
business. I pulled her onto the sofa and held both her hands.
She squirmed and fidgeted.

"Look, kid. You've done enough for one day. What do
you say we call Jenny and Charley and spend the weekend
on Fire Island?"

"Oh, no, Jack. We can't do that. We have an appointment tomorrow morning to look at houses in Westchester."

On Saturday we took an early train to wild and woolly Westchester to view real estate. We saw cathedral ceilings and
three-car garages, pseudo-saltboxes and split-level bath-
rooms, cosy cottages nestled into careful foliage allowed to
grow just so wild and no wilder, rambling ranches designed
from the same general all-purpose scheme for storing a standard quota of children in standard-sized boxes with a standard number of windows.

Mrs. Handiford, the real-estate saleswoman, efficient
and motherly, graciously hauled us around winding tree-
lined roads in her late-model battleship-on-wheels station
wagon, pointing out local amenities and landmarks: stables
here, swim club there, home of notable this and pillar of the
community that.

"And of course the public school system is one of the
finest in the state, although if you prefer private—"

"We haven't any children." Brenda was terse, border-
ing on rude, but Mrs. Handiford patted her neatly waved
silver-gray coiffure and bravely pressed on.

"Ah, well, you're young and there's no place better for

starting a family. I'm sure you'll find many activities here to interest you. There's the Arts and Crafts Guild. They have exhibits twice a year. And a very active chapter of the League of Women Voters. We have the Garden Club. They've done those very lovely plantings we saw in the village. Do you play bridge? We have several informal bridge groups, always looking for new members. Tennis and golf, of course. Oh, I'm sure you'll find lots to do, Mrs. Rollins."

"Yes. Well, I have a job. In the city." Brenda was obviously hating every minute of this grand tour of suburban glories.

Dammit, I thought. This was your idea. Let the poor woman get on with her spiel. And glared at her behind Mrs. Handiford's neat and businesslike navy-blue back.

Only momentarily dampened, Mrs. Handiford rallied swiftly and tried another tack.

"Well, if you're both going to be commuting, perhaps you'd like something closer to the station. I have a sweet little place, walking distance. Not much land, so it's easy to maintain."

The sweet little place near the station materialized as a Swiss chalet, replete with kitsch, cuckoo clock, and a grotto in the rear where recirculated water trickled over imitation moss on plastic rocks. Miraculously there were no gnomes. But I fully expected Shirley Temple as Heidi, or at the very least a nanny goat, to come bounding out of the garage-cum-cowshed exuding Alpine charm and the fragrance of edelweiss or Emmenthaler, take your pick. A tour of the interior offered us eaves to bump our heads on, which Brenda did, bottle-glass windows reducing the entrance of daylight to a minimum, low-beamed ceilings, and endless square feet of dark and intricately carved woodwork.

Brenda was breathing hard by this time, not saying much. Just breathing. And nursing the bump on her head. It was the bathroom that really finished her off. She opened

the door, quickly closed it, and tried to choke back a despair-
ing "Oh, God, no!"

She was not to be let off so easily. Mrs. Handiford bustled through the door, taking Brenda's arm as she went. I
followed in horrified fascination. There were the gnomes.
Frolicking on the vinyl wallpaper, in a landscape featuring
distant cows and Matterhorns.

"Of course, it's all custom designed," stated Mrs. Handiford, eyeing Brenda with grim satisfaction.

Indeed it was. The usual facilities were all encased in as
much wood carving as possible without interfering with
function. The tub-shower enclosure resembled a confessional box and the toilet-paper roll, when activated, tinkled
"The Sound of Music."

Revenge must be sweet to real-estate ladies spending
unprofitable Saturdays with obviously unsuitable clients.

"Sweet," gasped Brenda. "Utterly too sweet. But not
my—" She broke off, headed for the front door at an un-
gainly gallop, and narrowly missed impaling herself on the
staghorn doing duty as a coatrack in the tiny foyer.

Regrouped on the sidewalk, we all three tried to conceal our eagerness to split.

"We've seen so much . . . it's hard to decide."

"It's been a pleasure taking you around."

"We'll have to think it all over."

"If something new comes in . . ."

"Yes, please do give us a call."

"I'll drive you to the station."

"Oh, thanks. We'd like to walk. It's so close."

"Good-bye then. If I can be of help, don't hesitate—"

"Thanks again. Yes, we can find the station."

"Good-bye."

"Good grief!" snorted Brenda as Mrs. Handiford piloted
her dreadnought off to whatever suburban utopia she called
her own, which I devoutly hoped included a well-earned
double Scotch on the rocks.

"You were right, Jack. Absolutely right. I could never

hack this. Not in a million years. Where's that train schedule?"

By the time the train reached 125th Street, Brenda was
enthusiastically discussing plans for the erection of a ten-
foot-high solid redwood fence to take the place of the post
and wire affair currently separating our turf from Guttierez's.

Back home again, the late Saturday afternoon Brooklyn
streets basked in a golden glow. We bought Good Humors
from Maxie outside the subway station and walked home
munching and kicking prickle balls fallen from the huge old
chestnut tree at the corner.

"It's okay, isn't it, Jack?" Brenda mouthed around a
chunk of chocolate-chip ice cream.

"Sure it is," I replied from the midst of my toasted
almond.

"I don't really want to leave," she went on. "And I'm
sorry I made all those stupid phone calls. Maybe I should try
to talk to Mrs. Guttierez."

"Maybe you should just leave the whole thing
alone."

We let ourselves into the house, dim and cool and quiet.
Quiet, except for the muffled sound of a radio voice—the
unmistakable voice of the WHOM announcer blasting out
an Hispanic hard sell, exhorting his listeners to buy Vitarroz.
Suddenly the penetrating commercial message was
drowned, obliterated by a frantic frightened animal squealing. The squeals continued rising in pitch interrupted only
by an inhuman snuffling, a snorting attempt to breathe. In
the next moment this hair-raising noise was overridden by
cheers and laughter, quite definitely arising from human
throats.

"Jack, what's going on?" Brenda whispered. Her words
were normal, but her eyes had gone unfocused as she listened intently. "It's them again. I know it. What are they
doing?"

"Stay here, Bren. I think it's coming from the yard. I'll go take a look."

I strode off toward the back door, hoping Brenda would not follow. I didn't like the way she looked. Anything could set her off again.

The cheers and squeals had subsided, and WHOM had taken over with a burst of Latino music when I opened the door and stepped out into my garden. The first thing I saw was people. The neighboring yard was full of people. Young, old, and in-between, sitting on kitchen chairs and boxes, lying on blankets, leaning against the fence. One enormous old matriarch sat enthroned on a plastic-covered armchair. Guttierez was having a party.

All conversation stopped and thirty pairs of piercing black eyes turned full on me as I advanced to the center of my yard. Inquiry into the source of the frightful squealing was clearly unthinkable. A quick and furtive survey of Guttierez's yard disclosed a shallow trench filled with charcoal and a young man seated in a corner industriously whittling the end of a long wooden pole. The other end had already been shaped to a tapered point.

I turned to my rosebushes; Christian Dior was definitely drooping and I knelt for a closer look. Across the fence chatter and laughter resumed.

I didn't hear Brenda come out. I heard her gasp.

"My God! It's a pig!"

I turned. A pig it was. A small pig, not quite a suckling but not yet fully grown. I had missed it, lying under the hedge at the back of the yard, eyes closed and panting. A boy wandered over and began poking it with a stick. The pig gave a half-hearted squeal of protest, rose clumsily to its feet and trotted around the perimeter of the yard to escape its tormentor.

The boy trotted after the pig, and other children joined him. Several of the men rose and stationed themselves attentively around the yard. An anticipatory hush fell among the people; the radio was the only sound. The children stalked the pig; the men waited; we watched.

Guttierez marched out of his house, a gleaming, finely honed machete held lovingly in both hands. The waiting circle of guests tensed for the moment of truth. The children began to run. The pig scrabbled and galloped, turning to one side and then the other, seeking escape where there was none. And then the squealing began again.

The pig ricocheted off chair legs and people legs; the children shrieked and tumbled in the dust. The waiting stone-eyed man lunged and missed and lunged again. Guttierez stood motionless at the hub of the pig chase, the machete held ritually across his body. His moment would come. And rising above the shrieks and laughter of the children, the grunts and muttered comments of the men, the pig squealed its mortal terror.

In the corner of the yard the stake sharpener laid down his whittling knife. On light feet he moved, a thin sensitive-faced young man. Slowly and quietly, almost casually, he moved to a position some six feet behind the exhausted animal.

The pig stood at bay, its small wary eyes fixed on Guttierez and his shining blade. It did not sense the danger creeping up from behind. Suddenly the young man tensed, sprang, and soared across the intervening space. The full weight of his falling body flattened the protesting pig, splaying its slender dainty legs in four directions and cutting off its lament in mid-squeal.

A cheer rose from the spectators and the men and children crowded around the pair wrestling in the dusty arena. Guttierez flexed his sword arm and thumbed the edge of the blade. Two men struggled out of the writhing group on the ground, carrying the pig belly up. Its eyes rolled frantically as the men deposited it at Guttierez's feet, holding it immobile, throat exposed.

Guttierez imperiously motioned all others to stay behind him. The seated women drew in their feet and prepared to cover their eyes. The stroke, when it came, was almost anticlimactic. The machete swung upward, flashed once in the sun, and swung down. The hot pig blood spurted in a perfect arc and formed a puddle on the dried earth.

The women forgot to cover their eyes, but groaned instead in a kind of communal sensual satisfaction. The children capered around the carcass whose wound pumped a few smaller and smaller ribbons of blood, which finally subsided to a trickle. The smallest boy explored the puddle and squished his toes in the reddish mud.

The execution of the entire pigsticking must have taken no more than five minutes, but I felt as if I had been holding my breath for an hour. I sucked in a lungful of air, still heavy with the smell of fear and blood, and muttered to Brenda, "I wonder who's going to be awarded the pig's ear."

There was no reply. At some time during the slaughter Brenda must have fled indoors, unnoticed. I thought I'd better do the same.

I found her, tears streaming down her face, hysterically mouthing into the telephone.

". . . killing a pig . . . oh, God, the blood . . . all over the yard . . . come quick, he's got a machete."

I grabbed the phone from her hand and slammed it down.

"What have you done?" I demanded. "Not the police again?"

She was shaking uncontrollably, and now her head began a rhythmic nodding while the tears welled and splattered.

"Brenda. Brenda, they're having a barbecue. That's all it is. Brenda, snap out of it. Where do you think pork chops come from?"

I couldn't reach her. She would not be comforted. But while I was trying, thinking of calling a doctor, the sirens came. We stood at the center of a storm of sirens, more sirens than I thought existed coming from every direction.

In moments the doorbell shrilled, fists pounded at the door, voices demanded that we open up.

I ran to the door and opened it to a surge of blue uniforms with guns drawn, emitting a staccato battery of questions.

"Where is it? Where's the body?"

"Next door? Which side?"

"Is he armed? Is he still there?"

"How many are there?"

"You reported the cop killing?"

"One side. Let us through."

Cop killing! I ran after them, trying to explain. They raced through the kitchen out into the yard.

"It was a pig! Only a pig!" I shouted after them. Brenda, in the kitchen, was trying to stop one of them, held onto his arm, and was swept out into the yard. I followed, still hoping to explain the colossal mistake.

In his yard Guttierez stood facing the pig now strung head down from a low-hanging ailanthus branch. The blood-streaked machete was still in his hand; he was preparing to disembowel. The charcoal in the trench was flaming and the double-pointed stake stood ready to impale its victim.

Scores of policemen were swarming into all the neighboring gardens up and down the block, vaulting the fences, converging on the big party. Cop killing is not taken lightly in this town.

Brenda had not loosened her grip on the arm of the law. She clung, and with her free arm pointed to the hung pig; she chattered, gasped, and shook. Her words tumbled out in an incoherent stream. The policeman looked stunned; all the policemen looked blank and chagrined, their drawn pistols hung superfluous and obscenely naked at their sides. They had come to do battle for a brother and found only a barbecue.

In that momentary hiatus before explanations and recriminations must be made, in the silence before the full weight of embarrassment descended, understanding came to Guttierez. And with it fury. It swelled his chest and added inches to his height. His narrowed eyes sought Brenda, and the fury erupted from his throat.

"A-a-y-y! *PIG!*" he screamed.

And the machete flashed in the sun once more. It left his hand in a graceful arc, crossed the fence and seemed suspended in the still evening air for endless ages before it came to rest.

At almost the same instant a policeman standing near Guttierez fired once. He later said he was aiming for the up-swung arm but was too close and a split second too late. Guttierez lay beneath the hanging pig, the wreckage caused by a bullet in the brain mingling with the slow drip from the draining carcass.

Brenda sprawled at the foot of Christian Dior, the machete still quivering in her chest. The slowly spreading stain on her blouse matched the roses that drooped over her.

Somebody turned the radio off. And then the screaming began.

NORMAN AND THE KILLER

Joyce Carol Oates

Of her numerous short stories and novels, Joyce Carol Oates has said, "All of my writing is about the mystery of human emotions." In "Norman and the Killer" this theme is embodied in a gentle, ordinary man who is brought to violence by feelings that he cannot—and indeed does not attempt to—understand. Ms. Oates, who teaches English at Princeton University, won a National Book Award in 1970 for her novel Them, *as well as several O. Henry prizes for her short stories. A Guggenheim Fellow and member of the Institute of Arts and Letters, she is one of the most prolific and acclaimed writers of her generation.*

Because he was an ordinary man, whose reflection in mirrors and in incidental windows could have belonged to anyone, Norman had never thought of himself as involved in anything that could attract attention. He had no interest in going to see accidents or fires or other disasters because he would be pushed around by the crowd and would not complain, and because he had no heart to peer in, there, at the very center of the jostling, to see the exposed bleeding flesh suddenly catapulted out of the usual channels of life. Because he was a gentle man, a shy man, no longer exactly young, whose life had attached itself gently to his family, he was surprised at the professional hardness with which he was able to meet customers in the clothing store he managed, and at the violence of the love he was suffering through for a woman his brother-in-law had introduced him to. In his youth he had read much and was able to appreciate the spiritual hardness of the heroes of great fiction, who seemed to him to walk upon ropes stretched over nothing, dazzling and performing endlessly, without fear of death. Their absolution of their humanity made them heroes and for this Norman envied them but could not believe in them; they told him nothing about himself.

The young woman's name was Ellen and she too had read much in her youth, which her dark opaque eyes suggested had been an extension of the life she now led, sternly bleak and self-satisfied, a loneliness that had to be respected because it had been her own choice. She had been married for several years, in her early twenties, but of this Norman did not allow himself to think. He often frightened himself at the anxiety he felt for her: his desperation to protect her from whatever startled her eyes, whatever drew her mind away from him as if he were no more than an accidental accomplice to the caprices of her memory, calculated to

454

remind her always of other evenings, other years. Yet he knew he had no right to that desperation, for she did not belong to him. At times he disliked her for her power over him, but most of the time, during the long identical days at the store, his love for this woman—whom he did not really know—was so absurdly great as to overwhelm him, threaten him with an obscure, inexplicable violence, something that might have been building up in him through the years while he had lived at home, a child grown into a man without anyone really noticing. Waking each morning in his old room, in the old house, he would smell resentfully the odors of breakfast being cooked downstairs and would think that, if he did not marry Ellen, he would wake to this every morning for the rest of his life.

One afternoon they drove out of the city to a summer playhouse. The drive took two hours, and Norman was pleased at Ellen's friendliness. She spoke of the playhouse, some actors she knew, and this made him think idly that she was to him like the women he had been seeing in movies all his life: ethereal and majestic, following a script he did not know, could not anticipate, yet smiling out of the very graciousness of their own near-beauty, welcoming his admiration while not exactly acknowledging it. She wore white; the self-conscious pose of her profile distracted him from the road. She was talking now of her job. Norman thought of marrying her, of living with her, but at this his face flinched, for it seemed impossible that this should ever be; his very reflection, glancing down at him out of the rear-view mirror, the dusty reflection of a rather heavy, polite, stern face, with wisps of damp dark hair curled down on his forehead, caught his eye as if he were sharing a secret with it, a secret of perplexed failure. "I may have to leave this job, after six years," she said. He glanced over at her. "There are complications," she said.

He turned into a filling station to get gas. He did not want to ask her about these complications, but he knew she was anxious to continue. In the bright glare from the sun she

looked younger than she was; her youth had always seemed
to Norman like a weapon. They waited for the man to put
in the gas. "Always complications, involvements," she said.
"Personal relationships start off so cleanly but then become
too involved. Even business relationships . . ." She smirked
at something, some memory; for a moment her face was
unfamiliar, her nose sharp, her eyes darker with the intensity of a bemused unpleasant thought. Norman, unhappy,
turned to pay the station attendant. He peered up at a man
his own age, of moderate height, dressed in greasy clothes;
the man's face was smeared with dirt and perspiration. "Hot
day," said the man, with a smirk something like Ellen's.
Norman, staring at him, felt his heart begin to pound absurdly. The man's face was familiar, unmistakable. For an
instant they stared at each other. The man licked his lips, a
stout strong man yet a little startled by Norman's look, and
turned away. Norman stared at his back. He wanted to open
the door and get out, do something. Beside him Ellen was
talking, he could not understand her. Finally she touched his
arm. "Is something wrong?" she said. "I think I know that
man," he said. As soon as he said this something seemed to
assure him: he did not know the man, it was impossible, it
did not matter. Nothing mattered. "Know him from
where?" Ellen said. "I don't know, nothing. It doesn't matter," he said.

The man returned with Norman's change. Norman
tried not to look at him, for the intensity of his feeling had
alarmed him: he thought of his uncle, now institutional-
ized, who had been committed at last by his patient wife,
an ordinary man who could not stop talking. In that instant, as he first looked at the attendant's face, Norman felt
a kinship with that other, lost man, whom he had not
thought of for ten years. . . . But he did look at the station
attendant's face after all. The man was smiling without enthusiasm, a smile that stretched his lips to show discolored
teeth, leaving the rest of his face indifferent. He had a
rather plump face, he had obviously gained weight, Nor-

man saw, but still, out of that heavy, dirt-streaked face, another face confronted him, unmistakable. It was the face of a boy, maybe seventeen. "Here y'are, thank you," the man said. He had a dirty rag over one shoulder. It was strange, Norman thought, fumbling for the ignition, that the man had not offered to clean his windshield.

He drove away. His heart was pounding furiously. "Why didn't you ask him if he knew you?" Ellen said. "It seems to mean a lot to you." She sounded resentful, but he knew that if he were to continue she would lose interest. "No, nothing. A mistake," Norman said. Yet his mind flashed and dazzled him: he knew the face, of course, he might have been shuffling through a deck of cards to come to it, through a handful of old snapshots, waiting patiently for it to turn up. "You're driving rather fast," Ellen said. He slowed down. He glanced at his watch and was surprised to see that it was so early. A great block of time seemed to have passed, jerked away from him. Back at the garage, was the man staring after this car, his smile abandoned? Norman looked fiercely at the countryside. He shut his mind, pushed everything away. Aside. He would not think, he would not remember.

They had dinner at a country inn near the theater. It was dim and pretentious, but he saw that Ellen enjoyed it. In her white silk dress and dark necklace she looked clean, harshly clean and young, her shoulders poised against an unfamiliar background of rough-hewn wooden walls decorated with old wrought-iron objects Norman could not have identified. Yet Norman heard himself say, "Did you say you had a brother?" Yes, she had said. Why did he ask that? Why at this moment? She had a brother who lived in Europe, what did it matter? She was always antagonistic about families, friends, any relationships that belonged to the past. Norman wanted to touch her hand, not to comfort her but to ask for help. The darkness of his mind was released, flowing steadily, unhurriedly, and out of that flood of old faces his heartbeat anticipated the anguish of his revelation. "Excuse me," he said, standing. He caught her glance: she was thinking that he behaved strangely, he could not be trusted. He went to the men's room. There, his back against the tiled wall, he rubbed his eyes and waited until the turmoil ceased. He remembered the face now. He knew he had remembered it at once. Now it came clearly, a boy's face, dirty and hard, and rearing behind it a gray March morning, an indifferent mottled sky. "My God," Norman said aloud. He wanted to rush back to Ellen as if he had something joyous to tell her. But his legs were weak; he reached out to get his balance. Or he would go to a telephone. He would telephone the police. And his father—but his father was dead, had been dead for years. He felt strangely peaceful; something might have been decided. When he returned to their table, where this attractive young woman awaited him, concerned for him, he felt his fingers twitch as if he wanted to reach out to embrace her, to have her draw him to her so that he would no longer need to think.

One Saturday afternoon when he was fifteen Norman and his brother Jack were coming home from a movie. It was about four-thirty: late winter, the day already ending, a chill bleak wind. The Technicolor of the movie had dazzled Norman's eyes, so that the warehouses they passed now seemed to him unsubstantial and deceptive, not remnants of a world but anticipations of a fuller, greater world he would grow into. Invisible behind the vision of that movie had been flights of music, but here there was no music, only their hurrying footsteps. Jack, at seventeen, was not much taller than Norman, both were small for their ages, with meek, dark, defensive faces. There were other boys Norman preferred to be with—even his younger brother—but Jack never made friends easily, shrugged away the long days spent at the high school with a disdainful closed expression, so that only after his death did Norman find out, from other people, that Jack was considered a little strange—not slow, exactly, because he had always been good at mathematics, but not quite quick enough, not right enough, somehow inferior.

They went down by the river, Jack's idea, and here the wind was stronger. An odor of something rotting was in the air. Norman and his brother wore jackets that were alike, the same size, made of material like canvas, a dull faded green. Sitting at the end of one of the old docks was a middle-aged man in the same kind of jacket. He did not look around, he might have been asleep or drunk. "What's he doing out here, he don't have a fish pole," Jack said resentfully. They walked past the dock. Norman shared Jack's resentment, because it seemed to him something was wrong, something adult was out of place, and if this was so, then everything might be out of place. The familiar waterfront had become, in the poor light, parched with heavy clouds that gave to everything a strange lightless glare that hurt Norman's eyes. Jack, as if to comfort him, talked of what they would have for supper that night—he had smelled the spaghetti sauce cooking before they left. But Norman was watching something ahead—movement back by the unloading platform of one of the old warehouses, a giant monstrosity that had been abandoned for years. An immense exhaustion touched him suddenly, for this world was so banal a betrayal of the world of that movie, so unimaginative a failure, that he could not respond to it. A few more years, he thought, and his life would change: he did not yet know just how it would change. He would not be like Jack, begging to quit school, his side of the room cluttered with auto racing magazines. And he thought, glancing at Jack's worried face, that he could not admire him as an older brother, for Jack was not big or strong enough. He did not like Jack because Jack did not bully him; he pitied Jack because Jack at seventeen had to wear the same jacket he wore at fifteen, and the two of them, bored with each other, were doomed to be brothers forever and could do nothing about it.

"There's some guys," Jack said. Norman saw three boys on the dock ahead. Something was tilting, falling over. It was a hollow metal cylinder that was buoyed up for a moment on the water, then sank. "Do you know them?" Norman said. "Are they in your class?" "No, not them bastards," Jack said. As a child, Norman had always taken his responses from other people, and now, at fifteen, he felt Jack's sudden stiffened look pass over him at once. They kept on walking, Jack a little ahead. The three boys were laughing at something, their snatches of words incomprehensible and harsh, as if they spoke a foreign language. One, in a soiled flannel shirt, was lighting a cigarette. They were about Jack's age. As Jack and Norman approached they grew quiet, staring out at the water. Jack was looking straight ahead, but Norman could not help but glance at the boys—absolutely ordinary faces with identical blank, cautious expressions, their hair much too long. They stood with their legs apart, as if posing. The boy in the flannel shirt lit his cigarette and tossed the match out into the water. Jack and Norman passed by, were by them, and Norman felt his legs want to run—he did not know why—but Jack did not hurry. Norman's breathing had quickened. Nothing had happened, no one had said a word, yet just before he was hit something in him shouted at the back of Jack's head: You fool! You goddamn fool for getting us into this!

A board struck Norman on the right shoulder and he spun around, gaping. He saw the three faces lunge at him, serious and quiet. Then the pain exploded again, this time on his chest, and he felt himself falling, falling back into nothing; then he struck the water hard. It swelled upon him and he sank into its frigid softness with his eyes opened in terror at the sky. His arms jerked, his legs thrashed, but caught at nothing. It seemed queer to him that the water was cold and hard, yet could not support him. . . . Then he came to the surface, choking. Someone yelled, "Get that one!" and Norman tried to fling himself backward, anywhere. He did not know yet that Jack was in the water too. Something struck the water beside his head, he did not know what, and disappeared at once. Through the film before his eyes he saw one of the boys striking at the water by the dock with a long piece of rusty metal, his face hard and deliberate, as if he were chopping wood and counting the strokes. Norman pressed backward, out and backward, his heart pounding so violently that he could not see. Someone shouted—a word Norman did not recognize—and it seemed that in the freezing water words were shattered and had no meaning, did not matter, nothing mattered.

When he woke, it was with reluctance. Immediately the air assaulted him: he lay on his back against something hard, faces were peering down at him. Adults. He had been brought back. In curious alarm they stared at him and he at them; then he began to vomit. Someone held him. His body convulsed as if struggling against an invisible enemy, writhing and fleeing. They spoke to him, there was a siren somewhere, even a woman's voice, and though he could now understand their words he felt himself an intruder, someone returned from the dead who has no business overhearing anything. It was said later that he called for Jack at once, but he never remembered this. They had answered by assuring him that Jack was all right, he was already in the ambulance, but of course this was a lie.

During the play he could not sit still. He perspired heavily. Onstage, the actors moved through their lines without hesitation, pert and skillful, but Norman understood nothing. He might have been drowning again, drowning in air and words of another language, remote even from the woman who sat beside him. At intermission they went outside and he could tell from her silence that she was not pleased. They stared out together at a flower garden, some design of grass and flowers murky in the twilight but heavy with meaning, deliberate and plotted. "Would you like to go home?" Ellen said softly. As if guilty, Norman could not meet her eyes. He heard her words but could not make sense of them, for he was staring once again through that cold film at the boys up on the dock—secure and dry—the faces of two of them raw and blurred, but the other face now clear. He recognized it.

"Why don't we go home," Ellen said, touching his arm. Norman knew that if he broke down before her he would lose her, of course; her sympathy could not be trusted. "No, I'm all right," he said, almost angrily. "It's nothing."

He stayed at her apartment for only a few minutes. She was tired and distracted and apologetic, and she seemed not to see how he wanted to remain with her, he would have talked of anything, done anything, if only she would protect him against the violence of the past— After he left her he went to a bar for a while and then, dizzy and sickened, he went home. In bed old fragments of prayers taunted his mind, and now and then it seemed to him quite clear that he had made a mistake, that he was perhaps losing his mind. He would do nothing. He would not give in. In the morning he would wake as usual to the pleasant smells from the kitchen below, he would go to the store and call Ellen, he would never drive out to that part of the country again.

But he was unable to call her. He started to dial her number several times, but always something came up and he was relieved to put back the receiver. Once he caught himself walking somewhere very deliberately—to his desk in the back office. He opened one of the drawers and glanced in at the pistol there, half covered with papers. Trembling, he hid it with papers. He stood there, staring down at the drawer for a while. No one came in, nothing happened. The ordinariness of everything, the refusal of life to change at all, baffled and angered him. He felt nauseous but nothing happened. In the rest room, watching himself suspiciously in the mirror, he believed shakily that his reflection was that of a guilty man.

After the store closed he drove out to the country. The drive took less time than it had the other day. While he drove he thought of nothing, not even Ellen, who ought to have been sitting beside him. . . . If he returned to the gas station and saw the man again, and if he could assure himself that it was not the same man he wanted, then perhaps he would call Ellen from the station; he would do that. But as he neared the small junction where the garage was supposed to be, he found himself looking shrewdly around, at houses, down lanes, down side roads. He passed the garage. No one was outside. A shabby garage with dented Coke signs and signs with scrawled numbers on them advertising gas prices, and other signs advertising cigarettes and spark plugs. The drive was just dirt and gravel, not paved. They did little business, he thought, and this was good. Several miles farther he turned down a side road and drove slowly along: country without houses, wild fields unowned by people, woods gone wild. When he saw a shanty by the edge of a woods, half a mile back from the road, he stopped the car and got out.

The shanty was deserted. It was roofed with tar paper and its wood had turned black. Inside there were newspapers on the ground, an old dented pan, some rags, a few tiny anthills. Weeds blossomed everywhere. Norman tried to imagine what use the shanty had had, who might have built it. It seemed to him a mystery: built, abandoned, now ready for him and his brother's killer.

When he drove back he stopped at the garage for gas. The man who serviced him was not the killer, but Norman saw that there was another man inside, drinking soda pop. "What time do you people close?" Norman said. "Stay open till ten, summer," the man said. Norman hardly glanced at him. His eyes kept moving back to the open door of the garage. "That's all, thanks," he said, smiling. It was the first time he had smiled since having first seen that man.

He called Ellen from his home. At once his voice became anxious and apologetic, and her silence tormented him. "I know, I know what you said that time about not wanting to get involved with people you can't trust," he said hopelessly, "and how you don't want—you don't—" He fell silent. The vision of her that her silence evoked in him was transparent and unfamiliar; was she going to say nothing? How long had they known each other? "I am going to see you again, aren't I?" Norman said. "Yes, of course," she said faintly. "But I think you should get some rest or see a doctor. You don't seem yourself. . . ." "No, there's nothing wrong with me," Norman said sharply. She did not reply, as if startled. "When can I see you? Tomorrow?" Norman said. "No, not tomorrow, I forgot— I have something—" "What are you doing?" she said. "I'm sorry, I just can't make it then. The day after tomorrow?" Norman said. "Can I call you?" "Of course you can call me," she said meekly and coldly. Norman felt in that instant her strange hatred for him, for the force that drew him from her and before which he was so helpless; his eyes smarted with tears. "I'll call you, then," he said. He had the idea as he hung up that perhaps he would never see her again, and yet he could do nothing about it.

The next evening he drove out to the country again. Signs, barns, houses, side roads had become familiar. On the floor of the backseat were a small bag of groceries and two blankets and an old kerosene lamp he had found in the attic. It was nearly ten o'clock when he approached the garage. His heart was thudding dangerously, yet it did not upset him. He knew his body would not fail him, he could drive it as he drove the car. It was when he did not make himself think of the killer, when, out of disgust or fear, he tried to think of other things, that he felt the overwhelming guilt that had become for him the most extraordinary emotion he had ever felt. Now, prepared, everything ready and planned, he felt no guilt at all. With his car headlights off, he parked down the road from the garage, watching. Bushes screened him partly. There was his man—dragging a carton of empty soda pop bottles inside the garage. Norman waited. He had never before felt quite so free: the immensity of freedom to act and to act entirely without consequence. He wondered if that man and the two boys with him had experienced this same sweet suffocating freedom that afternoon sixteen years ago. . . . The garage darkened. Norman had no trouble making out the killer, who was taller than the other man and walked with heavy plodding steps as if he were overcome by the heat or by exhaustion. There was something self-righteous in that walk, Norman saw. The men went to their cars, the car doors slammed shut almost simultaneously, the other man drove off. The killer paused to light a cigarette. He tossed the match onto the gravel and Norman's lips jerked into a grin of recognition.

He stepped on the gas pedal and was able to head off the man's car just as it was about to turn onto the road. Norman leaned across the seat and waved into the glaring headlights. The man yelled, "What do you want? We're closed." But Norman had already gotten out of the car. "Something's wrong with my car, it's an emergency," he said. The man swore. His car engine roared and the car rocked impatiently back on the gravel as the man twisted the steering wheel. "You, wait," Norman said. "Not so fast." He took the gun out of his pocket and approached the man's open window. Behind the headlights he was helpless now, his face sagging at the sight of the gun as if he expected it. Norman's heart thudded viciously and he heard his own words as if from a distance. "I want to talk to you. I don't want to hurt you. You just get in this other car." The man did not move. Norman could hear him swallow. "Did you recognize me the other day?" he said. The man's eyes were fascinated by the gun. "There's no money in there," he said hoarsely. "Just some dollar bills. We made—we made a god-damned four dollars today—" "I don't want money," Norman said. "Get out. Get in my car." The man moved jerkily, then paused. Everything was still except for the noises of the insects. "You don't want any money?" the man said after a moment.

Norman sat beside him and the man drove. They went along slowly, down the dirt road, jerking and bouncing in the ruts. "They're waiting for me at home," the man said cautiously. "My wife and kids." Norman said nothing. When they reached the shanty—he had left a rag near the ditch for a marker—he had the man turn off the road and drive down an old cow lane and into the woods. The car churned and became entangled in underbrush. "Look, I don't know what you want," the man said, bowed over the steering wheel, "but I—I— Why don't you get somebody else for it, not me — My wife is—" "I'm not going to hurt you," Norman said. He was a little embarrassed at the man's fear: he had supposed the man would be the same as he had been sixteen years ago, cold and deliberate, without emotion. "I just want to talk with you," he said. "I want to get the truth from you. Where were you about sixteen years ago?"

He watched the man's damp face. It was an ugly, confused face, and yet its younger image had not been ugly, exactly. "I don't—I don't know," the man muttered. "Please try to remember," Norman said. "What's your name?" "Cameron," he said at once. "Anyone around here would know me— Look, what do you want? I don't know you. With that gun there—" "I'm not going to hurt you," Norman said softly. "Just tell me where you were sixteen years ago." "We come up from Kentucky, first me, then my mother and father," he said. Again he swallowed clumsily. "I was maybe twenty then. I don't know. Look, I think you want some other man, I mean, it looks to me you got some other man in mind—" "You never came up from Kentucky," Norman said. "Or if you did you were younger than that." "I don't know how old I was," the man said, "maybe I was younger—" His face rippled nervously. "You remember me, don't you?" Norman said. "You knew me the other day, too, didn't you?" "What other day?" the man said. In his heavy face this new, nervous rigidity contrasted ludicrously with the lazy slabs of flesh close about his jaws. He looked as if he were trying to shake himself free of the weight of his flesh. "I only want to talk to you, then the police will take care of it," Norman said. "Take care of what?" the man said at once. "You know what," Norman said. The man stared across at him. He supposes I am crazy, Norman thought. "So you don't admit it? That you remember me?" he said. He might have been speaking to a customer in the store, prodding and herding him on to a purchase, some clothing Norman himself looked at but did not see, had no interest in seeing because he had already seen it too many times before. "I'm not going to force anything out of you," Norman said. "I give you my word on that. We're going to have a long talk, nothing hurried. Because I've been waiting sixteen years—" "What's this sixteen years?" the man said. His voice was trembling and raw, a voice Norman had not yet heard from him. There was a certain edginess there too, a recklessness that made Norman draw back so he could watch the man more carefully. Nothing was going to go wrong. He had control. While insects swirled about the headlights and tapped against the windshield Norman felt strength course through him as if it were a sign, a gift, something supernatural. "Sixteen years ago you killed my brother," he said. "Sixteen years ago last March." "Killed your brother!" said the man. He made a whistling noise. "Look, mister, I never killed nobody. I told you before—it looked like you were after somebody else, something you said— You got the wrong guy here, believe me. I never killed nobody. Who was your brother? Am I supposed to know you? Were you in the Army with me or something?" Norman let him talk. The man's words tumbled from him as if stunned with shock; they meant nothing. Finally he stopped. The insects flicked themselves lightly against the car windows and disappeared. "Turn off the lights," Norman said. He had his flashlight ready. "What do you want?" said the man. "What are you going to do?" "Turn them off. All right, now get out. Get out," Norman said. "What are you going to do?" said the man. "Are you going to—going to— You said something about the police, why don't you call them or something? I mean, they got these things on record, could look it up and see when it was—they keep a record of all these things, mister, that would clear it all up— Because I never killed nobody, not even in the Army when we was overseas, and not even by accident or anything— Was your brother in the Army?" "Get out of the car," said Norman.

"Then where are we going?" the man said, gripping the steering wheel. "What are you going to do to me?" "I want to talk to you," Norman said. "You're crazy!" the man whispered.

They went in the shanty, Norman behind the man. Norman put the things down and shone the flashlight around from corner to corner. "What place is this?" the man said. "What are you going to do?" His teeth had begun to chatter; Norman was astonished. "Please sit down," he said. Cobwebs hung dustily from the ceiling. In the glare of the flashlight the weeds were stark and vivid, casting brittle shadows that froze in a complex, teethlike structure against the bottoms of the walls. The man sat, slowly, groping about. He looked gross and foolish sitting in the weeds, his fat stomach straining against his belt. About his forehead dark strands of hair were plastered as if arranged by hand. Norman crouched against the opposite wall. "I want the truth from you," he whispered. "The truth." The man's lips began to move, but he said nothing. "Try to remember," Norman said. "You killed a boy and he's dead, his life was ended in a few minutes, and now you're here with me and alive, you've got to see the difference between the two— He'd be just bones now, everything rotted away if you dug him up, and you're sitting here alive. He was seventeen when you killed him." The man brushed weeds away from him as if they were insects, in terror; then he stopped abruptly. "I think you do remember me," Norman said. "I was with him that day. You and the other two boys—"

"Other two?"

"Other two boys. All three of you. You pushed us in the river and wouldn't let us out. You hit Jack with something—when they found him his face was all slashed. I saw it myself. It was you and two other boys. I know your face."

The man began to shake his head. "My wife is waiting for me," he said faintly, "I can't talk too long. . . ."

"Where are the other two? Did they leave the city?"

"Mister, I got to go home— They're—"

"Shut up about that!" Norman cried. He waited until his anger died down. "I just want the truth. A boy is dead and you killed him and you're going to tell the truth before you leave here!"

"Mister, I never killed nobody—"

"But I saw you. I saw *you*. I saw your face."

"It wasn't me, it was somebody else."

"It was you."

"I got all kinds of cousins and guys that look like me—"

"Living up here?"

"Sure, around here, in the city too—"

"You said you were from Kentucky."

The man paused. His teeth chattered and he stared at Norman as if a flash of pain had overcome him. Then he said, "I am. They come up too."

"You all came up? When was this?"

"A while ago, I don't know—"

"You're lying," Norman said. "Goddamn filthy liar."

"I'm not lying!"

The man's lips twisted up into a terrified angry grimace. Norman felt his own lips twitch as if in imitation. "I want justice, nothing but justice," Norman whispered. He was shining the flashlight on the man's heaving chest so that the fainter halo of light illuminated the man's face, startling shadows upward from his nose and lips and the deep sockets of his eyes. "I've given up things to get here tonight," Norman said. "I'm going to get an answer from you, going to get justice. We must have justice." He might have marveled at what he said, at his strange talent, for where in the long tedious days at the store and in the evenings at home had he learned such things? Yet he felt the truth of what he was saying. It was true. He had been sent here, he could not turn away from it now if he wanted to. For this man he had given up Ellen, he would never break free and into her world now, he had given her up, killed her in himself. "There are things that have to be finished up, made even," Norman said. "If I turned you over to the police without a confession it wouldn't do any good. Nobody would care. Nobody knows about it anymore except me and my family and you. . . . Are you going to tell me the truth?"

The man sat staring down at his thick legs, motionless.

"You and two other kids, one Saturday afternoon," Norman said softly. "On the docks. You knocked us both in the water and wouldn't let us out. You hit Jack, cut up his face. His eye was cut. My brother drowned but I, I didn't, a man sitting down aways came over and got me. You read about it in the papers probably. You and them. You kept on reading it till it was forgotten. Nobody cared. And even me, I suppose I forgot it too. . . . Now are you going to tell me the truth?"

After several hours the man was sitting in the same position. Norman had lit the kerosene lamp and was sitting with his back against the wall, watching the man cautiously. When he asked the man about telling the truth, sometimes he answered and sometimes he did not. When he said nothing Norman had to fight down an impulse to strike him. He had to control his anger. "You son of a bitch," the man whispered. "Going to shoot me anyway, why not now?"

"I just want the truth," Norman said. "I want it written down and signed. Your confession."

"My confession . . ."

"On paper. Signed with your name."

"Then what?"

"I told you what."

"Then you're going to shoot me, aren't you?"

"No. I told you."

"Should I write it on paper or what? Do you have some?"

"Then you did do it?"

The man squinted. "Didn't you say you saw me?"

"Yes, I saw you."

"Then I must of done it."

"Do you admit it?"

The man's face looked paralyzed. "Do you?" Norman said, leaning forward. The bovine stupidity of that face—which he felt he had been staring at for years, hating—was suddenly too much for him. He slashed the back of the gun against the man's knee, for no reason, without really knowing what he had done. The blow did not hurt, the man seemed only baffled by it. Norman's face burned. "You made me do that," he said accusingly. "I didn't mean to—I didn't plan— You made me do it."

"Going to shoot me, why not now?" the man said dully.

"Nobody's going to shoot you, for Christ's sake," Norman said. "Will you just tell the truth for once? Will you stop lying?"

"My wife—"

"To hell with that!"

"My wife can tell you. Lots of people could, but you don't care. You want to kill me."

The man hid his face in his hands. Norman could still see part of his anguished teeth. "No," Norman said. "I only want justice." But the word "justice" struck him suddenly as a puzzle: what was he talking about? It evoked in his mind an uncertain image of a courthouse with a flag flying over it, not a picture of any court in town but one out of a movie or a book. The image vanished. Norman sat up. His head had begun to pound, he had not eaten that day, he cared about nothing except this man. "I don't need sleep," he said without pride. "I can keep going until I get the truth from you. I've waited sixteen years now."

"Sixteen years," the man whispered. His hands came away from his face and in that instant Norman saw unmistakably a flash of something like recognition. A droplet of perspiration tumbled down the man's face, from his forehead to his chin and then to his wet shirtfront, as if stunned by this recognition.

"Are you going to admit it?" Norman said.

"I'm not admitting anything!"

Norman's hand, holding the gun, jerked as if it had come alive. "What the hell do you mean?" he said. "A minute ago—"

"I'm not admitting anything!"

Norman waited until his heartbeat slowed. He felt on the precipice of terrible danger. Then he drew his knees up and watched the man silently. The emptiness in his stomach was turning into a kind of strength. While the kerosene lamp flickered indifferently, a cluster of moths and insects reeling about it, Norman and the man faced each other for a period of time. Norman was really not conscious of time passing; he might have been enchanted. "My brother and I were very close," he said softly. "He did things for me, stuck up for me. He looked like me only he was a lot bigger . . . he was going to go to college. Then one day you killed him. Just like that. For no reason." Norman wondered if the man was listening. "Why did you do it? For no reason, nothing, not even for money, just nothing. . . . Something in a murderer's brain must pinch him and make him do it, and everything is ruined. Lives are ruined. Nothing can be right and balanced again until justice is won—the injured party has to have justice. Do you understand that? Nothing can be right, for years, for lifetimes, until that first crime is punished. Or else we'd all be animals. The crime keeps on and on unless it's punished. Somebody like me gets caught in the middle and can't have his own life. Here I have to ruin myself to make it right and never had any choice—" The man's eyes were fascinated by Norman's face; he could not look away. When it began to get light Norman turned off the kerosene lamp. The man, slouched across from him in the weeds, looked rumpled and sick and aged. He really was not Norman's age after all, but quite a bit older. "Here," said Norman. He took an orange out of the grocery bag and tossed it at the man. It struck his knee and fell to the ground. The man seemed not to notice. "Eat that. You need to eat," Norman said. The man pushed the orange away vaguely, yet still without seeming to notice it. Norman wondered if something was wrong. The night had passed quickly for him, yet at the same time something had happened that had cemented him irreparably to this shanty, to this damp ground, to the man's rumpled body; surely it was the same way with the killer. This was something Norman could understand, after all. The woman he had loved—and he could not quite summon up her face—had been in another world where nothing was simple, nothing could be depended upon. Perhaps he had really feared and hated that world. But here, with the man obedient before him, he had only one other thing to keep in mind for both of them: that day in March. Nothing more. He did not need to think of anything further.

The man jerked his head up as if someone had called him. "Eat that orange," Norman said. "That's good for you." The man shook his head slowly. "I said eat it," said Norman. Muscles tensed in his jaw. He waited. The man did not move. "Eat that orange," said Norman, "or I'll kill you." The man's hand dropped and closed over the orange, as if the hand were part of a machine clumsily manipulated. He picked it up and peered at it. "Eat," said Norman. "Eat." The man brought the orange slowly up to his mouth. "Take off the skin first," Norman said. The man hesitated. "I can't eat it," he whispered. Norman saw tears in his eyes. "Take off the skin first," Norman said more gently. He watched the man peel the orange. Juice trickled down his big hands and fell onto his trousers and onto the bent weeds. "Now eat it," said Norman.

When the man finished, Norman said. "Are you ready now to confess?" The man made a sound something like a sob. He wiped his mouth; he stared down at nothing. Norman's heart beat so violently that his arms had begun to tremble. For an instant he felt faint; black spots appeared before his eyes, like insects. But he forced himself to say, evenly, "Are you ready to confess?"

"I never did it," the man whispered.

"But you did. You did something. You killed somebody."

"What?"

"You killed—" Norman paused. "Nothing. That wasn't — Never mind that."

"Look, I never— I never hurt—"

"Stop lying!" Norman cried. "Do you want to make me hurt you? Is that it? Want to bring me down to your level, a goddamn filthy animal? I waited sixteen years to get the truth from you—"

"What do you want me to do?" the man said. He lifted his sticky palms in a gesture of helplessness. "Where's the paper? What should I write? You said you'd let me go then—"

"I said what?"

"Said the police would have a record of it—"

"I never said that," Norman whispered.

"Yes, you said it, I heard you. We would go from here to the police and they would have some record. Have it written down. In a file. That's how they do it."

"Look, I don't want to do this to you," Norman said. "I don't want to be here. I have my own life, my own life, and here I am, over thirty already, and haven't done anything— haven't started yet—wasting my time with his troubles, and you sit and whine about yourself! You! You gave yourself up to me the day you killed him and there's nothing you can do about it."

"I got proof I wasn't up here—nowhere near here—"

"Like hell."

"We can go out and—"

"Don't you move," Norman said. His eyes throbbed. His vision itself seemed to throb with outrage and dismay. Only now had he begun to realize that this man had tried to kill him too. Had wanted him to drown. At one time that groveling man had stood safe on a dock and wanted him to drown. . . . There was the same face, Norman saw suddenly, as if by magic that young face asserted itself again within the older flabby face.

"If—if you got some paper or something—"

"You'd write it wrong," Norman said.

"No, I'll write it, then you check it, then I'll sign it—"

Norman laughed tonelessly. "You must think I'm crazy," he said.

"What?"

"Who'd believe what you wrote? When you had a gun pointed at you! How can I prove you did it, how can I prove anything? You have me trapped now like you did *then*—I could be drowning out in the water, it's the same thing, I feel like I'm drowning here, there's nothing I can do to get you —to get justice—" Norman's voice had become feverish. His hatred now was impersonal and ubiquitous; he hated without any object, without any catalyst. Even his brother's memory had become an annoyance.

"But what are you going to do?" the man said, licking his lips. "I think they'd believe a note," he said softly.

"They wouldn't. Not a jury."

"If I confessed it out loud to them—"

"No."

"If I said how I remembered it, who was with me, what you two looked like—"

"No, not even then."

"If I—if I got in touch with one of those two guys, and he said—"

"You're lying."

Stunned, baffled, the man stared at him. It seemed to Norman obvious that he was lying now, that he really could not remember anything but was only pretending, as if to make Norman feel better. It was not the lie Norman hated him for but his talent at not remembering: why had Norman not this talent, why had he been cursed with remembering when he had tried so long to forget?

"All right. You can go," Norman said.

The man did not move. "What?"

"You can go. Go."

"You mean leave here?"

His legs moved, experimentally, but he did not get up.

He was squinting at Norman. "You want me to go home?"

"Go home to your wife."

"Yes, all right," the man said. He got up slowly. His legs must have ached. Each of his movements was queer and gentle, as if he were still in a dream and feared overturning something fragile. "Yes," he whispered. The man tried not to look at Norman. He moved slowly, even his eyes moved slowly to the door, and it was finally his gesture of absurd fastidiousness—he paused to brush dirt and orange peels off his trousers—that overwhelmed Norman.

"You bastard, you killer!" Norman cried. "Going to walk out like that! It's in the newspapers every day how they kill people and walk out, nothing ever happens, nobody gets punished, nothing gets put right, and people like myself have to live under the shadow of it! Killers! What the hell do I care if you did it or not? If it wasn't you it was somebody else— Or even if nobody did it, if it was an accident or if I never even had a brother named Jack or anything—"

"Named Jack?" said the man.

Norman pulled the trigger. The shot was much louder than he had expected. When he opened his eyes the shanty was empty. He crawled to the doorway and looked out— there the man was, running, through the mist. He aimed the gun again and fired. The man stumbled, fell against a tree with his arms out in an embrace. Still on his knees, Norman fired again. "Everything I did for him," he sobbed, "everything ruined—my life ruined— He wouldn't give a damn anyway, that's how it always is. What do they care? I bring her home money every week, she forgets to say thanks, why should she say thanks? There's always more where that came from. Dirty bastards, killers, a whole world of killers, and that one there sitting all night long telling lies in front of me—as if I didn't know him right away!"

Something in him seemed to collapse. The earth beneath him tilted suddenly, and he felt spiky grass against his face; everything was dizzy, confused. His fingers grasped at the earth as if he believed his weight was not enough to hold him down and keep him from being sucked up into the depths of the morning sky. Minutes passed, Norman waited to regain his strength. "You there," he said bitterly. "Hey, you." The man did not answer. He must have been lying where he fell. Norman made a face, thinking of the day ahead, the airless routine: months, years of ordinary life, so sane and so remote from this field. He closed his eyes and felt his strength course slowly back into his body. Yet still he felt the numbed, beatific emptiness of one who no longer doubts that he possesses the truth, and for whom life will have forever lost its joy.

CATTAILS

Marcia Muller

A native of Detroit, Marcia Muller has published four suspense novels and has two more forthcoming. Most of these (Edwin of the Iron Shoes, Ask the Cards a Question, The Cheshire Cat's Eye, Games to Keep the Dark Away) *feature Sharon McCone, a female private investigator based in San Francisco. She has also written a nonfiction book and many short stories. Among her literary strengths are in-depth characterization and a feel for mood and atmosphere —attributes which make "Cattails," a story written expressly for this anthology, the fine, eerie tale it is. (B.P.)*

We came around the lake, Frances and I, heading toward the picnic ground. I was lugging the basket and when the going got rough, like where the path narrowed to a ledge of rock, I would set it down a minute before braving the uneven ground.

All the while I was seeing us as if we were in a movie —something I do more and more the older I get.

They come around the lake, an old couple of seventy, on a picnic. The woman strides ahead, still slender and active, her red scarf fluttering in the breeze. He follows, carrying the wicker basket, a stooped gray-headed man who moves hesitantly, as if he is a little afraid.

Drama, I thought. We're more and more prone to it as the real thing fades from our lives. We make ourselves stars in scenarios that are at best boring. Ah, well, it's a way to keep going. I have my little dramas; Frances has her spiritualism and séances. And, thinking of keeping going, I must or Frances will tell me I'm good for nothing, not even carrying the basket to the picnic ground.

Frances had already arrived there by the time I reached the meadow. I set the basket down once more and mopped my damp brow. She motioned impatiently to me and, with a muttered "Yes, dear," I went on. It was the same place we always came for our annual outing. The same sunlight glinted coldly on the water; the same chill wind blew up from the shore; the same dampness saturated the ground.

January. A hell of a time for a picnic, even here in the hills of Northern California. I knew why she insisted on it. Who would know better than I? And yet I wondered—was there more to it than that? Was the fool woman trying to kill me with these damned outings?

She spread the plaid blanket on the ground in front of the log we always used as a backrest. I lowered myself onto

480

it, groaning. Yes, the ground was damp as ever. Soon it would seep through the blanket and into my clothes. Frances unpacked the big wicker basket, portioning out food like she did at home. It was a nice basket, with real plates and silverware, all held in their own little niches. Frances had even packed cloth napkins—leave it to her not to forget. The basket was the kind you saw advertised nowadays in catalogs for rich people to buy, but it hadn't cost us very much. I'd made the niches myself and outfitted it with what was left of our first set of dishes and flatware. That was back in the days when I liked doing handy projects, before . . .

"Charles, you're not eating." Frances thrust my plate into my hands.

Ham sandwich. On rye. With mustard. Pickle, garlic dill. Potato salad, Frances's special recipe. The same as always.

"Don't you think next year we could have something different?" I asked.

Frances looked at me with an expression close to hatred. "You know we can't."

"Guess not." I bit into the sandwich.

Frances opened a beer for me. Bud. I'm not supposed to drink, not since the last seizure, and I've been good, damned good. But on these yearly picnics it's different. It's got to be.

Frances poured herself some wine. We ate in silence, staring at the cattails along the shore of the lake.

When we finished what was on our plates, Frances opened another beer for me and took out the birthday cake. It was chocolate with darker chocolate icing. I knew that without looking.

"He would have been twenty-nine," she said.

"Yes."

"Twenty-nine. A man."

"Yes," I said again, with mental reservations.

"Poor Richie. He was such a beautiful baby."

I was silent, watching the cattails.

"Do you remember, Charles? What a beautiful baby he was?"

"Yes."

That had been in Detroit. Back when the auto industry was going great guns and jobs on the assembly line were a dime a dozen. We'd had a red-brick house in a suburb called Royal Oak. And a green Ford—that's where I'd worked, Ford's, the River Rouge plant—and a yard with big maple trees. And, unexpectedly, we'd had Richie.

"He was such a good baby, too. He never cried."

"No, he didn't."

Richie never cried. He'd been unusually silent, watching us. And I'd started to drink more. I'd come home and see them, mother and the change-of-life baby she'd never wanted, beneath the big maple trees. And I'd go to the kitchen for a beer.

I lost the job at Ford's. Our furniture was sold. The house went on the market. And then we headed west in the green car. To Chicago.

Now Frances handed me another beer.

"I shouldn't." I wasn't used to drinking anymore and I already felt drunk.

"Drink it."

I shrugged and tilted the can.

Chicago had been miserable. There we'd lived in a railroad flat in an old dark brick building. It was always cold in the flat, and in the Polish butcher shop where I clerked. Frances started talking about going to work, but I wouldn't let her. Richie needed her. Needed watching.

The beer was making me feel sleepy.

In Chicago, the snow had drifted and covered the front stoop. I would come home in the dark, carrying meat that the butcher shop was going to throw out—chicken backs and nearly spoiled pork and sometimes a soupbone. I'd take them to the kitchen, passing through the front room where Richie's playpen was, and set them on the drainboard. And then I'd go to the pantry for a shot or two of something to warm me. It was winter when the green Ford died. It was winter when I lost the job at the butcher shop. A snowstorm was howling in off Lake Michigan when we got on the Greyhound for Texas. I'd heard of work in Midland.

Beside me, Frances leaned back against the log. I set my empty beer can down and lay on my side.

"That's right, Charles, go to sleep." Her voice shook with controlled anger, as always.

I closed my eyes, traveling back to Texas.

Roughnecking the oil rigs hadn't been easy. It was hard work, dirty work, and for a newcomer, the midnight shift was the only one available. But times hadn't been any better for Frances and Richie. In the winter, the northers blew through every crack in the little box of a house we'd rented. And summer's heat turned the place into an oven. Frances never complained. Richie did, but, then, Richie complained about everything.

Summer nights in Midland were the only good times. We'd sit outside, sometimes alone, sometimes with neighbors, drinking beer and talking. Once in a while we'd go to a roadhouse, if we could find someone to take care of Richie. That wasn't often, though. It was hard to find someone to stay with such a difficult child. And then I fell off the oil rig and broke my leg. When it healed, we boarded another bus, this time for New Mexico.

I jerked suddenly. Must have dozed off. Frances sat beside me, clutching some cattails she'd picked from the edge of the lake while I slept. She set them down and took out the blue candles and started sticking them on the birthday cake.

"Do you remember that birthday of Richie's in New Mexico?" She began lighting the candles, all twenty-nine of them.

"Yes."

"We gave him that red plastic music box? Like an organ

grinder's? With the fuzzy monkey on top that went up and down when you turned the handle?"

"Yes." I looked away from the candles to the cattails and the lake beyond. The monkey had gone up and down when you turned the handle—until Richie had stomped on the toy and smashed it to bits.

In Roswell we'd had a small stucco house, nicer than the one in Midland. Our garden had been westernized—that's what they call pebbles instead of grass, cacti instead of shrubs. Not that I spent a lot of time there. I worked long hours in the clothing mill.

Frances picked up the cattails and began pulling them apart, scattering their fuzzy insides. The breeze blew most of the fluff away across the meadow, but some stuck to the icing on the cake.

"He loved that monkey, didn't he?"

"Yes," I lied.

"And the tune the music box played—what was it?"

" 'Pop Goes the Weasel.' " But she knew that.

"Of course. 'Pop Goes the Weasel.' " The fuzz continued to drift through her fingers. The wind from the lake blew some of it against my nose. It tickled.

"Roswell was where I met Linda," Frances added. "Do you remember her?"

"There's nothing wrong with my memory."

"She foretold it all."

"Some of it."

"All."

I let her have the last word. Frances was a stubborn woman.

Linda. Roswell was where Frances had gotten interested in spiritualism, foretelling the future, that sort of stuff. I hadn't liked it, but, hell, it gave Frances something to do. And there was little enough to do, stuck out there in the desert. I had to hand it to Linda—she foretold my losing the job at the clothing mill. And our next move, to Los Angeles.

Frances was almost done with the cattails. Soon she'd ask me to get her some more.

Los Angeles. A haze always hanging over the city. Tall palms that were nothing but poles with sickly wisps of leaves at the top. And for me, job after job, each worse, until I was clerking at the Orange Julius for minimum wage. For Frances and Richie it wasn't so bad, though. We lived in Santa Monica, near the beach. Nothing fancy, but she could take him there and he'd play in the surf. It kept him out of trouble—he'd taken to stealing candy and little objects from the stores. When they went to the beach on weekends I stayed home and drank.

"I need some more cattails, Charles."

"Soon."

Was the Orange Julius the last job in L.A.? Funny how they all blended together. But it had to be—I was fired from there after Richie lifted twenty dollars from the cash register while visiting me. By then we'd scraped together enough money from Frances's baby-sitting wages to buy an old car—a white Nash Rambler. It took us all the way to San Francisco and these East Bay hills where we were sitting today.

"Charles, the cattails."

"Soon."

The wind was blowing off the lake. The cattails at the shore moved, beckoning me. The cake was covered with white fuzz. The candles guttered, dripping blue wax.

"Linda," Frances said. "Do you remember when she came to stay with us in Oakland?"

"Yes."

"We had the séance."

"Yes."

I didn't believe in the damned things, but I'd gone along with it. Linda had set up chairs around the dining-room table in our little shingled house. The room had been too small for the number of people there and Linda had made cutting remarks. That hurt. It was all we could afford.

I was on disability then because of the accident at the chemical plant. I'd been worrying about Richie's adjustment problems in school and my inattention on the job had caused an explosion.

"That was my first experience with those who have gone beyond," Frances said now.

"Yes."

"You didn't like it."

"No, I didn't."

There had been rapping noises. And chill drafts. A dish had fallen off a shelf. Linda said afterward it had been a young spirit we had contacted. She claimed young spirits were easier to raise.

I still didn't believe in any of it. Not a damned bit!

"Charles, the cattails."

I stood up.

Linda had promised to return to Oakland the next summer. We would all conduct more "fun" experiments. By the time she did, Frances was an expert in those experiments. She'd gone to every charlatan in town after that day in January, here at the lake. She'd gone because on that unseasonably warm day, during his birthday picnic at this very meadow, Richie had drowned while fetching cattails from the shore. Died by drowning, just as Linda had prophesied in New Mexico. Some said it had been my fault because I'd been drunk and had fallen asleep and failed to watch him. Frances seemed to think so. But Frances had been wandering around in the woods or somewhere and hadn't watched him either.

I started down toward the lake. The wind had come up and the overripe cattails were breaking open, their white fuzz trailing like fog.

Funny. They had never done that before.

I looked back at Frances. She motioned impatiently.

I continued down to the lakeside.

Frances had gone to the mediums for years, hoping to make contact with Richie's spirit. When that hadn't worked, she went less and spiritualism became merely a hobby for her. But one thing she still insisted on was coming here every year to reenact the fatal picnic. Even though it was usually cold in January, even though others would have stayed away from the place where their child had died, she came and went through the ritual. Why? Anger at me, I supposed. Anger because I'd been drunk and asleep that day . . .

The cattail fuzz was thicker now. I stopped. The lake was obscured by it. Turning, I realized I could barely see Frances.

Shapes seemed to be forming in the mist.

The shape of Richie. A bad child.

The shape of Frances. An unhappy mother.

"Daddy, help!"

The cry seemed to come out of the mist at the water's edge. I froze for a moment, then started down there. The mist got thicker. Confused, I stopped. Had I heard something? Or was it only in my head?

Drama, I thought. Drama . . .

The old man stands enveloped in the swirling mist, shaking his gray head. Gradually his sight returns. He peers around, searching for the shapes. He cocks his head, listening for another cry. There is no sound, but the shapes emerge. . . .

A shape picking cattails. And then another, coming through the mist, arm outstretched. Then pushing. Then holding the other shape down. Doing the thing the old man has always suspected but refused to accept.

The mist began to settle. I turned, looked back up the slope. Frances was there, coming at me. Her mouth was set; I hadn't returned with the cattails.

Don't come down here, Frances, I thought. It's dangerous down here now that I've seen those shapes and the mist has cleared. Don't come down.

Frances came on toward me. She was going to bawl me out for not bringing the cattails. I waited.

One of these days, I thought, it might happen. Maybe not this year, maybe not next, but someday it might. Someday I might drown *you*, Frances, just as—maybe—you drowned our poor, unloved son Richie that day so long ago. . . .

GREAT-AUNT ALLIE'S FLYPAPERS

P. D. James

*P. D. James, a former hospital administrator who began writing as a hobby, is best known for her novels featuring Chief Superintendent Adam Dalgliesh (*The Black Tower *and* Death of an Expert Witness, *among others), but her numerous short stories and two novels featuring Cordelia Gray, female private eye (*An Unsuitable Job for a Woman *and* The Skull Beneath the Skin) *are no less appealing. A Londoner who raised two daughters while pursuing a career as a civil servant, Mrs. James has received great critical acclaim for her work, including two Silver Dagger Awards from the British Crime Writers Association. "Great-Aunt Allie's Flypapers" presents Adam Dalgliesh's surprising solution to a sixty-seven-year-old murder by arsenic.*

"You see, my dear Adam," explained the Canon gently as he walked with Chief Superintendent Dalgliesh under the vicarage elms, "useful as the legacy would be to us, I wouldn't feel happy in accepting it if Great-Aunt Allie came by her money in the first place by wrongful means."

What the Canon meant was that he and his wife wouldn't be happy to inherit Great-Aunt Allie's fifty thousand pounds or so if, sixty-seven years earlier, she had poisoned her elderly husband with arsenic in order to get it. As Great-Aunt Allie had been accused and acquitted of just that charge in a 1902 trial which, for her Hampshire neighbours, had rivalled the Coronation as a public spectacle, the Canon's scruples were not altogether irrelevant. Admittedly, thought Dalgliesh, most people, faced with the prospect of fifty thousand pounds, would be happy to subscribe to the commonly accepted convention that once an English court has pronounced its verdict, the final truth of the matter has been established once and for all. There may possibly be a higher judicature in the next world, but hardly in this. And so Hubert Boxdale might normally have been happy to believe. But faced with the prospect of an unexpected fortune, his scrupulous conscience was troubled. The gentle but obstinate voice went on:

"Apart from the moral principle of accepting tainted money, it wouldn't bring us happiness. I often think of the poor woman driven restlessly around Europe in her search for peace, of that lonely life and unhappy death."

Dalgliesh recalled that Great-Aunt Allie had moved in a predictable progress with her retinue of servants, current lover and general hangers-on from one luxury Riviera hotel to the next, with stays in Paris or Rome as the mood suited her. He was not sure that this orderly program of comfort and entertainment could be described as being restlessly driven around Europe or that the old lady had been primarily in search of peace. She had died, he recalled, by falling overboard from a millionaire's yacht during a rather wild party given by him to celebrate her eighty-eighth birthday. It was perhaps not an edifying death by the Canon's standards, but he doubted whether she had, in fact, been unhappy at the time. Great-Aunt Allie (it was impossible to think of her by any other name), if she had been capable of coherent thought, would probably have pronounced it a very good way to go. But this was hardly a point of view he could put to his companion.

Canon Hubert Boxdale was Superintendent Adam Dalgliesh's godfather. Dalgliesh's father had been his Oxford contemporary and lifelong friend. He had been an admirable godfather, affectionate, uncensorious, genuinely concerned. In Dalgliesh's childhood he had been mindful of birthdays and imaginative about a small boy's preoccupations and desires. Dalgliesh was very fond of him and privately thought him one of the few really good men he had known. It was only surprising that the Canon had managed to live to seventy-one in a carnivorous world in which gentleness, humility and unworldliness are hardly conducive to survival, let alone success. But his goodness had in some sense protected him. Faced with such manifest innocence, even those who exploited him, and they were not a few, extended some of the protection and compassion they might show to the slightly subnormal.

"Poor old darling," his daily woman would say, pocketing pay for six hours when she had worked five and helping herself to a couple of eggs from his refrigerator. "He's really not fit to be let out alone." It had surprised the then young and slightly priggish Detective Constable Dalgliesh to realize that the Canon knew perfectly well about the hours and the eggs, but thought that Mrs. Copthorne with five children and an indolent husband needed both more than he did. He also knew that if he started paying for five hours, she would promptly work only four and extract another two eggs and that this small and only dishonesty was somehow necessary to her self-esteem. He was good. But he was not a fool.

He and his wife were, of course, poor. But they were not unhappy; indeed, it was a word impossible to associate with the Canon. The death of his two sons in the 1939 war had saddened but not destroyed him. But he had anxieties. His wife was suffering from disseminated sclerosis and was finding it increasingly hard to manage. There were comforts and appliances which she would need. He was now, belatedly, about to retire and his pension would be small. The legacy would enable them both to live in comfort for the rest of their lives and would also, Dalgliesh had no doubt, give them the pleasure of doing more for their various lame dogs. Really, he thought, the Canon was an almost embarrassingly deserving candidate for a modest fortune. Why couldn't the dear silly old noodle take the cash and stop worrying? He said cunningly:

"She was found not guilty, you know, by an English jury, and it all happened nearly seventy years ago. Couldn't you bring yourself to accept their verdict?"

But the Canon's scrupulous mind was impervious to such sly innuendos. Dalgliesh told himself that he should have remembered what, as a small boy, he had discovered about Uncle Hubert's conscience: that it operated as a warning bell and that, unlike most people, he never pretended that it hadn't sounded or that he hadn't heard it or that, having heard it, something must be wrong with the mechanism.

"Oh, I did accept it while she was alive. We never met, you know. I didn't wish to force myself on her. After all, she was a wealthy woman. Our ways of life were very different. But I usually wrote briefly at Christmas and she sent a card in reply. I wanted to keep some contact in case, one day, she might want someone to turn to and would remember that I am a priest."

And why should she want a priest? thought Dalgliesh. To clear her conscience? Was that what the dear old boy had in mind? So he must have had doubts from the beginning. But of course he had! Dalgliesh knew something of the story, and the general feeling of the family and friends was that Great-Aunt Allie had been extremely lucky to escape the gallows. His own father's view, expressed with reticence, reluctance and compassion, had not in essentials differed from that given by a local reporter at the time:

"How on earth did she expect to get away with it? Damn lucky to escape topping, if you ask me."

"The news of the legacy came as a complete surprise?" asked Dalgliesh.

"Indeed, yes. We never met except at that first and only Christmas six weeks after her marriage, when my grandfather died. We always talk of her as Great-Aunt Allie, but in fact, as you know, she married my grandfather. But it seemed impossible to think of her as a step-grandmother. There was the usual family gathering at Colebrook Croft at the time and I was there with my parents and my twin sisters. I was only four and the twins were barely eight months old. I can remember nothing of my grandfather or of his wife. After the murder—if one has to use that dreadful word—my mother returned home with us children, leaving my father to cope with the police, the solicitors and the newsmen. It was a terrible time for him. I don't think I was even told that Grandfather was dead until about a year later. My old nurse, who had been given Christmas as a holiday to visit her own family, told me that soon after my return home, I asked her if Grandfather was now young and beautiful for always. She, poor woman, took it as a sign of infant prognostication and piety. Poor Nellie was sadly superstitious and sentimental, I'm afraid. But I knew nothing of Grandfather's death at the time and certainly can recall nothing of the visit or of my new step-grandmother. Mercifully, I was little more than a baby when the murder was done."

"She was a music hall artiste, wasn't she?" asked Dalgliesh.

"Yes, and a very talented one. My grandfather met her

when she was working with a partner in a hall in Cannes. He had gone to the south of France with a manservant for his health. I understand that she extracted a gold watch from his chain and when he claimed it, told him that he was English, had recently suffered from a stomach ailment, had two sons and a daughter and was about to have a wonderful surprise. It was all correct except that his only daughter had died in childbirth, leaving him a granddaughter, Marguerite Goddard."

"And all easily guessable from his voice and appearance," said Dalgliesh. "I suppose the surprise was the marriage?"

"It was certainly a surprise, and a most unpleasant one, for the family. It is easy to deplore the snobbishness and the conventions of another age, and indeed there was much in Edwardian England to deplore. But it was not a propitious marriage. I think of the difference in background, education and way of life, the lack of common interest. And there was this great disparity of age. My grandfather had married a girl just three months younger than his own granddaughter. I cannot wonder that the family were concerned, that they felt that the union could not in the end contribute to the contentment or happiness of either party."

And that was putting it charitably, thought Dalgliesh. The marriage certainly hadn't contributed to their happiness. From the point of view of the family, it had been a disaster. He recalled hearing of an incident when the local vicar and his wife, a couple who had actually dined at Colebrook Croft on the night of the murder, first called on the bride. Apparently old Augustus Boxdale had introduced her by saying:

"Meet the prettiest little variety artiste in the business. Took a gold watch and note case off me without any trouble. Would have had the elastic out of my pants if I hadn't watched out. Anyway, she stole my heart, didn't you, sweetheart?" All this accompanied by a hearty slap on the rump and a squeal of delight from the lady, who had promptly demonstrated her skill by extracting the Reverend Venables's bunch of keys from his left ear.

Dalgliesh thought it tactful not to remind the Canon of this story.

"What do you wish me to do, sir?" he inquired.

"It's asking a great deal, I know, when you're so busy at the Yard. But if I had your assurance that you believed in Aunt Allie's innocence, I should feel happy about accepting the bequest. I wondered if it would be possible for you to see the records of the trial. Perhaps it would give you a clue. You're so clever at this sort of thing."

He spoke with no intention to flatter but with an innocent wonder at the peculiar avocations of men. Dalgliesh was, indeed, very clever at this sort of thing. A dozen or so men at present occupying security wings in Her Majesty's prisons could testify to Chief Superintendent Dalgliesh's cleverness, as indeed could a handful of others walking free whose defending counsel had been in their way as clever as Chief Superintendent Dalgliesh. But to reexamine a case over sixty years old seemed to require clairvoyance rather than cleverness. The trial judge and both learned counsel had been dead for over fifty years. Two world wars had taken their toll. Four reigns had passed. It was probable that of those who had slept under the roof of Colebrook Croft on that fateful Boxing Day night of 1901, only the Canon still survived.

But the old man was troubled and had sought his help. And Dalgliesh, with nearly a week's leave due to him, had the time to give it.

"I'll see what I can do," he promised.

The transcript of a trial which had taken place sixty-seven years ago took time and trouble to obtain even for a chief superintendent of the Metropolitan Police. It provided little potential comfort for the Canon. Mr. Justice Medlock had summed up with that avuncular simplicity with which he was wont to address juries, regarding them, apparently, as a panel of well-intentioned but cretinous children. But the salient facts could have been comprehended by any intelligent child. Part of the summing up set them out with admirable lucidity:

And so, gentlemen of the jury, we come to the evening of 26 December. Mr. Augustus Boxdale, who had perhaps indulged a little unwisely on Christmas Day and at luncheon, had retired to rest in his dressing room at three o'clock, suffering from a slight recurrence of the digestive trouble which had afflicted him for most of his life. You have heard that he had taken luncheon with members of his family and ate nothing which they, too, did not eat. You may feel that you can acquit that luncheon of anything worse than overrichness. Mr. Boxdale, as was his habit, did not take afternoon tea.

Dinner was served at 8 P.M. promptly, as was the custom at Colebrook Croft. Members of the jury, you must be very clear who was present at that meal. There was the accused, Mrs. Augustus Boxdale; there was her husband's elder son, Captain Maurice Boxdale, with his wife; the younger son, the Reverend Edward Boxdale, with his wife; the deceased's granddaughter, Miss Marguerite Goddard, and there were two neighbours, the Reverend and Mrs. Henry Venables.

You have heard how the accused took only the first course at dinner, which was ragout of beef, and then left the dining room, saying that she wished to sit with her husband. That was about eight-twenty. Shortly after nine o'clock, she rang for the parlourmaid, Mary Huddy, and ordered a basin of gruel to be brought up to Mr. Boxdale. You have heard that the deceased was fond of gruel, and indeed, as prepared by Mrs. Muncie, the cook, it sounds a most nourishing and comforting dish for an elderly gentleman of weak digestion.

You have heard Mrs. Muncie describe how she prepared the gruel, according to Mrs. Beeton's admirable recipe, in the presence of Mary Huddy, in case, as she said, "The master should take a fancy to it when I'm not at hand and you have to make it." After the gruel had been prepared, Mrs. Muncie tasted it with a spoon and Mary Huddy carried it upstairs to the main bedroom, together with a small jug of water in case it should be too strong. As she reached the door, Mrs. Boxdale came out, her hands full of stockings and underclothes. She has told you that she was on her way to the bathroom to wash them through. She asked the girl to put the basin of gruel on the washstand to cool and Mary Huddy did so in her presence. Miss Huddy has told you that, at the time, she noticed the bowl of flypapers soaking in water and she knew that this solution was one used by Mrs. Boxdale as a cosmetic wash. Indeed, all the women who spent that evening in the house, with the exception of Mrs. Venables, have told you that they knew that it was Mrs. Boxdale's practice to prepare this solution of flypapers.

Mary Huddy and the accused left the bedroom together and you have heard the evidence of Mrs. Muncie that Miss Huddy returned to the kitchen after an absence of only a few minutes. Shortly after nine o'clock, the ladies left the dining room and entered the drawing room to take coffee. At nine-fifteen, Miss Goddard excused herself to the company and said that she would go to see if her grandfather needed anything. The time is established precisely because the clock struck the quarter hour as she left and Mrs. Venables commented on the sweetness of its chime. You have also heard Mrs. Venables's evidence and the evidence of Mrs. Maurice Boxdale and Mrs. Edward Boxdale that none of the ladies left the drawing room during the evening, and Mr. Venables has testified that the three gentlemen remained together until Miss Goddard appeared about three quarters of an hour later to inform them that her grandfather had become very ill and to request that the doctor be sent for immediately.

Miss Goddard has told you that when she entered her grandfather's room, he was just beginning his gruel and was grumbling about its taste. She got the impression that this was merely a protest at being deprived of his dinner rather than that he genuinely considered that there was something wrong with the gruel. At any rate, he finished most of it and appeared to enjoy it despite his grumbles.

You have heard Miss Goddard describe how, after her grandfather had had as much as he wanted of the gruel, she took the bowl next door and left it on the washstand. She then returned to her grandfather's bedroom and Mr. Boxdale, his wife and his granddaughter played three-handed whist for about three quarters of an hour.

At ten o'clock, Mr. Augustus Boxdale complained of feeling very ill. He suffered from griping pains in the stomach, from sickness and from looseness of the bowel. As soon as the symptoms began, Miss Goddard went downstairs to let her uncles know that her grandfather was worse and to ask that Dr. Eversley should be sent for urgently. Dr. Eversley has given you his evidence. He arrived at Colebrook Croft at 10:30 P.M., when he found his patient very distressed and weak. He treated the symptoms and gave what relief he could, but Mr. Augustus Boxdale died shortly before midnight.

Gentlemen of the jury, you have heard Marguerite Goddard describe how, as her grandfather's paroxysms increased in intensity, she remembered the gruel and wondered whether it could have disagreed with him in some way. She mentioned this possibility to her elder uncle, Captain Maurice Boxdale. Captain Boxdale has told you how he at once handed the bowl with its residue of gruel to Dr. Eversley with the request that the doctor should lock it in a cupboard in the library, seal the lock and himself keep the key. You have heard how the contents of the bowl were later analysed and with what result.

An extraordinary precaution for the gallant captain to have taken, thought Dalgliesh, and a most perspicacious young woman. Was it by chance or by design that the bowl hadn't been taken down to be washed as soon as the old man had finished with it? Why was it, he wondered, that Marguerite Goddard hadn't rung for the parlourmaid and requested her to remove it? Miss Goddard appeared the only other suspect. He wished that he knew more about her.

But except for the main protagonists, the characters in the drama did not emerge very clearly from the trial report. Why, indeed, should they? The accusatorial legal system is designed to answer one question. Is the accused guilty beyond reasonable doubt of the crime charged? Exploration of the nuances of personality, interesting speculation and common gossip have no place in the witness box. Was it really possible after nearly seventy years that these dry bones could live?

The two Boxdale brothers came out as very dull fellows indeed. They and their estimable and respectable sloping-bosomed wives had sat at dinner in full view of each other from eight until nearly nine o'clock (a substantial meal, that dinner) and had said so in the witness box in more or less identical words. The bosoms of the ladies might have been heaving with far from estimable emotions of dislike, envy, embarrassment or resentment of the interloper. If so, they didn't choose to tell the court. But the two brothers and their wives were clearly innocent, even if it had been possible to conceive of the guilt of gentlefolk so respected, so eminently respectable. Even their impeccable alibis for the period after dinner had a nice touch of social and sexual distinction. The Reverend Henry Venables had vouched for the gentlemen; his good wife for the ladies.

Besides, what motive had they? They could no longer

gain financially by the old man's death. If anything, it was in their interests to keep him alive in the hope that disillusionment with his marriage or a return to relative sanity might occur to cause him to change his will.

And the rest of the witnesses gave no help. Dalgliesh read all their testimony carefully. The pathologist's evidence. The doctor's evidence. The evidence of Allegra Boxdale's visit to the village store, where, from among the clutter of pots and pans, ointments and liniments, it had been possible to find a dozen flypapers for a customer even in the depth of an English winter. The evidence of the cook. The evidence of the parlourmaid. The remarkably lucid and confident evidence of the granddaughter. There was nothing in any of it which could cause him to give the Canon the assurance for which he hoped.

It was then that he remembered Aubrey Glatt. Glatt was a wealthy amateur criminologist who had made a study of all the notable Victorian and Edwardian poison cases. He was not interested in anything earlier or later, being as obsessively wedded to his period as any serious historian, which indeed he had some claim to call himself. He lived in a Georgian house in Winchester—his affection for the Victorian and Edwardian age did not extend to its architecture—and was only three miles from Colebrook Croft. A visit to the London Library disclosed that he hadn't written a book on the case, but it was improbable that he had totally neglected a crime so close at hand and so in period. Dalgliesh had occasionally helped him with technical details of police procedure. Glatt, in response to a telephone call, was happy to return the favour with the offer of afternoon tea and information.

Tea was served in his elegant drawing room by a parlourmaid in goffered cap with streamers. Dalgliesh wondered what wage Glatt paid her to persuade her to wear it. She looked as if she could have played a role in any of his favourite Victorian dramas, and Dalgliesh had an uncomfortable thought that arsenic might be dispensed with the cucumber sandwiches.

Glatt nibbled away and was expansive.

"It's interesting that you should have taken this sudden and, if I may say so, somewhat inexplicable interest in the Boxdale murder. I got out my notebook on the case only yesterday. Colebrook Croft is being demolished to make way for a new housing estate and I thought I might visit it for the last time. The family, of course, hasn't lived there since the 1914–18 war. Architecturally it's completely undistinguished, but one hates to see it go. We might motor over after tea if you are agreeable.

"I never completed my book on the case, you know. I planned a work entitled *The Colebrook Croft Mystery, or Who Killed Augustus Boxdale?* But alas, the answer was all too obvious."

"No real mystery?" suggested Dalgliesh.

"Who else could it have been but the bride? She was born Allegra Porter, incidentally. Allegra. An extraordinary name. Do you suppose her mother could have been thinking of Byron? I imagine not. There's a picture of Allie on page two of the notebook, by the way, taken in Cannes on her wedding day. I call it 'Beauty and the Beast.'"

The photograph had scarcely faded and Great-Aunt Allie smiled plainly at Dalgliesh across nearly seventy years. Her broad face with its wide mouth and rather snub nose was framed by two wings of dark hair swept high and topped, in the fashion of the day, by an immense flowered hat. The features were too coarse for real beauty, but the eyes were magnificent, deep-set and well-spaced; the chin was round and determined. Beside this vital young Amazon poor Augustus Boxdale, smiling fatuously at the camera and clutching his bride's arm as if for support, was but a frail and pathetic beast. Their pose was unfortunate. She looked as if she were about to fling him over her shoulder.

Glatt shrugged. "The face of a murderess? I've known less likely ones. Her counsel suggested, of course, that the old man had poisoned his own gruel during the short time she left it on the washstand to cool while she visited the bathroom. But why should he? All the evidence suggests that he was in a state of postnuptial euphoria, poor senile old booby. Our Augustus was in no hurry to leave this world, particularly by such an agonizing means. Besides, I doubt whether he even knew the gruel was there. He was in bed next door in his dressing room, remember."

Dalgliesh asked, "What about Marguerite Goddard? There's no evidence about the exact time when she entered the bedroom."

"I thought you'd get on to that. She could have arrived while her step-grandmother was in the bathroom, poisoned the gruel, hidden herself either in the main bedroom or elsewhere until it had been taken in to Augustus, then joined her grandfather and his bride as if she had just come upstairs. It's possible, I admit. But is it likely? She was less inconvenienced than any of the family by her grandfather's second marriage. Her mother was Augustus Boxdale's eldest child and married, very young, a wealthy patent medicine manufacturer. She died in childbirth and the husband only survived her by a year. Marguerite Goddard was an heiress. She was also most advantageously engaged to Captain the Honourable John Brize-Lacey. It was quite a catch for a Boxdale—or a Goddard. Marguerite Goddard, young, beautiful, secure in the possession of the Goddard fortune, not to mention the Goddard emeralds and the eldest son of a lord, was hardly a serious suspect. In my view defence counsel— that was Roland Gort Lloyd—was wise to leave her strictly alone."

"It was a memorable defence, I believe."

"Magnificent. There's no doubt Allegra Boxdale owed her life to Gort Lloyd. I know that concluding speech by heart:

" 'Gentlemen of the jury, I beseech you in the sacred name of justice to consider what you are at. It is your responsibility and yours alone to decide the fate of this young woman. She stands before you now, young, vibrant, glowing with health, the years stretching before her with their promise and their hopes. It is in your power to cut off all this as you might top a nettle with one swish of your cane. To condemn her to the slow torture of those last waiting weeks; to that last dreadful walk; to heap calumny on her name; to desecrate those few happy weeks of marriage with the man who loved her so greatly; to cast her into the final darkness of an ignominious grave.'

"Pause for dramatic effect. Then the crescendo in that magnificent voice. 'And on what evidence, gentlemen? I ask you.' Another pause. Then the thunder. 'On what evidence?' "

"A powerful defence," said Dalgliesh. "But I wonder how it would go down with a modern judge and jury."

"Well, it went down very effectively with that 1902 jury. Of course, the abolition of capital punishment has rather cramped the more histrionic style. I'm not sure that the reference to topping nettles was in the best of taste. But the jury got the message. They decided that, on the whole, they preferred not to have the responsibility of sending the accused to the gallows. They were out six hours reaching their verdict and it was greeted with some applause. If any of those worthy citizens had been asked to wager five pounds of their own good money on her innocence, I suspect that it would have been a different matter. Allegra Boxdale had helped him, of course. The Criminal Evidence Act, passed three years earlier, enabled him to put her in the witness box. She wasn't an actress of a kind for nothing. Somehow she managed to persuade the jury that she had genuinely loved the old man."

"Perhaps she had," suggested Dalgliesh. "I don't suppose there had been much kindness in her life. And he was kind."

"No doubt. No doubt. But love!" Glatt was impatient. "My dear Dalgliesh! He was a singularly ugly old man of sixty-nine. She was an attractive girl of twenty-one!"

Dalgliesh doubted whether love, that iconoclastic passion, was susceptible to this kind of simple arithmetic, but he didn't argue. Glatt went on:

"And the prosecution couldn't suggest any other romantic attachment. The police got in touch with her previous partner, of course. He was discovered to be a bald, undersized little man, sharp as a weasel, with a buxom wife and five children. He had moved down the coast after the partnership broke up and was now working with a new girl. He said regretfully that she was coming along nicely, thank you, gentlemen, but would never be a patch on Allie, and that if Allie got her neck out of the noose and ever wanted a job, she knew where to come. It was obvious even to the most suspicious policeman that his interest was purely professional. As he said, what was a grain or two of arsenic between friends?

"The Boxdales had no luck after the trial. Captain Maurice Boxdale was killed in 1916, leaving no children, and the Reverend Edward lost his wife and their twin daughters in the 1918 influenza epidemic. He survived until 1932. The boy Hubert may still be alive, but I doubt it. That family were a sickly lot.

"My greatest achievement, incidentally, was in tracing Marguerite Goddard. I hadn't realized that she was still alive. She never married Brize-Lacey or, indeed, anyone else. He distinguished himself in the 1914–18 war, came successfully through, and eventually married an eminently suitable young woman, the sister of a brother officer. He inherited the title in 1925 and died in 1953. But Marguerite Goddard may be alive now, for all I know. She may even be living in the same modest Bournemouth hotel where I found her. Not that my efforts in tracing her were rewarded. She absolutely refused to see me. That's the note that she sent out to me, by the way."

It was meticulously pasted into the notebook in its chronological order and carefully annotated. Aubrey Glatt was a natural researcher; Dalgliesh couldn't help wondering whether this passion for accuracy might not have been more rewardingly spent than in the careful documentation of murder.

The note was written in an elegant upright hand, the strokes black and very thin but unwavering.

Miss Goddard presents her compliments to Mr. Aubrey Glatt. She did not murder her grandfather and has neither the time nor the inclination to gratify his curiosity by discussing the person who did.

Aubrey Glatt said, "After that extremely disobliging note I felt there was really no point in going on with the book."

Glatt's passion for Edwardian England extended to more than its murders and they drove to Colebrook Croft, high above the green Hampshire lanes, in an elegant 1910 Daimler. Aubrey wore a thin tweed coat and deerstalker hat and looked, Dalgliesh thought, rather like a Sherlock Holmes, with himself as attendant Watson.

"We are only just in time, my dear Dalgliesh," he said when they arrived. "The engines of destruction are assembled. That ball on a chain looks like the eyeball of God, ready to strike. Let us make our number with the attendant artisans. You as a guardian of the law will have no wish to trespass."

The work of demolition had not yet begun, but the inside of the house had been stripped and plundered. The great rooms echoed to their footsteps like gaunt and deserted barracks after the final retreat. They moved from room to room, Glatt mourning the forgotten glories of an age he had been born thirty years too late to enjoy, Dalgliesh with his mind on more immediate and practical concerns.

The design of the house was simple and formalized. The second floor, on which were most of the main bedrooms, had a long corridor running the whole length of the façade. The master bedroom was at the southern end, with two large windows giving a distant view of Winchester Cathedral tower. A communicating door led to a small dressing room.

The main corridor had a row of four identical large windows. The curtain rods and rings had been removed, but the ornate carved pelmets were still in place. Here must have hung pairs of heavy curtains giving cover to anyone who wished to slip out of view. And Dalgliesh noted with interest that one of the windows was exactly opposite the door of the main bedroom. By the time they had left Colebrook Croft and Glatt had dropped him at Winchester station, Dagliesh was beginning to formulate a theory.

His next move was to trace Marguerite Goddard if she was still alive. It took him nearly a week of weary searching, a frustrating trail along the south coast from hotel to hotel. Almost everywhere his inquiries were met with defensive hostility. It was the usual story of a very old lady who had become more demanding, arrogant and eccentric as her health and fortune had waned, an unwelcome embarrassment to manager and fellow guests alike. The hotels were all modest, a few almost sordid. What, he wondered, had become of the Goddard fortune? From the last landlady he learned that Miss Goddard had become ill, really very sick indeed, and had been removed six months previously to the local district general hospital. And it was there that he found her.

The ward sister was surprisingly young, a petite, dark-haired girl with a tired face and challenging eyes.

"Miss Goddard is very ill. We've put her in one of the side wards. Are you a relative? If so, you're the first one who has bothered to call and you're lucky to be in time. When she is delirious she seems to expect a Captain Brize-Lacey to call. You're not he, by any chance?"

"Captain Brize-Lacey will not be calling. No, I'm not a relative. She doesn't even know me. But I would like to visit her if she's well enough and is willing to see me. Could you please give her this note?"

He couldn't force himself on a defenceless and dying woman. She still had the right to say no. He was afraid she would refuse him. And if she did, he might never learn the truth. He thought for a second and then wrote four words on the back page of his diary, signed them, tore out the page, folded it and handed it to the sister.

She was back very shortly.

"She'll see you. She's weak, of course, and very old, but she's perfectly lucid now. Only please don't tire her."

"I'll try not to stay too long."

The girl laughed. "Don't worry. She'll throw you out soon enough if she gets bored. The chaplain and the Red Cross librarian have a terrible time with her. Third door on the left. There's a stool to sit on under the bed. We ring a bell at the end of visiting time."

She bustled off, leaving him to find his own way. The corridor was very quiet. At the far end he could glimpse through the open door of the main ward the regimented rows of beds, each with its pale-blue coverlet; the bright glow of flowers on the over-bed tables; and the laden visitors making their way in pairs to each bedside. There was a faint buzz of welcome, the hum of conversation. But no one was visiting the side wards. Here in the silence of the aseptic corridor Dalgliesh could smell death.

The woman propped high against the pillows in the third room on the left no longer looked human. She lay rigidly, her long arms disposed like sticks on the coverlet. This was a skeleton clothed with a thin membrane of flesh, beneath whose yellow transparency the tendons and veins were plainly visible as if in an anatomist's model. She was nearly bald, and the high-domed skull under its spare down of hair was as brittle and vulnerable as a child's. Only the eyes still held life, burning in their deep sockets with an animal vitality. And when she spoke her voice was distinctive and unwavering, evoking as her appearance never could the memory of imperious youth.

She took up his note and read aloud four words:

" 'It was the child.' You are right, of course. The four-year-old Hubert Boxdale killed his grandfather. You sign this

note 'Adam Dalgliesh.' There was no Dalgliesh connected
with the case."

"I am a detective of the Metropolitan Police. But I'm
not here in any official capacity. I have known about this case
for a number of years from a dear friend. I have a natural
curiosity to learn the truth. And I have formed a theory."

"And now, like that Aubrey Glatt, you want to write a
book?"

"No. I shall tell no one. You have my promise."

Her voice was ironic. "Thank you. I am a dying
woman, Mr. Dalgliesh. I tell you that not to invite your
sympathy, which it would be an impertinence for you to
offer and which I neither want nor require, but to explain
why it no longer matters to me what you say or do. But I,
too, have a natural curiosity. Your note, cleverly, was intended to provoke it. I should like to know how you discovered the truth."

Dalgliesh drew the visitor's stool from under the bed
and sat down beside her. She did not look at him. The skeleton hands, still holding his note, did not move.

"Everyone in Colebrook Croft who could have killed
Augustus Boxdale was accounted for, except the one person whom nobody considered, the small boy. He was an
intelligent, articulate and lonely child. He was almost certainly left to his own devices. His nurse did not accompany
the family to Colebrook Croft and the servants who were
there had the extra work of Christmas and the care of the
delicate twin girls. The boy spent much time with his
grandfather and the new bride. She, too, was lonely and
disregarded. He could have trotted around with her as she
went about her various activities. He could have watched
her making her arsenical face wash and when he asked, as
a child will, what it was for, could have been told: 'To
make me young and beautiful.' He loved his grandfather,
but he must have known that the old man was neither
young nor beautiful. Suppose he woke up on that Boxing
Day night overfed and excited after the Christmas festivi-

ties. Suppose he went to Allegra Boxdale's room in search
of comfort and companionship and saw there the basin of
gruel and the arsenical mixture together on the washstand.
Suppose he decided that here was something he could do
for his grandfather."

The voice from the bed said quietly:

"And suppose someone stood unnoticed in the doorway
and watched him."

"So you were behind the window curtains on the landing, looking through the open door?"

"Of course. He knelt on the chair, two chubby hands
clasping the bowl of poison, pouring it with infinite care into
his grandfather's gruel. I watched while he replaced the
linen cloth over the basin, got down from his chair, replaced
it with careful art against the wall and trotted out into the
corridor back to the nursery. About three seconds later Allegra came out of the bathroom and I watched while she
carried the gruel in to my grandfather. A second later I went
into the main bedroom. The bowl of poison had been a little
heavy for Hubert's small hands to manage and I saw that a
small pool had been spilt on the polished top of the washstand. I mopped it up with my handkerchief. Then I poured
some of the water from the jug into the poison bowl to bring
up the level. It only took a couple of seconds and I was ready
to join Allegra and my grandfather in the bedroom and sit
with him while he ate his gruel.

"I watched him die without pity and without remorse.
I think I hated them both equally. The grandfather who had
adored, petted and indulged me all through my childhood
had deteriorated into this disgusting old lecher, unable to
keep his hands off his woman even when I was in the room.
He had rejected his family, jeopardized my engagement,
made our name a laughingstock in the county, and for a
woman my grandmother wouldn't have employed as a
kitchen maid. I wanted them both dead. And they were
both going to die. But it would be by other hands than mine.
I could deceive myself that it wasn't my doing."

Dalgliesh asked, "When did she find out?"

"She guessed that evening. When my grandfather's agony began, she went outside for the jug of water. She wanted a cool cloth for his head. It was then that she noticed that the level of water in the jug had fallen and that a small pool of liquid on the washstand had been mopped up. I should have realized that she would have seen that pool. She had been trained to register every detail; it was almost subconscious with her. She thought at the time that Mary Huddy had spilt some of the water when she set down the tray and the gruel. But who but I could have mopped it up? And why?"

"And when did she face you with the truth?"

"Not until after the trial. Allegra had magnificent courage. She knew what was at stake. But she also knew what she stood to gain. She gambled with her life for a fortune."

And then Dalgliesh understood what had happened to the Goddard inheritance.

"So she made you pay."

"Of course. Every penny. The Goddard fortune, the Goddard emeralds. She lived in luxury for sixty-seven years on my money. She ate and dressed on my money. When she moved with her lovers from hotel to hotel, it was on my money. She paid them with my money. And if she has left anything, which I doubt, it is my money. My grandfather left very little. He had been senile for years. Money ran through his fingers like sand."

"And your engagement?"

"It was broken, you could say, by mutual consent. A marriage, Mr. Dalgliesh, is like any other legal contract. It is most successful when both parties are convinced they have a bargain. Captain Brize-Lacey was sufficiently discouraged by the scandal of a murder in the family. He was a proud and highly conventional man. But that alone might have been accepted with the Goddard fortune and the Goddard emeralds to deodorize the bad smell. But the marriage couldn't have succeeded if he had discovered that he had married socially beneath him, into a family with a major scandal and no compensating fortune."

Dalgliesh said, "Once you had begun to pay, you had no choice but to go on. I see that. But why did you pay? She could hardly have told her story. It would have meant involving the child."

"Oh, no! That wasn't her plan at all. She never meant to involve the child. She was a sentimental woman and she was fond of Hubert. She intended to accuse me of murder outright. Then, if I decided to tell the truth, how would it help me? How could I admit that I had watched Hubert, actually watched a child barely four years old preparing an agonizing death for his grandfather without speaking a word to stop him? I could hardly claim that I hadn't understood the implication of what I had seen. After all, I wiped up the spilt liquid, I topped up the bowl. She had nothing to lose, remember, neither life nor reputation. They couldn't try her twice. That's why she waited until after the trial. It made her secure forever. But what of me? In the circles in which I moved, reputation was everything. She needed only to breathe the story in the ears of a few servants and I was finished. The truth can be remarkably tenacious. But it wasn't only reputation. I paid because I was in dread of the gallows."

Dalgliesh asked, "But could she ever prove it?"

Suddenly she looked at him and gave an eerie screech of laughter. It tore at her throat until he thought the taut tendons would snap.

"Of course she could! You fool! Don't you understand? She took my handkerchief, the one I used to mop up the arsenic mixture. That was her profession, remember. Sometime during that evening, perhaps when we were all crowding around the bed, two soft plump fingers insinuated themselves between the satin of my evening dress and my flesh and extracted that stained and damning piece of linen."

She stretched out feebly toward the bedside locker.

Dalgliesh saw what she wanted and pulled open the drawer. There on the top was a small square of very fine linen with a border of hand-stitched lace. He took it up. In the corner was her monogram, delicately embroidered. And half of the handkerchief was still stiff and stained with brown.

She said, "She left instructions with her solicitors that this was to be returned to me after her death. She always knew where I was. She made it her business to know. You see, it could be said that she had a life interest in me. But now she's dead. And I shall soon follow. You may have the handkerchief, Mr. Dalgliesh. It can be of no further use to either of us now."

Dalgliesh put it in his pocket without speaking. As soon as possible he would see that it was burned. But there was something else he had to say. "Is there anything you would wish me to do? Is there anyone you want told, or to tell? Would you care to see a priest?"

Again there was that uncanny screech of laughter, but it was softer now.

"There's nothing I can say to a priest. I only regret what I did because it wasn't successful. That is hardly the proper frame of mind for a good confession. But I bear her no ill will. No envy, malice or uncharitableness. She won; I lost. One should be a good loser. But I don't want any priest telling me about penance. I've paid, Mr. Dalgliesh. For sixty-seven years I've paid. Great-Aunt Allie and her flypapers! She had me caught by the wings all the rest of my life."

She lay back as if suddenly exhausted. There was silence for a moment. Then she said with sudden vigour:

"I believe your visit has done me good. I would be obliged if you would make it convenient to return each afternoon for the next three days. I shan't trouble you after that."

Dalgliesh extended his leave with some difficulty and stayed at a local inn. He saw her each afternoon. They never spoke again of the murder. And when he came punctually at 2 P.M. on the fourth day, it was to be told that Miss Goddard had died peacefully in the night, with apparently no trouble to anyone. She was, as she had said, a good loser.

A week later, Dalgliesh reported to the Canon.

"I was able to see a man who has made a detailed study of the case. He had already done most of the work for me. I have read the transcript of the trial and visited Colebrook Croft. And I have seen one other person closely connected with the case but who is now dead. I know you will want me to respect confidences and to say no more than I need."

It sounded pompous and minatory, but he couldn't help that. The Canon murmured his quiet assurance. Thank God he wasn't a man to question. Where he trusted, he trusted absolutely. If Dalgliesh gave his word, there would be no more questioning. But he was anxious. Suspense hung around them. Dalgliesh went on quickly:

"As a result, I can give you my word that the verdict was a just verdict and that not one penny of your grandfather's fortune is coming to you through anyone's wrongdoing."

He turned his face away and gazed out the vicarage window at the sweet green coolness of the summer's day so that he did not have to watch the Canon's happiness and relief. There was a silence. The old man was probably giving thanks in his own way. Then he was aware that his godfather was speaking. Something was being said about gratitude, about the time he had given up to the investigation.

"Please don't misunderstand me, Adam. But when the formalities have been completed, I should like to donate something to a charity named by you, one close to your heart."

Dalgliesh smiled. His contributions to charity were impersonal; a quarterly obligation discharged by banker's order. The Canon obviously regarded charities as so many old clothes: all were friends, but some fitted better and were more affectionately regarded than others.

Then inspiration came.

"It's good of you to suggest it, sir. I rather liked what I learned about Great-Aunt Allie. It would be pleasant to give something in her name. Isn't there a society for the assistance of retired and indigent vaudeville artistes, conjurers and so on?"

The Canon, predictably, knew that there was and could name it.

Dalgliesh said, "Then I think, Canon, that Great-Aunt Allie would agree that a donation to them would be entirely appropriate."